NUMUNWARI

T0346649

"One of the best of the reptilian menace novels, this scores bonus points for its use of Aboriginal culture and religion, a fascinating subject not often encountered. The author knows his stuff and it shows, and in what is his first and only novel, he shows that he can also write a good tense yarn. It is surprising that most crocodile horror novels don't play up the gore aspect, and this is no exception, regardless of the lurid title. It is basically an extension of Webb's personal philosophy that crocodiles are feared mainly through public misunderstanding, and he makes a good case. Recommended."

– The Last Page Bookshop.

For Bunda-bunda and Agaral

NUMUNWARI

A Novel of
Aboriginal "Dreaming",
Crocodiles and Cultural Conflict

Grahame Webb

EER
Edward Everett Root, Publishers, Brighton, 2017.

EER

Edward Everett Root, Publishers, Co. Ltd.,
30 New Road, Brighton, Sussex, BN1 1BN, England.
www.eerpublishing.com

edwardeverettroot@yahoo.co.uk

Grahame Webb
NUMUNWARI
A Novel of Aboriginal 'Dreaming', Crocodiles and Cultural Conflict

ISBN: 9781911454373 Paperback.

First published in Australia by Surrey Beatty & Sons Pty Ltd, 1980.
This edition first published 2017.

Cover designed by Pageset Limited, High Wycombe, Buckinghamshire.
Printed in Great Britain by T.J.International Ltd, Padstow, Cornwall.

ACKNOWLEDGEMENTS

Although *Numunwari* is a work of fiction, many of the scenes depicted are based on the experiences of myself, colleagues or friends. They have been woven into a story which is imaginary, yet which could occur tomorrow.

To the many people who have assisted with *Numunwari,* I am grateful. Bunda-bunda and Agaral spent many, many nights trying to explain to me the ways of their people, and teaching me the rudiments of life in 'the bush'. I would particularly like to thank Bunda-bunda for permission to use a version of his name, Oondabund, as the name of a character in the novel.

Without the encouragement of R. D. Walshe, who read the earliest draft, the novel would not have been completed. Others who have contributed are: Chris Alexio, Hedney Webb, Margaret Tierney, Jim Jenner, John Barker, Dave Lindner, Mal Davey, Liza Muldoon, Jeff Lang, Tim Curnow, Jacqueline Kent, Karen Dempsey, Kim Weston, Michael Yerbury, Graham Gifford and Chris Dane.

Finally, my thanks are due to my wife Anna, and children Dudley, Catherine and Elizabeth, who, seeing me little enough as it was, had to put up with my writing when we were together.

Grahame Webb

AUTHOR'S NOTE

The intense reverence held by Aboriginals for certain animals, geological structures and areas, is, for the white man's sake, often referred to as 'dreaming'. The concept embodies an association between the people and their environment which even today few white people fully understand. To the best of my knowledge, 'dreaming' has nothing to do with sleep or conventional dreams, and 'extremely sacred' often seems an appropriate synonym.

PROLOGUE

From the corner of her eye, the receptionist watched the man approach the heavy glass door. She slid the soft-covered book beneath her desk as a gust of hot air rushed into the foyer, a reminder that Darwin's Museum had been effectively air-conditioned against the oppressive heat outside.

'Yes, sir?' she enquired as he neared the desk.

'Is Catherine Pope in?'

Lifting the phone, she scanned a row of white switches, selected one and pushed it in. 'Whom should I say is calling?'

'Harris, Steve Harris.'

After a short delay, the receptionist announced Steve's arrival and hung up. 'Dr Pope'll be down in a few minutes, Mr Harris; would you like to take a seat?'

Lowering himself into the closest of the six black, vinyl-covered chairs, Steve found himself staring at the display cabinet at the far end of the foyer. It contained a large, stuffed sea eagle, with its wings slightly spread and its head pointing forward. The eyes stared permanently at the glass doors—it was a hideous object. To the eagle's left was the door to the public galleries and exhibits, and to its right Harris saw the hallway leading to the Curator's offices and the reference collections. The foyer itself lacked movement, and the silence was consistent with the cold gaze of the eagle's glass eye.

'Steve!' came a cheerful voice from the eagle's left wing-tip. 'Come on in.'

The receptionist watched as Steve crossed the room. Although not particularly tall, he was solidly built, and with each step, leg muscles bulged within the tight-fitting woollen socks. His sunburnt skin contrasted markedly with his light khaki shirt and shorts.

Catherine Pope was a fifty-six-year-old anthropologist, considered a world expert on primitive art. She had been working at the Museum for nearly six months, describing and restoring a large collection of Aboriginal bark paintings, many of which had been damaged during Cyclone Tracy. Her planned two-month study leave had twice been extended, but she was still rushing to complete her work before returning to the University of Minnesota to start teaching.

Steve Harris had been helping her. A Senior Technical Officer with the Northern Territory's Wildlife Division, he was familiar with most of the animals depicted in the paintings she was working on. Steve's speciality was crocodiles, and his first three years with the Division had been spent in studying them in the vast Arnhem Land Aboriginal Reserve. During this time, he had lived and worked with Aboriginals continually, and had gained a full appreciation of their way of life, and the complexities of their culture. It was his familiarity with both the Aboriginals and wildlife, as well as his keen eye for interpreting meaning, that had first attracted Catherine Pope's attention.

'That's it over there,' she said, pointing from the office doorway to a metre-square sheet of bark on a desk near the window. 'See what you can make of it.'

The crocodile on the bark was obviously a saltwater crocodile, but the intriguing feature of the painting was the scene depicted. A single huge animal was surrounded by some twenty stick-like figures who appeared unarmed, and less than one-sixth as tall as the crocodile was long. The only colour used was white, and apart from a series of square objects in one corner, the background was unpainted.

'It's definitely a salty,' said Steve, absently running his fingers through his short black hair. 'They're not hunting, they haven't got any spears.'

'I've spent a couple of days on it and haven't got much further, Steve. The painting's typically western Arnhem Land style, stark figures and no background, but on the other hand, it seems to be trying to convey a rather complex story, more like the eastern style.'

'You don't know where it's from?' inquired Steve.

'We've got a general locality, but I'm not sure how accurate it is. The painting was part of a collection a Mrs Davenport donated after the cyclone. Her father surveyed Arnhem Land for potential cattle leases in the early 1900s, and to make money on the side he used to bring back artefacts and sell them to the southern museums. He ended up with a small collection himself, and she brought it all in to the Museum for safekeeping after the cyclone. This painting was one of seven good pieces. Fortunately there's a date on the back of it, and from his diaries we worked out he must have been between the Liverpool and Blyth Rivers at that time. He doesn't mention the painting specifically, but he does talk about arriving at a camp from which everyone had fled, and he mentions spending two hours "cataloguing".'

Steve had been staring at the bark as she spoke, and now pointed to the stomach of the crocodile, which in the painting contained three cone-shaped objects. Two of the stick figures were carrying similar objects, and there were more on the outside of the crocodile.

'I know what these are,' he said. 'They're the stones that collect in a crocodile's stomach. They help grind up the food, and some say they're taken in for ballast, but to the Aboriginals they're very sacred. This bloke's carrying one,' he continued, moving his finger to a stick figure. 'I'd say it represents a relationship of some sort between the crocodile and the men. They're helping him carry the stones.'

'What about this, Steve?' Catherine Pope pointed to a vertical rectangle in one corner, composed of three squares sitting on top of each other. Each square had a diagonal line across it, and on one side of the top square was an ill-defined but deliberately-painted white blob. There was another within the top square, and two more at the bottom of the rectangle but outside the lower square.

'It's just a bone pole, isn't it?' replied Steve, turning with a puzzled look on his face.

'I'm sure it is, in which case these would be frogs.' She pointed to the white blobs. 'Romallo, the animal that lives in the bone pole and keeps the "devils" away from the dead—that's all okay, but look at this.'

She put one finger on the top diagonal line of the pole, and with her other hand she traced a similar line on the crocodile. She then moved her finger to the horizontal line separating the top squares on the pole; there was a similar line on the crocodile.

'They're the same, Steve,' she said. 'The lines on the crocodile are the same as those on the bone pole. If the lines on the bone pole signify that it's the place where bones are kept, then the crocodile's been painted as though it had the same function.'

'Then the stones may take the place of the frogs,' suggested Steve.

'That's the way my thinking was going, too, but there's not much evidence in the literature to support the idea of a crocodile being used

3

to hold the bones of the dead. No bone poles are ever carved like crocodiles, at least none that I've heard of. This could be an important find, Steve.'

Steve nodded in reply. When he had been working on crocodiles in Arnhem Land, he had felt that the old people were unhappy about his catching large crocodiles, but nothing had ever been said about it. Oondabund, who had been his constant assistant in Arnhem Land, would have said something about it if it had been really important to his people—anything to do with the dead was always important.

'There's one more clue, Steve, on the label on the back of the bark,' Catherine said.

The label was brown with age, but the black-inked writing was as clear as the day on which it had been written: '20th September, 1905. "Noomoonwari".'

Steve mouthed the word three or four times before shaking his head. 'It doesn't ring a bell with me, Cath. It's not the name for crocodile, or the stones. Maybe it refers to some dreaming animal or place. If it's really important, there's a good chance that only the old people know anything about it. There's still plenty of well-kept secrets in that country.'

'Well, whatever it is, I'm not going to have time to unravel it this trip,' she replied quietly, still staring at the bark. 'Strange how huge the crocodile is in relation to the men. Normally the men would have dominated the scene, but here they seem almost insignificant.' She fell silent, and Steve looked at his watch.

'I've got to get going, Cath. Sorry I couldn't be of more help. If I get back out to Maningrida I'll see what I can find out about "Noo-moon-wari". When are you leaving?'

'Monday. I'll be out of a job if I don't get back.' She smiled. 'You've got my address. Drop me a line if you find out what it's all about; it's intriguing. By the way, Steve, thanks for all the help.'

'It's been a pleasure.' Steve shook hands and walked to the foyer. Within seconds he was outside in the heat, which seemed refreshingly warm after the coolness of the Museum. The eagle's glass eyes watched him descend the steps, while the receptionist again contemplated the novel she had replaced on her desk.

4

PART ONE

I

John Besser and Oondabund had been fishing in the small dinghy for nearly two hours before they heard the plane in the distance. Besser was seated in the bow with his rod out over the gunwale, its thin, taut nylon line running to a red-striped silver lure which darted and wobbled through the muddy waters of the Liverpool River estuary. In the stern, Oondabund manoeuvred the steering handle of the 9½-horsepower outboard engine, keeping the dinghy six metres or so from the muddy river bank. This was the most likely place for Besser to catch a giant perch, a barramundi—so far he had caught only one fish, a one-and-a-half-kilo threadfin salmon.

Neither man was distracted when the plane circled overhead. It was the regular twice-weekly flight from Darwin, which brought mail and perishable foodstuffs to the settlement of Maningrida. Besser thought only of the fish that he hoped would snatch the lure, while Oondabund searched the mangroves and mudbanks as he always did, taking note of birds, water goannas, crabs, and a multitude of signs of animal life in and along the river.

For Besser, lure fishing with a rod and reel was a new-found pleasure. He had originally arrived in Darwin in 1966, not telling anyone where he had come from, nor what work he did. However, the police knew that he had been involved in the protection rackets in Melbourne, and had had to flee the southern city after helping himself to his employer's funds. In Darwin, Besser teamed up with Bluey Noakes, a well-known fish poacher, and until six months before, they had worked together professionally. Besser was more accustomed to seeing hundreds of barramundi meshed in illegal nets across inland waters than to catching fish one at a time.

Time and beer had given Besser a covering of surplus fat, but it would have been unwise to think that he was soft. He was a tough and ruthless adversary, who would stop at nothing when in a tight corner. One of the main reasons he and Bluey had not been caught poaching was that no one had the courage to inform on him, regardless of what rewards had been offered.

Besser was equally well known in Darwin for his sense of survival, and when the Inspectors were conducting a blitz on most of the poachers, he and Bluey were usually on vacation down south. The reason he was in Maningrida now was that his sense had told him it was time to lay low.

He and Bluey had been poaching crocodiles while they waited for their nets to fill with fish, and this had brought Steve Harris on to the scene. Annoyed by the fatalistic attitude that the Inspectors seemed to have developed towards Besser and Noakes, Steve hounded the poachers continually for nearly four months. Knowing it was only a matter of time before they were caught, Besser had stopped their fishing operation and had taken a job at the Maningrida power house for the wet season.

Besser's introduction to lure fishing had come from his two fellow workers at the power house, Eric Smith and Jack Reynolds. Both were keen fishermen, and Besser had reluctantly borrowed one of their rods and joined them on a day's fishing. That day he caught five barramundi to their two, and from then on, lure fishing had become almost an obsession. Whenever Smith or Reynolds could not join him, he paid Oondabund to drive the boat while he fished. When he had had a good day, he would sell the excess fish to the Aboriginals, whom he considered almost subhuman, to offset the cost of hiring Oondabund.

Oondabund did not regard Besser or lure fishing as being particularly important. Driving the boat for the day gave him money with which he bought food and tobacco, and he enjoyed being out on the river. To Oondabund, the river was very special. He had been born on its banks some fifty to sixty years before (no one knew exactly when), and had spent his life learning its secrets. He had seen the white man come, and had watched and even helped in the construction of the settlement at Maningrida. He had seen the steady stream of people leave the bush and move into the settlement, and had watched the futile attempts to replace Aboriginal law with Christian ways. Oondabund said little, but he watched, and had seen a great deal. It was important that he should do so, for, since his father's death, Oondabund had been responsible for the sacred objects which together held his people's history—if Aboriginal law was to survive, he must know the ways of both the white and black man.

The dinghy continued upstream, until they approached the mouth of the Liverpool River's major tributary, the Tomkinson River. Here Oondabund directed the boat out from the edge and through the turbulence created by the merging of two outgoing water streams. His destination was neither the main stream of the Liverpool River nor the Tomkinson River, but rather a small creek, Mungardobolo Creek, the mouth of which was at the point where the two rivers flowed together. The dinghy stopped rocking as it slid into the creek, past the steep, glutinous mudbanks that looked deceptively solid to the novice. High on the banks were the twisted and interlocked roots of the mangroves, which were submerged at full tide. It would soon be slack low tide, and for perhaps fifteen minutes the waters would be still. Then Oondabund knew Besser would catch his fish.

After rounding the first bend in the creek, the boat suddenly slowed, and when Besser looked up he saw Oondabund's wiry black arm pointing upstream. Sixty metres away, something was floating in the middle of the creek.

'What is it?' he asked gruffly, reeling in the line to make sure it did not tangle in the propeller.

Oondabund made no response. Standing in the drifting boat, he raised two fingers to shield his eyes from the morning sun. The expression on his face would have indicated concern to those who knew him well; when he spoke, he did so quietly and without hesitancy.

'Him look like crocodile. Dead one maybe? We go look.'

As the small boat moved upstream, Oondabund knew he was right. It *was* a large dead crocodile, floating upside down, the checkered white belly skin above the water line.

They moved to within ten metres of the creature.

'Jesus Christ!' said Besser. 'It's a bloody big croc.'

Oondabund edged the boat in beside the bloated carcass and saw that the outside layer of the scales was separating from the skin, but there were no marks on the taut, swollen hide; nothing showed how the crocodile had died. He reached for his spear, which lay on the deck, and redirected the boat in beside the carcass. Extending the spear, he prodded the carcass on its far side, and as it began to roll, he gave it a second and then a third push. The white belly rolled beneath the surface and the black and yellow back emerged, with row after row of raised, armoured plates. He poked the spear at a gaping hole in the top of the skull, disturbing a small green crab which clambered from the wound and disappeared into the water. Any blood had long since been leached out.

'This one him die,' he said with authority, his eyes continuing to scan the body as the boat again drifted away.

'Smithy must have shot it,' said Besser, indifferent to the fact that shooting crocodiles was illegal. 'It'd take that .303 of his to make a hole like that. Must have got it yesterday when he was out with Reynolds.'

Although Besser saw only the hole he had been shown, Oondabund's search revealed two other clues to the way in which the crocodile had died. The front left leg was almost completely severed from the body, attached only by a thin sliver of skin. There was a second hole in the head, at the tip of the snout, some thirty-five centimetres from the hole he had pointed out to Besser.

With no apparent change of expression, he turned to the fisherman and said, 'We go home now.'

'What?' demanded Besser angrily, slapping at the sandflies which had covered his naked arms within minutes of the boat stopping.

'This bad place, this little creek. We go home.'

Besser glared at the man standing in front of him. As he spoke, blood flushed the pink skin of his face, emphasising the purple mole on his cheek. 'Listen to me. It's my boat, my engine, I've already paid you, and it's my day fishing. Now sit down and get going. You bastards are all the same. As soon as anything happens you reckon it's bad dreaming or bad devils—anything to go home and bludge. Well, we're not going home. Get going; these bloody sandflies are driving me crazy and I haven't even had a decent strike yet.'

Without answering, Oondabund engaged the gears and the dinghy continued upstream away from the carcass, which now lay motionless in midstream; it was slack low tide. His rod over the side and lure trailing in the water, Besser waited in anticipation of a strike; Oondabund was no longer relaxed. His brown eyes searched the muddy banks and each time the boat rounded a bend, his eyes strained to scan the distant shores, but he was no longer looking for goannas or birds.

Oondabund knew that the two holes in the dead crocodile's head had not been made by bullets. They were puncture marks, teeth marks. The only animal that could inflict such wounds on a crocodile was a larger crocodile, and the distance between the holes indicated the width of its snout; it was a huge reptile. The torn arm had been ripped from its socket during an unseen struggle, a battle that had culminated in the death of the crocodile they had just seen. Conflicts occurred whenever a large male moved into territory owned by another crocodile. Normally, one would bite onto a limb of the other, and by rolling over and over, tear it from the body. If the loser had not been killed, it would seek out a small backwater or gully in which it could wait undisturbed until the wounds healed; the winner remained in its newly-won territory, challenging any further arrivals.

As the small boat progressed upstream, Oondabund searched for signs of the new owner of Mungardobolo Creek.

Besser watched the lure dart back and forth across the small waves streaming back from the engine. He anxiously awaited the thrill of the strike; the dead crocodile meant little to him. If Eric Smith had shot it, Besser could confirm the kill, and this he considered to be of some importance. Dead or wounded, crocodiles usually sank when shot, and many a kill was never confirmed. Like most whites, he considered crocodiles vermin, their only salvation being that their hide was worth money. That they were protected was irrelevant to him, and every one he and his partners had drowned in nets while poaching had been duly skinned and the skins illegally sold. Shipping hides from Maningrida to Darwin, where the market was, involved too much risk, so he had not been skinning crocodiles for some time, though he shot every one he could when out of sight of the settlement.

Oondabund was tense, wishing he were away from Mungardobolo Creek. Suddenly he swung the boat into midstream. Something dark was floating there. Within a second of turning, he realised it was an uprooted mangrove.

'What the bloody hell?' roared Besser, thrown off balance and struggling to hold the line well out from the propeller.

Oondabund did not answer. His facial expression seemingly unchanged, he redirected the boat back towards the bank and continued upstream.

Where a corridor of flood plain passes through a mangrove forest, there results an exposed grassy bank on the edge of the river. Such sites are sheltered from wind by the mangroves, and are fully exposed to the warmth of the sun. As the dinghy entered a straight section of the creek, two events occurred simultaneously. Oondabund sighted such a clearing, and Besser's lure, which darted past a partially submerged tree trunk, was snatched by a four-kilo barramundi. As the silver-green fish leaped from the water, the lure firmly embedded in its mouth, Oondabund saw something on the clearing.

'Hold it!' shouted Besser, the thin line racing from his contorted rod. 'I've got one!'

Oondabund ignored him and swung the boat out into midstream. It lay there on the clearing, motionless in the sun. With a barely audible 'twang', Besser's line reached the end of the reel and snapped.

'Stop the fucking boat!' raged Besser, throwing his rod to the deck with such force that the reel shattered. The dinghy continued across the stream. 'Stop the fucking thing, you black bastard!' His face was flushed with anger and his lips quivered with rage.

The boat slowed. It was on the opposite side of the creek. Before Besser could speak, Oondabund's hand pointed to the clearing on the opposite side of the creek. The new owner of Mungardobolo Creek lay undisturbed in the sun.

'Christ,' whispered Besser, his mouth remaining open and his clenched fists relaxing. 'It must be thirty feet long.'

The enormous saltwater crocodile lay on the edge of the flood plain, about three metres above the water level. Oondabund noted that there were no tracks between the water and where the animal lay; it had taken up its position at high tide, before the sun came up, and had remained there while the water flowed out, watching its territory.

As the two men stared in amazement, the incoming tide steadily carried the boat upstream, gradually replacing the view of the crocodile with mangrove forest.

Besser grabbed for the plastic tackle box which lay on the deck. Beneath a tangled mass of lures, traces, swivels and hooks, he located an oil-soaked rag. Unwrapped, it left a .38 short-barrelled revolver in his hands, and when he pushed a metal button on its side, the chamber swung open. Six brass shells were in place and none had the punch mark of a spent cartridge. Snapping the chamber back in position, he looked up at Oondabund.

'You no kill him that crocodile!' said Oondabund angrily. 'Him dreaming crocodile maybe.'

'Dreaming be buggered.'

Besser's mind was filled with images: the reception he would get when he asked Eric Smith and Jack Reynolds to help him carry the head from the boat; the look on their faces when they first saw it; their eagerness to hear every detail of how it had been found and killed. John Besser felt surges of excitement he had never experienced before. He knew what he wanted.

'Turn the boat around,' he ordered.

'You no kill him that crocodile,' repeated Oondabund stubbornly.

'Turn the bloody boat around when I tell you!'

'Him dreaming crocodile. We go home—leave him.'

Besser turned on Oondabund, waving the revolver threateningly. 'You just turn the bloody boat around when you're told, feller. I'm going to get that croc and that's that. You've been mad ever since you saw that dead croc near the mouth.' He leant closer to Oondabund. 'Just calm down, old man,' he said quietly, raising the small hand gun. 'This'll make sure your dreaming crocodile doesn't hurt you.'

There was a momentary silence, before Besser raised the weapon and pointed it at Oondabund's broad squat nose. 'Turn!' he demanded, as the hammer clicked back into position.

Without moving his eyes from Besser's, Oondabund gently pulled the steering handle towards him, and the boat began to turn. They were a good hundred metres upstream of the clearing.

'Steve Harris him come from Darwin you hurt that crocodile,' said Oondabund. 'You go biggest gaol for ever and ever.'

Besser lowered the revolver and released the hammer. 'Harris'll do nothing, he hasn't been out here for months. You just steer the boat and shut up.'

Undaunted, Oondabund continued. 'Two ways you no finish him, that crocodile. One way, that cowboy gun like toy one for him, and two way, him dreaming crocodile—no white man can kill him.'

Besser ignored the comment, settling himself in the bow with the hand gun resting on the gunwale. They were about twenty metres from the crocodile, and already the gap in the mangroves could be seen.

'Switch the engine off when I tell you,' he demanded.

About twelve metres off, Besser signalled. The prize was coming into view, but they were travelling too fast. The engine was still going.

'You bastard!' hissed Besser, sitting up and turning as the engine cut out. The dinghy continued against the tide for a few seconds, before drifting to a halt directly opposite the clearing and some ten metres from it. The enormous crocodile was still motionless on the bank. Besser lay down and lined up the puny revolver.

With the engine off, the only sound in the creek was the gentle lapping of the rising tide on the mud bank. When the revolver hammer clicked into position, it sounded loud; but still the crocodile did not move.

'One shot,' thought Besser, as he lined up the square front sight of the revolver with the groove in the rear sight, and positioned them on the crocodile. 'One shot's all I'll get before he dives.'

For the first time since they had seen it, the crocodile moved. The massive head slowly rose and turned towards the boat. Narrowed against the sun, the two yellow eyes perceived a shape, a low-profiled shape, floating in the water with its back arched—an intruder.

The left front leg moved forward.

'Look out, him come now,' said Oondabund, quickly grabbing at the wooden shaft of the fish spear. His movement rocked the boat enough to spoil Besser's aim.

'Stay still!' hissed Besser, neither raising nor turning his head.

Oondabund searched the banks, absorbing the details of his immediate environment. The crocodile was turning; the giant head now pointed down the mud bank.

Besser fired.

The bullet sliced the skin between the crocodile's eyes, but was deflected along the heavy bones of its skull and disappeared out over the flood plain. At the same moment, the great claws drove into the ground, pushing the enormous animal down over the bank and into the creek, amidst a spray of water and semi-liquid mud.

Oondabund leaped to his feet, spear in hand. The crocodile was ploughing through the water towards the boat. Before Besser could fire again, Oondabund leaped over the side, causing the boat to capsize. Besser's second shot went into the water, and as he clambered to his feet, a mass of yellow with countless white teeth rushed towards him. He screamed as the boat moved from under his feet, the gunwale crushed between the crocodile's vast jaws.

A second later, he was on the animal's back, screaming uncontrollably. The crocodile's huge jaws released the crushed gunwale and instantly swung towards its back, slamming shut with a deafening report inches from Besser's head. Besser was off its back, swimming, clawing at the water, fighting within a screen of splashes, choking as he inhaled the brown saline waters as well as air. He concentrated every ounce of energy he had on regaining the bank somewhere in front of him.

Oondabund surfaced when he felt the bank under his feet, and ran across the thick holding mud that separated the water from the safety of the flood plain. He glanced back to see Besser swimming for his life, and watched the great crocodile violently shaking the boat, the intruder into its territory. The dinghy was almost completely submerged now, and as soon as the crocodile had released its grip, it disappeared. Only the fuel tank floated where, seconds before, there had been a complete boat and two men.

A couple of metres from shore, Besser was frantically trying to move through the shallow water and mud. The crocodile's head turned towards him, and after watching for perhaps a second, it sank below the surface.

Three steps through the mud saw Besser's ninety-kilogram bulk buried up to the knees, and going deeper with each movement. A vision of the head behind him forced him to keep struggling, his breaths coming in short sobs as his arms clawed into the viscous bank. The shaft of Oondabund's spear was before him and he grabbed at it wildly, his mud-covered hands fighting for a grip on the smooth wooden surface.

Three metres behind him, the head emerged.

Besser's legs came free and, gasping loudly, he slid and crawled to the firmer mud higher up the bank. Oondabund pulled him up the last couple of metres, over the edge and onto the plain. Besser's mud-covered body shook in an uncoordinated firing of signals to both muscles and nerves. When he sighted the crocodile's head in the water, he shouted loudly, trying to run on legs that collapsed beneath him. Oondabund grasped his arm and held it firmly, saying, 'Him no climb up here. Him too heavy.'

Besser lay where he had fallen, his chest heaving in and out as air rushed into his worn body. Each heartbeat resounded in his ears and he was aware that tears were running down his cheeks; he whimpered and sobbed, unable to calm his shattered nerves.

The great crocodile watched Besser and Oondabund, its only movement the irregular flick of membranes across the yellow orbs. Then, without warning, it submerged as noiselessly as it had appeared, a small surface wave being the only sign that the mighty tail had swept unseen through the dark waters.

Oondabund turned to Besser. They were alive and this white man had learned something he would always remember.

'We go home now,' he ordered.

Besser looked up from where he lay as the faintest trace of a smile vanished from Oondabund's stern face. Still gasping, his lips quivering, he tried to stand, but again his legs folded. He could see himself falling on the crocodile's back, and felt the raised scales which dug into him but which swirled from beneath him as they touched, the yellow mouth and solid teeth, the unearthly bang as the jaws slammed shut beside him. His hands clenched on tussocks of grass. Nothing was going to move him from the security of the plain.

Oondabund waited silently for almost five minutes, and then without speaking, strode out across the flood plain in the direction of Maningrida, leaving Besser where he lay. The realisation that he was being left behind sent a wave of fear through the white man, and he clambered to his feet. Oondabund could hear him staggering behind, but he did not look back; once Besser started walking he would soon recover.

Besser and Oondabund walked in silence, each man deep in his own thoughts. The fact that Aboriginals could walk off into the bush, yet always find the shortest distance between two places, was something all whites in Arnhem Land accepted without question, so Oondabund led and Besser blindly followed.

The route Oondabund chose meant wading a small tidal creek, and swimming the narrow but deep Tomkinson River. At the creek, Besser had to force himself down the bank, his heart pounding as once again he waded into flowing brown water. When he stumbled on a submerged mangrove, a scream surged in his throat, but he managed to suppress it to a muffled moan.

Swimming the Tomkinson River proved yet another trial. The incoming tide brought a strong current, and in midstream Besser began to tire, and was carried upstream. A burst of energy and fear drove his arms frantically until he felt the opposite bank, where he lay, momentarily catching his breath. Hauling himself up the bank, he saw Oondabund walking some fifteen metres downstream. A wallaby broke cover in the long grass close by and, terror-stricken, Besser jumped sideways, falling back down the bank. He wanted to stop where he was, but he knew that Oondabund was still walking; within minutes he would be very much alone. Sobered, he climbed the bank and started out after the steadily moving figure, half-hidden by the waving dry grass that covered the plain and had not yet been burnt.

Oondabund thought only of the crocodile, which was by far the biggest he had ever seen in the river. When a child, his father had taken him to a billabong in the upper reaches of the river, deep in the stone country where no white man had ever travelled. Here lived a monstrous crocodile, a dreaming crocodile of gigantic proportions. As he walked, Oondabund felt a surge of excitement. Could the crocodile they had just encountered be the same animal? Both were immense and both were very dark, the darkness being a sure sign that they were from fresh water. Only the very old men would know. They were clever, knowing the land as it had always been, and Oondabund resolved to see them as soon as he reached the settlement.

After leaving the river, Besser's thoughts passed through three definite phases. For nearly an hour, he saw the flash of yellow and white, and heard the terrifying snap of the crocodile's huge jaws closing. Every movement and sound that accompanied their trek made him jump.

When they left the flood plains and began walking through the open forest, Oondabund was usually only about five metres in front, and Besser's thoughts began to centre on him. The black man had warned him not to interfere with the crocodile, and had remained calm when he panicked; he had seen the whimpering and tears, the fear and panic. Within a day, all the Aboriginals in Maningrida would know what had happened, and Besser could already see the children pointing and laughing, the adults smiling mockingly. Fortunately, he consoled himself, Oondabund's ability to relate the story in English was limited, so if he told the whites his version first, they might never know the whole truth.

In the last stage of their journey, they walked on the timbered high country. Besser began to plan his entrance into Maningrida, deciding that his first action would be to confront the Superintendent, Greg Jackson, and demand that a hunting party be sent out to kill the crocodile. The Superintendent would have to contact Wildlife Division for permission, but they would not be able to refuse—it was definitely a man-eater. Besser smiled to himself at the thought of Steve Harris in Darwin giving permission for him, John Besser, to kill what was perhaps the biggest crocodile left in the Northern Territory. Steve Harris didn't like anyone killing any crocodile, and the thought of John Besser legally killing this one would be abhorrent. The corners of Besser's thin mouth formed into a wry smile—maybe he would organise a photograph of himself and the dead crocodile, just for Steve Harris's benefit.

After seeing the Superintendent, Besser planned a long, hot shower, a change of clothes, and a good dozen cans of beer. By the time his two fellow-workers, Smithy and Reynolds, returned, he would be ready to tell them all about what happened on the river, and the version he told would be completely up to him. They would be eager to listen, as it was by far the most exciting thing that had happened during his stay in Maningrida, and within the past six months they had told each other the highlights of their lives at least twice over.

The last segment of the eleven-kilometre trek was much easier walking. Oondabund brought them out onto a soft sandy track which led to the outskirts of the settlement. When they reached the first of the buildings, Oondabund stopped and indicated that he was going down to the far camp. It was here that the old people lived, and he needed to see them urgently.

'I'm going to see Greg Jackson,' Besser answered, adding, 'Thanks,' after obvious hesitation. But Oondabund didn't hear him, for he was already striding away through the grass, anxious to reach the small group of tin shelters that housed the most elderly of his people.

The Superintendent was startled when the office door banged open to reveal Besser, his clothes torn and covered in dried mud, his hair matted and erect. The sweat from his forehead had streaked lines across his nose and cheeks. His bare legs were black and scratched from the burnt vegetation through which he had walked. The identity of the intruder was masked until the Superintendent saw the telltale mole protruding through the thin coating of dirt. Completely unused to walking in the heat, John Besser had lost almost a stone in weight.

'What the . . .'

'You've got a man-eating croc in the river, Jackson, a thirty-footer.

18

It attacked me and Oondabund down in that middle-arm creek. Nearly got both of us.'

The word 'nearly' echoed in the Superintendent's ears, contrasting markedly with his initial visions of blood and torn limbs, screams and panic.

'*Nearly?*' he repeated. 'Did it take anyone?'

'No,' replied Besser, 'but not from lack of bloody trying. Missed me by inches and chewed the bloody boat to pieces.'

'What about Oondabund? Where's he?'

'He's okay. He's just like the rest of 'em. He was over the side as soon as the thing started coming. Shit scared. Left me there on me own, the bastard.'

The two men stared at each other in silence. For the Superintendent, the problem represented a precedent, and he was unsure what to do about it. He had never been happy about the ban on killing crocodiles, because he considered them a potential hazard to the people, but in two years at Maningrida they had caused no trouble. Until now.

'You'd better come in and sit down, John. Tell me exactly what happened. I'm not sure just what to do.'

'I'll tell you what to bloody do!' said Besser loudly, as he pulled up a chair. 'We've got to get a hunting party together.'

'But they're protected . . .'

'Protected be buggered!' cried Besser. 'Nothing's protected when it kills people. Steve Harris in Wildlife, he's the man to contact. Tell him what's happened and that you're sending out a hunting party.'

Again there was an uneasy silence for perhaps twenty seconds. The Superintendent finally said, 'Tell me exactly what happened, and then we'll get on to what we're going to do about it. Like you say, the crocodile's got to go.'

For twenty minutes, Besser related an abridged version of what had happened. There was no mention of Oondabund's attempts to make them leave the creek after seeing the dead crocodile. He did not refer to his own attempt to kill the crocodile with a revolver. According to Besser, when they first sighted the giant crocodile, it was heading down the bank towards them. Oondabund promptly leaped over the side, leaving Besser on his own. When the crocodile hit the boat, he was thrown into the water and the crocodile tried to take him, as it did again when he was trying to climb up through

19

the mud to where Oondabund was safely standing on the plain. Besser concluded with, 'We'd better get a hunting party together so that we can leave as soon as it's dark.'

'Just hang on a bit, John. I'm going to have to contact Darwin to get permission from Wildlife.'

'*Permission!*' repeated Besser, scornfully. 'Just tell Harris you're doing it. He can't say anything.'

'Let me do it my way, eh? You go home and clean up and I'll get in touch with ... Harris, was it?'

'Steve Harris. But don't *ask* him for permission—*tell* him.'

'For Christ's sake, John, I've got to get permission. Go home and I'll come around.'

Besser stood to leave. 'If it'd been one of your precious Abo kids you wouldn't be bloody worried about permission. You lot make me bloody sick!'

2

Steve Harris was in the small office of the Darwin research station, adding the finishing touches to a progress report he had spent most of the day writing. At thirty-six he was reasonably happy with the course his life was taking, though it had not been carefully planned —it had just happened that way.

Originally from Sydney, Steve had spent the previous six years as a Senior Technical Officer with the Northern Territory's Wildlife Division. He now considered himself a Territorian, and much of his life prior to heading up north had become distinctly hazy. His present duties were varied, taking in anything from pure research and public relations to field enforcement of the Wildlife Act, but the variety made the position continually interesting. He was unmarried, and enjoyed the freedom of being able to pursue whatever he considered important, whenever it came up.

He had not always had that freedom, nor had he always wanted it. After graduating with a basic university degree, Steve had joined a research team studying wild pigs in western New South Wales. Steve and wildlife research suited each other, and after three years, when the team leader was promoted, Steve was offered the position, which he gladly accepted.

The following three years saw major changes in his life. Instead of spending most of his time in the bush, he was expected to be in Sydney most of the time and to direct others in the field. Implicit in the new position was the responsibility of representing the Department at certain conferences, and it was at one of these that he first met Mac Wilson, Director of the Northern Territory Wildlife Division. Steve and Mac soon became the closest of friends, and Mac and his wife Anne flew the several thousand kilometres between Darwin and Sydney when Steve and Susan eventually decided to marry.

At twenty-nine, Steve thought his life was well mapped. He was married and still deeply in love with Susan, he had a four-year-old son upon whom he doted, a permanent job that he liked, and the ever-present prospect of promotion. But an automobile accident robbed him of Susan and his son, and with them went much of his purpose in living.

The four months after the accident saw an accelerating loss of interest in all aspects of Steve's life. He sold the house and bought an apartment close to work, but it was empty, lacking the warmth that only Susan could have brought. He started drinking heavily after work and during weekends, and forced himself to seek out new companions and a social life. None of it worked. A smile, a flash of teeth, a swirl of blonde hair or the sight of a young boy were perpetual reminders of what he had lost, all the things he knew were gone for ever.

He resigned his position, intending to move away from Sydney completely, and to start a new life. At this point Mac and Anne arrived in Sydney for four weeks' holiday. Appalled at the state in which they found Steve and his dwelling, Anne set about making the apartment a home, while Mac tried to get Steve out of his depression. During one of their many conversations, Mac happened to mention the vacancy they now had in their Division—they needed someone to work on crocodiles. Steve jumped at the opportunity, and although Mac emphasised that he was over-qualified for the Senior Technical Officer position available, it made no difference.

Within two months, Steve Harris was a member of the Northern Territory Wildlife Division, and, after an additional month, he found himself stationed at Maningrida, on the north coast of Arnhem Land. Here he studied saltwater crocodiles, keeping very much to himself, and appearing to confide in only one person, Oondabund. The relationship between the two men was built on mutual respect and understanding. For Steve, who had never really known full-blood Aboriginals, Oondabund represented an encyclopedia of knowledge, which made his own expertise with wildlife seem ludicrously inadequate. Oondabund knew that the young white man was genuinely interested in his people and the crocodiles, and was always willing to listen and learn.

Steve stayed in Maningrida for three years, by which time he had essentially completed the field aspects of the crocodile research. In this time he had learned a great deal about the Aboriginals, and he felt he understood them better than most, though he realised that their cultural and spiritual beliefs were so complex, and that many secrets were so strictly guarded, that he could never hope fully to understand them.

When he returned to Darwin, Steve became involved in more of the day-to-day tasks associated with crocodiles. A considerable public relations effort was required, because, although they were protected and few in number, the occasional crocodile appeared in populated areas, or took someone's pet dog. An illegal market in hides had developed, and poachers were taking their toll of the recovering juvenile crocodiles, which had never been hunted and were not wary of man.

Further research was needed on captive crocodiles, and Mac had acquired two houses and a block of land on the outskirts of Darwin, which Steve had converted to a small research station for this purpose. Here he kept crocodiles in pens, and had an office as well as a modest Government home.

He was in the office when the phone rang and he found himself connected to the Superintendent at Maningrida some five hundred kilometres away.

The Superintendent related the events John Besser had described, and Steve listened carefully and jotted down the occasional note. When he had finished, Steve asked for a description of Besser, and for the name of the Aboriginal who had been with him. To the Superintendent's suggestion of a hunting party, Steve replied with a definite 'No,' saying that such a group would only succeed in wounding the crocodile, or making it wary. He agreed to come out on a charter flight at first light in the morning, and emphasised that no one should go near the area until then.

Steve always investigated reported crocodile attacks personally, because, although some were genuine, the majority resulted from a combination of imagination, fear and ignorance. It had taken a considerable public relations effort to win any support for the fact that 'protection' was essential if the crocodiles, which had been grossly over-exploited for their hides, were to survive. Each time an attack was reported, some of this support was lost, and this did not depend on whether the attack was genuine or not.

Within minutes of terminating the conversation, Steve phoned Mac Wilson at the main Wildlife Division Office.

'Looks like there's been a croc attack at Maningrida, Mac. Just had a radio sched with the Superintendent out there. No one's been hurt, but a boat and engine were lost and he wants something done about it.'

'Who is the Superintendent out there? Do you know him?'

'Never met him. Jackson's his name. He's the bloke that wrote in about a permit for the Abos to start killing crocs and selling the skins. You remember, he arrived about a year after I left.'

'I remember,' replied Mac after a short pause. 'What about the attack, Steve? Sound genuine?'

'Well, it does, but there's something strange about it. Besser was the bloke who reported it, and he was supposed to have been with Oondabund when it happened.'

'John Besser?' repeated Mac incredulously. 'What's he doing out there?'

'Supposed to be working at the power house—has been for six months.'

There was another pause before Mac answered, 'Guess that explains why you haven't had any trouble from him for a while. Wonder what the hell he's really up to out there?'

'Something pretty strange. According to the Superintendent, Besser had the day off and he went lure fishing for barramundi! Oondabund was driving the boat for him.'

'You're joking. It can't be the same man.'

'It's him, all right, even down to that growth on his cheek.'

'You going to go out and have a look around, Steve? Sounds like it'd be worth it.'

'Told the Superintendent I'd be leaving at first light. Besser reckoned the croc was thirty feet long! He's seen enough to know a big one from a little one, so it does sound a fair size.'

'Like the thirty-footer at Gove, I'll bet,' murmured Mac. 'Anyway, if you have any trouble, let me know over the radio. See if you can find out what Besser's been up to—Oondabund'll know.'

'Okay, Mac, see you when I get back.'

Steve was smiling broadly when he replaced the phone. The first croc attack report he had investigated on his return to Darwin from Maningrida was a purported monster nine metres long in a small creek near Gove Peninsula; it had 'attacked' two fishermen. Having never seen a crocodile longer than five metres, Steve let his enthusiasm run wild, and arrived in Gove armed with his rifle, plus a large case of photographic equipment, tape measures and preserving equipment. If such a crocodile had to be destroyed, he was going to make sure that it was fully-documented and preserved for science. At Gove, Steve learned that the two men had not actually *seen* the crocodile: they had heard it roar, and made a narrow escape. A survey revealed that there were no crocodiles over two metres long in the area, and, although the sound might have been made by a crocodile, many other animals could also have been responsible. Steve and Mac had often laughed about the episode since, though it had been a very practical lesson.

It was almost half-past six in the evening when the Superintendent arrived at the single men's quarters where Besser lived. He had tried to locate Oondabund en route, but had been told that he was 'at business' with the old men—something with which few people were welcome to interfere. After a light tap on the door, he entered the communal lounge-cum-dining-room, which served the three bachelors employed to maintain Maningrida's power house.

'Come on in,' called Besser, who was slumped in a cane chair with a beer can in his hand. 'Help yourself—there's a beer in the fridge. Smithy and Reynolds have gone down to Roy's place to get some grog for tonight. It'll be cold out there on the river.'

After retrieving a beer, Jackson lowered himself into a chair opposite Besser. At least a dozen empty beer cans were strewn on the once highly-polished but now badly-scarred wooden floor. Piles of newspapers and magazines were everywhere, and the three ashtrays in sight were all brimming full and spilling out onto the table and the floor. The remains of three meals were among the filth on the table. Besser seemed unaware of the state of the house; perhaps he was used to it.

Besser himself had changed considerably. Clean shorts and singlet and a complete loss of the mud had made a considerable difference. His legs were covered with a hundred small lines, marked with red; a tribute to the walk he and Oondabund had done through virgin bush.

'Smithy and Reynolds are coming,' said Besser, excitement in his voice. 'We're leaving just after dark. How'd you go with Wildlife?'

'Got on to them okay. That Steve Harris bloke's going to come out at first light in the morning.'

'He'll be a bit bloody late,' replied Besser, grinning to himself. 'I'd say we'll have the bastard by midnight. Maybe we'll have the head to welcome Harris with.'

'John,' the Superintendent said slowly and quietly, 'they've told us to leave it alone until Harris arrives. No one's to go out tonight.'

'What d'you mean?' snapped Besser.

'Simply that. Harris said specifically not to let anyone go out after the croc until he arrives. Reckons we'd wound it or scare it.'

'I suppose you told him it was me that got attacked,' said Besser, his face flushing with anger. 'Yeah, bloody Harris wouldn't like that at all. He won't kill a crocodile the size of this one. He thinks more of crocodiles and Abos than he does of half the white people in the Territory.'

'I'm sorry,' said Jackson, realising there was more in the relationship between Besser and Harris than met the eye. 'But that's the instruction.'

Besser continued as though he hadn't heard Jackson's last statement. 'Bloody waste of taxpayers' money, that's what it is. Harris just doesn't want me to kill it. That's what it's all about. I've killed hundreds of crocs and he knows it. He just doesn't want me to have a go at this one. Well, what if I do? What can he do about it?'

'Come on, John, don't make life difficult. We've just got to do what we're told. Like you say, it seems pretty stupid, the croc could be miles away by tomorrow—but there it is.'

Besser ignored Jackson's consoling words. He stared blankly at the wall, his face flushed, the purple mole prominent among the short stubble of his unshaven face.

'Now, don't do anything stupid,' cautioned Jackson, becoming apprehensive about the atmosphere in the room.

'Stupid?' yelled Besser. 'I nearly get killed by a fucking croc, and you think I'm stupid because I want to kill it? You're as bad as Harris.'

'Don't get me wrong,' said Jackson. 'I'd like to see the bloody thing dead as much as you would. I'd prefer it if every croc was dead. But there's nothing I can do about it.'

'Yeah, well, there's something I can do about it,' said Besser, who appeared almost in a trance.

The Superintendent finished his can of beer and stood to leave. By the door he stopped and turned to face Besser, who appeared unaware of his departure.

'Look, John,' he said, 'I've told you what they told me. If you do go and do anything, I don't want to know about it. Right?'

Jackson was out of the door before Besser answered, his voice barely above a whisper. 'For Christ's sake, piss off.'

When Eric Smith and Jack Reynolds returned to Besser's house with the extra beer, they were both inwardly relieved to learn about Steve Harris's instructions. Neither had been looking forward to hunting a nine-metre crocodile from Smithy's four-metre aluminium dinghy, although they had agreed to do so in a spirit of mateship.

Besser was obviously extremely bitter, and still determined to go out after the crocodile, but after a little encouragement from Smithy and Reynolds and at least a dozen cans of beer, he became absorbed in a card game. This was followed by their nightly darts championship, and by half-past ten, it seemed that the crocodile attack had been largely forgotten.

Jack Reynolds brought the subject up again. He was curious to know whether in fact Besser had really 'kept his cool' when the crocodile attacked. Although Besser answered him in the affirmative, with enough emphasis to prevent him from seeking further information, Besser's mind was once again directed to the crocodile.

Ten minutes later, he said, 'Come on Jack, Smithy, let's go get that bloody crocodile. I'm not going to wait for Harris. We'll take your .303, Smithy.'

'It's pretty late, John,' said Smith. 'Why not leave it till morning?'

'Yeah,' agreed Reynolds. 'I was only joking before, mate. Let's not bother about it now.'

'Leave it be buggered,' replied Besser emphatically. 'I'm not going to have Steve Harris tell me whether or not I can blow over a crocodile that tried to kill me! Come on, you two, let's get the battery and light into the boat.'

'For Christ's sake, John! Jack was only joking, mate—taking the micky out of you. Let's all have another beer—maybe another round of darts,' urged Smith.

'I'm not worried about what Jack said. I want to get the croc, that's all. You pair don't have to come if you don't want to.'

There was a momentary silence in the room before Eric Smith spoke again. 'Look, John, let's be bloody sensible. We've all been drinking and, like you say, it's a bloody big croc. Why not wait till morning, like Jack says? If you want to, you can get going before Harris gets here.'

'I'm going,' said Besser stubbornly. 'I thought you two would like to join in the fun—you know, something to tell your grandkids about. But you don't have to, I can do it on my own.'

Neither man answered as Besser looked from one to the other. 'Well, I'm off,' he announced. 'See you in the morning.'

Reynolds was the first to speak when Besser had left the room. 'We can't let him go out alone, Smithy.'

'Why not? He'll sober up and come back. Do him the world of bloody good—get the croc out of his system.'

'We can't, Smithy. It's hopeless out there on your own at night. Come on, we'll have to go. Anyway, he's shot a lot of crocs and it might be fun.'

'Those stories of his about being a croc shooter and fish poacher are probably bullshit, you know.'

The sound of the engine starting outside cut into their conversation. They looked at each other in silence, then both began to stand simultaneously.

'Bugger the stupid bastard. Grab the grog and let's get out there before he backs the bloody truck into me boat.'

Oondabund was sitting alone on the beach when he saw the headlights of the Toyota moving onto the barge landing. When he noticed the manoeuvring of a boat trailer into the water, he rose and walked towards it in the darkness. From the shadows, less than forty-five metres from the landing, he watched the men at work.

The tide was ebbing, and some fifteen metres of sand lay between the landing and the water. Besser had driven the truck on to the sand, and in the lights of the vehicle, the three men dragged the boat to the receding water. Two men returned, picked up gear from the back of the truck and switched off its lights.

'What about taking the truck and trailer up on the landing, John?' asked one of them.

'No, it'll be okay,' came the answer. 'We'll be back well before the tide comes in.'

In the moonlight, Oondabund watched as two of the men climbed into the boat, and the third pushed it out through the shallow water. He saw the outboard lowered when the water deepened, and heard the three pulls of the starting cord before the engine burst into life.

He watched the phosphorescence of the bow wave, created by a billion disturbed micro-organisms, as the boat streamed out from the shore and turned upstream into the river. Oondabund recognised each of the men, and he saw the rifle.

The realisation that someone was knocking lightly on the door gradually drew Greg Jackson from sleep. His watch indicated twenty minutes to one, and the gentle repetitive tap was definitely that of an Aboriginal; hesitant to disturb, but determined to do so.

On seeing Oondabund through the screen, he knew it was no minor matter. Something important had happened, at least something important to Oondabund.

'Those white men go try finish him that crocodile,' said Oondabund. 'Them leave by landing now. In small boat belong that Mr Smith man.'

'Besser's mob?' inquired Jackson.

'That Mr Besser and them other ones. They take rifle and light; them try finish him all right.'

'Well, what would you like me to do about it, Oondabund?'

The Aboriginal merely shrugged his shoulders. It was not his job to determine actions taken against Europeans.

'Do you think they'll have a chance of finding the crocodile?' asked Jackson.

'Maybe find him, but them no finish him that crocodile. No white man can kill him, that one, him special Aborigine crocodile, dreaming crocodile.'

'Well, why don't we wait till they get back? I'll see them in the morning. They were told not to go, and they'll get into trouble for disobeying.'

'Them get into trouble from that crocodile if they find him. That one, he not frightened that white feller—not like all other crocodile.'

On the river, Besser, Smith and Reynolds had been searching with the spotlight for what seemed hours; when Smith checked his watch, it showed 3.05 am. The beer had long since gone, and for the last hour their vision had been restricted by a light mist rising from the water's surface. They had searched where Besser thought the attack had taken place, though Smith doubted whether it was possible to distinguish one bend in the creek from another in the daytime, let alone at night. They had sighted five crocodiles, but all were less

29

than two metres long. Reynolds had suggested they shoot these and go home, but Besser thought the shots might scare the one crocodile he wanted.

'Don't you think we'd better be getting back, mate? It's after three,' called Smith, shivering in the stern.

'Yeah,' added Reynolds. 'I'm as cold as a witch's tit; it's the only thing keeping me awake. Let's give it away.'

Besser continued scanning the light without answering. Going home had been suggested two hours before, when the beer ran out, and had come up every half-hour since then. Their chances of seeing anything in the mist were slight, but every time Besser considered turning for home he felt the urge to find and kill the crocodile. Besides, Steve Harris would learn that they had gone out, and to return empty-handed would be even more embarrassing.

'Come on, John,' repeated Smith. 'Let's call it a night.'

Besser relented. 'Another half-hour. If we don't see anything by then, we'll go home.'

Smith automatically checked the time again, deciding to remind Besser exactly when the half-hour expired.

'Take her up in there,' said Besser, pointing to where a minor tidal creek entered the river. 'Looks good.'

The entrance was barely nine metres wide, and after slowing the engine Smith directed the boat into the narrow channel. Rounding the first corner, Besser immediately saw what he had been waiting for—red points of reflected light. Without diverting his attention from the red glows, he spoke—not loudly, not softly, but with a seriousness that startled his companions.

'Keep it on his eyes,' he muttered, passing the warm light to Reynolds, while moving his other arm up and down as a signal for Smith to slow down. As the engine revs dropped, Besser picked up the rifle, and, still staring at the reflections, worked the first bullet into the chamber. The boat was barely moving as he crouched and lay the rifle on the bow; forty-five metres away, their quarry lay motionless.

The crocodile had been in the water since sunset. It had drifted out of Mungardobolo Creek on the fall tide, after the disturbance with Besser and Oondabund. By chance it had approached and entered the small creek, where it crawled out on a low mudbank to catch the last rays of the afternoon sun. When temperatures began to fall with the onset of night, it slid back into the water, which was comparatively warm, and positioned itself among the limbs of a partly-submerged dead mangrove. If left undisturbed, it would wait here until the tide changed, and let the rising water level lift the great body to the level of the high bank. Only then would it crawl out and orient itself to catch the morning sun.

It had heard the engine vibrations over an hour before, perceiving them only as a disturbance among the normal night sounds. It had seen the spotlight beam before the boat rounded the corner, but had not responded until the light shone directly into its yellow eyes. Then, in a fraction of a second, the pupils contracted from a black sphere to a very narrow slit. Momentarily blinded, and with the engine vibrations now throbbing into its primitive head, its protective ear flaps began to vibrate irregularly. The great crocodile was not frightened, because it feared nothing, but it was confused and thankful to be well hidden in the wet branches where it intended to remain until the disturbance passed.

When Reynolds saw the outline of the head, he realised that Besser had not exaggerated the crocodile's size. 'Look at the bloody thing. Christ, let's leave it—it's too big.'

'Shut up and keep the light on it,' hissed Besser, determined not to fire until they were at point-blank range.

As the distance between the boat and crocodile gradually decreased, Reynolds saw the head getting bigger and bigger.

'For Christ's sake, leave it, John!' he repeated in a wavering voice.

'Keep the bloody light steady!' snapped Besser, still not taking his eyes from the reflections, now barely eighteen metres away. A sharp sideways gesture of his arm, and Smith, who had not yet seen the crocodile, switched off the engine.

When the engine stopped, Jack Reynolds panicked, thinking that the engine had stalled and that they were helpless.

'What's up?' he yelled frantically, standing in the small boat and swinging the light to the engine. 'Get it going!'

Blinded by the intense beam, Smith shielded his eyes as Besser grabbed the light and cast the beam back out in front; there was no reflection. As the boat stopped rocking, he passed the light back to Reynolds and released the safety catch on the rifle. Accepting the light without question, Reynolds again began to search up and down the small creek, the wave of panic slowly passing. It was deathly quiet, with not even the splash of a small fish. Smith's vision slowly returned.

The crocodile's huge eyes, blinded by the light, registered only an increase in light intensity as the boat approached. The engine vibrations had stopped, and then the light shifted position. The giant pupils expanded in the darkness to see the movement fourteen metres in front, and the small splashes of the rocking boat rushed through the turbid waters—prey, struggling prey.

One sweep of the tail and the body was dragged backwards and down, the ear flaps shut and the valves of each nostril closed; the animal's heart rate slowed from twenty beats per minute to three as it dived.

'Switch the torch on, Smithy,' said Besser slowly and with authority.

The small beam cut a thin line through the mist as the boat drifted in the quietness, passing the tangled mass of mangroves that had held their prize. The stillness and dancing shadows emphasised to each of them that he was vulnerable, and in danger.

'Let's get out of here,' said Besser, nervously.

Smith did not need to be told twice, and, putting down the torch, he reached for the starting cord. As he flexed to pull the plaited cord, he felt a disturbance in the water. Besser and Reynolds turned as the nasal valves opened and air hissed from the crocodile's deflating lungs. Besser saw the massive sculptured head for the second time in twenty-four hours, and this time it was moving fast. As he swung the rifle to his shoulder, the crocodile's tail ploughed through the water, driven by over half a tonne of muscle. The crocodile was rising at the stern, its jaws opening wide. Besser fired, and the boat rolled right over, but Eric Smith was screaming, his thighs crushed and pinned in the grip of the vice-like jaws that no human being could release.

In the creek, Besser felt warm salty water covering his face. Reynolds panicked, but his struggling attempts to swim were futile; he sank beneath the surface, water rushing into his lungs as he tried to call for help. The thrashing tail beside him smashed into his side, the tail that was rolling the giant reptile's body, dragging Smith beneath the surface and extinguishing his cries.

Reaching the bank in three strokes, Besser frantically clambered through the mud in the darkness. He could see nothing, but his arms fought wildly to grip the mangroves, and once he had found them, he crawled, pushed and fought his way among them, knowing only that he was moving away from the water. When he stopped, his heart pounding, he listened, hopeful of a sign from his companions.

Suddenly the silence was shattered by an unearthly scream of terror. The crocodile had surfaced with Smith, still conscious, trapped between its jaws. A frenzied explosion of splashing and the creek was still once more.

'Smithy!' yelled Besser into the darkness, but there was no response. 'Jack! Jack!'

Overcome by the desire to get further away from the water, he again fought the entwining vegetation, and slowly progressed inland.

It was 3.35 am, exactly half an hour after John Besser had said they would go home.

In Maningrida, slow repeated knocking on the Superintendent's door again roused him from sleep. At the front door, he squinted in the morning sun.

'What is it now, Oondabund? It's only 6.30.'

'That white man, Mr Besser, him not come home this place yet. Him still up along river there maybe, but him truck proper wet one now.'

Greg Jackson rubbed his eyes. 'What did you say about the truck?'

'Him all wet. That white man him leave truck near landing.' Oondabund held up a loosely clenched fist to signify the truck. 'Big tide him come up now.' Slowly he raised his other hand up the side of his fist.

'Oh, shit,' said Jackson, picturing the government Toyota being swamped by the incoming tide.

Oondabund was smiling. 'Him look like boat, that truck. All the kids them laugh.'

'Besser's outboard's probably broken down up the river. Do you want to take the Department boat and see if you can find them?'

Oondabund looked at the ground without answering.

'It's an official job, you'll get paid. I'd go myself only there's a bloke from Wildlife due out here.'

'What him name, that man?' asked Oondabund, his smile gone.

'Harris, Steve Harris.'

Oondabund's face burst into a broad grin. 'Good one him come

33

that man. Him know crocodile proper well, and him know Aborigine too. Me work crocodile with him long time.'

'Okay, you take the boat and see if you can find them, and I'll go and meet him.'

Oondabund's twelve-year-old son sighted Besser on the edge of the mangroves after a two-hour trip. There was no sign of Smith's dinghy. Skilfully Oondabund manoeuvred the boat into the bank, so that the bow pushed into the mud below where Besser stood. He clambered down the bank and climbed over the bow, spreading mud everywhere. He was wet and exhausted, his eyes bloodshot and sunken.

'The c-croc,' he stammered. 'It got Eric Smith and Jack Reynolds. They're both dead.' Tears welled in his eyes.

'You been try finish him, that crocodile,' said Oondabund, his voice lacking sympathy.

Besser stared at the Aboriginal before him, but could not interpret the expression in the piercing brown eyes. He sensed that Oondabund, his son, and his nephew were not particularly worried about the fate of Smith and Reynolds.

'Get me back to Maningrida, quickly.'

'Where that boat?' asked Oondabund, refusing to be hurried.

'It's gone,' yelled Besser, raising his arms in the air. 'Your fucking crocodile tipped it over, sank it.'

'Proper bad luck,' replied Oondabund, shaking his head. 'Him been good boat, that little dinghy.'

The boat trip back to Maningrida took barely thirty minutes. Oondabund and his son and nephew chatted continually in their native language, but Besser remained silent. He stared out over the waters, but saw nothing; he could hear nothing but Smithy's terrifying screams, and again felt tears building up in his eyes.

When they were about two kilometres from Maningrida, Oondabund saw the light aircraft lift off from the airstrip, circle, and head back towards Darwin. Steve would be there, and he felt a twinge of excitement at the prospect of once again seeing the white man whom he thought of as a son.

Long before the boat anchored, Oondabund recognised Steve, who was waiting at the landing with the Superintendent. He waved and excitedly pointed him out to the others, although Besser showed no sign of having understood. The anchor thrown, Oondabund was in the water wading ashore. Steve left Jackson on the landing and came onto the beach to meet his Aboriginal friend, and as they came together, the two men embraced firmly for perhaps five seconds.

'How you going, old man?' asked Steve, smiling and looking into the sparkling brown eyes. Oondabund didn't answer; a broad grin and a simple nod of his head sufficed. Laying his hand on Steve's wrist, he squeezed it tightly—there was no need for words.

Steve's smile vanished with the realisation that John Besser was standing beside them. When their eyes met, Steve felt a surge of tension through his body. He glanced out at the boat, but it bobbed lightly on the anchor line, and the only people in sight were the two Aboriginal boys wading ashore. His eyes met Besser's again, but still no words were spoken. For a second time Steve glanced out at the boat, searching for the two men who had accompanied the wreck of a man standing before him.

'They're dead, Harris,' snarled Besser, his bloodshot eyes wide open and his fists clenched so tightly that his arms were shaking. 'They're fucking dead. Both of them.'

Steve was lost for words. Again he looked out at the boat, but it was empty. He looked down at Oondabund, who was no longer smiling.

'Them been try finish him that crocodile,' he said sternly. 'I been tell him—*leave him that one, him dreaming crocodile*—but him no listen.'

Steve looked into Besser's face again, feeling rising anger. 'Looks like you've done it well and truly this time, Besser.'

'Me!' shouted Besser. 'What are you talking about? That fucking crocodile.'

'You were told to stay away from the thing,' said Steve, fighting to control his feelings.

'What the hell are you talking about, Harris? The *crocodile* killed 'em—not me.'

'Sure, Besser,' said Steve quietly, not taking his eyes from Besser's. 'And how did they happen to end up where the croc could get them? I suppose the poor buggers kept at you to go out, did they?'

'Shut your mouth, Harris!' yelled Besser. 'Just shut your bloody mouth.'

'They should have put you away long ago, Besser,' taunted Steve, his hatred of the man beyond control.

'I don't have to take this shit from you, Harris,' snapped Besser. '*You* go get the croc. It's killed two men now, and it's your problem.'

The two men stared at each other in strained silence. Nothing more could be said. Both were tense, their fists clenched, their eyes wide open, each ready for any movement from the other. Steve turned to move away, and, as if programmed, Besser's fist flew back to his shoulder. Within a fraction of a second the two men faced each other again, no longer for verbal combat.

'Try it, Besser,' said Steve slowly. 'Just try it.'

Very slowly, Besser's fists were lowered, and once again the two men found themselves silently staring at each other.

'Hey, what's going on?' asked Greg Jackson, who had walked down to the beach. He looked out to the boat, then back and forth along the sand. 'Where's Smithy and Reynolds?'

'Ask Besser,' said Steve, without turning.

'Where are they, John? Where's Smithy and Reynolds? I told you blokes not to go out last night, didn't I?'

Besser's eyes turned from Steve to Jackson, who was still awaiting an answer. 'They're dead, Jackson. The croc got 'em.' Without waiting for a response, he turned and began walking up the beach.

'What's he talking about?' demanded Jackson, a look of horror on his face. 'Where *are* they?'

With Besser gone, Steve calmed almost immediately, and told Jackson the essence of what Besser had told him. When the Superintendent appeared to have absorbed the news, Steve suggested that they work out just what needed to be done. He and Oondabund decided to walk rather than drive to Jackson's office; Steve felt he needed time to think about the whole thing, and he also wanted to have a quiet talk with Oondabund.

There now seemed little doubt that there had been a fatal crocodile attack, the first in the Northern Territory for perhaps twenty years. Still, the whole thing rested on Besser's word, which was far from reliable. However, the crocodile had been reported as having taken two men, so it was no longer just a Wildlife problem. The police in Darwin would have to be informed as soon as possible.

Given that the attacks were genuine, recovery of the victims' bodies was the next priority. Parts of the bodies might still be found at the site of the attack, but most of them would be in the crocodile's stomach. This meant that the animal would have to be caught and killed. Steve hated having to damage any large crocodile, but he had resigned himself long ago to the fact that if and when a fatal attack did occur, it was imperative that his priorities be in line with those of the public. Oondabund's describing it as a 'dreaming' crocodile presented an unforeseen problem, but Steve hoped that he and his Aboriginal friend could resolve the point one way or another.

Mac would have to be given all the details urgently, because the story could be expected to be headline news in Darwin within twenty-four hours, and Wildlife Division would be plagued with enquiries.

Perhaps Steve's most difficult problem was that someone had to find out from Besser exactly what had happened and where, so that they could get down there as soon as possible.

Steve then turned his attention to Oondabund, and asked him about the previous day's attack. Oondabund told him exactly what had happened, and his account differed considerably from the story that Besser had told Jackson. Besser's revolver and the attempt to shoot the crocodile were particularly important; not only had the crocodile's attack been provoked, but hand guns were illegal throughout the Territory.

'Oondabund,' said Steve, as they reached the Toyota parked outside Jackson's office, 'the crocodile may have to be killed—finished.'

The Aboriginal's silence and cold stare made Steve hate himself for what he knew he had to say. 'It's killed two men, and the police are going to want to find the bodies. You know where they'll be.'

'Him dreaming crocodile, that one,' said Oondabund sternly. 'Him important to Aborigine man. Them white feller try and finish him— he finish them. That fair one.'

Steve was momentarily lost for words. He reached into the back of the truck where his suitcase lay, opened it, and removed a brown paper package that clearly enclosed a square bottle of rum. Bringing alcohol on to a settlement was always frowned upon, but Steve had done it anyway, and Oondabund gladly accepted it.

'I've got a problem, Oondabund. Blackfeller way says, "no kill him", white man's way says, "kill him". I don't want to hurt the croc, but I've got to do what I'm told.'

Steve was surprised to see Oondabund smile. 'Well, you have him your way, and you try kill him. But you not get him that one. Him

37

proper old one, that crocodile, and him smart like old people. You white men can't finish him. Him dreaming crocodile of all the Aborigine people. I know all him story—old people they tell me.'

'I'd better get into the office and start getting things organised. I'll be heading up the river later to see what I can find.'

'Me come with you,' said Oondabund, still grinning. 'That crocodile him no hurt you if me there.'

The two men stood in silence, smiling at each other. Again Oondabund held Steve's wrist and squeezed it; then he was gone, walking towards the tin shelter that was his home, the brown paper package tucked beneath his arm.

Radio reception between Maningrida and Darwin was particularly good, so Steve had no trouble relaying the news of what had happened. The police said they would try to get a charter flight out during the afternoon, and urged Steve to get up the river as soon as possible, to try and locate the bodies.

Mac's response to the news was a request for Steve to repeat it, then silence for thirty seconds, followed by a slow but distinct, 'Oh, shit'. Steve outlined the plan of campaign, rejecting the offer of additional support. Given that the police were sending out people, he would have enough, he said. Mac emphasised that the croc had to be killed as soon as possible, which Steve knew only too well, and asked to be kept in touch.

Armed with a map of the river, Greg Jackson reluctantly went to John Besser's house. At first, Besser was very reluctant to discuss the episode, but, realising the seriousness of it, he eventually did so. Between frequent expressions of abuse, mainly directed at Steve, he told Jackson all he could remember. He was not sure where they had actually been attacked, though it had not been far from where Oondabund had picked him up; probably within a kilometre.

The obvious hatred between Besser and Steve had aroused Jackson's curiosity, and back at the office he asked Steve what it was all about, making it clear that he had little sympathy for Besser. Steve filled him in briefly on Besser's background as far as he knew it.

At 11.45 am, Steve drove to Oondabund's tin shanty to pick him up. The place was deserted, but a shout attracted his attention to a group of people in the shade of a small bushy tree some hundred metres away. Oondabund was on his feet hurrying across towards him, fish spear in hand, but Steve caught sight of a lone hand waving from the group. It was Nancy, Oondabund's eldest daughter, the one girl in the settlement for whom he had ever felt strongly. He was returning the wave, when Oondabund reached the truck.

'That Nancy there,' he said smiling. 'She happy for see you.'

'She's a pretty girl,' said Steve quietly as he climbed into the truck.

Preparations for leaving took them nearly half an hour. Oondabund waded out from the beach and brought the boat in, then they loaded fuel, some ropes, a light in case they needed to stay out at night, and finally Steve's gun case. Oondabund looked derisively at it, but said nothing. Steve wanted to see the site of the first attack before looking for the bodies, so they headed upstream to Mungardobolo Creek. At the clearing where the crocodile had first been sighted, Oondabund pointed to the tracks and nosed the boat into the soft mud.

There was a furrow some two metres wide where the animal had pushed itself down over the mud, and on each side of the furrow were deep grooves where the claws had dragged. In the middle was a swaying channel where the enormous tail had lashed back and forth, helping to drive the massive bulk into the water. Oondabund pointed to one very clear impression of a hind foot. It was on the edge of the flood plain, where the mud was firmer.

'Take him up,' called Steve, a small field tape measure in his hand. Oondabund revved the engine, and the boat pushed into the soft mud beside the track, the bow climbing the bank to where Steve could jump to the flood plain. He quickly measured the track. It was twenty-eight centimetres wide, ten centimetres wider than the biggest he had ever measured before. He looked at Oondabund, who was grinning broadly, knowing full well Steve had not believed that the crocodile was so big.

Oondabund pulled back into the stream, but Steve pointed to a second set of tracks, human tracks, leading from the water to the flood plain.

'Me make that road,' said Oondabund, proudly tapping his chest. 'Me and Mr Besser, we go there.'

'How big's that crocodile's head, Oondabund?' asked Steve, still coming to grips with what the tracks were telling him.

Oondabund held his hands nearly a metre apart. Had he been estimating the length of the head, they would have been talking about a crocodile nearly six metres long, but Oondabund was indicating width; it was the way all Aboriginals summarised the size of an animal.

'Well,' said Steve after a delay. 'Guess we'd better try and find where the attack occurred last night.'

Oondabund started downstream again, heading to where they had found Besser in the morning. Steve said little. He was aware of a burning desire to see the great animal.

'Where is that crocodile, Oondabund?'

Oondabund shrugged his shoulders, then pointed downstream. 'Maybe this way, or maybe him this way.' He pointed upstream. 'Him belly full tucker now, maybe him sleep somewhere.'

As the boat moved back towards the mouth of Mungardobolo Creek, both men searched for any sign of the crocodile. They saw two small crocodiles slide down the bank and scurry off into the water, but large tracks were nowhere to be seen; they saw no tracks of any crocodile over two metres long.

'There him boat!' called Oondabund suddenly as they passed a small tidal gully.

John Besser's boat was wedged upside down in the gully. As they approached it, Steve examined the hull for signs of damage, but none were evident. It was only when they pushed into the mud beside it that Steve saw the tooth marks in the gunwale; two rows of puncture marks some thirty-eight centimetres in diameter.

Steve climbed over the side and waded through the mud to where the bowline was tangled in mangrove roots. After pulling it free he threw it to Oondabund, who secured it to their boat. Oondabund then reversed out into the stream, and, with Steve pushing, the boat suddenly came free and slid down the bank. When it cleared the mangroves Oondabund brought the boat back in and Steve rolled Besser's dinghy over. There were a further series of scored marks where the crocodile's head had lashed sideways and its teeth had raked the inside of the boat.

With Besser's boat in tow, they progressed out of Mungardobolo Creek and started across the main river channel to where Oondabund had picked up Besser. Steve searched continually, hoping at least to catch a glimpse of what he now knew was probably the largest living crocodile in the country—perhaps the largest in the world. Just upstream of a small nameless side creek, Oondabund pointed to Besser's tracks and the mark where he had pushed the boat into the bank to pick him up.

'That must be the creek,' said Steve, pointing to the break in the mangroves lining the river bank. 'We'll tie his boat up and have a look in.'

Oondabund manoeuvred their boat under an overhanging mangrove, and Steve secured the bowline from Besser's boat to it. They then backed off into the stream again, and headed towards the small creek mouth.

'Do you think he's still in there?' asked Steve.

'Maybe him there,' replied Oondabund, with a simple shrug of his shoulders.

As they entered the mouth, Steve unclipped the two latches on the gun case and withdrew the rifle. Opening the breach, he checked that the bullets were in the magazine, trying to ignore an icy stare from Oondabund. With the engine idling just enough to give steerage, they moved into the creek, both sets of eyes scanning the banks in a silent search for any information about the fatal drama that had occurred there the previous night.

On the second bend, Oondabund pointed to what could only have been Besser's tracks in the mud. Beside them were the same huge crocodile tracks they had seen in Mungardobolo Creek. Without stopping, they progressed upstream very slowly, looking, watching, waiting.

'There!' called Oondabund, startling Steve, who instinctively slammed the rifle bolt home. Caught in the mangroves and half buried in mud, was a body, a bloated mud-covered body.

Oondabund pushed the bow into the mud, and Steve tied it there with the bowline. They both jumped out and plodded towards the head. Thousands of small crab tracks radiated out from it in all directions, but the body itself seemed intact. A flapping noise startled them both, but it was only a large sea eagle flying from the opposite bank and landing on the top limb of a mangrove. From here it could watch undisturbed—it had also found the body, but as yet hadn't touched it.

'It Mr Reynolds,' said Oondabund, lifting the head by gripping the wet, mud-covered hair.

Although barely twelve hours old, the body was swollen and surrounded by swarms of blowflies. Those parts of the skin not covered with mud looked blue and bruised, and were covered in the white egg masses of the flies. The face, swollen and grotesque in death, was barely recognisable; the warm tropics had acted quickly.

'What we do?' asked Oondabund, letting the head flop back into the mud and sending a wave of revulsion through Steve.

'We'll have to take it home,' he replied quietly, unable to drag his eyes from it.

When they pulled the body from the mud, a hundred small crabs which had sought shelter beneath it scurried across the bank in search of shade. Oondabund was less affected by the task than was Steve, and when they got the body to the water he spent some five minutes washing off its excess mud so as not to mess up the boat too much. Steve was unable to help at first, but eventually joined Oondabund in heaving the body up over the gunwale, whereupon it slithered down on the deck.

'We go home now?' inquired Oondabund, when they were both once again in the boat.

'We'd better look up further,' replied Steve, wishing he were miles away.

On the next bend, Oondabund sighted the fuel tank from the boat, which was caught up in the mangroves. Steve retrieved it, and it seemed undamaged. The crocodile's tracks were everywhere on the banks, and Oondabund did not need to explain to Steve what the circular swirls in the mud indicated. This was where the crocodile had thrashed about with its prey, tearing and pulling in order to dismember it for swallowing. Steve tried to imagine the event, and found himself hoping that Eric Smith had died quickly.

When Oondabund next pushed the bow into the bank, Steve was caught unawares. He searched the bank in front of him but saw nothing, and it was only when he looked back to Oondabund that he saw the direction in which the black arm was pointing. Only about a metre away, completely buried in mud and barely recognisable, was a shirt. When Steve leaned out and pulled it, he suddenly became aware that it contained the remains of an arm, and in indistinguishable mass of tissue which was in fact Eric Smith's right shoulder. Steve's stomach heaved in revulsion, and he vomited over the side. As he sat in the boat with his head in his hands, he was barely aware that Oondabund came up beside him and retrieved their find. When he did look back, the Aboriginal was washing the mud from it, much as he would from any object that had fallen in the glutinous deposit of tidal rivers. Again he vomited, and with his hand he signalled Oondabund to start the boat and get out of the creek.

Oondabund pulled the boat alongside the dinghy they had tied up. With no visible signs of emotion, he picked up the shirt and mass of tissue, which had since separated, and dropped them into the boat they would tow. He then tapped Steve on the shoulder, and without speaking, indicated he should help move Reynolds's body into the dinghy also. With a deep breath, Steve obliged, managing to stem the flow of juices which surged in his throat.

'Let's get going,' he said softly, when Oondabund had again connected the towline. 'Back to Maningrida. We can look for the croc tonight.'

3

The shoreline at Maningrida differs from that of the rest of the river in that it is composed of sand. About two hundred metres of white beach sand is bounded on both ends by mangroves and mud. The whites never swim there because the brown murky waters contain at least ten species of shark as well as the deadly box jellyfish, which floats on the surface and can paralyse a man in minutes. The Aboriginals are not worried about sharks, and know the migration patterns of the jellyfish, which arrive in the wet season. Thus, during the dry season, it is not unusual to find groups of children playing in the water, under the watchful eye of an adult who is usually sitting higher on the beach in the shade.

As Steve and Oondabund started for Maningrida with Reynolds's body and what remained of Smith's, five naked Aboriginal children were splashing and playing in the water, watched by two women talking in the shade, their six dogs sprawled lazily on the warm sand. No one noticed the distant drifting object, which, about four hundred and fifty metres from shore, was slowly moving towards the river mouth. In response to the splashing, the huge head turned towards the beach, and disappeared beneath the surface.

On the beach, one of the dogs approached a woman and, grabbing a half-eaten fish, ran up the bank, away from the water. Both women jumped to their feet yelling at it, then, stick in hand, one ran up the beach after it. The children, hearing the commotion, momentarily stopped splashing and laughed and giggled as the emaciated dog avoided its pursuer.

Two hundred yards away, the crocodile surfaced, replaced its air, and dived again.

With the chase on the beach over, the two women again adopted their positions in the shade, while the dog, in full view, finished eating the fish. The children lapsed back into the games they had been playing, their dark wet skins glistening in the sun.

The child farthest from the beach felt a swirl as the tail swept through the water beside him, and instinctively cried out. Both women and dogs were on their feet as the children stopped playing, and turned. The child, still crying loudly, was thrashing through the water to shore as the women began running.

The head emerged among the group of four. Two saw it breaking the surface and immediately began yelling and rushing towards the sand, but the third, less than two metres from the crocodile, did not even cry. His small brown eyes stared into enormous yellow orbs, as water ran down the sides of the aged head and the jaws parted, revealing the full extent of the prehistoric teeth.

The women were screeching hysterically when they reached the water's edge, for as they watched the head was moving. The dogs barked and growled in defiance as the first child reached the beach and ran screaming from the water.

Propelled by a single sweep of the tail, the distance between predator and prey closed. Three metres away, the women forced their bodies through the shallow water, their vision blurred by the tears streaming down their faces. But they were too late—the child did not move as the mighty jaws closed, causing a muffled cry as air rushed from the collapsed chest. Then, except for a swirl, there was nothing.

Waist-deep in water, the women frantically searched, their cries mingling with screams from the beach. Suddenly the crocodile emerged some forty-five metres from shore. The great head rose above the waterline with the body hanging sideways between the jaws, limp and dead. Unaware of the cries, the crocodile's head jerked back and its mouth flashed open, throwing the body into the air, only to recatch it. The small body was being oriented for swallowing. Two final movements and the body was gone; within seconds the crocodile disappeared. Along the beach people were moving, running, grabbing children in tearful embraces while the older women wailed, already mourning the dead child.

On the river, the streaming fresh air cleared Steve's mind, although thoughts of Eric Smith and the giant crocodile were ever present. He found himself unable to look back at the dinghy in tow, unsure what his reaction to its cargo would be. It puzzled him that Reynolds's body had not been savaged by the crocodile, and had apparently not even been touched. For Oondabund, the situation was clear.

'Debils them been take him.' he said. 'Him try finish him that croco-dile and them debil get him.'

They were perhaps a kilometre from the beach at Maningrida when Oondabund's eyes fixed on the strip of white sand. Following his line of sight, Steve saw the activity, but was unable to read an explanation in Oondabund's face. As they came closer, Oondabund stood alert, his eyes scanning up and down the beach where his children played. He began to whimper and tears trickled down the deep furrows of his cheeks and over the corners of his mouth.

'What is it?' asked Steve, seeing emotion he thought his friend incapable of showing.

Ten metres from the beach, Oondabund stopped the engine and immediately leaped over the side. Half-swimming, half-running, he ploughed through the water to his people.

'Wailing!' thought Steve as the mournful sound carried out across the water. His heart started to beat faster; he, too, searched the beach for an answer.

As Oondabund left the water and run up on the sand, he could see that only three of his four children were sitting with his wife. High-pitched cries were coming from everywhere and he ran towards an older woman, naked from the waist up, with heavy tribal scars run-ning across the wrinkled skin beneath long-dried breasts. The face of his youngest daughter popped out from behind her. Sweeping her into his arms, he held her tightly, crying aloud with relief.

His daughter perched on his shoulder, Oondabund was at the water's edge when Steve waded ashore after anchoring the boat.

'What's happened?' Steve asked urgently.

'Him been here that crocodile. Him been here Maningrida and take little boy. Poor thing.'

Steve looked back and forth between the mourners and Oondabund, unable fully to comprehend what he now knew had happened. He looked out to sea for no particular reason. It was calm and the waters were still. Their boat drifted at anchor with Besser's dinghy still in tow, lying low in the water.

The police arrived late in the afternoon, and the remains of Smith and Reynolds were sent back on the plane to Darwin. By sunset, a plan for the night had been formulated and most preparations com-pleted. Four boats would take part in the hunt, leaving Maningrida on the falling tide, around half-past nine, and systematically search-

46

ing the river system. Attempts to enlist Aboriginal support had failed dismally, the people apparently not being interested in helping to kill the crocodile. Given that one of their children had been taken, Steve found their attitude hard to understand. Oondabund, who had originally agreed to go with Steve, opted to remain behind. He was needed for the 'business' associated with the child's death, something Steve knew was extremely important.

Earlier that afternoon, Steve had contacted Mac Wilson by radio, with the news that the bodies had been recovered and that there had been another attack. Mac had sounded almost beside himself with worry. The details of the attacks on Reynolds and Smith were now all over Darwin, and his phone had been constantly ringing. Rex Barrett, his immediate superior and the direct link to the Minister, had demanded a report, which, although only a hand-written summary, Steve had sent on the plane returning the bodies to Darwin.

Steve had told Mac about the size of the crocodile and about its apparent significance to the Aboriginals in the area. There must have been something in his voice that intimated hesitancy about killing it. 'It's got to be killed, Steve,' Mac had said sternly, 'the sooner the better.'

The reason why Jack Reynolds's body had had no marks on it became clear when Steve looked through his personnel file in the power station office. Underlined in it was the statement that he could not swim and was not to be given duties requiring travel in small boats. He had in fact drowned.

John Besser had drunk himself into a stupor by midday, having decided that his stay in Maningrida had come to an end. Jackson had organised a seat for him on the next plane back to Darwin. He was not even aware that a hunting party was going out at night, something that pleased Steve, who foresaw problems if Besser had wanted to participate.

On Maningrida's beach, the wailing continued throughout the afternoon. One woman, the grandmother of the dead child, had been taken to the hospital with a gaping self-inflicted gash across her thigh—a form of mourning difficult for the whites to understand.

By nightfall, over a hundred Aboriginals had congregated, and were huddled around the glow of three fires. The women cried into the night, while an old man sang, a song that none of the whites, and few of the Aboriginals, had ever heard before. It was a mournful song which consisted of the old man talking in time to the beating of the clap sticks and slow, pulsating drone of the didjeridoo. Without warning the tempo would increase and the didjeridoo, which was being played by another old man, would be blown three times, like a hunting horn. As if responding to a signal, the singer's croaking voice would stop and he would begin swaying back and forth, chanting the same words over and over; after a few minutes, the whole cycle would be repeated.

Steve, who had heard the singing, walked along the beach towards the group; he felt decidedly uneasy close to the water's edge, but doubted that the people would have been there if there were any real risk. As he approached the fires, an individual stood and walked towards him. Steve failed to recognise Oondabund at first; his body was naked except for a piece of cloth wrapped between his legs and tied in a knot on each hip. White clay was daubed in no obvious pattern on his face and chest.

'You never hear that old man sing before,' he said to Steve, betraying no sign of the grief suggested by the wailing. 'Him real good singer, that old man. Long time him no sing, but now him sing. Old time song, old custom song.'

Steve found it hard to comprehend that Oondabund, although involved in the wailing, did not seem sad, or in the least disturbed. He was further amazed when Oondabund suggested that Steve should get a tape recorder and record the old man singing; something they had often done during happier times.

'Oondabund,' said Steve, 'why won't your people help get the crocodile now that it's eaten one of your children?'

'Him sick one, that little boy. Maybe that why him eat him.'

The answer signified a sense of values totally different from Steve's; as he had done many times before, he wished he understood the people.

He suddenly became aware that a third person had silently joined them, and turned to see Nancy's face, smiling in the moonlight. A small child nuzzled into her breast which protruded from her loosely-fitting, brightly-patterned dress.

'Hello, Steve,' she said cheerfully, gently touching his arm.

'Who's this?' asked Steve, pointing to the infant.

'My little girl,' replied Nancy, proudly looking down at the baby. 'Her name Susan.'

Susan, thought Steve. If only his Susan had still been alive. How would she react to such a namesake? Would she understand his feelings towards these people? Would she have wanted their son to play hand-in-hand with the bush children?

'She nearly one year old,' continued Nancy. 'Born here, Maningrida.'

'She looks very pretty,' said Steve.

Unlike Oondabund, Nancy had spent a good part of her childhood in the settlement, and had attended school irregularly for six years. She had a good command of English, and could both read and write. When Steve had been in Maningrida before, she had often sat with him and Oondabund while they talked, because, although Oondabund could always make his point clear in English, it was very much a second language. If he was trying to tell Steve a complex story, the flow was frustrated by his trying to think of the appropriate words within a limited vocabulary. They had found it much easier for him to tell Nancy the story in their language, and then for her to tell Steve in English, with Oondabund listening to make sure that she had it correct. Most of what Steve knew about Aboriginal mythology had come from Oondabund via Nancy.

But the relationship between Nancy and Steve had become deeper than just that of a translator and listener, and now Steve felt a little embarrassed about it. When Nancy had turned seventeen, she had been forced to become the wife of a man to whom she had been promised when a child; the man was over fifty years old, and already had two wives. Steve had tried to intervene. It was the only time he could remember when his relationship with Oondabund had been threatened. 'This Aboriginal law,' he had shouted. 'You must stay away. This nothing for white man's business.' On the night that Nancy left Maningrida for the Cadel River, Steve had sat on his own and drunk a bottle of rum.

As he looked at her now, he realised that she had changed little in the three years since they had last met.

'Nancy,' said Steve, hopeful of a clearer understanding, 'what's so special about this crocodile? Why does Oondabund here worry about it so much?'

Oondabund knew what Steve was asking, and seemed thankful that Nancy was there to translate what was a complex story. He spoke to her for nearly ten minutes in their native language, before smiling at Steve and nodding his head.

'More easy she tell you that crocodile story. Him hard one,' he said.

It took Nancy a few seconds to prepare the words, but when she started talking, Steve listened carefully.

'That crocodile belongs to this river here, this Liverpool River, but not here from Maningrida. He comes from way upstream in the stone country, from his own big billabong. For long, long time he's camped at that billabong. That place my daddy's country,' she pointed to Oondabund, 'it's his father's country. When my daddy was little boy, his father took him to that billabong and called out to the crocodile. It swam over, but on the surface, not under the water. When it come, Oondabund's father talk to the crocodile, then sing to him—all the time that crocodile lie there, quiet. That crocodile didn't try to eat them, because it can't eat Aborigine—it's a quiet one. Other crocodiles they can eat white man, black man, anything, but not this one.'

Steve's mind raced to the child who had been taken that afternoon, but he did not interrupt.

Nancy continued, 'That crocodile is the boss man of all that stone country, and all this Liverpool River. But he's not always been a crocodile. Long, long time ago, he was a black man, like this man.' Again she pointed at Oondabund.

'At that time, there was no Liverpool River, just a little billabong. That man him hungry and cold—no wallaby, no goose, no turtle, no emu, nothing for him to eat. Okay, that man take his firestick and he hold it between his legs, in his bum, then he dive into the billabong and become a crocodile. Here there big mob fish, crab, mussel for his tucker, and he eat plenty. But he still little crocodile that time, not big one like now.

'Because him little, them other crocodiles chase him, and he run everywhere trying to find somewhere to hide. First time, he go long way up towards stone country, and he make that big river, Liverpool River. In that stone country him run everywhere, making all them little creek.' She paused momentarily, reorienting the infant, who had slipped from its source of nourishment.

'That crocodile not little one any more. All that work make him strong and big, but him tired too. He make one last billabong, for his own camp, and since then he live there all the time. Plenty tucker at that place, wallaby, rock kangaroo, bird, fish—he not worry for food again. Sometimes other crocodiles go up to his billabong but he chases them away—sometimes him finish them.

'This man Oondabund,' she said, pointing to her father, 'when his father finished, long time ago before I was born, two bones of him they take to that crocodile and them give to him. Even though him finished, that old man not really dead because him live inside that crocodile—like spirit. That crocodile he owns all this Liverpool River and all that stone country. This man, Oondabund, he responsible for that crocodile, and when him finished, me, Nancy; I'll be responsible.'

She paused and looked at Oondabund, then back at Steve. 'That's the story he wanted me to tell you.'

The story had explained a great deal to Steve. It told him why everyone was reluctant to help kill the crocodile and why Oondabund, though not openly recognised as a leader in the community, was often the man who had the last say about many issues. Oondabund was responsible for the crocodile, which in turn had formed almost all the Liverpool River and all the many branches which ramified through the Arnhem Land escarpment.

'Why did the crocodile leave the billabong?' asked Steve.

Oondabund answered, 'This all him river, that crocodile. Biggest rain that last wet season so easy one for him to come and look his country. When he find that crocodile in Mungardobolo, him kill him. He remember that one—same one who chase him from that billabong when him little boy. Him teach him lesson. That Mr Besser and them white men, they try and finish him that crocodile. Him teach them lesson too.'

'What about the little boy?' asked Steve. 'He was an Aboriginal.'

'Sick one, that little boy. Him bad chest and always him in hospital. That why that crocodile take him.'

Steve paused before asking the next question, and, with both Oondabund and Nancy smiling, he felt much as he had done three years before. 'Are you sure it's the same crocodile?'

'It same one,' Nancy assured him. 'There are no crocodiles that big anywhere, and same colour too, black. All the old men they know that crocodile.'

Oondabund spoke to Nancy in their language, and she in turn

told Steve in English. 'He says that when the crocodile attacked the boat it tried to get Besser, not Oondabund.'

In the background, the singing died down. There was no longer any sound from the clap sticks or didjeridoo, only the croaking voice of the old man, who sang a single word, over and over: 'Numunwari, Numunwari . . .'

'That him name that crocodile—Numunwari.' Oondabund leaned closer to Steve and slowly repeated the word: 'Num . . . un . . . wari, Num . . . un . . . wari'.

Awkwardly Steve repeated the word, 'Noo . . . mon . . . wari', but Oondabund shook his head and leaned closer.

'Not Noo, Num . . . Numunwari.'

After several attempts, Steve could pronounce the word to Oondabund's satisfaction, which was again reflected in a broad grin.

'What does it mean, Oondabund? What does Numunwari mean?'

'Just him name, like you and me. That crocodile him name Numunwari and him have that name for long time.'

As they stood in silence, Steve repeated the name to himself, wondering where he had heard it before. Suddenly, his mind cleared. The painting, he thought. It was the name of the painting that Catherine Pope had shown him in Darwin, with the giant crocodile depicted.

'Did anyone ever paint that story, Oondabund?' asked Steve.

'No one allowed paint that one,' answered Oondabund immediately. 'That my father's dreaming. They get biggest trouble if they paint that one.'

'What about your father? Did he paint it?'

'Him good painter, that old man,' answered Oondabund. 'He paint that story long time ago, and when I little boy he show me that story. Now him finished only me can paint that story.'

Oondabund turned to Nancy and spoke rapidly in their native language for perhaps three minutes. She in turn spoke to Steve.

'Oondabund says that long time ago, when his father young man, white men ride into camp and everyone run away. When they come back those white men gone but them take many things, business things. They take painting of that crocodile story, too.'

'Were the people worried about losing it?' asked Steve.

'That mob biggest worry for that crocodile story,' replied Nancy.

'But then that Oondabund's father him paint new one and everyone happy.'

Steve decided not to pursue the matter further. There was no doubt in his mind that the painting that he and Catherine Pope had tried to interpret in Darwin had been the same one as Oondabund's father had painted many years before. The story was the story of Numunwari.

There seemed no obvious solution to the conflict that was now raging within him. The crocodile, Numunwari, was an extremely important cultural object to Oondabund and his people—perhaps the single most important object left. Yet he, Steve Harris, was supposed to destroy it. Scientifically, the crocodile was perhaps the largest reptile alive, yet he had been told to kill it. After years of protecting and studying crocodiles, he had finally come across one that was indeed a giant, a relic of the past that might have been over a hundred years old—and it had to be killed. His friendship with Oondabund would end with the death of the animal. He could never see Nancy again.

Steve put his arm around Oondabund's shoulder and looked into the knowing brown eyes. Oondabund had to be told; somehow he had to accept what had to be done.

'I've got to go out tonight and try to . . . get the crocodile. Did you know that?'

'You no kill him that crocodile,' said Oondabund confidently and without anger. 'Him not there no more. Him gone now.'

Bewildered, Steve stared at Oondabund, wondering how he could be so sure. 'Oondabund,' he said quietly, 'if I find that crocodile, would it attack me?'

'Him no kill you. Not that Numunwari,' replied Oondabund, shaking his head. 'Him know you friend those Aboriginal people. Him can tell from your eye. But you not see him, him gone.'

'Where to?' asked Steve, completely confused as to why Oondabund believed the crocodile would be able to distinguish him from Besser, Smith or Reynolds. 'Where's he gone to?'

'Him little bit fright now that crocodile. Him go long way, maybe to Darwin for holiday.' The broad smile told Steve that Oondabund was joking, which was reassuring. In the moonlight, highlights emphasised the strong cheekbones, the white teeth and eyes. If

53

Oondabund was right, they would fail to find the crocodile and Steve would not be able to kill it. Steve hoped he was right.

Behind them, the wailing increased in intensity, and to the sound of the clap sticks and didjeridoo, the old man was singing.

'I go now,' said Oondabund. 'That mob want me for dancing now. Crocodile dance for that Numunwari.'

Steve watched him walk back to his people, before looking down at Nancy. She was as beautiful as he remembered, and as their eyes met, she gently placed her hand on his, and very gently squeezed it. Steve could not be sure, but thought he saw a tear trickling down her cheek.

'Be careful,' she whispered. 'That old man Oondabund he still believe all those old custom stories. You look out for that crocodile.' Saying no more, she released her grip and followed her father towards the glow from the fires.

Steve stood alone for perhaps a minute. Once more he had been made aware of the intensity of Aboriginal beliefs, and of just how little he really knew about them. Why had Oondabund not told him about Numunwari before? Perhaps it was because Steve had never asked. As he looked along the beach, he saw the headlights of three vehicles approaching the landing.

The four boats, each in radio contact, left Maningrida on schedule at 9.30 pm. They were manned by the three policemen, four of Besser's friends from the construction group, three teachers and Steve. They carried an assortment of rifles, revolvers, torches, lamps and spotlights, and when they left, there was a general atmosphere of excitement, with everyone apparently confident that they would find and kill the crocodile; everyone except Steve, who wondered whether the crocodile was still in the river.

The boats had been loaded by the lights of three parked Toyotas, and during the loading, the old man stopped singing. Steve felt the people sitting silently round the fires, watching every movement; it was as though they were all watching him and ignoring the others. Having always respected the fine line between reality and dreamtime, he now felt that he was letting them all down, and was relieved when the boats finally pushed off. When they were barely ninety metres from the beach, the old man started singing, and all attention once again centred on the songs.

Alone in her thoughts, Nancy watched until the boats could no longer be seen.

By midnight, the enthusiasm and excitement of the men in the boats had waned considerably. There was no longer a startled jump at the eyeshine of a small crocodile; it was just pointed out and the search continued. The air had cooled, and most of the men were both damp and cold, their eyes tired and strained from peering into the light beam.

It was not until four hours later that Steve finally called a halt to the hunt. The mist was rising, restricting visibility to less than thirty metres, and he considered the chances of finding Numunwari to be minimal. Within seconds of hearing his voice on the radio, the four boats were heading for home. It was a tired, weary and disappointed group who waded ashore, having searched some two hundred kilometres of river, creek and stream, for a total sighting of fifty-eight crocodiles, none of which was over two metres long.

Steve, his eyes bloodshot and sore, was relieved that no one had sighted the great crocodile. He would have liked to have seen it himself, just once, to verify its existence beyond all doubt. But on the other hand, the thought of lining the animal up in the telescopic sight and squeezing the trigger sent a shiver down his spine. As he walked up the beach carrying the rifle, he wondered whether Oondabund was right—maybe the crocodile had left the river; he hoped it had.

The hunt for Numunwari continued in vain for the next two days and nights. Eric Smith's boat, from which he and Reynolds had been thrown, was found half buried in mud over two hundred metres from the creek in which it had sunk. The search for more remains of Smith's body was fruitless, and Steve had no doubt that the crocodile had eaten it.

The men had had only one difference of opinion, which resulted in an immediate flareup of tempers. Some of Besser's friends decided to set hooks for Numunwari. They found a colony of flying foxes and shot two dozen, and in each one they positioned a large shark hook attached to a two-metre length of chain and a six-metre length of rope. They intended to hang these from mangroves so that the flying foxes dangled just above high tide mark, a standard method used by hide hunters to catch the few remaining crocodiles in the river, those so scared that they could never be approached by boat.

Steve exploded with anger when told of the plan, and managed to stop it before the hooks were set.

He had seen crocodiles caught on hooks many times before, and the sight was sickening. While they fought for their freedom, the chain trace snapped off almost all their teeth, and with each struggle, the hook drove deeper and deeper into the stomach and intestines, ripping and tearing indiscriminately inside. If the crocodile did escape, it died a slow agonising death, rotting from the inside out.

If set in the Liverpool River, the hooks would catch the few remaining adult crocodiles there, those which were keeping the population alive; there was a very remote chance of catching Numunwari.

On the morning of the third day, Steve decided to call off the hunt. He contacted Transport Section over the radio and organised a charter flight to take himself and the police back to Darwin. Numunwari had eluded them, and there were mixed feelings of disappointment, despair and relief.

Steve was the last to climb over the wing and into the small plane. He had thanked Jackson for the help he had given them, and suggested an occasional look up the river for Numunwari's tracks. Oondabund had agreed to help, on the understanding that if the tracks were sighted, Steve would come back out to Maningrida. However, Oondabund was equally convinced that the crocodile had gone, and that they would be wasting their time.

Seated next to the pilot, Steve lay back and prepared for a well-earned sleep on the flight back. He did not even see the woman carrying a child in her arms who had joined her father to bid him farewell.

PART TWO

I

In Darwin, Steve woke when the plane pulled up outside the charter company hangar. He found it an effort to raise himself from the seat and climb down to the tarmac, and now back in Darwin, he hoped he would be able to get the sleep he knew he needed. There would no doubt be reports and interviews, and he anticipated a major fight to justify the continued protection of crocodiles, animals that most people viewed with revulsion and hatred, especially now, but it could all wait until he had had a night's sleep.

After the noise of the aircraft, it seemed unnaturally calm and quiet as he walked across the tarmac to the telephone box, but the calmness broke the moment he dialled the six numbers needed to connect him with Mac's office.

At fifty-three years of age, Mac Wilson had considered himself perfectly happy in his present position. He had no ambitions for promotion, and anticipated eventual retirement in Darwin itself, or in one of the suburbs on its outskirts. Unlike Steve, he had learned to restrict his work to office hours, and he enjoyed each weekend and evening at home. He was a dedicated family man, who preferred the company of his wife and their five-year-old son to that of all his acquaintances.

The previous three days had seen his routine suddenly altered, for in Steve's absence, he had personally been handling all enquiries about crocodile attacks. It was a thankless task, and it had to be done with considerable discretion because the protection of any large predator was always a controversial issue. However, in twenty years of Wildlife work in the Northern Territory, he had never seen so much public interest generated in any animal as had arisen because of this crocodile and its attacks. Everyone seemed interested, wanting facts and figures on all aspects of crocodiles—especially, of course, the size and sex of Numunwari. Mac had attempted to answer all questions, while at the same time being careful not to commit the Wildlife Division to any change of policy.

The biggest problem had been Darwin's senior public servant, Rex

Barrett. He had been ringing Mac at all hours, badgering him for progress reports, and seeming to insinuate that, because a crocodile was causing all the trouble, Wildlife Division was to blame for the furore that now occupied large amounts of space in each of the northern papers, as well as a good proportion of the television news broadcasts.

With dark circles under both eyes and with his brown hair already receding, Mac felt as though he had aged five years. Maybe, he thought, I'm just getting too old to handle tense situations. He longed for Steve's return, to share the burden and to discuss just what they were going to do.

He was working on the tenth of a large pile of written enquiries when the phone rang.

'You're back !' he cried gladly as he recognised Steve's voice. 'Where are you?'

'Down at the charter office, Mac,' replied Steve. 'We just got in.'

'Damn Barrett wants to see you as soon as you arrive. The Minister must have been onto him again, because he's been giving me a hard time. What say I get a car down to pick you up and bring you back here? Then we can go round to see him after we've had a talk. He's in a pretty foul mood, judging from what he's been saying to me.'

'OK,' replied Steve, resigning himself to the fact that he was not going to be able to get any sleep for a while. 'How have the media played it up?'

'Haven't you seen any papers?' asked Mac in surprise.

'Heard a few radio broadcasts,' replied Steve, 'but the papers hadn't got out there yet.'

'It's been worse than we ever anticipated. It's been headline news up here and in most of the southern papers. There's three film crews from current affairs programmes in town and lots of phone calls. We're going to have trouble keeping the crocs protected. Besser arrived yesterday and he's really been giving us a hard time; your name's been mentioned a number of times.'

'Right, Mac,' said Steve after a pause. 'Guess we're just going to have to get into it. See you in a while.'

It took Steve an hour and four mugs of coffee to tell Mac all that had happened in Maningrida. When he finished, Mac told him about the public reaction to the attacks, producing newspaper headlines to support his story.

The first attack, when Besser had been tipped from his boat, had had surprisingly wide news coverage. In Darwin itself, it rated headline status—CROC ATTACK IN ARNHEM LAND—but it also rated space in the first three pages of most southern papers. Two current affairs programmes had contacted Wildlife Division about the feasibility of covering the story, but on finding out the logistics of getting into Arnhem Land, they had opted not to pursue the matter. The general trend of the Darwin coverage was that croc attacks on boats were definitely increasing in frequency, and that the authorities should reconsider the whole question of crocodile protection. One paper had been quite adamant that 'nothing would be done until someone was killed'. Rex Barrett had inquired about the details, but had not been overly concerned, as on the average, there had been less than one crocodile and boat incident per year over the previous decade.

When news of Smith's and Reynolds's deaths reached Darwin, the initial reaction had been shock—what many people had thought about as a remote possibility had finally become reality. The front page of every Darwin newspaper was devoted solely to the attack, the headlines being KILLER CROC IN ARNHEM LAND and MEN KILLED BY SALTWATER CROCODILE. The local radio talk-back sessions began canvassing opinions and interviewing anyone remotely connected with crocodiles.

Again, the news had had a surprisingly wide coverage in the southern states, meriting headline news in at least four papers. Television current affairs teams had chartered planes up to Darwin, and there was a continual stream of phone calls from various divisions of the news media. Rex Barrett had become deeply concerned, or so it seemed, as he demanded a complete report on everything known about the incident, while at the same time making it obvious that he considered Wildlife completely responsible. The central theme in most news coverage was, 'When and where would the crocodile attack next?'

News of the Aboriginal child being taken seemed to stun everyone except those associated with the media. The incident was on the front page of almost all Australian papers and mentioned in many of those overseas; the crocodile was clearly Australia's public enemy number one.

The Wildlife Division telephone exchange was jammed with incoming calls. The film crews that had arrived were temporarily blocked from going out to Maningrida by the Northern Lands Council, so they began interviewing the people in Darwin. The lobbying to have crocodiles taken off the protected list began in earnest, led by the Sporting Shooters' Association and the Cattlemen's Association.

Rex Barrett had sounded almost hysterical when Mac phoned the news of the last attack through. He spoke openly about how the Minister had been demanding that the problem be solved and out of the papers. Barrett had agreed that the Tourist Bureau could place a $3,000 bounty on the crocodile's head—they were concerned that the media coverage would have a direct effect on the number of tourists heading north. In fact, both airlines had reported cancellations, though the empty seats had been quickly filled by reporters. The bounty had caused more problems than it had solved, because at least fifty people had enquired about how they could get out to Maningrida with their rifles.

'It's been a real shambles, Steve, much worse than we expected,' said Mac over coffee. 'Everyone's scared stiff of the croc and just waiting to hear who it attacks next. Where is the thing, anyway?'

'Like I told you over the radio, Mac, I just don't know. There are no tracks in the river and no one's sighted it since it took the kid. Oondabund thinks it's drifted out of the mouth with all the disturbance.'

'What if it did? Where would it go?'

Steve shrugged his shoulders. 'Your guess is as good as mine. There are plenty of small creeks opening out onto the coast. He's probably just picked one of them. Hopefully he'll head back upstream and we'll never hear of him again.'

Mac looked into his friend's tired face. 'Well, let's hope it does. I haven't had a good night's sleep since it tipped Besser out of his boat, and you look completely buggered.' He glanced at his watch. 'Okay, I'll ring Barrett and let him know you've arrived—he'll want to see us right away.'

While Mac phoned, Steve thought about the coming meeting. There was little doubt that the crocodile attacks had caused Barrett a few sleepless nights, too, and serve him right. Rex Barrett's ambition to secure a high administrative post in Canberra dictated his every action. He appeared to go to any lengths to ensure that his record in the Territory was unblemished, and this resulted in a ruthlessness with people more typically associated with big business enterprises. Being well aware of the power of the press, he was frequently interviewed about current developments in Darwin, and his public image was good—it contrasted markedly with the very small circle of people who knew him well, most of whom disliked him intensely.

Still, Barrett was not the type of person to be perturbed by a lack of close friends. He was more concerned with the many acquaintances who could help him realise his ambitions in some way, and on these people he lavished considerable attention and time.

His most important 'acquaintance' was the Minister, the single person who could make or break him. Steve smiled to himself when he thought of the flack that the Minister must have been getting from the Ministers for Aboriginal Affairs, Environment and Tourism, because it would no doubt have been passed on to Barrett.

'He wants us down there right away,' said Mac, replacing the phone. 'The bastard's in a foul mood.'

When Steve and Mac arrived at the multi-storeyed office block, they went straight to Barrett's office. He was standing with his hands clasped behind his back, looking from the window of the large, conservatively-decorated office. He was relatively short, with broad shoulders and well-trimmed black hair, though his arms seemed unnaturally long for a man of his height. Dressed in a suit, Barrett looked quite different from most senior public servants, who wore tailored shorts and long socks, but that was the way Rex Barrett wanted it to be.

When Mac and Steve entered, he did not turn, nor acknowledge their presence in any way. On the desk lay the morning newspaper with the headlines: SETTLEMENT LIVES IN TERROR AS HUNT CALLED OFF.

After perhaps thirty seconds, Barrett slowly turned, staring for a moment at each man before walking to the padded red chair behind the desk. As he lowered himself into it, the small piercing eyes beneath the receding hairline fixed themselves on Steve.

'Now, for Christ's sake, tell me what the hell's been happening out there.'

It took Steve twenty minutes to relate what he had told Mac less than an hour before. While he spoke, Barrett slowly rotated a gold pen between the fingers of his right hand; his eyes never left Steve's, and his cold expression remained unchanged.

When Steve finished talking, Barrett held the pen tightly and tapped it firmly on the desk.

'I supported you people when crocodiles were first protected,' he almost shouted, 'and twice since then when there was talk of opening a shooting season. The last time there was a hell of a lot of opposition from the station owners and it took nearly a year to get some of them back on side. My decision then was based on information you two supplied, namely that there were virtually no records of whites having been taken by crocodiles in the last fifty years.

'There have been more people killed by that crocodile in the last few days than have been killed on the roads in the whole of the Territory. I hope you two understand what that means. In less than a week, I've been made to look like an absolute bloody fool, and all because of your damn crocodiles. Personally, I agree with the people. It's time the whole question of protection was looked into again.

'Here's the press release that's going out this afternoon,' he continued, passing a single sheet of paper to both men. 'In it I've said that there'll be a detailed report on the whole incident before the end of the week and that the question of protection for saltwater crocodiles is under review, pending a thorough investigation of what happened at Maningrida. What I need from you two is a detailed written report on everything that's happened. I want it on my desk at 8.30 am tomorrow.

'There's one more thing. My phone hasn't stopped ringing, and as from now, all calls about crocodiles are going to be redirected to Wildlife Section. You two can start taking the load for a change.'

'Mr Barrett,' said Steve, his face flushed with anger, 'you seem to think we're responsible for what's happened. I don't think that's fair.'

'Personally, Harris, I don't give a damn what you think. I've got a Wildlife Section that's supposed to look after crocodiles, and when three people get eaten, who do you think is responsible—me?' There was a short pause before he continued. 'You give me one good reason why crocodiles should be protected, anyway.'

'*One* good reason!' repeated Steve angrily, aware that his voice was gradually becoming louder. 'Well, what about their world status, for a start? There are twenty-seven different types and twenty-two of those are critically endangered. Australia's the only country left that has viable populations of saltwater crocodiles that aren't being hunted. For two hundred million years there has been a crocodile-type animal around. Two hundred million years, and man's brought them to the brink of extinction in *twenty*.'

'So what?' replied Barrett coldly. 'Most people couldn't give a damn if they were extinct.'

'Okay,' snapped Steve, 'what about their commercial value? Australia's probably going to end up the largest producer of crocodile hides in the world—a multi-million dollar industry for the north.'

'Well, if the protection's lifted, maybe we could start getting some of that cash, instead of talking about it.'

'You can't start harvesting our crocs yet!' snapped Steve. 'They had the hell shot out of them before protection, and if you start now, you'll just take every one that's appeared since. It takes time for a population to recover.'

'I'm not convinced, Harris,' replied Barrett sharply. 'When you have crocs killing people, you just can't tolerate them around. It's no good trying to tell me or anyone else that in the future they'll be worth money.'

Steve glanced at Mac momentarily before once again looking into Barrett's cold eyes. 'What about the tourist industry? The Asian croc farms make more out of tourism than they do from the hides. People just like looking at crocs.'

'Don't talk to me about bloody tourism!' Barrett shouted, raising himself out of his chair. 'They've been on to me continually since this thing started. Christ, they've put a $3,000 bounty on the bastard's head!'

Before Steve could answer, the phone on the desk rang, and Barrett snatched it from the hook. 'I thought I told you I wasn't to be disturbed!' he snapped. After a short pause, he brushed his hair back with one hand, although it was not noticeably out of place, and lowered himself back in the chair.

'Hello, Barrett speaking,' he said, in a suddenly melodious voice. 'Yes, Minister, the whole issue is in hand, and I've personally spoken to the papers. I'd say it's over up here now, just the dying embers to put out.' Steve looked at Mac, whose mouth had twisted in a slight but knowing smile.

'Yes,' continued Barrett. 'That's right, sir, they're back now and there's no sign of the crocodile. Like I say, it's over. Yes, we'll be looking forward to it, and I'll try and arrange a few days' fishing for you. Same to you, sir, my regards to your wife. Goodbye.' When Barrett hung up, he seemed momentarily at a loss for words, and when he did speak, he no longer looked at either Mac or Steve, but stared at a note pad on his desk. When he spoke, his voice was sharp again.

'I've got no more time to discuss this matter. If there's any more trouble with crocodiles, they'll go on the pest control listing—I'm sick to death of them. You two had better get on to that report.'

'Where do we arrange for the calls to be transferred?' asked Mac. Barrett looked up and fixed him with an icy stare.

'Where do you bloody well think, Wilson?'

'Okay,' replied Mac, 'we'll see your secretary.'

Barrett didn't acknowledge the statement, but just stared at Mac for perhaps ten seconds before again looking down at the pad. Steve and Mac saw themselves out.

'Why don't you come over to our place, Steve?' asked Mac when they were in the car. 'Anne'll get you something to eat, and you can have a sleep in the spare room. I'll look after any inquiries this afternoon and we can get on to the report tonight.'

'Yeah,' replied Steve, stretching, 'I'll take you up on that. He's a nasty bastard, that Barrett, a real pig.'

'Guess it's thrown a spanner in his works. Did you hear him with the Minister?'

Steve nodded his head. 'Something else, isn't he? It hasn't been a ball for anyone, but to talk to him you'd think we'd been on holidays.'

'Don't worry about him. He's getting pressure from above and passing it on—probably makes him feel better. Anyway, you're buggered. Good feed and a sleep and you won't know yourself.'

'I hope so,' added Steve, yawning. Again they lapsed into silence, the sort of silence that close friends can endure without feeling uncomfortable.

It was five o'clock the following morning before Steve and Mac finished their hand-written report. They had included every detail Steve could remember, and concluded with a section emphasising the abnormal nature of Numunwari. All evidence indicated that the crocodile had lived most of its life away from people, and had therefore never been hunted. Unlike most crocodiles, it was unafraid of boats and human beings. When it had attacked Besser's boat, it had been defending its territory rather than trying to obtain food; most crocodiles would have been terrified by the sound of the engine, and would have dived well before the boat arrived.

When it took Smith and the child, it attacked them as it would normal prey. It was not frightened by the spotlight, nor by the activity at Maningrida; again, most crocodiles would have been extremely wary of both, and this caution was the only reason they had avoided getting shot before protection. Numunwari was definitely atypical, not a crocodile by which the remainder of the population could be judged.

Mac read the report aloud, and after making some minor corrections, both agreed it should suffice. Within ten minutes, each was in bed asleep.

The report was delivered to Barrett as promised, then Mac and Steve spent the rest of the day in the office answering phone calls and giving interviews to reporters. Though Steve had expected enquiries, he was amazed by the number of phone calls, especially overseas ones, which accounted for almost ten per cent of the total. Even the compilers of the *Guinness Book of Records* contacted them, interested in the size of the crocodile and the time interval between attacks. Three television interviews were recorded, one for the local station and two for the southern news media. By the end of the day, Steve was finding it difficult to concentrate, and at exactly 4.20 pm, he joined the Public Service exodus from work; he was asleep by eight o'clock that evening.

The next three days were no different. Steve managed to answer over fifty letters, only to find that twenty-five more had arrived. He began to wonder when it would all end.

Interest in crocodiles was rekindled when Barrett issued a comprehensive summary of the events at Maningrida, as well as decisions on the future of crocodiles in the Territory. To the delight of Steve and Mac, he emphasised the unusual nature of Numunwari, and found no evidence to alter in any way the current legislation by which saltwater crocodiles were protected. Barrett's reversal of opinion had in fact been directed by the Minister. In Canberra, both the Queensland and Western Australia Wildlife Authorities had strongly protested about the possibility that the ban on hunting crocodiles in the Territory would be lifted. If this occurred, they argued, there would be widespread poaching throughout their States, with the hides being sold in the Territory. The Australian Conservation Foundation had also taken up the issue, causing the Minister even more embarrassment.

Barrett's press release generated considerable public debate in Darwin itself, though not throughout the rest of Australia.

By the end of two weeks, interest in Numunwari had almost completely waned. There was no longer mention of crocodiles in the press and no further phone calls. The letters were slowly answered, and for Steve and Mac life gradually returned to normal.

When the mail arrived on the morning of the fifteenth day after Steve's return, he did a preliminary sort into overseas letters, local letters and window-faced envelopes. The overseas letters were normally the most interesting, because they were mainly from people working on crocodiles in other parts of the world; Steve usually opened them first. The local letters, often from children, were normally general enquiries about wildlife, and these he opened second. He always left the bills until last.

On this day, there was a single overseas letter, from a research team in Venezuela. They had an opening for a Senior Research Officer to work on caymans, the small South American crocodiles, and Steve's name had been suggested to them by a visiting American scientist. Steve made a note to ask for more details as a check on what crocodile specialists were worth overseas, but then went on to the local letters.

That morning, he didn't get to the bills. He was on the telephone after reading the third local letter.

'Mac, it's Steve. I've got a letter you'd better hear.'

'Who's it from?' asked Mac, instantly worried by the tone of Steve's voice.

'Father Metz on Goulburn Island. I'll read it to you.
"Dear Mr Harris,

"You may remember that when you visited our mission in 1973, you asked if I would inform you of anything interesting concerned with crocodiles which occurred on the island.

"During the last three years nothing has happened; however, yesterday something did.

"At approximately 10.30 am (Friday the 20th) some children

asked me to hurry to the beach to see a big crocodile which had come ashore. By the time I arrived, some fifty people had congregated and were 'talking' to the biggest crocodile I have ever seen. It was lying on the sand, appearing to take no notice of them.

"The animal had come ashore with the rising tide and crawled up the bank into a small gully created by the overflow from our fresh water bore. It stayed in the same position for three hours before crawling back to the water and swimming away, on the surface.

"While on the beach, some of the older men offered it barramundi on the end of a fish spear. It did not grab at the fish, but rather opened its mouth and waited until they were placed between its jaws. It then raised its head and seemed to manoeuvre the fish in its mouth before swallowing. Altogether five barramundi were eaten.

"According to the old men, the crocodile had been travelling at sea and come ashore for fresh water. Three of the men are convinced that they know the crocodile, and they say it comes from the Maningrida region. Their name for it is something like 'Noomunwari'.

"I did not, of course obtain an accurate measurement of its length. However, by noting where it lay on the sand and measuring that distance after it had left, I approximated it to be just over seven metres. The head itself seemed about a metre in length.

"One interesting fact was that the tail was complete. In the big crocodiles I have seen in the past, the tails have always had the end damaged. The only injury we could see was a cut between the eyes, which it probably got while coming through the reef.

"I wondered whether it was possible that this crocodile was the same one that caused the tragic loss of life at Maningrida recently. It seemed so placid that I seriously doubt it, though the people looked quite concerned when I asked them about this possibility.

"I hope this information will be of assistance to your studies. We look forward to seeing you out here again.

"With best wishes, Fath. J. Metz".'

Steve waited for Mac's reaction to the letter. There was a thoughtful pause before Mac said, 'It's the same bloody croc, isn't it?'

'Sounds like it. In fact I'd say it is, for sure. Oondabund said that when Besser shot it, the bullet cut the skin between its eyes.'

Mac didn't reply immediately. He was trying to picture the crocodile lying on the beach, surrounded by people. 'Why didn't it have a go at them, Steve?'

'I guess it's just not bothered by people. When you think about it, there's probably nothing anywhere it's afraid of. In that billabong it would have only had wallabies and birds around, and when it got washed downstream it came into a region where most of the animals have been shot. The first real food it had a chance at was probably Smith. Big crocs can't really move much on the land, they're too heavy; their real hunting area's the water's edge.'

'I wonder where the bastard is now?' asked Mac.

'God knows. Hang on a bit, Mac, and I'll have a look at the map and work out how far it had to go to get to Goulburn.' Using a ruler, Steve measured the distance between Maningrida and Goulburn Island on the wall map, then held the ruler against the scale on the lower edge. 'In a week it's come about a hundred and twelve kilometres. Actually, it's probably more than that, because it most likely moved around the coast.'

'Come over, Steve, and bring the letter and map with you. I hate to say it, but I think we'd better tell Barrett about this.'

Mac re-read the letter when Steve arrived, and asked more questions which Steve was unable to answer. He examined the map, traced the course from Maningrida to Goulburn Island, then followed the coastline to the west around Cobourg Peninsula. Noting the geography, Mac had a sudden thought.

'Steve . . . the bastard couldn't swim around to Darwin, could it?'

'It'll probably go up some creek, find another billabong and settle down to fifty years of married bliss,' replied Steve, cheerfully avoiding the question.

'Could it swim to Darwin? Can they go that far at sea?'

Steve stared at Mac for a moment before answering. 'I don't really know, Mac. I suppose it could, but it would be pretty unusual. As far as I know, they'll go out of rivers into the sea, but they normally just travel round the coast close inshore and go up another river. But there are records of them travelling long distances at sea. One turned up at the Eastern Caroline Islands, about sixteen hundred kilometres from the nearest known population.'

'If that croc got into Darwin Harbour, Steve, it'd make what happened at Maningrida look like a game of tennis. Christ, what about all those hippies down on the beach? What about people swimming, fishing?' Mac's voice was getting louder as the implications ran wild in his mind.

'I'll get on to Barrett right away. God knows what he's going to say, but if there's any more trouble with that croc there's going to be hell to pay.'

Mac picked up the phone and asked for a line to Barrett's office. Steve went to the urn for two cups of coffee.

'I'm sorry, Mr Wilson, he's in conference at the moment. I don't expect him to be free for another hour,' said the secretary.

Mac thanked her and hung up. Five minutes later, when they had half-finished their coffee, the phone rang.

'Wildlife Section, Wilson here . . . yes, he's here beside me.' He passed the phone across. 'It's for you, Steve. Larkins Barge Company.'

Steve was on the phone for five minutes, his side of the conversation being restricted to short answers. Mac was thinking of ways to break the news to Barrett. There were two possibilities—direct and indirect. He generally preferred working around to the point rather than coming straight to it, though he knew the direct approach would be quicker and have less chance of being confused. When Steve put down the phone and turned, his face betrayed a new worry.

'That was John Skillet, the skipper of the *Cape Croker*. Guess what he saw on the way back to Darwin yesterday?'

Mac stared at Steve, hoping for the faintest sign of a smile, but there was none. 'If it's a joke, Steve, it's a rotten one.'

'Fifteen miles NNE of Croker Island, John Skillet and every member of the crew saw the biggest croc any of them have ever seen. Skillet's shot thousands of crocs along this coast, Mac. He's kept accurate records and I've seen them; he doesn't lie and he's not even prone to exaggeration.' Croker Island was one hundred and twenty kilometres west of Goulburn Island.

The sharp sound of the telephone bell startled them. 'That's probably Barrett,' said Mac, reaching for the phone. 'What in the bloody hell am I going to tell him?' A pause. 'Wildlife Section, Wilson speaking.'

'What's the problem, Wilson? I'm on my way to the airport.' The tone of Barrett's voice implied that the problem, whatever it was, could not be important. Mac realised as he began to answer that he was using the indirect approach.

'Ah . . . Mr Barrett, we've had a letter. A letter from . . . Father

71

Metz from Goulburn Island.' Mac hesitated. Barrett's reply was quick and cutting. 'You lucky devil. What the hell's it got to do with me?'

'Yeah, I'm sorry. We've just had a bit of bad news. Just before you rang.'

'For Christ's sake, Wilson, what's going on? I'm in a rush.'

'The croc. The bloody croc. It's been at Goulburn and Croker. It's on its way to Darwin!' Mac realised he had switched to the direct approach.

There was silence on the phone for a second. When Barrett answered, he spoke slowly, but with a deliberateness that implied a threat. 'You and Harris get over here. I'll expect you in ten minutes.' He hung up.

Barrett was reading when Steve and Mac walked in. They waited in silence while Barrett's attention was taken by a document on his desk. After a second, Barrett looked up.

'I've had a bloody gutful of crocodiles. If there's another incident like that one at Maningrida, as far as I'm concerned they can shoot every croc in the Territory. Now, what's in that damn letter you told me about?'

Steve passed Father Metz's letter across the desk, and for the first time noted the picture of Barrett's family on the shelf beside the window. It seemed out of place; Barrett hardly seemed the type to enjoy a family. When he had finished reading it, Steve told him the essence of John Skillet's sighting off Croker Island.

'Is it the same croc?' Barrett asked sternly.

'Sounds like it. There just aren't many crocs that size around,' replied Steve.

'You both realise that the bloody croc's got to be killed, don't you?'

Mac replied with a simple 'Yes', which Barrett didn't seem to hear.

'If it takes anyone else, our heads are going to be chopped right off. That croc's got to go.' Barrett lapsed into silence, rereading the letter while Steve and Mac stared at him. The next question was directed at Steve.

'Right. How are we going to find the bastard? Could you spot it from a plane?'

'Suppose so,' said Steve, trying to visualise the area in which the croc would be and the practicality of finding it. 'If the weather's fine and you spent enough time you might find it, but there's a big area to search. I guess it'd be worth a try.'

'What about a chopper?'

'You'd need a chopper if you're going to try and shoot it,' added Mac, 'but you'd be better to search from a plane. You need the speed to cover the area, but even then it'd still be like looking for a needle in a haystack.'

'Which settlements are to the west of Croker?'

'None,' answered Steve. 'There are a few people on Cobourg, but there's no real settlement. The closest would be Snake Bay, round the top of Melville Island.'

'And if it doesn't go round the top of Melville Island, I suppose it's going to head towards Darwin. Could it swim to Darwin, Harris?'

'Hard to say,' replied Steve quietly. 'I reckon it'll move up some creek or river along the coast, but I suppose it *could* swim to Darwin. The currents go that way.'

'That does it. We're going to start searching. I don't care how long it takes, but we've just got to get that bastard. How do we get a search going?'

Although Steve felt the same uneasiness about killing Numunwari that he had felt at Maningrida, he was acutely aware that there was nothing he could do about it. He thus participated in the twenty-minute discussion in which it was decided to do the initial searching with a light aircraft, and if they found the crocodile, to take out a helicopter to shoot it from. As the direction of the currents was well-known, Steve assumed that there would be no trouble relocating the crocodile once it had been sighted from the aircraft, though he hoped and felt quite sure that it would not be sighted. Barrett emphasised that the press was not to know what was going on, and suggested that Mac assisted Steve, rather than involving anyone else.

'That's all okay,' said Mac, when the plan had been finalised, 'but there's still one problem. The Wildlife budget can't afford the charter costs.'

'It can come from the Administrator's fund,' snapped Barrett. 'Let my secretary know on the way out.'

'I think you should be clear on one thing,' said Steve. 'Our chances of finding the crocodile are really remote, even if it has come around the peninsula. There's a lot of water out there, and just one croc.'

'Just keep flying till you do bloody well find it,' answered Barrett sternly. 'I'm simply not going to tolerate any more trouble with that crocodile. Last time it was only inter-State politics that saved crocs, and if there's any more trouble, the Territory will take the matter into their own hands. Understood?'

As they walked from the office, Steve thought of Numunwari. Somewhere the huge animal was drifting, unaware of the preparations being made to terminate its existence.

Barrett's instructions were simple: 'Keep searching till you find it, then kill it.' No one seemed to appreciate the animal for what it was, yet surely whether such a unique animal lived or died was an important issue; too important for Mac, Steve and Barrett to resolve in minutes, although they had. If the crocodile created any more trouble, it could be political suicide for Barrett, of course. His attitude was understandable, but Mac, even Mac, didn't seem to realise the gravity of the decision they had just made. Evereyone seemed only to want the problem removed—out of sight, out of mind.

As long as the status quo was restored, nothing else mattered, and Steve felt bitter that there was so little he could do about it.

Steve took the first day's survey, which was planned to follow a search pattern that he and Mac had worked out during the night. They were to fly to Cobourg Peninsula, then begin searching eastward towards Maningrida, in case the crocodile had turned back. Steve knew the area well, and was confident that, if Numunwari were sighted, he could pin-point its position for the helicopter to find later.

The search proved fruitless, although they spent the whole day in the air, except for a brief landing at Croker Island to refuel and to ensure that there had been no further sightings of Numunwari. Two crocodiles were sighted, both on exposed mudflats near the mouths of small creeks, but both were about three metres long—definitely not the giant they were searching for. Steve thought he saw it once, some eight kilometres offshore, but when they flew down to one hundred metres and circled, they saw only a large floating mangrove, washed from a coastal river.

Mac was waiting at the airport when they landed, and walked out to the plane.

'How'd you go?'

Steve shook his head. 'All's quiet. Not a sign of him anywhere.'

'Well, things haven't been too quiet in here, I can tell you. John

Skillet thought his sighting was worthy of the local press, and the phone's been ringing since four o'clock. Have a look at this.' He passed the afternoon newspaper to Steve.

The headlines read ANOTHER MONSTER MAN-EATER AT CROKER ISLAND. Below was a short double column of newsprint with a half-page photo of a captive saltwater crocodile.

The story read: 'Captain John Skillet, master of Larkins Barge Company's *Cape Croker* and a resident of Darwin for over 27 years, yesterday reported sighting the biggest crocodile he had ever seen, moving at sea between Croker Island and Cobourg Peninsula . . .' Steve did not read the rest of the article. In the bottom left-hand corner was a photograph of one of the so-called crocodile shooters constantly called upon by reporters to make comments about crocodiles. Steve could imagine the story. 'There's too many crocs around . . . the big ones are all man-eaters . . . they can run faster than a horse . . . when they come in to attack they can swim faster than a boat with a 40-horsepower engine . . .'

'What'd Barrett say?' he asked.

'Haven't seen him yet,' replied Mac. 'He was at a meeting all afternoon.'

Steve yawned and stretched. 'Well, I guess I can sort it out with him tomorrow while you're flying. It really buggers you, Mac; I don't know how these pilots keep it up.'

The following day, Mac carried out the search, flying the region between Cobourg Peninsula and the Alligator Rivers, then up on the north coast of Melville Island. By the end of the day, he began to wonder whether he would recognise Numunwari even if he saw it. At least twice he had considered telling the pilot that it was hopeless and to fly back to Darwin, but the thought of explaining his actions to Barrett brought him back to reality, and the search continued.

Steve, who spent the day in the office, was once again reminded that saltwater crocodiles were news. There were a number of inquiries from the news media, just checking that nothing serious had happened. He now felt sure that if there should be another attack, protection for crocodiles would have to be lifted. Numunwari represented a threat to the species as a whole, and Steve began to wonder whether or not it would be better for all concerned if the huge reptile was dead. One thing was for sure: Numunwari had created unexpected interest in crocodiles, and Steve pondered whether or not this would be beneficial in the long run.

The following day, he surveyed the coast between Darwin and the Alligator Rivers, checking the mouth of each small creek they passed, but without success. He then flew north to Cobourg Peninsula again, and after landing at Croker to refuel, the plane began zig-zagging across the open sea between Melville Island and the main-land. The only sighting of interest was a fishing boat anchored in a small tidal creek, surrounded by nets set from one side of the creek to the other. Steve asked the pilot to report the illegal fishing over the radio, in the hope that Fisheries Section could catch the poachers, but he doubted that they would; helicopters were needed for such enforcement work, and their budget was too limited for such a luxury.

By 5.30 pm, Steve was finding it difficult to concentrate, and he had to force himself to keep searching while his mind wandered. As his strained eyes moved from the horizon to the water below, he caught a glimpse of something on the surface, something long and black.

'Turn her round, over on the port side!' he yelled to the pilot, raising himself to look out the rear window for another glimpse, as his heart began to pound. As the plane turned and began to descend, excitement surged through his body; he was alert and aware, all tiredness gone. As the plane levelled, he scanned below, suddenly doubtful. But there, about six hundred metres in front, was the black floating object.

'Down there!' he yelled above the background noise of the engine and radio, as he leaned forward and pressed his face against the clear perspex.

As they passed overhead, Steve had his first view of Numunwari. The giant crocodile was on the surface, slowly swimming westward with leisurely movements of the tail. It was huge and dark-skinned, with the massively broad head that is found only in the largest of crocodiles. Unconcerned, the great animal continued, its head held high, slightly above the water and out of the small waves.

'That's him!' Steve yelled excitedly. 'Take her round again.'

As the plane circled and came in again, Steve had his second view of the crocodile, while the pilot had his first. A simple 'Christ!' and a wide-eyed stare at Steve expressed his feelings.

'We'll have to move fast to get the chopper out before sunset,' said Steve, as the plane accelerated and climbed.

'There won't be enough time,' replied the pilot, directing the plane on to the shortest course for Darwin. 'You'll have to wait till morning.'

Steve checked his watch: it was 5.47 pm, and even if the chopper was ready to leave by the time they arrived back in Darwin, it would be almost dark by the time they got back to where the crocodile was. At present it was high tide, and for the next six hours the water would be running against the crocodile. Then it would change, and for the six hours after that it would make progress towards Darwin much easier. They would need to be ready to leave by first light.

On the pilot's map, Steve circled the area where they had just seen the crocodile. It was five kilometres north of the Adelaide River, and barely fifty-five kilometres from Darwin Harbour. He spread the map on his knees and marked each of the locations at which Numunwari had been sighted, with the date of sighting next to each. In the first week it had moved at least a hundred and twelve kilometres, and in the next three days, a hundred and thirty; in the last four days it had come almost two hundred and twenty-five kilometres.

Steve was not surprised that there was no answer from Mac's office phone because, regardless of the trouble with the crocodile, it was an accepted Public Service tradition that at least the first hour of Friday evening was spent in one of the local hotels, forgetting the week that had just passed. Steve phoned a taxi to take him to the Great Northern Hotel, where Wildlife Section met.

As expected, Mac was in the lounge with two men from Forestry, and upon seeing Steve at the door, he waved for him to join them.

'You're half an hour early. I was going to come down and pick you up.'

'We ran short of fuel, so I decided to give it a miss.'

'Feel like a beer?' asked Mac, in an attempt to detach Steve momentarily from the remainder of the group.

As they walked to the bar, Mac asked him whether he had seen anything, and when he heard Steve's affirmative answer, he stopped in his tracks and stared in disbelief.

'Where?'

'Off the mouth of the Adelaide. It was too late to get the chopper out, but we'll have to be in the air by first light—it's only fifty-five kilometres from Darwin.'

'Shit . . . okay, one quick beer and we'll get cracking.' Mac looked at his watch and back at Steve. 'We'll have to find Barrett and tell him. You're sure it's the same croc?'

'Certain. It's really big, Mac, and black. There couldn't be two of them like that. It's the same one, all right.'

Steve's explanation to the others was that he had been aerial surveying all day, and was only going to have one beer before going home for a sleep; Mac invented a dinner guest, and the two of them left together, barely twenty minutes after Steve's arrival.

At the office, Mac made strong black coffee and explained the delay to his wife by telephone, while Steve spread out the map he had marked in the plane, and gathered tide charts and additional maps. He wrote the expected times of high and low tide for the next two days on a pad, then unfolded a more detailed map of the coast near the Adelaide River mouth; on it he circled the area in which Numunwari had been sighted. He then transposed the last three sightings to a nautical chart, which contained the depth soundings of the complete region.

'All these sightings are in the deep channel running around the coast, Mac. If he stays in it, he'll drift straight past Darwin.'

'But if he gets out of the channel he'll end up in Darwin Harbour,' added Mac, watching Steve trace the meanderings of the channel.

'Depends whether he goes north or south, I guess. I wish there were some way we could make sure it was north.'

'What about finding it again, Steve? What are the chances?'

'Well, we've got all the information on currents and tides in this region; we'll just have to work out all the possibilities. I don't think we'll have too much trouble, as long as we're on to it first thing in the morning.'

For the next hour, they related information on currents, channels and tides to the crocodile's sighted position, as well as the known rate at which it had been moving. At the earliest, it could reach Darwin in twenty-four hours, though between thirty and forty was more likely—if it moved out of the channel. There was not much time, and, regardless of the fact that a large portion of Darwin's male population would be at parties or in hotels, everything would have to be organised immediately. Having decided to arrange the helicopter before contacting Barrett, Mac turned to the air charter section of the yellow pages in the telephone, and after a number of advertisements saw one for 'Helihire, helicopter services throughout the Northern Territory'.

While Steve organised more coffee, he dialled, and after a short delay spoke to a child, then hung up.

'The manager's down at the Workers' Club, Steve. Having a few drinks before going to one of the pilot's places for tea; a Cliff Robinson.'

By the time Mac had found the new number and dialled, the manager had already left, and it took four further phone calls before he finally had him on the line. The manager immediately made it clear that he was not anxious to spend Friday night talking about chartering helicopters, nor Saturday morning in the air at daybreak. He did, however, remember agreeing to the possibility of a short-notice charter, and after some pleading on Mac's part, he relented and agreed to locate his pilots and try and arrange something. He asked Mac to phone back in an hour.

After some discussion, Steve and Mac decided that if the manager's reply was negative, they would just have to tell him the exact reason for the charter. If the pilots knew why the helicopter was needed so urgently, they would probably be eager to fly. Barrett had to be notified, and Steve agreed to phone him, although he was not eager to tell him that the crocodile could be in Darwin within twenty-four hours. A woman answered Barrett's telephone after four rings.

'It's Steve Harris speaking, from Wildlife Section. Would it be possible to speak to Mr Barrett, please?'

The reply sounded like a taped answering service: 'Mr Barrett is engaged and will be so for the remainder of the night. I suggest you phone his office on Monday morning, after nine.'

'Certainly,' replied Steve, equally crisply. 'I would appreciate it if you could tell him that the crocodile was sighted today and is expected in Darwin Harbour tomorrow night. Goodnight!' He replaced the phone and turned to Mac, who looked horrified. 'Bloody bitch, sounds just like him—"Mr Barrett is engaged, I suggest you ring him Monday morning"—who the hell does she think she is?'

A few seconds later their phone rang. Steve let it ring nine times before answering with a simple, 'Harris'. Although he was three metres away, Mac could hear Barrett shouting.

'What the hell's the idea of insulting my wife? And what the fuck's this about the croc being in Darwin Harbour?'

'We found the croc today, just before sunset, off the mouth of the Adelaide River,' Steve said evenly.

'Why the bloody hell wasn't I informed?' Barrett yelled.

'We wanted to get everything arranged for the morning first. Didn't want to bother you earlier than necessary.'

'Bother me!' screeched Barrett, 'my whole bloody career's at stake and you're concerned about *bothering me*? For Christ's sake, Harris, what's wrong with you?'

'I'm sorry.' Steve was just as angry. 'We've worked out where we reckon the croc'll drift to, and we're getting the chopper organised for first light in the morning.'

'Getting?' repeated Barrett.

'The manager of Helihire's trying to arrange it, but it's pretty short notice. I think we'll be all right.'

'You damn well tell him that if it's not all right he won't get another charter contract from the Government. You got that?'

'Okay,' replied Steve, hoping he would not need to use Barrett's name.

When Barrett spoke again, his voice had lost its aggressiveness. 'Would there be room for me to come?'

Stunned, Steve placed his hand over the mouthpiece and turned to Mac. 'He wants to come!'

'Nothing we can do about it,' whispered Mac, shrugging his shoulders. 'He's the boss.'

Steve nodded and resumed his conversation. 'I don't think there'll be room, Mr Barrett. It's a pretty small chopper.'

'Tell them we want two, then! Tell them I said we need two choppers. How's that?'

'Guess it would make it easier to find the croc,' agreed Steve, realising he was beaten. 'Two choppers would be better than one.'

'Right, then, that's that. I'll get my things ready. What time in the morning?'

'We'll pick you up round six.'

'Good. You ring me, Harris, if there's any trouble with the helicopters. I'll see you in the morning.' He hung up.

'That's bloody terrific,' said Steve, slamming the phone down. 'That's all we need.'

'He'll be okay, Steve, don't worry about him. Nice try about the room in the chopper, though.'

'Well, it didn't work, and now I've got to get two choppers. To think I was worried about the cost of the charter.'

'He's probably just bored with life in the office. Wants to come out and get in on the action for a change; get where the excitement is.'

'Well it's not a picnic, Mac. There's a damn serious side to this whole thing.'

'I'll say there is. The bastard's eaten two people and been responsible for a third drowning.'

'Smith and Reynolds asked for what they got, and it's up to the Abs to decide what they want to do about the kid. In their own way, the Abs have got more sense than we have.'

'If Barrett wants to come, Steve, there's nothing we can do about it. He runs the north,' Mac pointed out.

'It's not whether he wants to come or not; it's his attitude. To him it's a crocodile hunt, the last of the great safaris, paid for and delivered by the taxpayer. I can't see that you, me or Barrett has any damn right to decide whether Numunwari lives or dies, anyway.'

'Any right!' repeated Mac, staring at Steve. 'What are you talking about?'

'Well, you just think about it. There's probably one crocodile like that left in the world. Just one. It's as unique as the bloody Harbour Bridge. You can't tell me three people could sit in a room and decide to get rid of that, can you?'

'You've got your priorities wrong, Steve. That crocodile's killed people. I can buy all the arguments about protecting the saltwater crocs, but, Christ, not that one.'

'I just don't know any more,' said Steve. 'There're people getting killed every day all over the country. Take the Aboriginals—they can die of a hundred diseases and no one gives a damn. The bloody crocodile takes one and everyone wants to make a big deal out of it. Not for the Aboriginals—no, nothing so straightforward. They make a big deal out of it to sell newspapers and the like. Take Barrett. Do you really think he's interested in the crocodile or the people? Come on, Mac, who's he interested in?'

'Look, I don't like him either, but there's nothing you and I can do about it. If he comes, he comes—there's no sense us shouting at each other.'

'I'm sorry, Mac,' said Steve after a pause. 'He really bloody annoys me, and I just don't like the idea of him being there if we do kill it. I don't see it as something to be proud of.'

'Changing the subject, I wouldn't have minded being a fly on the wall when Barrett's wife told him about the croc in Darwin Harbour.'

Steve was smiling when the phone rang. It was the manager of Helihire.

'There's not a hope in hell of getting two choppers for you, mate,' he replied after Steve informed him of the change in plans. 'We've got one two-seater and Cliff Robinson's agreed to take it up for you.'

'Rex Barrett's coming with us now, and we've got to get two; one of them has to have room for two passengers.'

'Hold the line for a minute,' came the immediate reply. The mention of Barrett's name obviously threw a new light on the matter. Companies like Helihire existed on Government charters, and because of the expense involved, Barrett's approval was usually sought for each one; it would be unwise to antagonise Rex Barrett.

'There's a six-seater we can use, and I'll fly it myself,' said the manager. 'What time do you want to leave, and exactly where do you want to fly?'

For the next hour, Steve and Mac packed the equipment they would need: two rifles, Steve's .270 and a military 7.62 millimetre automatic that Wildlife Section had acquired for pest eradication; two packs of twenty shells for the .270 and four for the 7.62; two field radios for communication between the helicopters; three pairs of binoculars and an assortment of maps and charts. On two maps, they drew in the survey lines for both helicopters, the plan being to start at Darwin and work out to the channel, from where they would zig-zag to the mouth of the Adelaide River. It was almost midnight when they drove home.

2

By 5 am, Steve was up and eating a light breakfast of toast and coffee. After a last check through the gear packed on the Toyota, he drove to Mac's house, and was knocking on the door by 5.40 am; he could hear the radio, and when Anne opened the door, he saw Mac finishing a cup of tea at the table.

'He won't be a tick, Steve, come on in.' Steve guessed that the square package on the table was food. Anne usually prepared enough for them both, knowing that field work could be made far more pleasant by some realistic preparations which the over-eager often overlooked.

'Got time for a cup of tea?' she asked, expecting a negative reply.

'We're running a bit short on time, Anne. Wouldn't mind coming round for something to eat tonight, though—if you'd like to invite me.'

'We'll expect you,' she replied, smiling. 'What are you doing up?' she continued, turning to their five-year-old son who had just walked into the kitchen rubbing his eyes. 'You should still be in bed.'

'Where are you going, Dad?' he asked, approaching Mac in the hope of being picked up.

'Steve and I are going out to try and find a big crocodile.' Mac lifted the small boy and sat him on his knee.

'How about I take you fishing tomorrow if we find the crocodile. How'd that be?' The small boy cuddled into his father without answering, but his smile showed that he would be looking forward to it.

Mac carried his son to the door, passing him to Anne after giving her a light kiss on the cheek. The sun was not yet visible, but the sky was light, and the air pleasantly cool.

'You look after him, Steve,' she said, smiling as they walked to the truck. 'He's not a youngster any more.'

They drove to Barrett's house and, in response to Steve's firm knock, Barrett himself answered the front door. He was dressed in a bright red-checked woollen shirt, the type normally associated with advertisements for American hunting products, and on his head he wore an orange cap, with an insignia demonstrating that he was a member of an exclusive Victoria hunting lodge. Around his waist was a leather belt containing a single row of new shining brass bullets which belonged to the highly-polished rifle slung on one shoulder. A large pair of binoculars and a camera hung from his neck, and the khaki tailor-made trousers fitted neatly into the tops of tightly-laced black rubber hunting boots.

'Give me a hand with the Esky, Steve. Mrs Barrett packed some food and wine for the trip.'

Following Barrett to the Toyota with the large container in hand, Steve caught Mac's eye and shrugged his shoulders, while raising his eyebrows.

The two pilots were talking when Steve pulled up at the hangar; he and Mac had spent the ten-minute drive listening to Barrett's monologue about his prowess and experience as a hunter. His rifle, a custom-built .460 Weatherby magnum, was one of the best in the world, but by the look of it, it had rarely been used. Steve decided that, no matter what, Mac and Barrett could go together in the big helicopter, and he would go alone in the small one.

Twenty-five minutes after arriving at the airstrip, they were in the air. Steve was thankful that the waters below were calm, and except for two trawlers on the horizon moving towards Bathurst Island, the sea was deserted. Visibility was good, and he felt confident that they would find the great crocodile.

For the first hour, nothing was sighted. Seated next to the pilot, Barrett continually moved and fidgeted, barely able to contain his childish excitement. Behind him, Mac could see only out of a small side window, but he searched regardless, catching an occasional glimpse of Steve's helicopter almost two kilometres away, flying on a parallel course.

By the end of the second hour, one hundred and twenty-eight square kilometres had been searched in vain. Barrett caused some excitement when startled by six creatures breaking the surface in unison.

'There it is !' he shouted, reaching for his rifle.

'They're dolphins,' yelled Mac, over the noise of the engine.

It was 9.05 am when Barrett caught sight of a dark shape some

84

thirteen hundred metres in front. He wanted to announce the find and to demonstrate his keen eyesight, but he waited until they were closer to be sure it wasn't another false alarm.

'What's that?' yelled the pilot, pointing ahead.

'It's him, it's the bloody croc!' shouted Barrett, tangling his arm in his camera strap as he reached for the rifle. Mac leaned forward for his first view of Numunwari, only to receive a savage smack on the chin from Barrett's rifle, swinging dangerously in the cabin.

As it had been on the previous day, Numunwari was on the surface with its head slightly raised and its giant tail sweeping steadily from side to side. Because of the calmness of the sea, small but distinct bow waves streamed back from each side of the sculptured head.

Mac was on the radio to Steve, still rubbing his chin, as they passed over it.

'We've got him, Steve, below us now, on the surface. You'd better get over here quickly.'

'How do you open the door?' yelled Barrett frantically over the engine noise as he fumbled with a handful of bullets, trying to fit them into the magazine.

'Are your belts done up?' asked the pilot, giving Barrett's webbing strap a sharp pull. 'Turn the handle vertically and let the door back ... *slowly.*'

Barrett swung the red handle from the horizontal to the vertical position, and began to slide the door back as the helicopter slowed. The first rush of air took him by surprise, and he lost control of the door, which flew back along the guide rail, stopping with a bang as the helicopter made a violent sideways slip. The pilot said nothing, but Mac noted his anger as he controlled the craft.

'Where is it?' yelled Barrett, rifle in hand.

'Four hundred yards to your left,' replied Mac, eagerly hoping to see Steve's helicopter approach.

The helicopter descended rapidly while moving to the left, finally hovering some sixty metres above the massive animal, which continued moving, unconcerned.

Barrett extended the rifle out the door, awkwardly working the action back and forth to bring the first bullet into the chamber.

'Okay, I've got him now,' he yelled as Numunwari flashed to and fro across the telescopic sight.

'Steve's getting ready now!' shouted Mac, having seen the smaller helicopter approach, with Steve in the doorway, his rifle up to his shoulder.

Mac jammed his fingers in his ears as the first shot exploded from Barrett's rifle. The barrel moved violently as he fired, and the noise of the discharge was deafening. The rifle had been shaking so much that Mac was surprised to see Barrett pull the trigger; there was little possibility of precise aim.

'Just missed him!' yelled Barrett, as the second bullet entered the chamber.

Steve swore when he saw Barrett's shot hit the water six metres to the rear of Numunwari's tail, and watched helplessly as the great crocodile dived. Another shot landed in the water in the general vicinity of where the crocodile had been, the report catching Mac unawares as he strained to see the crocodile through the small side window.

'Don't move next time!' yelled Barrett at him. 'I nearly got him.'

Steve almost shouted over the radio, 'Take them up to one thousand feet and wait there.' Mac knew he would be furious, as he had often heard him criticise the fact that amateurs were allowed to shoot at any wildlife, let alone Numunwari.

The door closed and the helicopter climbed as Barrett turned. 'I had him right in my sights when you moved, Wilson. Guess we've lost him now.'

The helicopters circled for nearly fifteen minutes before Steve's machine suddenly dropped and his voice came over the radio.

'He's up, five hundred yards on the port side.'

Quick to respond, the larger helicopter descended rapidly, turning as it came down to place the crocodile on Barrett's side. After working another bullet into the breach, Barrett laid his hand on the door lever, looking to the pilot for the signal to open. As they levelled off, the pilot raised his thumb, and Barrett slid the door back and began to raise his rifle. Less than ninety metres away, Steve's helicopter was just beginning to hover, the door not yet open.

'Where is it?' yelled Barrett, searching frantically.

Mac leaned forward to look, seeing Steve position himself to fire. 'It must be below us,' he answered above the engine noise.

Leaning out against the safety harness, Barrett immediately began to raise his rifle, but as Mac blocked his ears, he saw the puff of smoke from Steve's rifle, a fraction of a second before Barrett jerked the trigger and there was a muffled explosion.

Steve's shot missed the head by less than a metre, while Barrett's landed a good three metres further out. The crocodile dived while Steve cursed himself for being hasty in trying to fire before Barrett. 'Take them up again,' he yelled, over the radio.

Annoyed at not having sighted the crocodile earlier, and furious that Steve had radioed after beginning his descent, Barrett let fly with a string of abuse, to which Mac did not respond.

After hovering for some five minutes, Steve's voice came over the radio. 'How's your fuel, Mac? We're getting low, only enough for another five minutes.'

After a consultation with the pilot, Mac replied that they had enough for ten. Steve checked the coastline, and marked their new position on the map, twenty-four kilometres from Darwin Harbour, on the landward side of the channel.

Numunwari failed to reappear, and within ten minutes both helicopters were on their way back to Darwin. They landed within twenty minutes, and, while the pilots arranged immediate fuelling, Steve, Mac and Barrett heatedly compared experiences.

'I'd have got him, if Wilson hadn't moved. Had him right in my sights when I fired,' asserted Barrett.

'Probably would have been a better idea if you'd waited till I was ready. Would have doubled our chances of getting it.'

'I was worried it'd dive,' replied Barrett, justifying his actions. 'Anyway, why the hell did you go down before you told us where the croc was? That wasn't what you'd call co-operation. Not fair at all.'

'Fair!' repeated Steve angrily, 'this isn't a bloody competition, you know. Fairness has got nothing to do with it. I'm in a small chopper which takes a lot more time to manoeuvre. If there's any chance of us both shooting together, I've got to start earlier.' He was lying, because he knew full well that he had hoped to shoot before Barrett was ready.

'Don't yell at me, Harris. You just remember who you're talking to! I'm the one with the ultimate responsibility for this, and if I think I can kill the bloody thing I'm not going to wait for some two-bit amateur to get ready.'

Steve's face showed the anger that raged inside him, but fortunately Mac changed the subject, pointing out that the fuel truck had arrived, and that perhaps they could hasten the process by helping. The suggestion was accepted in silence, and in ten minutes both helicopters were again ready to fly.

'Try and shoot together this time,' suggested Steve as he walked towards his helicopter. Barrett did not reply.

Steve spotted Numunwari within minutes of reaching the survey area. It was now well out of the channel and drifting on the surface only three kilometres from the coast.

'There!' he yelled over the radio, 'a thousand yards in towards the coast.' The crocodile dived as both helicopters descended.

'He's getting spooky, Mac, take them up again.'

After five minutes, both Barrett and Steve saw the crocodile break the surface, but again it dived before the helicopters could approach it.

'He's really wary now,' called Steve. 'Looks like we'll have to try and anticipate him. Next time we go down, stay at two hundred feet and we'll wait there for him to surface.'

When Numunwari surfaced again, he was three hundred and sixty metres to the landward side of the helicopters, but again he dived before they reached him. This time both helicopters hovered at sixty metres, both men waiting with their rifles ready for the crocodile to appear.

There could be no co-operation now; the crocodile would not allow it. The first man to see it would have to shoot immediately, and Steve and Barrett watched the silt-laden coastal waters, hoping the crocodile would emerge closest to them.

After three minutes, the pilot of Barrett's helicopter saw the enormous head surface ninety metres on the far side of them. He swung the craft around as the crocodile's great eyes opened and the signals to dive ran through the primitive body—but its muscles were too slow to respond.

Barrett glimpsed the animal in his telescopic sight and jerked the trigger.

'Got him!' he screamed. 'Got the bastard!'

'Steve, we've hit him. I can see blood in the water,' called Mac.

'Got the bastard!' repeated Barrett, hysterically.

'Where'd you hit him, Mac?' asked Steve.

'Where'd you hit him?' Mac repeated to Barrett, who was searching the water below in the hope of getting confirmation.

'I don't know. I was aiming at the head, probably got him there.'

'He thinks he got him in the head, Steve. Can you see any sign of him?'

'No. Take the choppers up and we'll have a good look.'

As the helicopters climbed, Barrett turned excitedly to Mac for praise, a wide smile across his face. Mac tried to ignore him, and continued searching, far from convinced that the crocodile was dead. After ten minutes Barrett was certain the crocodile was dead, and was sure that he in fact *had* shot it in the head. 'He's dead, Wilson. We won't see him again. Let's go home.'

Mac relayed the message to Steve, whose answer was immediate.

'Let's stay out a bit longer, just in case. We can't afford any mistakes.'

After a further five minutes, Barrett was no longer searching, convinced the crocodile was dead. 'It's dead, Wilson,' he said. 'Tell Harris we're going back.'

'Steve, we're going in, mate.'

'Okay, Mac, I'll stay until our fuel's down, about another half-hour. See you in there.'

Not wanting to leave without Steve, Barrett grabbed the microphone from Mac. 'Harris, let's go in. That bloody croc's dead and we've already run up a large bill. They're bloody expensive, these things.'

'I'd rather wait,' replied Steve. 'It might only be wounded.'

'Wounded, my arse!' shouted Barrett. 'We're going back, Harris. That's not a request, it's an order. The crocodile's dead. I know, I shot it.' Steve did not answer; he put down the microphone and signalled the pilot to head for Darwin.

Barrett was relieved to see the small helicopter moving, and his own shortly followed suit. He had shot the crocodile; had beaten Steve Harris to it. The kudos was his and his alone, and with Steve now on his way back to Darwin, there was no hope that any stories could spread about the wounded crocodile surfacing and Harris having to finish it off.

When they landed, he almost ran to meet Steve. 'How'd you like that, Harris? Not bad for a bloke who spends most of his life in an office. You never really lose the touch, do you?'

'That was a good shot, no doubt about it. Hope you killed it, though.'

'Hope?' repeated Barrett, holding up his rifle. 'With one of these things in its head it's as dead as a concrete slab.'

Steve concentrated on the rifle to avoid Barrett's smiling face; it was a magnificent weapon, too good for its owner. 'I guess you're right. Congratulations.' He walked away, his mind fighting to accept the fact that Numunwari was probably dead.

It had happened. At first he had doubted Barrett's shot, but Mac had seen blood, and the crocodile would have surfaced in the time they had waited, if it had been only superficially wounded. It hurt to allow Barrett the pleasure of killing Numunwari, because Steve felt quite strongly that if the crocodile had to be killed, he would have liked to do it himself, with perhaps a little dignity, as befitted its importance to Oondabund.

'That's a pretty bad case of sour grapes,' Barrett mumbled, as he watched Steve walk away.

Mac and Steve enjoyed the dinner Anne prepared that evening. No matter how often they ate barramundi fillets, they always enjoyed them, especially the way Anne did them: fried slowly in butter, with liberal sprinklings of black pepper.

Neither of them had spoken much since returning, though they did have a further discussion about the right of people to kill an animal like Numunwari. Mac tried to convince Steve that the action was justified by the threat to the species that this individual represented, but Steve found this difficult to accept; his depression was obvious.

When Steve was opening the second bottle of wine, Anne noticed that it was 7 pm, and switched on the aged black and white television set to catch the news. Mac half turned to watch it, but Steve lapsed back into thoughts of Numunwari. It just didn't seem right that there were thousands of millions of people on the earth and one unique crocodile; one dead unique crocodile shifting back and forth on the bottom of the sea, with only the sharks for company. Perhaps it would float to the surface in a few days, bloated and repulsive, with the scales lifting from the aged hide. And what about Oondabund? His father had talked to the crocodile about forty years before, and perhaps his grandfather had done the same, well before the white man made an impact in Arnhem Land. How could Steve ever tell Oondabund why Numunwari had had to be killed? He would never understand or forgive—to him, the old people lived inside the crocodile and, by killing the crocodile, Steve had essentially killed the people yet again.

'Steve,' called Mac, without raising his eyes from the television set. An old picture of Rex Barrett, taken well before his face wrinkled and his hairline receded, flashed on to the screen.

A voice-over said, 'Rex Barrett, one of Darwin's most popular personalities, today saved the city from what may well have been yet another series of attacks by a man-eating crocodile. The crocodile, estimated to be eight metres long, was shot from a helicopter barely thirty-two kilometres from Darwin Harbour. It is believed to be the same crocodile responsible for the attacks in Arnhem Land earlier this month.'

'The bastard,' said Steve, as the scene changed from the single photograph to Barrett's garden. Barrett was still dressed in his red-checked shirt and ridiculous orange cap, and clasped in one hand was the .460 Weatherby magnum.

'We've been following it ever since the attacks at Maningrida, Bob,' Barrett said calmly to the interviewer. 'It was sighted off Goulburn Island, then off Croker Island, and that's when we started daily searches from light aircraft. When we found it, I took a helicopter out to shoot from. It was quite a cunning reptile, took nearly four hours to get.'

'Shooting from a helicopter, Mr Barrett, is it difficult?'

'Not really, Bob. When I was a young fellow I used to do a lot of hunting, and I guess these old experiences help. The difficulty with this particular animal was that it was extremely wary after being hunted by the Wildlife Officer at Maningrida. It wouldn't stay on the surface long, and you had to be quick to fire before it dived. Took quite a few shots before one hit the head.'

'What does this mean for crocodile protection, Mr Barrett? Many people were outraged by your recommendation that crocodiles remain protected after the last attacks.'

'The question of crocodile protection is an exceedingly difficult one, Bob, and I know that many of the people of Darwin thought my decision unwise. However, the facts at that time dictated my action. You see, when crocodiles were protected, the numbers were down to an all-time low from overhunting. Not one professional hunter was making his living solely from crocodiles, and tremendous pressure was brought to bear on the Government to rectify the situation, so they were duly protected. Since that time, the populations have recovered considerably, and we've been monitoring this recovery. In my last report, the available evidence suggested that it was still too early to begin harvesting, and that's what I recommended. But in view of the public interest in the issue, I've decided to establish a Committee to re-evaluate the whole issue in detail.'

'Have you decided who'll be on the Committee yet, Mr Barrett?'

'We haven't finalised it yet, Bob. John Conners from the Cattlemen's Association and Mike Smith from the Sporting Shooters' Association have both generously agreed to be on it. We'll have a representative from Wildlife Division, and probably someone from the Tourist Bureau.'

'How do you think the conservation groups will respond? In the past they've been quite vocal about such matters.'

Barrett smiled knowingly. 'You know the situation as well as I do, Bob. There are some people around who didn't want this particular crocodile killed because they considered it too *valuable*. I can sympathise with their concern and listen to their opinions, but they just don't appreciate the local situation. It's easy to be wise about crocodile conservation when you haven't got them living in your own backyard.'

'Well, Mr Barrett,' said the interviewer, who was facing the camera, 'thank you for talking to us, and I'm sure I speak for the whole of Darwin in offering my congratulations for your efforts today.'

The scene switched back to the studio, where the newsreader continued with the next item. Mac got up and switched the set off, then looked across at Steve, who was silent. Anne felt the tension within both men, and quietly waited for one of them to break the silence. She could never tell either of them that she thought crocodiles were the most loathsome creatures on earth, and that, like most other people in Darwin, she hated them.

'You know, he's a real bastard,' said Steve eventually.

'Regardless,' said Mac, 'most people in Darwin would have believed every word he said and be right behind him. You've got to give him one thing, he's a smooth operator. It's hard to believe that's the same man that was talking to us in his office.'

They again lapsed into silence, and Anne took the opportunity to get coffee.

'It just seems a hopeless battle sometimes, Mac,' said Steve after a while. 'You put years of work into learning enough about crocs so that they can be managed and eventually harvested, and one bastard like Barrett ends up making the final decision. What about his bloody Committee? Real unbiased group—Conners and Smith have been lobbying to get the legislation changed for years.'

'Yeah. I thought his statement about you blokes making the croc wary and him having to outsmart it were a bit gross, too.'

Steve nodded in reply, and looked at his watch. Of the two things that had shaped his life in the North, Oondabund and crocodiles, both were in jeopardy; Oondabund would not be able to forgive anyone for killing Numunwari. He felt as though he wanted to be on his own, just to think about everything that had happened.

'Sorry I've been such a rotten guest, Anne.' Steve finished his coffee and forced a grin. 'I'll get going now. Thanks for dinner. I always enjoy the old barra.'

After he left, Anne curled up beside Mac and laid her head on his knees. 'Barrett really upsets him, doesn't he?'

'Pretty easy to understand,' replied Mac, giving her a gentle squeeze. 'You should have seen Barrett in the chopper. Christ, I thought he was going to shoot *me* for a while. It was just luck that he hit the croc anyway, and only because Steve directed him to where it would come up. I wish I was as sure as Barrett is that he shot it in the head.'

'Poor Steve,' said Anne. 'Since Susan died, he takes everything so seriously. I wish he'd find someone and settle down.'

'I thought he was interested in Oondabund's daughter for a while, but nothing came of it. Wonder how Susan would have taken to the idea of Steve and a black girl?'

'I wonder,' repeated Anne quietly. 'I guess if she thought Steve loved her and that they'd be happy, she wouldn't have minded.'

'Well,' said Mac smiling and looking at the clock on the wall, 'I suspect we're going to have a long day tomorrow. Once Steve starts thinking how to keep the crocs protected he'll come up with something. Come on, let's go to bed.'

When Steve woke the following morning he was immediately aware that he had forgotten to drink a large quantity of water before going to sleep. He had a splitting headache, a dry and 'fur-lined' mouth, and a craving for fluid which was not satisfied by either cold milk or tomato juice, both of which he drank in copious quantities. As soon as he had arrived home the previous night, he had opened a bottle of rum, and by the time he had gone to bed at about 2 am, he had drunk most of it.

He still felt bitter about Barrett and for at least the first hour he had thought about confronting him with an imaginary word-perfect oration which would leave no room for answers. Later his thoughts had wandered back to Maningrida, to Oondabund and Nancy, who would both soon learn what had happened. It had been close to midnight before his thoughts had turned to what he could do to thwart Barrett's attempts to change the protective legislation. By the time he had gone to bed, although quite drunk, he had felt confident he was on the right track.

At midday, he phoned Mac. 'I've got something worked out, Mac, what say we get together?'

'Sure. Why not come over for lunch? How you feeling?'

'Terrible.'

Mac laughed into the phone. 'We went to bed just after you left, but we thought you might make a night of it.'

'I did, and I'm regretting it,' Steve assured him. 'See you in a while.'

After their lunch together, Mac showed Steve the morning paper. The front page had a photo of Barrett, still in his 'hunting' clothes, as well as a longer version of the interview they had listened to the previous evening. There was a picture of a local crocodile shooter beside the skull of a large saltwater crocodile which had been killed before protection, and yet another report about how crocodiles were plentiful again. The paper also featured a short interview with John Besser, who, according to the paper, could now rest at ease with the knowledge that the animal that had taken his close friends was now dead. In the article about Barrett, it was promised that the so-called 'era of marauding crocodiles' was over, and that the Committee to determine the new policy would be formed within a week. The immediate priority, according to the newspaper's editorial, was to eradicate all saltwater crocodiles within a thirty-five kilometre radius of Darwin.

Having read all that, Steve sighed. 'Well, it looks like real problems, Mac. They'll be shooting crocs before the next wet season unless we get cracking.'

'What have you got in mind? I'm not too sure there's much we can do.'

'For a start,' replied Steve immediately, 'we can expand and update the report we did for Barrett, and have it all ready to publicise if it's needed. There's a file I put together in case this sort of thing came up, and it's got all the notes we've made, plus most of the literature records on the ecological importance of crocs. It's also got predictions about the commercial value of crocs if they're managed properly, as against the uncontrolled shooting that Barrett's precious Committee is likely to aim for.'

'And we just sit on the report?' queried Mac.

'Yeah. Barrett may change his mind like he did last time, and we don't want to fire all our guns unless they're needed. If they really try and change the legislation, I'll send copies of the report to every conservation group in the country.'

'You can't do that, Steve!' replied Mac, horrified at the suggestion. 'You're a public servant.'

Steve smiled. 'Maybe not, but let's get it ready anyway. With Barrett on the opposite side it's not going to be easy, and I've decided that if worst come to worst I'll resign. Then I can say what I like to whom I like.'

Mac stared at Steve in silence before speaking. 'Well, I hope it doesn't come to *that*.' The subject was dropped.

After a further cup of tea, Mac and Steve drove out to Steve's office, where they spent the rest of the afternoon extracting information from files and compiling an ordered list enumerating the positive aspects of maintaining the current legislation and keeping crocodiles protected. Their points ranged from a projected $15 million industry within fifteen years to a supposed correlation between the disappearance of crocodiles and the decline in barramundi numbers. Neither Steve nor Mac believed that there was any relationship between the statistics, but this was not the time for scientific ethics.

Steve also prepared a detailed account of the spiritual and cultural aspects of Numunwari, and its importance to Oondabund. Although he did not tell Mac, he intended to send this to one of the southern weeklies, where it was sure to be published, if events became critical. He also summarised exactly what had happened in the helicopters when they shot the crocodile, just in case there was a need to get Barrett's role straightened out.

At 8.15 pm, Mac went home, leaving Steve confident that they had made realistic progress in what could develop into a major conservation issue. He was also more than ever determined that, if necessary, he would put his job on the line.

3

At just after 8 pm the same night, Roger Blunt staggered from the door of Darwin's Waterfront Hotel, having been drinking since midday in one of the back rooms. Theoretically, trading on Sundays was restricted to specific hours, but everyone in Darwin, including the police, knew that he could always get a drink in the Waterfront's back bar; it seemed to be open twenty-four hours a day, every day.

Blunt was a regular, who drank whatever he could whenever he could. As soon as he got his pension cheque, he drank beer, and when his finances ran low he switched to wine; when they were gone altogether, he would beg, borrow or steal enough money to buy methylated spirits. At fifty-six years of age, he was beyond help, and when sober he realised this himself.

His cheque having arrived the previous Friday, he had spent the Sunday drinking beer, knowing that by Monday he would be on wine. Still, beer kept his spirits up, and as he staggered from the door he was happily drunk. At the footpath, he stumbled on his bad leg, the limb which had never fully recovered from being crushed in a trucking accident. This had brought him his pension and had heralded the start of his drinking. The fall did not worry him, and he merely picked himself up, reoriented himself to the route home, and continued.

The roadway he walked on, Fishers Road, had been reclaimed from the mangrove swamps that had once bordered the harbour; it was lit by amber street lights, and one side fell steeply to the waters of Darwin Harbour. Blunt knew the road well, and happily lurched along, straddling the white line which divided it into two lanes.

Ninety metres away, in the harbour, two eyes barely fifteen centimetres above water level watched the movement down the hill. Although the tide was running in rapidly, slow movements of the tail held the massive body in one position.

Singing to himself to ward off his loneliness, Blunt neither heard nor saw a blue Holden sedan coming over the crest of the hill. Because his full-length grey woollen coat merged with the colour of the bitumen road, the driver did not see him until he was barely forty-five metres away, and he had to swerve to the right-hand side of the road to avoid colliding with him. Instinctively Blunt's worn body responded to the sound of danger, and he flung himself to the narrow footpath, but his crippled leg collapsed and he slid over the embankment. When Blunt looked up, the footpath was three metres above him.

Leaving barely a ripple, the great croocodile sank beneath the surface.

The three-metre climb to the road proved difficult, Blunt's left leg refusing to support the full weight of his body. Twice he slipped, but gradually he approached the path, and as his hands reached it, Numunwari surfaced six metres below, about a metre from the edge of the embankment. Gasping for breath, Blunt climbed over the top and sat on the edge of the road. The climb had been strenuous and he rummaged for and found the stubbed end of a cigarette in his coat pocket. After five deep puffs, he staggered to his feet and continued along his way, this time walking on the footpath.

Numunwari was in deeper water with two strokes of his tail, and there he lay watching the movement on the road. Twice he saw Blunt stumble and fall, and twice he dived and swam to the edge, only to see the movement continue out of reach. He was not bothered by the waiting—it was normal for a successful attack.

Singing once again, Blunt failed to notice a green Hillman sedan appear over the crest and start down the hill. The driver, Margaret Tierney, and her fiancé Dennis Waters had been at a party all day and were both tired, but they saw Blunt staggering along on the footpath.

'Look at that old bloke,' she said, pushing the horn button. 'He'll get hit if he's not careful.'

Startled by the sudden noise behind him, Blunt again jumped, but this time when he tripped and fell, he rolled over the embankment and down over the rocks and gravel to the water's edge. Margaret slammed on the brakes, causing the car to skid to a halt.

Blunt, sobered but uninjured by the fall, started to climb back to the road, but when he was three metres above the water, his leg collapsed and he slid back to the edge. Behind him, the water parted as a rounded snout widened to a grotesque triangular head, on which the nostril valves opened and the membranous eyelid slid across the eye.

'You okay, mate?' yelled Dennis from above.

Two metres from the water, Blunt stopped climbing and looked up. 'Yeah, I guess so. What'd you do that for?'

The head rose slowly in the water with the jaws slightly gaped, the amber lights reflecting from the rows of teeth. Margaret suddenly realised she wasn't looking at just another boulder which had rolled out from the embankment.

'Look out!' she screamed, 'crocodile!'

The head was moving across the water separating it from the bank as Blunt looked to see why she had screamed; he turned and just moved his leg, as the teeth and jaws slammed shut, fifteen centimetres from his foot. Frantically his fingers clawed at the ground as the huge crocodile slid back down the steep grade upon which it had launched itself unsuccessfully. With just an occasional flick of the membranes, the yellow eyes watched the prey move steadily away.

Blunt clambered frantically up the bank. At the top he crawled and staggered out across the road as he rose to his feet, and stopped only when Dennis grabbed his shoulder. He was yelling, 'You all right?' as Numunwari slipped noiselessly out into deeper water.

'You saw it, didn't you? You saw it? It was a big croc, wasn't it?' Blunt demanded, his whole body shaking.

'A bloody big croc, mate. You're lucky it didn't get you—Christ, it was huge.'

'Dennis!' called Margaret from the path. 'It's still out there; look.'

Dennis ran to the edge, but at first saw nothing. Slowly his eyes became accustomed to the light and he recognised the evil shape, some forty yards out, motionless, watching the road. Placing his arm around Margaret, he gently eased her back from the edge.

'It's watching us, Dennis! It's watching and waiting for one of us to fall down there!'

'Come on, sweet, we'd better go and tell the police before someone *does* get taken.'

'The police!' repeated Blunt. 'What'd we have to do that for?'

'So they can get rid of the bloody thing before it takes someone.'

Blunt was silent, still trying to convince himself that it wasn't all a drunken hallucination. 'I suppose you're right. It was a big croc, wasn't it?'

It took seven minutes to drive to the police station, but when they entered, the officer on duty, Constable John Wiley, merely smiled when he saw Blunt.

'Don't tell me Blunty's been causing trouble again?'

Blunt lowered his head and stared at the floor; Dennis began to understand his reluctance to report the incident to the police. 'We brought him in from Fishers Road. A big croc nearly got him.'

'Him?' Wiley emphasised, pointing and smiling widely. 'Did he tell you that?'

'We saw it,' said Margaret, irritated.

'It's true, officer,' added Blunt, trying not to sway on his feet. 'It nearly grabbed me leg. I slipped down the bank and there it was, a real big bastard. But these people saw it; it's true.'

'Is this all true?' asked Wiley, his smile almost gone.

'Well, we both bloody well saw it,' answered Dennis. 'It came out of the water at him and missed his legs by inches. It was huge, the head looked about five feet long and, Christ, you should have seen the bloody teeth.'

'I'll have to ring the sergeant on this one,' replied Wiley, whose smile had now disappeared. 'Just hang on a bit, will you?'

After identifying himself on the phone, Wiley summarised the events he had just been told. From the repetition of details it was clear that the sergeant also doubted the story, and both Dennis and Margaret found themselves getting angry.

After three minutes, Wiley hung up. 'Seems it's a Wildlife Section problem, not a police matter. You'll have to contact them.'

'You've got to be joking!' said Dennis, making no attempt to hide his anger. 'Listen, mate, there's a bloody big croc down there that nearly killed this old bloke, drunk or no drunk. Now we've reported it to the police, and if you think we're now going to drive all around Darwin trying to find Wildlife Section, whatever it is, on Sunday night, you're mistaken. We've told you; it's your problem.'

Privately Wiley agreed with Dennis; he had joined the police force to protect people from danger, and what could be more dangerous than a man-eating crocodile? But the sergeant had made it clear that it was not a police problem, so officially there was nothing he could do. He wished the sergeant were in the office now, facing these people. Wiley looked at his watch; it was 9.50 pm.

'Between you and me,' he said quietly, 'I agree with you. I'm off duty in ten minutes, and if you could just wait till then, I'll come down and you can show me where it all happened—that be okay?'

Dennis nodded acceptance reluctantly. 'We'll wait for you outside,' he said.

'There's no need for me to hang around, is there?' said Blunt, when they got outside. 'I might just walk home from here. I don't like the police much.' He stumbled away.

Wiley came out in exactly ten minutes, and, in his Morris 850, followed Dennis and Margaret to where the attack had occurred. Standing on the footpath, Dennis pointed to where Numunwari had come out of the water. 'It was just over there, to the right of that boulder down from the lamp post. The old bloke was level with the boulder when the croc came out, and afterwards it just slid back into the water and swam over there somewhere. It seemed to be staying in one place, watching us.'

Wiley switched on his torch and shone it along the edge of the embankment, but saw nothing. When he looked down to where the crocodile was supposed to have attacked Blunt, he saw that the bank was still wet, and obviously disturbed. Moving the light beam back and forth over the water, he caused a fish to jump, which startled them all, but there was no sign of a crocodile. They walked down the path in silence. Wiley continuing to scan with the torch, and had only gone a hundred yards when Wiley caught the faintest glimmer of a reflection.

'That's it!' said Margaret, when he pointed it out to them. 'That's it, I'm sure.'

Wiley and Dennis ran down the path a further forty-five metres, and when they shone the torch out into the bay, there was no mistaking the bright red glow just above water level. About twenty metres out, Numunwari lay motionless, watching them and confused by the intense beam, which initiated signals to dive.

'Take the torch,' Wiley whispered, passing it to Dennis as he fumbled with the safety strap that held his revolver in its holster. 'I'll see if I can get a shot at it.'

Pupils contracted in the light, temporarily impairing his vision, Numunwari caught only glimpses of activity on the bank. Stronger signals to dive spread throughout its primitive body. There was a flash and a splash in the water barely twenty centimetres from his head. Instinctively he swung sideways, the jaws opening to close rapidly where the splash had been, as the sound from the revolver reached him.

'Christ!' said Dennis, not taking his eyes from the crocodile.

'It's enormous,' agreed Wiley. 'Hold the light steady and I'll have another go. That one went close.'

Before Wiley could squeeze the trigger, Numunwari dived. There was no single reason for the action, just an instinctive behaviour, the reason that crocodiles survived for millions of years when their contemporaries died out. When he surfaced, he was sixty-five metres from the embankment.

'Damn him!' hissed Wiley, 'he's too far out. We'll have to go down to the edge of the water.'

Margaret's intuition urged her to stop Dennis following, but she said nothing as they climbed over the edge and slid down the slope. In the darkness, Numunwari's pupils expanded and he watched their movements coming closer and closer. The huge tail began to move and the body cut across the tidal stream towards the bank, diving when the beam once again reached his eyes, and he was forty-five metres from shore.

'There!' whispered Dennis, picking up the eyeshine. But in the short time taken for Wiley to lift the revolver, it had gone.

'He's dived,' said Wiley, lowering the hand gun. 'We must have made too much noise coming down. Damn it!'

Dennis directed the torch as far as the beam would carry, and began moving it back and forth across the water, while both he and Wiley strained their eyes to pick up the faintest reflection—but there was none, and the waters were quiet, except for the continual gentle lap of water at their feet.

Intent on the beam, neither Wiley nor Dennis saw the head begin to emerge three metres away, but both heard the rush of spent air. They suddenly realised that they had been skilfully hunted, but they were too late. Dennis swung the beam down to the approaching crocodile and Wiley prepared to fire, but the revolver was barely raised as Numunwari's jaws slammed shut around Wiley's legs, hurling him sideways and causing the revolver to fire uselessly into the water. A short-lived scream of terror was muffled as Numunwari dived. Dennis dropped the torch and, panic-stricken, fought his way up the bank.

Wiley lived for two seconds longer, his skull cracked against a rock during the first explosion of struggling. When Numunwari surfaced eighteen metres out, the limp body trailed in the water with its legs held firmly in the steel grip. Neither Margaret nor Dennis heard the splashing as the body was thrown about and repositioned, and they did not see the giant claws anchor in the prey as the head jerked violently sideways to separate it into two pieces. The body torn in two, connected only by a twisted cord of cloth and skin, Numunwari moved back to the embankment, where the prehistoric jaws opened, closed, jerked and pulled until the two sections separated. Each was manoeuvred down the giant gullet, leaving a twisted mass of intestines spilling out over the teeth.

Within five minutes, Numunwari swam back out to deeper water and drifted with the outgoing tide, content in his success.

Steve was asleep when the phone started ringing, and only half-awake when he stumbled into the lounge room to answer it. When the policeman on duty at the station told him what had happened, he considered the possibility that he was dreaming, but knew it was misplaced hope.

'Did anyone see it?'

'Two people, and they both said the crocodile was really huge, over thirty feet long.'

'*Thirty?*' repeated Steve.

'Yes, they reckon the head was five feet long, and they were right there.'

'Oh God, no,' replied Steve quietly, after a pause. 'Give me twenty minutes and I'll be down; I'll pick up Mac Wilson on the way.'

Steve stood by the phone and thought of Barrett's television interview. 'Took quite a few shots before one hit it in the head,' he had boasted.

'I hope you're bloody satisfied now, you bastard,' Steve mumbled to himself as he dialled Mac's phone number.

Mac was asleep in the lounge chair by the television set when the ringing woke him. When he heard the tone of Steve's voice, he knew instantly that something catastrophic had happened.

'The croc, Mac. The bloody croc's in Darwin Harbour. It just grabbed a cop down by the embankment on Fishers Road.'

Mac stared at the wall in disbelief. 'It can't be. It's dead!'

'It's *not* bloody well dead! Two people saw the whole bloody thing and they reckoned it was thirty feet, its head's five feet long. It's the same one, Mac. It's Numunwari.'

'Christ, no,' said Mac, rubbing his eyes. 'When's all this going to end?'

'They want me down at the station right away, and I think it's probably better if we both go. We might be out all night trying to get it, so you'd better put on some warm clothes. I'll bring my rifle and pick you up in a few minutes.'

'What about Barrett, Steve? Does he know yet?'

'Well I'm certainly not going to tell the bastard. He's caused enough trouble, and this time I want to do it my way.'

On the drive through Darwin to the police station, both Mac and Steve noticed spotlights scanning the water near the embankment. When they arrived, there were three patrol cars parked outside, and as they entered the station, a uniformed officer approached them.

'What's the problem, fellers? We've got an emergency on our hands, can it wait?'

'We're from Wildlife, mate,' answered Steve, 'Mac Wilson and Steve Harris; a Constable Clemson asked us to come down.'

'Are we glad to see you,' said the officer. 'I'm Clemson, and the Inspector's been expecting you. He's down the hall, second office on the left.'

Mac and Steve both knew Inspector John Smythe well, so Steve merely knocked and entered, to see him standing by a wall map of Darwin. He was a big man, nearly two metres tall, and weighing at least ninety kilograms, with a mop of red hair and an extended bushy moustache. His red cheeks indicated too much whisky.

'Steve, Mac. Looks like a big croc's taken one of our men. It's been lurking off the embankment, and had a go at an old drunk about nine o'clock. One of our constables, John Wiley, went down to investigate, and it grabbed him, round ten o'clock. A young couple saw the whole thing. They're in the next office.'

'How big was the croc?' asked Steve. 'Does anyone really know?'

'It's evidently enormous, Steve. Exaggerations aside, it's obviously really big, just like the one Rex Barrett shot.'

'Well there's a bloody good chance it's the same damn croc!' replied Steve. 'I saw spotlights on the way in; what's going on down there?'

Smythe turned to the map. 'As near as we can determine the croc took Wiley here, where the red pin is, on Fishers Road.' Steve followed the road around the edge of the harbour, to where it ended at the wharf. Smythe continued, 'We've got two cars with lights down there now, trying to find some sign of Wiley, but so far they haven't seen him or the croc. We've contacted the Water Police, and they've got the launch ready to leave whenever we want it. I didn't want to start too much till you got here, Steve. As far as I'm concerned, you can run the operation from here on in.'

Steve looked from the map to Mac. 'I hate to say it, but there's not much chance of Wiley being found if the croc got him. This one's quick and accurate, your man wouldn't stand a chance. People are just going to have to be kept away from the water's edge until we find it, or we'll lose someone else.'

'Should we have it broadcast over the radio and television stations?' asked Mac. 'It might just bring everyone out to see what's going on.'

Steve thought of the prospect of people wandering near the water trying to catch a glimpse of the crocodile. 'Why don't we just keep things quiet for now? If we get it tonight, there'll be no problem, and if we don't, we can make sure warnings are put on the morning news.'

'And what if we don't get it tonight, Steve?' asked Mac.

'We'll just have to keep everyone away until we do. Anyone would be taking a big risk going near the water's edge with that thing out there; it's as simple as that. Anyway, if we take the launch out as soon as possible, we might be able to get it in an hour or two. We can worry about the rest later.'

Steve turned to the Inspector. 'If your men could patrol the shores by car, it'd help. There's a chance they'll see the croc and they'll be able to keep people away from the water. For Christ's sake, make sure that nobody just shoots on sight; if they see it, tell them not to shoot unless they're certain of hitting the top of the head, with a high-powered rifle.'

'What about Barrett?' asked Mac. 'We'd better phone him.'

'Could you ring him after we're gone?' Steve asked the Inspector, after a glance at Mac. 'We don't want him lousing things up again.'

'No problem. Do you think it's a good idea to have a quick talk to my men before you go? Tell them what to do, just in case?'

Steve agreed, and the Inspector assembled the available police officers in the mess room. The talk was brief. Steve explained how a crocodile attacked, and emphasised that this particular crocodile was not afraid of people. He almost pleaded with them not to shoot unless they were absolutely certain of hitting either the square platform on the top of the head, or the area behind the front legs; the latter being unlikely, because it was normally under water. After a few minor questions, Steve and Mac left the group and drove to the small Customs jetty, where the police launch was moored.

Drifting with the outgoing tide, Numunwari rounded the point, saw the lights on the main wharf and felt the vibrations of the fishing trawler engines. With a slight increase in the rate at which his tail waved, he changed direction and effortlessly glided across the tidal stream towards the wharf. Using the increased current in the deep channel beside the wharf, he drifted out past the end piers.

Seven people were on the wharf fishing, but none saw the animal at the outer edge of the area illuminated by the jetty light; they were concentrating on their thin lines which streamed out into the channel below to tempt passing fish.

The crocodile turned sharply when it passed the far end of the jetty, and, in the strong current, it used its powerful tail to push it against the tide. Noiselessly it slid in under the wharf, moving slowly among the oyster-covered pylons until it found a main bearer, over a metre in diameter, behind which it was essentially out of the current. Gentle strokes of the tail maintained its position, and its relaxed limbs hung limply in the water. Six trawlers were berthed at the wharf, and vibrations from their engines resounded in its primitive ears, but they did not cause alarm. Numunwari had eaten, and now desired only to wait undisturbed until morning, when it could crawl out in the sun and warm its huge body to facilitate the digestion of what filled the bag-like stomach.

Above the crocodile, on the wharf, there was virtually no movement. A school of queen fish had passed through over an hour before, and everyone fishing caught at least three, but since then no one had caught anything. The trawlers were equally quiet, with the crews either asleep or in one of Darwin's many hotels.

The quietness was shattered by a taxi, which rattled along the loosely-fitting boards until it was opposite the end trawler on the landward side. Alerted, Numunwari listened as the rattling stopped and a door opened and closed. There was a brief exchange of words, and again the rattling started—then there was nothing but the continual throb of the engines.

Peter Collins was the skipper of the *Shindy*. He had been on fishing boats since childhood and was widely recognised in the north as the trawler skipper who always came home with a good catch, be it fish or prawn. After seven days off the north coast of Melville Island, he had returned with over two thousand kilos of prawns. This was a good catch for that time of year, and something worth celebrating, which was what he had been doing since 4 pm. Having agreed to relieve the deckhand at midnight, he had returned in a taxi, and as he climbed down the narrow rusted ladder to the trawler's deck, his thoughts centred on the cheque he would receive in the morning; that would make it all worthwhile.

Numunwari watched Collins's legs on the ladder, for although recently fed, instinct ruled the great body lying five metres away; an instinct which demanded that a predator must never ignore easy prey.

Peter Collins jumped the last few rungs to the deck, and within seconds disappeared through the doorway to the small mess area. Every movement had been watched and Numunwari had now turned his head just enough to watch the steel door without placing it in the current outside the shelter of the bearer.

The young deckhand was asleep at the table, with the radio blaring and eight empty beer cans strewn over the table. Taking a full can from the refrigerator, Collins opened it and sat beside him. Had he stayed there for only two minutes, he would have heard the music interrupted by a news flash about the crocodile attack on Wiley; one of the policemen had phoned the radio station, for a small fee. But it was hot in the small room, and with the tide falling, the mooring ropes needed letting out, so Collins decided to finish his beer on deck in the cool night air.

At the Customs jetty, Steve and Mac followed two police officers down the ladder to the deck of the twelve-metre launch. It was a boat Steve had often seen, but never been on, and he looked forward to being shown over it. Powered by twin Volvo Penta diesels, and with an array of navigational and radio equipment, as well as two large spotlights on the flying bridge, it was an ideal vessel for work in the north.

The skipper looked over the charts with Steve, and they decided to search the embankment area before following the coastline around to the headlands, going out on the east bank, and if necessary coming back on the west bank. At 12.14 am, the ropes were cast and the sleek launch glided out into the swiftly-flowing current.

At 12.15 am, Peter Collins climbed out the door to the deck, to be immediately refreshed by the cool sea air. He walked to the bow, and on the port side released three turns on the mooring rope, and then did the same at midships and at the stern, before resting against the wire guard rails to finish his beer. In the water below him, he watched the schools of small fish dart between the darkness of the wharf and the illuminated water beside the ship. He looked up to the wharf, but there was no sign of life, and then his eyes fixed on the superstructure of his boat—its design was good, the main reason for his success as a trawler skipper. His life was a lonely one, but in success there was pleasure, and in success there was money.

As his eyes moved to the fittings on the starboard boom, the fittings he had designed and built, small fish frantically dispersed in all directions. A single sweep of his tail and Numunwari appeared from beneath the wharf; six metres behind the trawler's stern it oriented its sight on the moving arm which carried the half-empty can of beer to Collins's lips. Within seconds, the crocodile had dived.

Collins's first reaction was to jump forward when he heard the small but unnatural splash behind him, but simultaneously the huge teeth ripped into his left leg, pinning it to the wire. Within a fraction of a second he had seen the yellow eyes deep in the head which protruded through the stainless steel wire, and was slipping backwards into the water. Reefed against the wire, the supports started to bend as the great crocodile rolled its tail and body, bringing its complete body weight to bear on the head, which held its prey, and began to turn. The teeth tore through the muscle and Collins was free, blood gushing from the gaping wound as he pitched himself forward, only to hear and feel Numunwari lunge up on to the deck again, grasping the steel wire between the pipe supports. Collins turned as the strained clamps broke, and the crocodile and wire crashed back into the water.

Gripping the stern winch, Collins pulled himself up on his right leg in time to see Numunwari lying motionless behind, with just his head above water. There was blood on the snout, Collins's blood, but as he watched, the immense head sank below the surface.

'You right, mate?' came a voice from the wharf.

'I need help, quick!'

As the fisherman clambered down the ladder, Collins ripped his own shirt off and wrapped it tightly around the shredded muscle. The cloth rapidly darkened as it soaked up blood, and Collins frantically hoped that the bleeding would be stemmed.

'What happened?' yelled the bearded fisherman, confronted with Collins amidst a sea of blood.

'A fucking croc just had a go at me. Leapt up the back of the boat. Look at the wire.'

The bent iron posts and broken wire told their own story. 'Jim! Bill! Come over here quickly.'

From behind the bearer, very gently moving its tail, Numunwari watched the three men struggle to get Collins up the narrow, rusted ladder.

Some four hundred metres out, the police launch cruised by, heading for the arm of the harbour from which Fishers Road had been reclaimed.

'Those buggers must have got a big one,' said Steve, pointing to the group of fishermen struggling to get Collins over the top rung on to the wharf. 'Look at them.'

'They get big skinnies off there every now and again,' replied Mac. 'But they seem to spend a hell of a lot of time for each one they get.'

As the launch rounded the point, blocking the view of the wharf, Steve and Mac saw the police headlights scanning the water. Mac switched on the launch's lights, and as Steve signalled to the skipper to slow down, they began systematically searching the bay.

'Base on the radio, Steve,' came the skipper's voice over the intercom. 'Anything to report yet?'

'Not yet,' answered Steve, his eyes fixed on the beam which slowly progressed along the shoreline.

Siren blaring, Constables Jones and Buckley drove the patrol car on to the wharf. They had been closest when the radio message about Collins was broadcast, nearly thirty minutes after the attack. Two of the fishermen who had helped Collins were still there, waiting by their lines, but they stood and signalled to the car, which pulled up beside them. Buckley was carrying a torch and rifle when he jumped out. 'Which one's the *Shindy*?'

'That's it there, mate, beside you,' replied the bearded fisherman pointing to the ladder. 'What took you blokes so long?'

'The hospital just let us know,' said Buckley stepping to the ladder. 'Christ! Get a load of this, Jonesie.'

'Did you blokes see it?' asked Jones as his eyes took in the carnage on the trawler's back deck.

'We were first there, helped the poor bastard up the ladder.'

'What about the croc, any sign of it?'

'Nothing. We've been here ever since, and haven't seen a sign of it. With all the noise it would've taken off, but the bloke that got grabbed reckoned it was bloody huge—thirty feet at least. How is that poor bugger, anyway?'

'They've stopped the bleeding and they're sewing him up. He's lucky it missed the bone and only got the muscle.'

Buckley shone the torch out over the water, lighting up the area beyond the jetty lights, then brought it back to the trawler, and finally to the ladder, the narrow rusty ladder. 'Is that bloody thing safe? Looks pretty damn rusty.'

'It'll be okay,' replied Jones, giving it a quick glance. 'Let's get down there and have a look around.'

Jones climbed carefully but rapidly down the ladder, jumping the last few rungs, and was at the stern examining the bent posts when Buckley started down. Hesitant to carry the rifle on the ladder, Buckley left it on the wharf.

Behind the main bearer, Numunwari remained out of the current, which had increased even more as the tide continued ebbing. He had heard the sounds of the car arriving five metres above, but had made no movement; he had also watched the renewed activity on the ladder and deck without any apparent response. However, as Buckley jumped to the deck, the massive body turned into the current, and with three rapid strokes of the tail cruised out from the darkness thirty-five metres behind the trawler.

Jones did not know what made him look up, it was just a feeling. 'The croc!' he screamed as he grabbed for the .357 magnum revolver strapped to his belt. Numunwari was swimming fast in the current, and slid across the water's surface heading for the darkness that lay beyond the jetty lights.

'Don't shoot unless you're sure, don't shoot unless you're sure,' crashed through Jones's mind as he levelled the square open sights along the moving body to the head; it was almost in the darkness.

'Shoot!' yelled Buckley, his revolver in hand.

In the bad light, the head could not be clearly seen and Jones refrained from pulling the trigger as a shot exploded behind him, then another.

'Shoot!' screamed Buckley, again, as he fired twice more into the darkness. Jones lowered his hand gun; Numunwari disappeared towards the mouth of the harbour.

'Why the hell didn't you fire?'

'You heard what Harris said—don't shoot unless you're sure. I couldn't be sure. Get on the radio and let the launch know, quickly!'

When the news that Collins had been attacked at the wharf reached the launch, the skipper immediately swung the boat around and opened up the engines; when Buckley's message was relayed, they were only three kilometres away, with Steve furious about the original delay in communication.

'He's a cunning bastard, this croc,' he said to Mac. 'I've never come across anything like it. It's no wonder he's lived so bloody long.'

'The press is going to go absolutely beserk tomorrow.'

'And all because of bloody Barrett. The whole thing could have ended yesterday in the choppers if that stupid bastard hadn't been there,' raged Steve. Mac did not bother to reply.

From the four police cars on the wharf, spotlights probed the darkness in all directions while at least forty people milled around. When the launch approached, three of the lights waved up and down in the one direction. Steve pressed the intercom button. 'Follow the lights, skipper; that must be the way he went out.'

Mac shone the light among the pylons as they passed, but there were no reflections. The bent guard rails confirmed what they had heard over the radio, and as they watched, bright flashes of light indicated that photographers were already present, recording the scene for the morning paper. With the engines slowed, the launch gradually moved away from the wharf. Mac scanned every bit of water in their path, but they saw nothing.

Three kilometres from the wharf, Mac caught the momentary glimmer of a reflection which suddenly disappeared. When Steve checked along the beam he could see nothing, but he had the skipper slow right down to an idle and switch off all lights other than the spotlights. Heads together, he and Mac concentrated on the beam, and this time both of them saw it appear and just as suddenly disappear, a good three hundred metres in front.

'Keep the light on it, Mac, that looks like him,' Steve whispered. 'He could be swimming away from us and only get the light occasionally.'

Pressing the intercom, he passed news of the sighting on to the skipper, who was unable to slow down any more, as Steve had requested.

'There!' whispered Mac, as the reflection appeared again.

'It's him,' Steve replied. 'It must be.'

Steve picked up the .270, and while resting the barrel on the railing surrounding the bridge, he worked the action to bring the first of five bullets into the chamber. A slight wind was blowing, and, as the tops of small waves danced in the light, Steve realised that tension was mounting within him; the end might be near, but he had to remain calm. Taking deep, slow breaths, he consciously worked on controlling the excitement that flowed through his body, knowing he could not afford to miss an opportunity, least of all have a badly-placed shot as the result of a shaky hand.

'There it is again!' whispered Mac.

Steve spread his legs and bedded the rifle against his shoulder, moving his eye just close enough to the telescopic sight to gain a full field of view. With the small waves, the reflection darted across the sight, and he waited to see it clearly, still breathing slowly and deeply. With his thumb, he released the safety catch.

A hundred metres away, the first doubts ran through Steve's mind; there was something odd about the way the reflection moved with the waves. When they were eighty metres away, his grip relaxed and his finger left the finely-grooved trigger. When they were sixty metres away, he stood up and began to remove the bullet from the chamber. 'It's a stinking beer can,' he said to himself. He relayed the message to the skipper, and as the lights flicked back on, the revs picked up again.

'What a bastard,' said Mac. 'I thought we had it that time.'

'It's happened before,' said Steve, laying the rifle back in its case. 'You can usually tell by the way they float, cans go up and down with the small waves whereas a big croc steams straight through them. I should have picked it up earlier, but I guess I'm not quite myself with old Numunwari.'

The search along the eastern bank of Darwin Harbour to its mouth proved fruitless, so they crossed to the western shore and followed it back upstream until level with the wharf again, though six metres from it. In desperation, they cruised out to the mouth, this time in midstream, and on returning, they went back in around the wharf and embankment, but nothing was sighted. Numunwari had eluded them.

As the first rays of morning sun lit the night sky, Steve and Mac both knew it was hopeless. Using the launch radio, Steve had planned a day search, utilising two light aircraft and a helicopter, manned by police and other Wildlife Section personnel; it was due to start at 6.30 am. The police had made preparations to restrict boat activity in the harbour, and warnings were already being broadcast on both radio and television.

As the launch approached the Customs jetty, the welcoming committee of some fifteen men and women, mostly reporters from the local papers and representatives from the southern news media, congregated around the narrow stairwell that led from the jetty to the water level. Steve looked at Mac and managed a smile. 'I hope they don't keep us long. I'm buggered, and you look the same.' To both men, it seemed like weeks since they had hunted Numunwari from the helicopters, though it was barely forty-five hours ago.

Steve climbed the stairs first, and as he reached the jetty platform, Rex Barrett met him.

'Why didn't you let me know what was going on last night, Harris? Who the hell do you think you are, taking charge of the hunt?'

Without answering, Steve stood to his full height and fixed his weary and bloodshot eyes on the smaller man before him. Barrett still wore his hunting clothes, which now infuriated Steve, and over his shoulder was the Weatherby .460, well polished and truly magnificent. Steve felt none of the uneasiness of their previous meetings; now he was angry, wild, and fighting for control. He heard the cameras repeatedly clicking and knew that he must move away. Without answering, he turned and walked down the jetty, ignoring the reporters, who fired questions at him.

'Wilson!' Barrett shouted, as Mac reached the jetty platform. 'Why didn't you inform me? You're supposed to be able to handle a responsible position.'

Tired and weary, Mac's mind fumbled and hesitated, sending garbled messages to his moving mouth. 'We ... ah ... I mean ... we didn't ... have time.' Blushing and embarrassed, he found he could no longer look into Barrett's small piercing eyes, and ashamed at the public rebuke, he lowered his head, not knowing what else to do. Steve stopped walking.

'You two haven't heard the end of this,' continued Barrett, appearing to disregard the reporters around him, but actually spurred on by their presence. 'I just hope for your sakes you haven't spooked *this* one; you caused me enough trouble with the other bastard.'

Steve had almost reached Barrett when he finished talking, and he pushed past the remaining reporters to confront him.

'I want to talk to you, Barrett. Now!'

'Don't speak to me in that tone, Harris.'

Steve looked from Barrett to the reporters and then to Mac, who was staring at him with bloodshot eyes.

'We can talk on the launch. Won't be a minute, Mac.' Steve pushed past the remaining reporters and climbed down the stairs to the launch. Barrett followed, still with his rifle slung on his red-checked shoulder. They both walked past the skipper into the combined kitchen and eating area; once inside Steve slammed the door.

'Now you just listen to me, Harris,' Barrett blustered. 'I don't know what's going on in that addled brain of yours, but you don't talk to me like that in public. I'm not your bloody equal.'

'Shut your mouth, Barrett.'

'Have you gone mad or something? You don't tell *me* to—' Barrett barely saw the fist that crashed into his shoulder, knocking him against the bulkhead. His rifle clattered to the floor. Barrett lay there, stunned and holding the shoulder which beneath the shirt was rapidly bruising. Tears of anger and fear rose in his eyes as Steve took a step and stood above him.

'Just shut your mouth and listen, Barrett.'

'You're mad; you've gone crazy.'

'Mad!' Steve repeated. 'I'm bloody mad all right. If you hadn't been such a bloody pig-headed idiot in the chopper, we wouldn't have the trouble we've got now.'

'What are you talking about? It's not the same croc.'

'Of course it's the same bloody croc, you stupid bastard. How many crocs that size do you think are around? If you hadn't tried to be a bloody hero, the croc would have been killed. But no, you couldn't miss that chance, could you? Well, I hope you're happy, mate, because you killed Wiley as surely as if you shot him yourself, and I'd say Collins would be pretty unhappy if he knew about the great Rex Barrett, too.'

'You're mad, Harris. They'll be locking you up when I get out of here.'

'You say that once more, Barrett, and you bloody well won't get out of here. I'm sick to death of you. If we still didn't have to get that croc, I'd give you a hiding you'd never forget.' Barrett stared up at Steve, but didn't answer, and the room was silent for some thirty seconds.

'Now no one's seen what happened here, Barrett, and what's done about it is completely up to you. But I'll tell you one thing. If you start on me I'll tell the bloody world about what happened in the choppers, and you can say what you like. There are plenty of witnesses. Now just lay off us until we get that croc and don't interfere.'

Without waiting for an answer, Steve walked from the cabin and closed the door. On the jetty, Mac was waiting with a frightened look on his face.

'What happened?' he whispered as the reporters began to crowd around Steve.

'Nothing. Let's go.'

'Mr Harris, how about telling us what happened last night?'

'Not now. There'll be a statement issued later.'

'Mr Wilson said it was as big as the one Rex Barrett shot. Have you any comment on why there's so many big crocs around?'

'Look, I said not now. You'll just have to wait.'

Steve and Mac pushed past the group, and walked to the parked Toyota. Within seconds, they were driving off.

'What happened down there, Steve?'

'I told him to stop bothering us,' replied Steve, managing a smile, but so tense that he thought his body would burst.

'Shit. What'd he say?'

'Nothing, and as long as the croc's around and we're needed to get it, I'd say he'll leave us alone and won't say a word. But, by Christ, I'd like to place a bet that my next promotion takes a while to come through.'

'Am I glad to see you two,' said the Inspector when Steve and Mac walked into his office. 'You both look terrible.'

'Don't remind us, we know it,' replied Steve, pulling up a chair. 'Okay, what's been happening in here?'

'It's almost a state of emergency. News of the attacks got on to the late night radio and television, and there've been regular broadcasts since transmission started this morning. The whole of Darwin's waiting for news about the croc. We told one of the radio stations that you'd be landing at the main wharf, and people flocked down there. I think they thought you'd be bringing the croc in with you. The Director of the Tourist Bureau has put a $5,000 reward on its head—he phoned about fifteen minutes ago and it's on the radio and television already.'

'How's the bloke who got grabbed at the jetty?'

'Collins, Peter Collins. His leg's a real mess. All the muscle was torn off the bone and just hanging there. They're not sure how much of it will be saved, though at least he won't lose his leg. Sorry you didn't get the message about that attack earlier, but the hospital didn't contact us until they'd found doctors and had the bleeding under control.'

'What have the official releases said? What are the people being advised to do?'

'I've got copies of what we've told them, but it's essentially what you said over the radio. There's a large saltwater crocodile in the harbour that's attacked three men and should be considered highly dangerous. On no account are people to go near the water's edge anywhere in the harbour, and all small craft are to stay out of the water unless they have written permission to do otherwise from us.'

'And none of your men saw anything last night?' queried Steve.

'Nothing. A couple of young blokes took a shot at what they thought was a croc down at Rapid Creek, but it turned out to be a dog. The last sighting of the croc was when it swam out from under the wharf.'

'Did you have any problems getting the charters for the search?'

'Not really,' replied the Inspector. 'The chaps with the helicopters were a bit reluctant to start at such short notice but Rex Barrett fixed it up. By the way, he was bloody furious when I rang him after you'd left. He abused the hell out of me and said he was going to chew your arses off when you got back. He reckoned he should have been told what was going on from the start.'

'Yeah, he's a bit hard to take,' agreed Steve. 'Still, that's not our problem at the moment. We've got to find that croc and make sure no one else gets attacked.'

'There's been a suggestion we organise an emergency committee,' said the Inspector.

'Committee!' repeated Steve angrily, with visions of a large group of people all having their say on how best to get the crocodile.

'Mainly to co-ordinate the developments in here,' added the Inspector. 'Someone's got to police the water and keep everyone informed of what's going on. Remember, it's only 7.30 am, and there're probably still thousands of people who are just hearing about the croc for the first time. There's panic around the place, I don't mind telling you.'

'It's standard practice, Steve,' added Mac. 'It won't interfere with any plan to get the croc.'

'Who'd be on it?' asked Steve, still hesitant.

'Not decided yet, but you, Mac and myself; Rex Barrett's indicated he's going to be on it. One or two other people should be sufficient. Maybe some of the old croc shooters. You'll head the group. I've already told Barrett that.'

'I guess it does make sense,' admitted Steve after a pause. 'We've had problems with crocs before because too many people were involved; I'd hate to see it happen again.'

'What about the shooters?' asked Mac. 'Do you think that's wise?'

'I think we'd be better off without them,' replied Steve. 'Some of those guys really know what they're about, but you run the risk of a lot of conflict. I think it'd be better to seek advice if and when we need it, but not to get them in on the decision side. Let's keep the party small.'

'Is there anyone in particular that you want on the Committee?' asked the Inspector. 'Any of your blokes from Wildlife?'

'Not really,' replied Mac, looking to Steve for confirmation.

'There's one man,' added Steve, after a pause. 'He knows more about crocs than anyone else in the Territory, present company included, and I don't only want him involved, I think we need to get him involved.'

'Well, who is it?' asked the Inspector, whose puzzled look matched Mac's.

'He's an Aboriginal from Maningrida. Oondabund's his name. He used to work for you blokes about twenty-five years ago when the early patrols were going into Arnhem Land. What he doesn't know about crocs isn't worth knowing. If someone can get a message out to the Superintendent at Maningrida, he'll organise Oondabund at that end. All we'll have to do is get a charter flight to pick him up. He could be here within a few hours.'

'Well, if you think we'll need him, we'll get him.' said the Inspector, picking up a pencil and paper. 'What's his name again?'

'Oondabund,' replied Mac, before turning to Steve. 'How's he going to take to killing the croc, Steve?'

'I'm not sure, but we've just got to try him. We've got to get that croc before it does any more damage, even if it is going to hurt Oondabund.'

'What do you mean?' asked the Inspector, who seemed bewildered by their comments. 'You mean this bloke won't want to kill it?'

'How about letting me worry about it?' suggested Steve. 'The crocodile's all part of his dreaming. It's a spiritual thing. But, on the other hand, he knows enough about crocs to increase our chances of getting it.'

Not to be deterred, the Inspector continued, 'You're serious aren't you? You want to bring an Abo in, knowing that he's not going to help you kill it?'

'Just leave it to me,' said Steve, firmly. 'It might sound a bit strange, but believe me, we're going to have problems without him.'

'Okay then,' agreed the Inspector, obviously not convinced. 'If you want him we'll get him, but I hope you know what you're doing.'

'I do,' Steve replied. 'Well, there's not much more we can do at the moment, so we'll go and get a few hours' sleep. It's 7.45 now. What say we meet again at 1.30?'

'Where'll you be in case it's sighted?' asked the Inspector.

'My place,' replied Mac, looking across at Steve. 'It'll save running around and we'll both be on the same phone number. Besides, Anne can get us some food; I'm starving.'

They drove to Mac's place, to be greeted by Anne. 'Mac, I've been so worried,' she said, stepping back after giving Mac a prolonged hug. 'It's been all over television and it's on the radio all the time. The phone's been ringing since six this morning with people wanting to know what's going on. I started to get frightened of the damn thing. It sounds awful, Mac. That policeman and the man off the trawler.'

'I know,' said Mac, giving her a hug. 'We looked everywhere for it, but just didn't find it. We'll be going out again tonight. We haven't got a lot of time, sweet, can you get us something to eat? Then we'll bed down for a while.'

'Did you get it, Dad?' asked Mac's small son, who was busily devouring a bowl of breakfast cereal at the table.

'Not yet,' he replied, gently ruffling the boy's blond hair.

'Darling, you both look shocking,' said Anne as she studied both Steve and Mac. 'Have you had a look in a mirror?'

'It's been a long night, love. We've got to be back down there by 1.30.'

'Can't someone else go out? Why do you two have to do everything?'

'Sweetie, how about something to eat?'

'It makes me mad, Mac. Nobody thanks you for what you do.'

Mac kissed his wife gently on the forehead and smiled at Steve. 'Not now, love, we're hungry.'

After a hearty breakfast, Steve and Mac had no trouble sleeping, and while they slept Anne listened to the radio as she washed up the dishes. The friction between Barrett and Steve on the jetty was mentioned, and she wondered what had really happened. The memory of Steve's reaction to the television interview was still fresh in her mind. At 8.20 am, her son toddled off to Kindergarten, excited about his Dad, and his Dad's best friend; Anne smiled at the innocence of his imagination.

At 12.40 pm, Anne gently shook Mac's shoulder. 'You'd better get up, love,' she said, 'it's nearly time to go.'

She had to shake Steve five times before his eyes suddenly sprang open, and he lay there staring into her face. 'Anne, it's you!' He sat up and rubbed his eyes. 'Funny, I thought it was Susan. I'd been dreaming about her.'

'It's going on for one o'clock, Steve,' said Anne gently. 'Mac's already up and there's a cup of tea and some sandwiches on the table. You'd better get cracking.'

At 1.20 pm, Steve and Mac arrived at the police station, where they had to push past a group of about twenty reporters to get to the doorway. Fortunately, they were almost through before one of the reporters recognised them, and the policeman at the door was quick to let them in before they were swamped with questions. The Inspector was on the telephone at the front counter, and his face left little doubt that the emergency was far from over.

'That was the airlines,' he said, when he recognised the two men standing before him. 'It seems there's two film crews arriving between two and three o'clock, and another lot's on its way up in a private charter. It's been bedlam in here.'

'I take it nothing's been sighted,' said Steve.

'Not a sign of it anywhere. The chopper's been all over the harbour a dozen times, and the planes have been back and forth along the coast and out to sea. No one's seen a damn thing.'

'How'd you go with Oondabund?'

With a broad smile, the Inspector pointed over Steve's shoulder to a lone figure sitting in one corner. 'He's hardly said a word since he got in. By the way, Barrett's out back too. He wanted to see you as soon as you got in.'

'Okay,' said Steve, as he strode across the room to where Oondabund was standing to meet him. 'You're here,' Steve said excitedly, as they firmly clasped hands.

'Me hear that story him crocodile,' said Oondabund. 'Mr Jackson him say that Numunwari proper big worry all you white people here Darwin.'

'We need your help, Oondabund. He's been causing a lot of trouble.'

'Him no trouble that one,' Oondabund replied, mockingly. 'You white men no understand him. We catch him, you see.'

'You're a confident old bugger, aren't you? Do you remember Mac? That feller over there.'

'Me know him. He come Maningrida long time, when you there.'

'Yeah, that's him. Come over and say hello. I've got to go down here and see someone. I'll be a few minutes.' They walked across to the counter.

'You remember Oondabund, Mac.'

'How could I forget him?' replied Mac, shaking hands.

'Look after him for a few minutes, while I go and see Barrett,' said Steve, striding away.

He knocked once on the door and walked in, to see Barrett seated at the table. He looked up when the door opened.

'I want to talk to you, Harris,' he snapped immediately.

'There are a few things I want to talk to you about, too.'

'Your job's on the line. You know that, don't you?'

'I couldn't give a damn about my job, Barrett. I'm worried about one thing: the croc.'

'Well you won't have to worry about it much longer.'

Steve had to control the anger building up inside him. 'I didn't come down here to argue, Barrett. I reckon you asked for what you got down there.'

'It happened to be assault, Harris, and they don't take too kindly to that in the Public Service.'

'If it makes you feel any better, I'm sorry. I was in no mood to be yelled at, and neither was Mac. We've got a lot of work in front of us and it's not going to go any easier with you and me at each other's throats. What say we sort out our personal differences later.'

'Well, I'm not going to forget it, Harris.'

'Neither am I,' Steve assured him. 'But it's a bit bloody irrelevant when you've got a croc that could be taking someone while we're arguing. Now, for Christ's sake, let's start worrying about what's important.'

Barrett glared at Steve, but said nothing.

'I think we should get the Committee together now, and work out a plan,' said Steve. 'If it hasn't been sighted by nightfall, we're going to have to go out again.'

'Well, everyone's been contacted,' snapped Barrett. 'They've been waiting for you and Wilson to arrive.'

'I'll get them together then,' said Steve, leaving the room.

'How'd you go?' asked Mac.

'He's still pretty stirred up, but don't worry about him. Who'd they end up with on the committee?'

'They've kept it small. You, me and the Inspector, Oondabund, Barrett and two other police officers; they're both sergeants.'

'Sounds good. What say we get together where Barrett is, and work out what in the hell we're going to do?'

A few minutes later, the committee was assembled, waiting expectantly.

'There's no sense going over everything that's happened,' said Steve to the six men seated at the table. 'You all know as much as I do, and the big problem seems to be what we're going to do if they don't sight it from the planes or choppers.'

'Well, it can't just disappear,' said Barrett. 'Where do you reckon it is?'

'I don't know. It was last seen heading towards the mouth, so it may have left the harbour altogether. On the other hand, it could be lying in the mangroves somewhere. When we finish here, I'll take Oondabund around to where the croc's been sighted and see what he thinks. He knows a lot about them, that's why he's here.'

'What if we don't find it, Steve?' asked Mac. 'We can't just keep the harbour closed indefinitely.'

'Yeah, I know. I'd say we keep everyone away until at least tomorrow, and if we still haven't found it, we'll have to work something out then; but let's not worry about that now.'

'There's one thing no one seems to have considered,' said Barrett. 'John Wiley fired two shots at the bastard before it grabbed him, and the officers down on the wharf fired a couple more. One of them might have got it—the bastard could be dead.'

There was silence in the room; it was a possibility that no one had seriously considered. 'Wiley *might* have hit it,' said Steve, 'but I doubt whether it would have been a fatal shot. When it attacked Collins it seemed okay, and that was over an hour later. The other two, Jones and Buckley, didn't think they hit it themselves, so we can't count on it being dead.'

'No one's saying we should count on it, Harris,' snarled Barrett. 'It's just something that hasn't been considered.'

'Right. Well, now we've considered it,' replied Steve angrily.

One of the sergeants asked, 'If they spot it from the plane, how are they going to get it?'

'The men in the helicopter have rifles,' replied Barrett. 'They'll shoot it.'

Steve and Mac both looked at Oondabund, whose smile had vanished. He was staring at Barrett. 'What you mean?'

'Shoot it?' Barrett raised his arms as though holding a rifle. 'Bang, bang . . . you know, rifle, gun.'

Oondabund looked at Steve, seeing only a stranger, a stranger who had deceived him. The room fell silent.

'What's the matter?' asked Barrett, intrigued by the change in atmosphere.

Oondabund was glaring at Steve, and when he spoke his voice clearly betrayed his feelings. 'You lie to me,' he snapped. 'You white men think you clever ones to trick this Oondabund. You want finish that crocodile, don't you?'

'What's going on?' demanded Barrett. 'What's he talking about?'

'Shut up, Barrett!' snapped Steve.

Oondabund was on his feet, glaring down at Steve. 'Me go home Maningrida.'

'Just hang on a minute,' said Steve, his mind fighting for a solution. He quickly glanced at each of the men in the room, before speaking quietly. 'I need some time to talk to Oondabund. How about leaving us for a few minutes?'

'Why?' retorted Barrett. 'Why should we go?'

'Just bloody well go, Barrett,' snapped Steve angrily, in response to which everyone began to stand. 'I'll come and get you in a few minutes.'

Barrett and Steve stood glaring at each other in contempt. Each man bore a hatred for the other, yet in different ways each needed the other. To keep crocodiles protected, Steve needed Barrett on side, and he knew it. On the other hand, Barrett needed Steve to solve the present crocodile problem and to ensure that the last attacks were in no way publicly linked with the crocodile he had supposedly shot from the helicopter.

Eventually Barrett turned, and left with the other men. Alone in the room with Oondabund, Steve suggested by a hand signal that Oondabund sit, but the man less than two metres away did not move, and his eyes were fixed on Steve.

'I know what you're thinking, Oondabund, and you've got good reason. But the crocodile is killing people, and I've got to stop it. I don't want to hurt it, but I've got no choice.'

Oondabund didn't answer, and after perhaps twenty seconds, Steve spoke again, sounding desperate. 'For Christ's sake, Oondabund, try to understand.'

'Me understand,' retorted the Aboriginal. 'That Numunwari, him take bad man, now you want finish him.'

'He didn't take bad man, he took good man. A policeman.'

'In Maningrida they been tell me this story but you know Numunwari, him not take good man.'

'Oondabund,' said Steve, after a pause. 'That short bloke, Barrett. He's my biggest boss and if he tells me I've got to do something, I've just got to do it. The crocodile's got to be stopped before it takes anyone else.'

The look on Oondabund's face had not changed, and Steve knew that argument was futile. Still, he tried again. 'We can't just leave it out there, Oondabund. Right now it might be hunting some little kid that's down on the beach. The whole of Darwin's scared stiff—everyone's terrified.'

'You try finish him, that Numunwari, and him get you. You listen my word very carefully because you die from that one.'

'What the bloody hell else can I do, Oondabund?' said Steve in exasperation.

'You been lie me. In Maningrida, that Mr Jackson him been tell me that story from Numunwari in Darwin and him been say, "You Oondabund, that Steve him need you for catch him that Numunwari." I been think myself, poor thing that crocodile. Him home in Maningrida and him lost and lookem for him camp but no can find there Darwin. So I been say okay, I go to Darwin, we catch that Numunwari and we bring him back Maningrida.'

'Catch him!' repeated Steve. 'Alive?'

'That what them tell me.'

'And take him back to Maningrida?' Steve did not hear Oondabund's affirmative answer. Slowly, as though afraid to think positively of what had been suggested, he began to explore the possibility. When he spoke next he did so quietly, hesitantly, looking deeply into the intense brown eyes.

'Could we . . . could we catch him alive?'

'Easy one, that Numunwari,' replied Oondabund, his look of anger gone. 'Him proper quiet one.'

'How could we get him?'

'Harpoon.'

'You're sure? He's bloody big.'

'Proper easy one that Numunwari.' Oondabund spread his fingers five centimetres apart. 'Little harpoon all you need that crocodile. Not matter him big one, him skin still soft one. Little harpoon catch him.'

Steve grinned at Oondabund. 'You've hit the answer, the perfect bloody answer. We'll catch the bastard.'

'Him good idea that one?' questioned Oondabund, a smile on his face.

'It's a terrific idea. Those other men probably won't like it, but don't you worry, I'll talk to them. I think you've solved the whole damn problem.'

Thoughts raced through Steve's mind as he walked from the room to find the others. Oondabund's suggestion was the first light in a rapidly darkening situation. No one had ever considered catching Numunwari alive, yet Oondabund was confident it could be done. No sophisticated equipment was needed, just the harpoons normally used to catch crocodiles. The problems of where to find him, how to restrain him, how to move him and how to get him back to Maningrida, all seemed trivial—Numunwari could be saved, and removed from Darwin Harbour.

The men were talking when Steve joined them.

'I've had a talk with Oondabund,' he said. 'He'll help us, but there're a few problems we've got to work out. Why don't we go back inside?'

They obediently filed in. Steve remained standing while the others sat at the wooden table.

'As I said out there, Oondabund's agreed to help us get the crocodile, but he's got a price. He wants the crocodile.'

'That seems fair enough, what's the problem?' asked Barrett.

'He wants it alive.'

'Alive?' repeated Barrett. 'What do you mean?'

'That's what he wants. He wants to catch the croc alive.'

'If we can't even shoot it, how in the hell are we going to catch it alive?' inquired Barrett sarcastically.

'I think you've hit it right on the head,' replied Steve. 'We can't even shoot it. Oondabund's confident he can find it and catch it, but his deal is, either we take it alive, or he goes back to Maningrida and we're on our own. We haven't got a choice.'

'Well, I think we've got a bloody big choice,' snapped Barrett. 'Send him back to Maningrida. If we keep looking, we've got to find the bastard eventually.'

'And if we don't?' asked Mac.

'If we don't, we don't.'

'Who's going to tell everyone it's safe to go back in the water, Barrett? You?' demanded Steve.

'What are you getting at, Harris?'

'What do you bloody well think I'm getting at? You're the bloke who said it was safe on Saturday night. You seem to have forgotten that.'

'Right, you pair,' said the Inspector. 'Why don't we get back to the problem on hand?'

'Well, what do *you* think?' asked Barrett, directing his attention to the Inspector. 'The bloody croc eats half a dozen people and these bastards want to treat it like royalty. They've gone mad.'

Barrett lowered himself back into his chair, furious. Steve said, 'I'm chairman of this committee, and if Oondabund's price is the crocodile, there's nothing we can do about it. I say we give it to him.'

'It's not all that simple,' replied the Inspector. 'There's a moral issue at stake. The crocodile's killed people, and that makes things different.'

'People are getting killed every day. What happens when a truck hits someone? Do they get rid of the truck?'

'No, but they get rid of the driver if it happens a second time,' said one of the sergeants. 'And another thing, can you imagine what would happen if the croc escaped after you caught it?'

'More to the point,' said Steve angrily, 'what if we don't find it? Next week, it might just cruise back into Darwin, and what are we going to say? That we sent the man who had the best chance of finding it away because he wanted to catch it alive?'

Mac said. 'It seems to me we're arguing about the future, the "if this" and "if that".' He looked from the Inspector to Steve and to Barrett. 'Our problem's not next week, it's now. We've got to get rid of the croc now; and if Oondabund's price is the croc, it doesn't matter a damn if it's alive or dead, as long as it's caught.'

'That's all okay,' said the Inspector, 'but what about the people here in Darwin? How do you think they're going to react if you've got the croc alive somewhere? They'll tear the place apart to get to it.'

'Well, don't bloody well tell them!' shouted Steve.

'You're mad, Harris,' said Barrett, standing. 'You've gone off your bloody head since this croc turned up. You've forgotten who in the hell we are—we're the Public Service, not the Secret Service.'

'I'm sick of your comments, Barrett,' snapped Steve, also standing with his fists clenched in anger. 'You come up with a better plan.' He grabbed at a chair and sat, not taking his eyes from his enemy.

After a short silence, Mac spoke. 'Do you think it could be caught anyway, Steve? I'm no expert, as you know, but it seems a pretty tall order.'

'Oondabund's confident we can find and catch it,' said Steve, shifting his attention from Barrett to Mac. 'He reckons harpoons are all that're needed, the same sort we use to catch normal crocs. And believe me he knows what he's talking about.'

'Just say we got it, Steve, what then?'

Steve looked around the group, then back at Mac. 'It'd have to be kept hidden, I suppose, at least for a while. I can't see how you could explain it to the people in Darwin.'

'That's all very well,' said one of the sergeants, obviously agitated. 'But just how do you hide a live thirty-foot croc?'

'What about the old breeding pen?' suggested Mac, after an uncomfortable silence. 'It's big enough and it's empty now.'

'And it's on it's own,' continued Steve, 'away from all the other pens. If you kept it hidden there for a month or two, maybe you could fake another capture. No one would guess in a million years it was the same croc. Especially if you assured everyone it had been killed, once you did catch it.' Steve looked from man to man, but only Oondabund was smiling.

'Well I'm taking no responsibility for any of this,' snapped Barrett. 'It's preposterous!'

'Has anyone asked you to?' said Steve. 'I'll take it. Let's just catch the bloody croc.'

'What Rex says goes for us too, Steve,' said the Inspector. 'There's no way we could have anything to do with this.'

'I'm not asking anyone to take responsibility. The only thing I want is everyone's word that they'll shut up if we catch it.'

'Why don't we work that last bit out when and if we do catch it?'

asked the Inspector, reluctant to commit himself. The room went silent.

Steve turned to Oondabund. 'We're going to try and catch it alive.'

'Me want piece of paper story.'

Steve stared at the black man, suppressing a smile. 'I'm head of the committee; I'll write you one.'

'What's he after now?' asked Barrett suspiciously.

'He doesn't trust us. He wants a written statement that the crocodile is his.'

'Well, I'm certainly not signing it,' snapped Barrett.

'You don't have to. I am,' said Steve, scribbling a short note on a piece of paper. 'Here you are. "As payment for services in catching the rogue crocodile I hereby agree that if caught, the crocodile belongs to Oondabund. All attempts will be made to catch it alive. Steve Harris, Chairman, Emergency Committee".' He passed it to the waiting black hand. Without answering, Oondabund folded it carefully and slipped it into his shirt pocket.

'That's about it,' said Steve standing. 'Mac and I'll take Oondabund to everywhere the crocodile's been sighted—should take us about an hour. What say we meet then and decide on tonight's schedule?' Everyone agreed, some grudgingly, and the meeting broke up.

Steve and Oondabund drove to the site of Numunwari's first Darwin attack. At the embankment, it was low tide and exposed mud tapered out from the base of the steep grade. From where Oondabund stood, he could see five sets of tracks in the soft mud, spread over an area of about three hundred metres.

'Him been hunting something, that Numunwari,' he said, cheerfully.

At the place where Wiley had been taken, there were deep claw marks and an area of churned-up mud where the crocodile had rolled and thrashed with its victim. Oondabund noted a small mound of mud to one side of the disturbed area and leaned down to it. He stood up with Wiley's mud-covered revolver in his hand. Steve snapped open the chamber to see that only two of the six bullets had been fired.

Further along the shoreline, Oondabund located a piece of khaki cloth, matching the regulation material of police shirts; it was beside a second area of churned-up mud a few metres from the bank.

'This where that crocodile eatem policeman,' he said. 'Him come in here from fast water so not lose him food when open mouth.'

Although they searched, there were no other signs of Wiley's body, and given the myriad of small roadways and tracks over the smooth mud, Steve presumed that the scavengers of the shoreline had long since removed any fragments of tissue.

At the wharf, they climbed down the ladder to the deck of the *Shindy*, where the iron pipes were still bent towards the water. Oondabund spent about two minutes looking in under the wharf, and Steve did not know whether he was checking to make sure whether Numunwari was still there, or was trying to reconstruct the way in which the crocodile had moved during the night. In fact, he was doing both. Back on the wharf, Steve pointed out the direction in which the crocodile had been seen leaving, and the general area in which they had searched for him. Oondabund merely smiled and nodded his head knowingly.

On the drive back to the police station, Oondabund said little as he pieced together the segments of the puzzle. It was only when they pulled up and were climbing from the Toyota that Steve noticed the Aboriginal grinning.

'What's so funny?' he asked.

'Me know where him be, that Numunwari,' replied Oondabund confidently.

4

In the station, Steve and Oondabund talked for nearly half an hour in one of the offices. Oondabund had trouble in relating the details of his story in English, and Steve wished that Nancy had been there to translate. After numerous questions, he felt confident that he knew what Oondabund meant, and his assessment of what had happened. They walked out to the others, and within minutes the group was again seated at the wooden table.

Steve started straight into it. 'As far as we know the crocodile's been at sea for three weeks, and the only fresh water he's had was at Goulburn Island. Oondabund thinks it left the deep channel and came into the harbour to find water, not to hunt. He reckons it was searching for water by the embankment, when the old chap, Blunt, came staggering along on the road. The movement caught the croc's attention and it attacked; Blunt was lucky. Wiley wasn't. After it took Wiley, it swam back around the point and saw the lights and movement on the wharf. The croc isn't frightened of people and it's naturally inquisitive. When it moved in under the wharf, it was probably trying to find somewhere to wait, out of the current, because after eating, it would normally wait until the sun came up, then crawl out on to a bank to warm up. When Collins started to walk around on the deck, the crocodile attacked by instinct. For a big croc, food is food; they take as much as they can whenever they can, because there are times when they may have to go months without any.

'If Oondabund's right and it did come in looking for water, it'll need it much more now, because it would have swallowed a lot of salt water when it attacked Wiley.

'He thinks it was confused by the lights when it was under the wharf and so it just swam out with the current which was flowing towards the mouth; but, once out of the glare, it could see where it was and turned back upstream. That's why we didn't see it last night —we were searching in the wrong area.

'Oondabund's sure it would have laid up somewhere today, either in mangroves or up some small creek, somewhere where the sun was shining, but where there was no wind. According to Oondabund, tonight it'll keep moving upstream trying to get fresh water. If it's up in the mangroves, it'll come down on the falling tide, then wait until the tide changes so that the current can carry it upstream. This is when we've got to be ready.'

'Couldn't the croc be amongst the mangroves near the mouth, like you suggested before?' asked Barrett, making it obvious that he was going to question Oondabund's appraisal.

'It could, but if it went that way last night I'm sure we'd have seen it. We went back and forth across that area and saw nothing, and what Oondabund says makes a lot of sense; it fits all the facts.'

'What's the plan for tonight then?' asked Mac.

'I haven't worked all the details out yet, but the basic plan is to get all the catching gear together plus a small boat, probably a fourteen-foot fibreglass dinghy, then take it all to the police launch and go upstream against the falling tide tonight. On the way up we can search with the spotlights and if we find it, well and good, but if we don't, we'll anchor in the part of the bay that constricts into the river. When the tide changes, we'll drift upriver in the dinghy, with the small spotlights and catching gear; we'll have a radio and if we do harpoon it we can call the launch for assistance. I think there's a damn good chance of getting it now.'

'What if you do get it?' asked Barrett. 'How are you going to move it?'

Steve looked at Mac. 'I'm not really sure, but if we could organise one of the forestry low loaders, we could leave the croc somewhere near a landing up the river and bring the truck in later. It'll be awkward to manoeuvre, but we'll have the croc anaesthetised and should be able to haul it up with the winch.'

'What about ropes and things like that?' asked Barrett.

'All at my place. I'll work out exactly what we need this afternoon.'

'Who's going, Steve?' asked Mac.

'Oondabund, myself, and I'd like you to come if you would.'

Mac nodded in reply, aware of a tingle of excitement.

'I might be a bit naïve,' the Inspector said, 'but it seems a bit bloody silly to have three men going out in a fourteen-foot boat to catch a twenty-five-foot croc. Sounds like taking on a tank with a pushbike.'

'It's not as bad as it sounds,' Steve assured him. 'With a bigger boat you lose manoeuvrability with oars; you'd need an engine which might scare the croc. And as far as the croc's concerned, it's not going to be interested in us once we've got a harpoon in—it'll just want to get away, and tire itself trying.'

'You hope,' was Barrett's comment.

Like Mac, Steve was aware of a sense of excitement building up within him, and he hoped it did not show. To shoot a crocodile, any crocodile, did not necessarily require skill, nor much knowledge of the animal, but to catch a crocodile alive was a different matter. It was an exciting undertaking which involved just enough risk to deter most people from even contemplating it. To catch Numunwari alive was truly challenging, and Steve would not have even considered it, had not Oondabund been confident it could be done. In his own way, Steve looked forward to the night, and having Oondabund there made him doubly confident of success. The fact that the problem could be solved without having to kill the crocodile had removed the conflict which had been nagging him continually.

'What time do we leave?' asked Mac.

'Let's get everything down to the launch by 9.30 and start up the river round 10. Low tide where we anchor should be about 12.30.'

'I'd like to come on the launch,' said Barrett.

Steve looked intently at Barrett, and hesitated before answering. 'Okay,' he said at last, 'but only on the launch.'

'I'm staying here,' said the Inspector. 'Someone's got to run this end, and I've got no desire to become a statistic just yet. I'll get on to a press release right away, because the media are eager to know what we're doing. I'll tell them you'll be going out tonight to look for the croc.'

The meeting finished. Steve, Mac and Oondabund began writing a list of what was needed, and Rex Barrett drove back to his office, where he anticipated a mountain of enquiries requiring his urgent attention. Although everyone except Steve and Oondabund had serious doubts about whether the crocodile could be caught, they all seemed a little more relieved than they had been a few hours before.

5

At the Newcomer Inn, there was silence throughout the bar when the news flash about the meeting was broadcast on television. No one listened more carefully to it than the two men seated in one corner, one of whom had a protruding mole on his cheek. John Besser and Bluey Noakes, the man whom everyone had regarded for years as Besser's closest friend, listened to every detail of the broadcast.

Since returning from Maningrida, Besser had once more teamed up with Noakes and they had started fish poaching again. They had already made three runs, with Besser calling the tune as usual, and Bluey Noakes doing more or less as he was told.

Unlike Besser, Bluey was a Territorian by birth who had started poaching when the rivers had first been closed to netting some fifteen years before. Although at that time there were no inspectors, and it was a lucrative business, Bluey always worked with someone else; someone who would make the decisions.

When Besser had first arrived in Darwin, he was very much a loner, as he still was to some extent. But Bluey Noakes had gradually made friends with him, and had actually introduced him to poaching. Within three weeks, Besser was running the two-man operation, which had continued for years, and which after a six-month delay was once again getting off the ground.

The news broadcast to which they listened was very explicit. It said that Wildlife Division would be sending Steve Harris, Mac Wilson and Oondabund out after the crocodile that night, and that there was an injunction against small craft operating anywhere in the Darwin Harbour region without appropriate permits. When the broadcast finished, Besser looked across at Bluey until he caught his attention.

'With no bastard in the water except Harris's mob, there'd be no chance of running into any Fisheries Inspectors. What do you reckon, Blue?'

'What you figuring on?' asked Bluey.

'The thought just crossed me mind that it's a long time since any bastard put a net across Buckleys Creek. Could you think of a better time to do it? Everyone scared shitless about the croc, and that bloke on TV promising us there'd only be one boat on the river.'

'What about the croc?'

'What about it? I'm not worried about the bastard, it's got the whole harbour to cruise around in. Anyway, it's not going to go near Buckleys. On the news they reckoned it was out near the mouth somewhere.'

'What about your mates at Maningrida?' asked Bluey, doubtfully. 'The croc's eaten a pile of people; even a cop. No, thank you, not a thirty-foot croc. Bloody Harris's still trying to get us anyway, and he's the one who'll be out looking for the croc.'

'I'm not saying we will go, Blue, mate, I'm just looking at the possibilities. What I've said is that there'll be no Fisheries bastards around, and Buckleys Creek hasn't been netted in months. On the surface it looks as though we could get at least a thousand bucks for a night's work. I'm not saying we'll go, though.'

Bluey didn't answer, and catching the barman's attention he ordered two more beers. They chatted about other things, but twenty minutes later Besser brought up the subject again. 'Bluey, I think we better go down and net that creek off.'

'What about the croc?' was Bluey's final expression of disapproval, knowing Besser had made his mind up.

'There're hundreds of small creeks off the bay; he's not likely to pick Buckleys just cause we're there. Anyway, I've got a bit of a policy on big crocs now. I'd sort of like to find it.'

'What if he hears the fish and comes into the net?'

'Christ, Blue, you're like an old woman. Come on, have another beer.'

By late afternoon, Steve, Mac and Oondabund had assembled most of the gear they would need. Oondabund had spent nearly an hour filing the harpoon points until they were needle-sharp, and had also hollowed out the end of each harpoon pole just enough for the harpoons to fit snugly. He showed them to Steve with pride, a hunter proud of the tools of his trade.

Over the telephone, Mac arranged to have a Forestry low loader fuelled and parked outside the Wildlife office, using as an excuse that they might need to move a ten-metre launch. The truck organised, he then set about binding with leather the rowlocks of the smaller boat they intended using to prevent them squeaking. Steve had already checked over the 9½-horsepower outboard engine they were taking; if they managed to spear the harpoons into the crocodile, they would need the engine to manoeuvre the boat while the crocodile tired, and the engine needed to be one hundred per cent reliable.

With the work finished, the three of them hoisted the boat up on to the Toyota, and tied it in position, then, as Mac read from a list, they packed all the other items carefully into the truck, and later again, would check each item into the dinghy. Steve had learned long before that the margin between success and failure was often very fine.

Unlike Steve and Mac, Anne felt nothing but apprehension about the rapidly approaching night. She had heard all the reports about the crocodile and it was unimportant to her what Steve, or even Mac said about it; it was a killer. When she had first met Mac, nine years before, he was lying in hospital with his leg opened up by a buffalo—another Wildlife job he had volunteered for. When they married, he had agreed not to become involved in any more danger-ous field work, and until then he had kept his word. But tonight he was going out in a small open boat after a known killer, an animal of which the whole of Darwin was terrified. Why did it have to be Mac? Precious Mac who had already given years of his life to the public? Why couldn't Steve get someone else?

The prospect of Oondabund joining them for a meal before they went out did not relieve her worries at all. She admired Aboriginals and appreciated the problems that bush people were having with white society, but this was different; Oondabund and Steve were conspiring to take Mac from her, and she resented it. Mac had mumbled something about the only reason he was going was that Oondabund 'knew' the crocodile, and specifically wanted Steve and Mac to help him get it. She was not to know that Mac had twisted the truth to justify the shattering of his seven-year-old promise.

During the meal with Steve, Mac and Oondabund, Anne was quiet and rarely smiled. Her mind was tense with worry, and to make matters worse, she became preoccupied with Oondabund and felt a continual urge to stare at him. They had never had an Aboriginal in their house before and it was the closest she had ever been to one of the people of whom she had often talked. Now, each furrow and line of his character-laden face held her undivided attention, and her inability to ignore it annoyed her.

Mac's young son had a similar problem, but without his mother's inhibitions. He just walked around the table and stood beside Oondabund, staring up into the dark face. When Oondabund looked down and smiled, he jumped back in fear, and looked as though he was about to cry; Anne opened her mouth to chastise the child, but Oondabund held up a finger, signalling her to say nothing. Taking a match from the box in his pocket, he turned to the boy and, smiling broadly, pushing the match through the hole in the septum between his two nostrils, so that it stuck out on either side of his nose. The boy's look of fright changed to a smile and he started to giggle; all at the table laughed, and even Anne smiled with the break of tension.

The meal finished, the three men moved to the more comfortable lounge chairs, to relax by the television as they waited. Mac's son sat with Oondabund and kept pestering him to put matches into the hole in his nose, and each time he did so, the small boy broke into fits of laughter. Eventually Mac put a stop to it; it was time for the boy to go to bed.

Mac and Steve both dozed off, leaving Oondabund sitting forward in his chair, watching every movement of the actors in a television movie.

When Anne came in, after finishing the dishes, and saw everyone asleep except Oondabund, she decided to sit in the kitchen and write to her mother in Sydney; that was something that always calmed her down. Her letter was almost finished when she noticed it was 8.45 pm, and, after making a large pot of tea, she went back to the lounge room and flicked on the light. Oondabund did not budge, his eyes following the antics of two cowboys fighting in a saloon. Mac woke immediately, but she had to shake Steve twice before he did.

'There's food on the table,' she said, upset by the realisation that within twenty minutes they would be gone. Mac saw the signs of tears, and followed her out to the kitchen. When he gently turned her around, she fell into his arms and grasped him tightly.

'What is it, sweet?' he asked, though knowing the answer.

'I'm frightened, Mac,' she whispered, holding him still tighter. 'I hate damn crocodiles and I always have. And this one—God, Mac, it's a real monster, a man-eater. I don't want anything to happen, Mac, not now. We're just too happy.'

'We'll be all right, darling,' said Mac, giving her a momentary squeeze and looking into the wet eyes he loved. 'Oondabund knows crocs backwards, and you know Steve does. I'm only going to be driving the boat. Nothing can happen.'

'I'm sorry, love,' said Anne, drying her tears. 'I don't know what's got into me these last few days. I never seem to know if you'll be coming home or not, and it throws my routine out.' She wanted to say something more, but couldn't find the right words, so she gave Mac a quick squeeze before walking past him and back into the lounge room.

'Now, you look after him, Steve,' she said, as she poured the tea. 'He's not as young as he used to be.'

At ten minutes past nine, Steve stood, and indicated it was time they left. Only Oondabund seemed reluctant, saying, 'Him proper good fighter that cowboy man. Biggest mob Indians him fight all on him own.'

They all laughed, but within minutes were in the Toyota and driving through Darwin.

At the jetty, Steve was surprised to see the roadside lined with vehicles, and at least five hundred people crowded around the smallish landing. Two police officers were keeping people and vehicles away from where the launch was tied, so they were able to drive up to it, but lights were set up and three television cameras recorded their arrival. Rex Barrett was already there, and had spoken with each interviewer in turn, and Steve was thankful that there were few questions left for him. Those that were asked related to whether or not he or Mac were frightened; Oondabund was largely ignored.

The unloading of the gear was filmed, and Barrett assisted in passing it down to where Mac was stacking it with the assistance of the launch skipper. Steve checked each item, ticking them off as they were passed down. When the last was stowed, they all climbed down to the deck, giving a cursory wave to each of the cameras.

On the deck, Steve followed Oondabund's glance upwards. The sky was clear, but, more importantly, there was no moon. He had learned, initially from Oondabund and later from experience, that it was usually hopeless to try and catch big crocodiles when there was a full moon, because they were skittish and could not be approached.

He had once thought that it was only because crocodiles had been hunted with spotlights, and that when the moon was full it was a continual reminder of past experiences with hunters, but since then he had found that even crocodiles in captivity behaved the same way; the reason remained a mystery.

'Him good night tonight,' said Oondabund as they leaned on the railing around the deck. 'We get that Numunwari, you see.' Oondabund turned and walked over to the doorway leading to the small mess area. Steve stood on his own, looking out over the water momentarily before becoming aware that someone had joined him. He looked up to see the skipper.

'I'm ready to leave when you are, Mr Harris,' he said.

'We're right,' replied Steve. 'Let's get going.'

The skipper leaned closer to Steve, and, looking to see that Oondabund was not present, passed over a small object. 'The Inspector sent this down,' he whispered. 'Thought you'd at least better have one with you.'

Steve glanced at the .357 magnum hand gun before slipping it beneath his shirt and tucking it into his belt. He had meant to bring his own, but had deliberately failed to mention it when they made out the list, and had subsequently forgotten it.

'Thanks,' he replied, pocketing a handful of shells. 'As you say, I hope we don't need it, but it's nice to have it along.'

At 10.10 pm, the launch slid out in the darkness and headed upstream against the ebbing tide. It would take two hours to reach their anchorage.

Elsewhere in Darwin, John Besser and Bluey Noakes were tying the last rope which secured their three-and-a-half-metre aluminium dinghy to the tray of Bluey's Land Rover. Beneath the boat lay the compact icebox and neatly rolled gill net. The twelve-centimetre mesh net was new, and had been air freighted to them from Sydney. It was a strong net, and they hoped it would last the whole season.

Within minutes of latching the last rope, they were driving onto the highway leading out of Darwin. Twenty kilometres further on they intended to turn south on a dirt track, and follow it until it branched into three; there they would take the right fork, which would finish at Buckleys Creek, about thirty miles from Darwin.

Besser estimated that the trip would take them an hour, if Bluey's vehicle did not break down.

When the launch was almost a mile from the jetty, Steve walked out on deck and rummaged through the stack of catching equipment until he found the stiff leather case that contained the tranquilliser gun and darts, and the small wooden box with the anaesthetic and spare gas cylinders for the gun. In the cabin, he opened the leather case and spread out the six darts, three green and three red. Using formulae from a research publication, he had estimated the approximate weight of a seven-metre crocodile as 1,587 kilos; the amount of drug needed depended on the body weight. From the wooden case, he took the anaesthetic and after measuring it out, poured a full dose into the body of each of the red darts, and a third of a dose into each of the green ones. It was easy to kill a crocodile by using too much anaesthetic, so Steve liked to fill the darts himself.

Theoretically, one red dart would be enough to anaesthetise Numunwari, and the two spare ones were in case Steve missed. After a red dart was in, he would wait fifteen minutes, then, if the crocodile showed no signs of becoming sluggish, he would fire in a green dart. The main risk with tranquillising a crocodile was that if the darts hit home, and the crocodile struggled and freed himself from the harpoon lines, he would succumb to the drug, sink to the bottom and drown; it was important to pull the harpoon lines and ropes firmly before firing in the drug.

The darts sealed, Steve slipped them back into the pockets of the leather case. When he replaced the bottle of anaesthetic, he took out a fresh gas cylinder, and, unscrewing the knurled knob on the end of the gun, slipped it into the chamber and tightened it in position. The gun was ready.

When Steve returned to the deck, he dragged out a red plastic fish crate containing a variety of ropes and twines, each selected for a specific purpose. He tipped them on to the deck and systematically checked each one before coiling it in such a way that it could be easily uncoiled in the dark.

The catching ropes were all-important. Once a crocodile was harpooned, it could be played much as a fish on a line, but eventually it had to be brought in close to the boat and the mouth tied. The head of a crocodile was like a triangle, so no matter where a rope was tied, it would usually slip off once the crocodile began to struggle.

There was only one place where a rope could be tied to hold a big crocodile—around the top jaw, just behind the bulbous front of the snout. The main catching ropes were specially made for this purpose. On one end was a length of plastic coated steel cable, formed into a noose with a one-way locking snare clip. When a harpooned crocodile was sufficiently worn out, it was pulled in close to the boat and tapped gently on the snout with the end of the harpoon pole. This usually made the jaws open just enough to slip the cable noose in, and it was possible to manoeuvre it among the teeth until it was level with the constriction behind the snout, then the noose could be jerked closed, and, with the clip locked in position, it would not loosen. Only then could the anaesthetic be used, because there was little chance of the crocodile escaping.

Steve checked each of the cables to make sure there were no rough edges on the plastic coating, which could foul the small metal clips. He checked each clip to make sure it locked correctly, and finally checked the join between the cable and rope; all were in good condition.

Steve liked to get at least two cables around the snout, so five were checked and packed into the fish crate. Once two were in position, normal rope nooses could be used to surround the jaws and lock them together, but these nooses alone could never hold the weight of a crocodile; they were only used temporarily, until the thin braided cord could be wrapped around both jaws and tied tightly. Only then, with the jaws immobilised, could the crocodile be handled with safety, and to facilitate this, it was normal to then slip on a variety of rope nooses round the neck, trunk and tail. Steve checked the spliced eyes in some twelve securing ropes, and cut a long length of braided twine into ten smaller lengths, each a little less than two metres long, which he loosely tied to the side of the fish crate where they could be found in the dark.

Satisfied with the preparations, Steve and Oondabund climbed to the flying bridge where Mac, with Barrett beside him, was moving the light back and forth across the waters of Darwin Harbour. Apart from an occasional flying fish, they had seen nothing worthy of note.

Besser and Bluey Noakes arrived at Buckleys Creek at 11 pm. They unloaded the boat and, after throwing the net into it, pushed it down the muddy bank to the water's edge, where the tide was still running out.

Besser unravelled a coil of rope, tied one end to the buttress of a mangrove tree and dropped the remainder in the boat, then pushed the boat into the water and held it against the tide while Bluey climbed in. Besser waited until Bluey was seated with both oars in his hands, then gave the boat a strong push into the current. Three strokes with the oars, and the boat pushed into the mud on the opposite bank nearly twenty metres away, while the rope trailed in the water from one bank to the other. Bluey secured the boat and pulled the rope until it was taut, then tied his end to a mangrove. Holding on to the rope, Bluey pulled himself and the boat back across the creek to Besser, who was pinpointed in the darkness by the glow of his cigarette. Throughout the operation, they had barely spoken a word; when it came to poaching, they were true professionals.

Besser tied one end of the net's float line to the tree to which he had tied the first rope, then he and Bluey got in the dinghy, and as Bluey pulled the boat across the creek, Besser let the net out. When they reached the opposite side, and Besser tied the other end of the net to a tree, the net effectively blocking the whole creek.

Besser laughed in the darkness. 'Well, Bluey, let 'em come. There's not many of anything that's going to get through that little baby.'

The two poachers pulled themselves back across the creek, and on reaching the other side, Besser switched on a torch and checked the tide. 'About an hour and a half to run, Blue, then she'll start coming in,' he said. 'I'd say we check it around twelve, then again round one. That'll keep us busy.'

Both men knew that they would get some fish while the tide was falling, with a rush at slack tide. There had been times in the past when they had had to haul the net out at slack tide because it was so full of fish, and once they had had to use the truck to pull it up the bank. It wasn't the right time of the year, so neither Bluey nor Besser expected a mighty catch, but each man expected to make at least $500, which meant over two hundred and twenty kilos of fillets each.

They tied up the boat and climbed the bank to the Land Rover, where Bluey found two cans of warm beer. Sipping them quietly in the darkness, they waited for the fish to come.

In the silence on the bridge, Steve and the others were startled by the skipper's voice on the intercom.

'We're just about there, Mr Harris; be anchoring in a few minutes.'

Steve confirmed the message, and after Mac had had one further scan with the light, they switched it off and replaced its cover. As they climbed down to the deck, the engines slowed to an idle and the anchor chain rattled over the side.

'Well, Steve,' said Mac, 'guess this is it.'

'Sure looks like it. Give us a hand to pull the boat, eh?'

Together they pulled on the rope towline, in response to which the fibreglass boat slid in beside the launch. Mac climbed down into it, while Steve secured its lines, then picked up the list of equipment.

'I'll mark everything off as Oondabund passes it down,' said Steve.

'Christ, Steve,' protested Mac, 'have we got to go through all that again?'

Steve smiled. 'We sure do. Anyway, the tide hasn't changed yet, so we've got to do something.'

The fuel, battery and radio were placed in the stern, where Mac, who would be rowing or driving as the situation demanded, could reach them. The fish crate, which contained the ropes, cord, two torches, two knives and a spare spotlight, was placed in the middle of the boat where everyone could reach it. The revolver lay beneath the ropes where Oondabund could not see it. The leather case was opened, and, with the tranquilliser gun exposed, a red dart already in the breech, it was slipped under the front seat.

Oondabund climbed into the boat to arrange the harpoons and harpoon lines personally. He put one harpoon pole down the length of each side of the boat, and made two coils with the lines, one on each side of the bow. He then checked the four harpoon heads before selecting two, and attaching them to the ends of each line; the connection checked, he jammed one in the end of each pole, and pocketed the two spares.

The harpoon heads were made from three small shark hooks, straightened and bound with wire around a short wooden rod, so that the barbs pointed inward; on the side was a wire loop to which the line was attached. When punched into a crocodile, the needle-sharp points pierced the skin, and the blunt barbs locked beneath it. Although they rarely came out, with Numunwari there could be no chances; they intended to get two harpoons in before risking hauling on a line.

'Will I check the engine again, Steve?'

'Yeah. Do the lights, torches and radio, too.' Steve turned to Barrett and the skipper. 'We're just about ready to go.'

'Anything you want us to do?' asked the skipper.

'Nothing, just wait. We're going to drift off with the tide and keep looking around with the light every few minutes.'

'What about the radio?' asked Barrett. 'Want us to check with you every hour?'

'For Christ's sake, no. It'd be just our luck to be coming in on him when the radio went. Don't call us at all. If we get him on the harpoons and get the drug in, we'll give you a call, because we'll probably need the launch to handle him.'

'Well, don't take any unnecessary risks,' added Barrett. 'It's a crocodile, remember.' Barrett looked genuinely concerned, which surprised Steve. As they stood looking at each other, the launch swung at its anchor. The tide was changing.

Steve climbed into the boat and sat in the bow beside Oondabund, who gave him the spotlight. Steve flicked it on and off, testing, then looked around the boat. Everything was where he wanted it. Oondabund could reach the harpoons at a moment's notice and Mac could use either the oars or the engine. The outboard was propped up out of the water, waiting unused until they got the harpoons in.

'Untie you?' asked the skipper.

Steve nodded and as the ropes were released the boat drifted out from the launch and into the darkness. The hunt for Numunwari had started again.

On the first inspection of the net, Besser and Noakes took fifteen minutes to remove twenty-six barramundi, three small sharks and one catfish. The barramundi were between three and six kilos each, and with one to three kilos of meat per fish, and with barramundi selling for at least a dollar a pound and rising all the time, they had made over a hundred dollars on the first haul. The sharks were discarded, but not the catfish. Carefully filleted, the meat resembled barramundi, and if packed in the middle of barramundi fillets, no one ever picked it. To Bluey and Besser, catfish were as valuable as barramundi.

They filleted the fish by a small fire beside the Land Rover. Both men were experts, and with their razor-sharp knives it took them less than a minute per fish to separate edible flesh from non-usable carcass. They stacked the fillets on a tarpaulin and threw the carcasses on the ground.

At 12.20, they checked the net again, and took out fifteen barramundi and three catfish. One of the barramundi weighed nearly twelve kilos—worth nearly fifteen dollars on its own. As they filleted the catch, there was more activity in the net as fish hit and struggled to force their way against the cords that bit into their gills.

Fish in the net were like an iceberg—a small amount on top and a lot below. If one could hear or see five fish on the surface, there were fifty beneath the surface. Besser shone the torch across the net, and counted six barramundi meshed on the surface, lying still as though dead. Yet, when one struggled, they all did. The red reflection from their eyes looked like that of a crocodile.

By 1.30 am, the small boat containing Steve, Mac and Oondabund had drifted three kilometres from the launch, and with an occasional sweep of the oars, Mac had managed to keep it in midstream. No one had spoken since their departure from the launch, and every two or three minutes Steve switched on the light and searched a full three hundred and sixty degrees before switching it off.

They had seen one crocodile, a small one, perhaps a metre long. It was lying in shallow water on the edge of a mud bank and appeared undisturbed by the boat; when small prawns flicked to the surface, the crocodile swung sideways at them, snapping into the water.

Each time the light went out, it took nearly a minute for the men to adjust to the darkness. It was quiet on the river, the only sounds being the cracks of pistol prawns stranded in mud by the falling tide, and the occasional splash of a fish. Steve began to wonder whether they would see the crocodile, but Oondabund had no such doubts.

Besser and Bluey caught sixty-two barramundi on the first haul after low tide, three of them weighing at least twelve kilos. Carrying the fish to the vehicle involved three separate trips, slipping and sliding across the soft muddy bank. The knives dug into the quivering flesh, the fish not yet dead as the filleting began, but this was no time for idleness; fish would be hitting the net continually for the next two hours.

By 2.30 am, the boat was eight kilometres up the river, and although they had sighted another juvenile crocodile, there was no sign of Numunwari. Oondabund tasted the water and spoke for the first time.

'Little bit fresh now, that water. Numunwari him up here somewhere, maybe.'

They passed two small side creeks and Steve shone the light as far up each as he could, but saw nothing. The weariness of the last few days, the quietness of the river and the calmness of the drifting boat were all sleep-inducing, and he found it an effort to keep his eyes from closing.

Normally they would use the outboard engine and cruise up the river until they saw a crocodile, and only then, with the harpoon at the ready, would they switch the engine off. Catching crocodiles that way was quick and stimulating, and one never felt tired. But this night was different. The engine was not being used in case it scared Numunwari, yet the quietness was slowly sending the hunters to sleep.

'What that?' said Oondabund, grabbing the light from Steve and startling him into wakefulness.

The light beam shone to a floating log, and as they drifted nearer, Oondabund pointed to a large barramundi nestled against it, just below the surface, slowly moving its tail from side to side. If he had had a fish spear, it would have been an easy mark. He switched off the light and passed it back to Steve, who was now wide awake.

The sound of an animal crashing through the mangroves startled all three of them. Steve flashed on the light in time to see a large splash on the edge of the water with a wave nearly a metre high moving out from it. On the mud bank was a slide mark almost two metres across.

'That him,' said Oondabund excitedly. 'That Numunwari. Him been up there them bushes.'

Excitement surged through Steve's body, and he moved the light around in the hope of catching the great red reflections he had been waiting for. The wave from Numunwari made their boat rock when it reached them, and suddenly the crocodile was there. Some sixty metres in front the two eyes watched, the red glow unnatural in the stillness. Oondabund's hand slid up the harpoon pole to check that the head was still wedged in the end. Steve switched the light off, his heart pounding.

Oondabund wrapped the first five metres of line into three loose coils, which he let hang from his left hand. Grasping the pole in his right hand, he noiselessly stood, and without needing to look down, touched Steve's shoulder. The spotlight, still pointing in the direction of Numunwari, flashed on, and the eyeshine was there, a hundred metres upstream. Numunwari was drifting sideways in the river, the quiet, still river.

The light died with a seemingly loud click, when Oondabund again touched Steve's shoulder.

Taking care not to touch or bump the side of the boat, the Aboriginal swung the harpoon pole around, so that the end with the harpoon in it pointed towards Mac, sitting behind him. Oondabund gently lowered the opposite end into the water and effortlessly shook the long pole, so that the end danced in and out of the water for two seconds. He stopped for five seconds, then repeated the splashing. It was an action Steve had seen before; the splashing resembled the sound of an injured or trapped fish, a sound to which crocodiles and many other predators are immediately attracted. At night, a crocodile's response was normally to turn and face the disturbance, then slowly swim along the surface towards it, even though the spotlight was on. During the day more care had to be taken, because a crocodile would dive after sighting the disturbance and reappear within striking distance.

Oondabund gave five bursts of splashing, then waited motionless in the drifting boat for a full twenty seconds, which seemed like hours, before touching Steve on the shoulder.

The light flashed on, revealing the reflections from both eyes; Numunwari had turned towards them. Still a hundred metres away, he was looking at them when Steve switched the light off.

Again Oondabund splashed the harpoon pole in the water, and when Steve switched the light on, Numunwari was closer, perhaps eighty metres away, swimming slowly on the surface against the tide and towards the boat which was itself being carried towards Numunwari by the tide.

When Oondabund finished splashing the next time, he stood erect, swung the pole around so that the harpoon faced the front and extended the pole to its full length. He touched Steve with his foot and the light flashed across the water, but there was no reflection —Numunwari had dived.

Oondabund arched his back and held the harpoon with his right hand on the end and his left in the middle, supporting the weight. The coils of the first length of line hung from his left hand, as he scanned the water in front of the drifting boat.

'Him maybe come up close now,' he whispered calmly, without lifting his gaze from the water.

'He's down, Mac,' called Steve. 'Switch the torch on, and keep a check behind.'

Mac switched it on and began moving the beam back and forth behind the boat, his body quivering with the expectation of the next few minutes.

They searched in silence for almost a minute before Numunwari surfaced, about forty metres in front of them. Steve and Oondabund saw it as soon as it appeared, whereas Mac only realised it had surfaced when he saw Steve's light stop moving, and fix on one spot.

The huge crocodile lay motionless, facing them, unafraid, curious.

After a further minute Oondabund leaned down without appearing to relax his stance. 'Little torch, little torch,' he whispered in Steve's ear. Steve reached behind without moving the spotlight, and felt in the crate until he found the torch. Pointing it in the direction of Numunwari, he switched it on and the spotlight off; the bright red reflection dropped to a faint red glow.

Very slowly, Oondabund lowered the harpoon pole and slid it further back in his hands. Without taking his eyes from Numunwari's, he swung it around and let the end touch the water, making three short splashes. Numunwari began to move, and Steve and Oondabund watched as the powerful tail swept from side to side. Within seconds, the distance between the small boat and the crocodile began to close. Mac reached into the basket for the revolver, feeling secure with it in his grip, though he dared not pull back the hammer for fear the click would be too loud in the tense silence.

Twenty metres away, Numunwari seemed to speed up, then he stopped swimming, looked at the boat, and dived.

The spotlight flashed on as Oondabund yelled, 'Big light!' while swinging the pole around and positioning himself ready to drive the harpoon in. Steve felt the tension in the muscles of the man beside him, like an overwound spring waiting for release. If Numunwari surfaced, Oondabund's whole body would explode in a single co-ordinated effort, to drive the harpoon forward with enough force to break through the skin.

A fraction of a second before the light, Oondabund swung to the right. The huge head was looking at them, air leaving the nostrils with a hiss.

No one moved. Only the head was above water level. The neck and tail, the only sites that will take a harpoon because their heavy skin is not strengthened with bony plates, were beneath the surface. Oondabund waited for Numunwari to move, to expose either position.

Steve slid the centre of the beam from the giant eyes to a spot almost a metre to the right of Numunwari's head. When he wiggled his hand, the light flickered on the water. Mac placed his thumb on the hammer of the revolver.

Within two-tenths of a second, the massive head swung towards the flickering light, the jaws opened and the tail ploughed through the water, turning the great animal on its side. The spring beside Steve released, driving the pole forward into the writhing mass. It hit ten centimetres behind the head on the upper surface of the neck, the points punching through the skin, making holes barely six millimetres in diameter, and burying in the muscle below. Jammed between the barbs was a piece of heavy hide and from it, running back to the boat, was the thin green line.

As soon as the harpoon hit, Numunwari almost completely submerged, spraying water over the boat from the frantic and powerful crashing of its tail through the water. Within a second it was gone.

'Start 'em engine!' yelled Oondabund, throwing the pole back into the boat. Steve shone the light on the coil of line—there was still plenty to call on. Mac released the hammer of the hand gun, having pulled it back without realising.

Oondabund let the line run through his fingers. It was not moving fast, but with a steady strength that he dared not restrain.

Seventy metres of line were out when Mac got the engine started and the boat began to move, Oondabund taking in the slack line as they approached the animal swimming unseen below the surface.

'Slow one!' he yelled as the boat sped forward; 'Stop him!' It started to overrun his line.

Mac slammed the engine into neutral, while Oondabund frantically pulled in slack line. When he felt the heavy moving weight he yelled, 'Move him up,' while giving the line a gentle tug; the harpoon was well in. Numunwari swam upstream beneath the surface, and they followed in the boat. It was essential to get the second harpoon in before they pulled the lines, and brought the crocodile to the surface; then it would not matter if one harpoon came out because the other would hold until the first could be replaced.

Pursued, Numunwari swam faster. 'Speed 'im up!' shouted Oondabund as the line ran from his hands, and the boat responded. 'Slow one now, slow one,' he called quietly as he gathered in the slack— the line tightened, the harpoon was still in.

'Stop 'im! Stop 'im!' yelled Oondabund once again, as the boat overran the line and he rapidly gathered in the slack. When the line tightened, it was no longer moving; the crocodile had stopped and was on the mud six metres below, and for the first time since the harpoon had been in, the line ran vertically into the water.

'Him camp now,' said Oondabund, passing the line to Steve, who let it gently run across his hand while the boat drifted back. Oondabund reached for the second harpoon, and after checking that its line was free of tangles, stood on the seat.

'Little pull,' he said to Steve, as Mac turned the boat to where the line disappeared into the brown waters, and slowly edged it forward.

Pulling in the line with one hand, Steve gave it a light pull—all was well. 'Hold it there, Mac,' he called, when they were above the line.

Suddenly the line went slack, then tight, then slack again. 'He's rolling!' yelled Steve.

'Slack one! Slack one!' ordered Oondabund immediately, as the line ran from Steve's hand.

In a desperate struggle to free itself, Numunwari rolled over and over beneath the surface, wrapping the line around its head, neck and body. It stopped, but within seconds was rolling in the opposite direction.

Pulling in the slack line, Steve waited nervously for the struggling to cease, and was relieved to feel the line tighten and begin moving forward again; the single harpoon was still in, and Numunwari was once again swimming upstream beneath the surface. 'Forward, Mac!' he shouted, as the line disappeared over the side of the boat.

The line went slack again. 'That's it, hold it!' he called, gathering in the loose cord. Still the cord came, and Steve knew something was happening. Either the harpoon had come out, which was unlikely given the steady pull on it moments before, or the great crocodile was surfacing.

'He's coming up!' yelled Steve.

Standing tensed with the harpoon, Oondabund waited as the slack line was retrieved, his eyes scanning the water. The line pulled taut, but did not move.

'He's on the bottom again,' said Steve, relieved.

'Pull him up slow one,' ordered Oondabund quietly, as Mac slipped the engine into neutral.

'Give us a hand up front, Mac,' called Steve. 'He's on the bottom.'

Leaving the idling engine, Mac pocketed the hand gun and took the two steps necessary to bring him to the bow, where Steve passed him the light. With the three men standing together, the boat dipped forward, dangerously out of balance and saved only by the engine, fuel and radio in the stern.

In the silence, Steve pulled gently but firmly on the line, while Mac directed the beam to where it disappeared beneath the surface. The line went slack.

'He's coming up!' called Steve, pulling in the slack with both hands.

As the great head broke the surface less than three metres from the boat, the harpoon pole flashed through the air. The dull thud as it buried itself in the skin very close to the first harpoon was unmistakable proof that it was firmly in.

Numunwari felt a panic response to dive, and its body erupted in activity, cascading water over the three men, as without its much-needed breath the huge crocodile swirled into the depths, leaving both lines running from the boat.

'We've got him now, we've got him!' shouted Steve in excitement.

Oondabund replaced the pole and, smiling broadly, passed the second line to Mac and took the light. He shone it out in front, but saw nothing.

'Put a bit of weight on the line, Mac, only let him take it slowly. If the harpoon comes out, yell!'

With each thrust of the mighty tail carrying through the lines as a distinct tug, the boat began to move faster through the water; Numunwari was towing it. Suddenly the lines went slack, then tightened, then went slack again.

'He's rolling again,' Steve called to the much-relieved Mac who was about to signal that his harpoon was out.

'Him come up now soon. Him proper buggered, that Numunwari,' said Oondabund.

Mac's line went slack. He pulled in a yard, then a few yards as Steve gently pulled on his, to feel it go taut.

Underwater the lines had wrapped around Numunwari when it rolled, and Mac's line was holding the great head on one side; when the crocodile straightened, using the powerful muscles of its back and neck, the harpoon was ripped from the skin.

'Mine's out!' screamed Mac; Steve let his line run.

Oondabund gave the light to Steve and pulled in Mac's line until the harpoon was in his hand.

'We'll need the motor,' called Steve, as Oondabund picked up the pole and slid the harpoon into position, and Mac clambered back to the stern. As the boat moved, Oondabund again stood with his harpoon ready, the first few yards of line hanging limply from his hand. Steve pulled in the slack as they gained on the steadily-swimming Numunwari, now urgently in need of air.

'Slow it,' yelled Steve as the boat began to overtake the line. 'He's on the bottom; he's stopped!'

Steve pulled strongly on the line as the boat drifted forward, and the dead weight slowly moved, the immense animal rising from the mud on which it lay; Oondabund tensed as the line slowly came in.

'He's moving,' called Steve, feeling the tugs as the giant tail swung. 'Get the boat going!'

Numunwari surfaced six metres in front. The pole flew from Oondabund's hands and the harpoon buried itself in the neck as the crocodile exploded in a frenzy and disappeared beneath the surface.

'Him in good one strong now,' said Oondabund, smiling, as once again both lines ran over the bow. Mac joined Steve to take one line while Oondabund searched with the light. It shot out in front; Numunwari was on the surface swimming, but stopped when the beam reached him. The long fight had taken its toll. Regardless of a desire to dive and swim, the crocodile could no longer ignore a basic need for air, and it lay on the surface gazing at the light as air rushed into its lungs in deep breaths, hearing but not responding.

Steve said, 'Hold the lines, I'll get the gun.' A rapid check that the red dart was still in position, and Steve squatted in the bow and rested the tranquilliser gun. 'Pull him in slowly,' he whispered, when settled.

It was important that the dart should hit and penetrate muscles that were continually circulated with blood. Otherwise, the injected anaesthetic would remain in a local pouch, and not be distributed throughout the animal, not reaching the primitive brain. The tail butt represented such a region, because the animal used the tail continually, and thus kept it circulated with blood, but it was a relatively small target, and the crocodile had to be closer to ensure hitting it.

Very carefully, Oondabund and Mac dragged the lines in, gradually diminishing the distance between the boat and Numunwari, as both drifted upstream. Oondabund could clearly see both harpoon heads in the neck, and both lines were wrapped once around the top of the head. The crocodile jerked its head against the lines and momentarily headed back upstream as Steve's grip relaxed, but as they pulled, the great head again swung to face them.

'Keep him coming,' whispered Steve quietly.

Without warning, Numunwari's head rose above water level and snapped viciously at the lines, grasping them between its jaws and pulling them violently as its head shook from side to side. Then it dived. The force of the dive was enormous and Mac and Oondabund were unable to stop the lines running. 'We're going to need the engine, Steve!' shouted Mac. 'He's really off this time!' Steve clipped on the safety catch, and, placing the gun on the seat, took the line from Mac, who immediately headed to the stern.

For fifteen minutes, Numunwari swam beneath the surface, before finally coming to rest on the muddy bottom once again. Mac moved back up to the bow, and with Oondabund began to lift the crocodile as Steve prepared the gun.

The lines went slack.

'Him come up now!' yelled Oondabund, hauling in the slack.

Mac saw the head a fraction of a second before it broke the surface less than thirty centimetres from his side—instinctively he jumped. The boat rolled and Steve's attempt to point the gun was futile as both he and Oondabund were thrown sideways in the rocking boat. Numunwari's jaws flew open and slammed shut on the gunwale, the great teeth tearing through the thin fibreglass. The head shook from side to side as the tail swept through the water and the crocodile started to roll. Mac screamed as he went over the side, while Steve and Oondabund were thrown helplessly to the moving deck, which flooded with water as one side submerged. Dropping the tranquilliser gun, Steve fought for a grip, the lighting extinguished as the spotlight crashed against the seat amidst a flash of sparks. Suddenly it stopped.

'Mac!' Steve shouted.

'I'm here!' came from the stern, where Mac clawed his way back into the boat over the idling engine. Oondabund was on his feet, grabbing for the lines, both of which were rushing from beneath him.

'Where's the bloody light?' yelled Steve, frantically searching in the darkness.

'Him finished,' came the answer as Oondabund fought to separate the tangled lines.

Steve groped around till he found a torch, and, when he switched it on, he saw that a thirty-centimetre square section of the boat's side was missing. Mac was shaking uncontrollably, sitting huddled on the deck which was covered in water. Beside him the radio lay three-quarters submerged. He felt the line tighten.

'It's round my leg,' Steve called, falling to the deck.

Oondabund threw himself between Steve's leg and the bow, while Mac grabbed for Steve's shoulders. The line tightened further and began to drag him forward, while at the same time Oondabund pulled on the lines, his feet wedged beneath the bow for purchase. The boat started to move. It stopped. The pressure on Steve's leg relaxed and the lines went limp.

'Him fall out,' said Oondabund dejectedly.

Aghast at the realisation that the harpoons had come free, Steve lowered his head into his hands. He didn't even notice Oondabund's capable hands loosening the line from his leg, and hauling it back into the boat. The two harpoon heads clattered as they ran over the bow. Mac pressed the rubber-covered button to stop the engine, causing the boat to fall silent as it drifted.

'You okay, Steve?' he asked.

'I guess so,' said Steve quietly, after a pause. 'What about yourself?'

'I'm all right. Bit wet, but that's nothing.'

Mac picked up the torch. Although water flowed from within it, it was still working. They looked around the boat to see what damage their quarry had caused in his short-lived anger. The catching basket was overturned and the neatly coiled ropes swilled back and forth in the water which covered the deck. When Steve picked up the spotlight, he could see that the glass and globe were smashed beyond repair. He found the spare one, but even as he lifted it he knew the worst; its glass and globe were also smashed. He lifted the radio out of the water and held it while it drained; when he switched it on there was nothing but an unintelligible buzz, unchanged by pressure on the handpiece switch.

'What about the gun, Steve? How's that?' asked Mac as he moved the beam around searching for it.

The leather case and darts were still beneath the seat, but the tranquilliser gun was not to be found; it had gone over the side when Steve dropped it.

Mac felt for the revolver which had been tucked in his belt when he went over the side, but it too was gone; gone also was one of the oars. There was a gaping hole in the side of the boat, fortunately above the waterline.

'Steve,' asked Mac quietly, 'are we still in the race, mate?'

There was no immediate answer. Steve thought of what they had left and tried realistically to assess their chances of continuing. The torches, ropes and harpoons were the essential items needed, and they were still there. To restrain such a crocodile without drugs was a different matter; that could be risky, especially in view of the crocodile's last demonstration.

'If we give it away now, we might never get near him again, Mac,' he said.

'But what about the gun and radio? Have we got enough gear left to do it?'

'We have, but only just. The radio's not so important, it's more the tranquilliser gun. I think once we got the ropes on, we'd be able to handle it somehow; it'd be a bit risky. I don't know, Mac, I guess I'm bloody reluctant to give up now.'

'Okay, then, we'll keep after it. But let's get this bloody shambles cleaned up.'

Using the hard plastic covers from the spotlights, Steve and Mac began baling out the water. Oondabund untangled each of the harpoon lines and coiled them back in the bow. Then, with one of the torches, he scanned the water, but saw no answering reflection. When he switched it off, the outline of the mangroves on the bank appeared as a black band against an otherwise clear starlit night. As they drifted, he noticed one area where the sky penetrated the mangroves to water level; it was the mouth of a small tidal creek.

'Little creek there,' he said pointing to it.

'Which one's that, Steve?' asked Mac after discerning the irregularity in the shoreline.

'Not sure; there's two of them round here somewhere. One's Marna Creek and the other's . . . I forget its name. It's the one where the road finishes.'

'I know it,' replied Mac, 'Buckleys Creek.'

6

Besser and Bluey had caught over two hundred barramundi, and more were hitting the net. On the last haul they had got fifteen, all weighing around four kilos, but as they filleted them, there was a sudden loud burst of splashing from the net, lasting barely a second before there was silence.

'What the fuck was that?' asked Bluey, straightening up.

Besser looked for the torch and found it half-buried under the pile of filleted carcasses, but as his hand touched it, there was a second violent thrashing in the net. Both men jumped to their feet and Besser switched on the torch, but nothing moved on the creek. Almost all the floats on their net were underwater, and the ropes tying the net to the mangroves were taut.

'Shit!' said Bluey. 'What the hell've we got?'

Besser concentrated on the light beam which he moved back and forth across the creek where the line of net floats should have been. 'Maybe it's a saw-shark,' he suggested.

'Maybe it's that fucking crocodile,' said Bluey.

As the two men watched, the rope pulled tighter than either would have thought possible without breaking as whatever was in the net struggled beneath the surface. As suddenly as the splashing had started, the ropes went slack and the floats popped back to the surface. The torch beam reflected the red glow from the eyes of a single barramundi caught near the surface. Whatever it was had broken through the net; it was gone.

Besser shone the torch upstream, then down, but saw nothing. 'Well whatever it was just got out, Blue. I'll bet it's put a bloody great hole in the net.'

'It must be that bloody croc. What else could it be?'

'No croc could break that net, not even that big bastard.'

'Well it wasn't a saw-shark. He'd never have got out.'

'Listen, Blue, the chances of that bloody croc being up here are bugger all; it's down near the mouth somewhere. I don't care what was in the net anyway, the main thing is it's gone and probably left a bloody great hole, right in the middle. Let's finish filleting this lot then we'll clean it out again and patch up the hole.'

Bluey Noakes didn't answer. He sat beside the half-filleted fish, picked up his knife, and slid it back into the flesh. The thought of the crocodile frightened him : Besser could say what he liked, but as a child Bluey had seen the marks crocodiles left on cattle and horses —a seven-metre crocodile was something to be reckoned with, and Besser, more than anyone else in the Territory, should have realised it.

On the river, Steve, Mac and Oondabund drifted in silence. The boat baled out and the harpoons ready, they again waited for Numunwari. There was only one harpoon pole left. The other had been lost when Oondabund launched it to get the second harpoon in, when they had Numunwari on the one line, and he was angry with himself for not having retrieved it; but at that time they had been confident of success.

As before, Steve scanned with the torch every two or three minutes, and, as before, he felt tiredness creeping back into his body, and doubts about whether they would see Numunwari again.

Noakes and Besser found the hole, two-thirds of the way across the net, and were surprised to see that it was at least a square metre in area—something big had been caught and had forced its way through. As they tied the broken strands together to prevent fish by-passing the meshes, Besser found himself wondering what had been caught. He had seen plenty of crocodiles caught in nets, but almost invariably the net had been twisted and knotted where the trapped animal rolled and rolled, trying to free itself; the hole they had just patched up was unlike that; it was a clean break. If it was not a crocodile, it could have been a shark, a big shark, whaler or tiger, though they rarely came upstream. Closer to the mouth, saw-sharks were sometimes caught, and they occasionally moved upstream; but as Bluey had pointed out, their rows of flat teeth were almost designed to get caught in nets—once caught, one could never have escaped from this net. Of course, it could have been a very large hammerhead shark. They often got caught, and often broke through the nets, but usually the broken strands were frayed, not cleanly snapped like these had been.

The haul of fish had produced twenty-one barramundi, again about four kilos each, a good commercial size. Having hauled the fish up the bank, and admired the pile of fillets already on the tarpaulin, Bluey and Besser again began filleting. The naked carcasses now covered an area some three metres square.

The filleting went quickly, and within fifteen minutes they reached the last fish. Besser wiped his bloody hands on his trousers, before reaching into his pocket for a tobacco pouch, while Bluey started on the last fish.

There was an explosion of splashing in the net, and both men jumped to their feet. Besser switched on the torch.

'Fuck the bastard!' said Bluey. 'It's come back.'

The floats were all underwater and the ropes tight as they stood and watched, waiting for whatever it was to surface.

Without struggling, the huge head, tightly wrapped in a veil of netting, surfaced. It's eyes opened, revealing two red orbs in the beam of the torch, as air rushed from the nostrils with an audible hiss. The first time the net had broken, letting Numunwari through; this time, it was meshed tightly.

'It's the fucking croc!' yelled Bluey. 'Look at the size of the bastard!'

The massive tail lashed into the water rolling the gigantic body over and wrapping more net tightly around its head, as the floats sank and the ropes jerked tight on the mangroves but the cords did not break.

Besser felt a surge of fear at seeing the great head yet again. But the fear passed quickly and was replaced with anger. He was angry at seeing the crocodile after he had told Bluey it could not be there, and he was angry at the mass of animal tearing their new net apart. But as he flashed the torch back and forth across the creek, he began to think of Smith and Reynolds, of the panic he had felt in the water, of Oondabund laughing at him.

'I'll tell you one fucking thing, Blue, this bastard's not going to get any more people. That I'll promise you,' he said grimly.

'What do you mean?' Bluey asked.

Before Besser could answer, the water erupted as the wildly-rolling crocodile broke the surface in frantic attempts to free itself. The peg-like teeth were tangled in masses of net, and Bluey knew that the crocodile could not escape, for although the lower jaw was free, the head and top jaw were tightly meshed. Numunwari stopped struggling and slowly sank beneath the surface.

'I'm going to do something for the people in Darwin, Blue, and something for me mates from Maningrida. I'm going to axe the bastard. Four people he's killed, four bloody people.'

'Don't you think he's just a bit big to be buggering around with?' Bluey was nervous. 'He's only got to hit you with that tail, mate, and he'll knock your bloody block off. *You* should know.'

But it was no use talking. Besser's mind was made up, and nothing was going to stop him killing the giant crocodile now. He strode to the Land Rover and rummaged in the back until his hand found the smooth, rounded handle of the axe.

Numunwari again thrashed violently in the water, the lower jaw slamming shut against the ball of netting wrapped around the top jaw, the ropes straining as he fought in vain to free himself from the hundreds of cords which held him securely. When Besser shone the torch out, the movement stopped; the two eyes stared out from amongst the mesh before sinking beneath the surface.

'Come on, Blue, let's get the bastard before he gets out.'

'I'm serious, John,' said Bluey, knowing Besser was determined. 'That bloody croc's huge, mate. It's not like other bastards we've caught. This one can really smash you to pieces, kill you. Why not just leave it there until it drowns? Come on, let's not repeat what happened at Maningrida.'

'Yeah, sure, and what about the bloody net? What's it going to be like by the time he drowns? Be in a great state. Now for Christ's sake, Blue, stop carrying on like a fucking kid and give me a hand. Anyway, there's a five grand reward for the head, and the skin's got to be worth $1,500. Come on, Blue, that's six-and-a-half grand.'

When Besser reached the boat and realised he was alone, his temper began to flare. Shining the torch back up the bank to where Bluey stood firm, he snapped a command: 'Fucking well get down here, Blue, or I'll come up and bloody drag you down—I've had enough of this bullshit.'

Bluey Noakes didn't need to be told twice. He had only heard Besser talk like that once before, just before he had bashed two men until they were unconscious, and both men had had reputations for being tough. The crocodile was unknown territory, but Besser was not.

'Keep your pants on, I'm coming,' he shouted as he started down the slope.

The net floats were up on both sides of the creek, and down in the middle, but the net was motionless. Numunwari was not struggling.

Besser placed the axe in the front of the boat, and untied the bowline. 'Now, Blue, I'll get in the front and you pull the boat out along the float line. Just take it bloody easy, and when the bastard comes up for a breath I'll let him have it.' Besser shone the torch in his partner's face. 'For Christ's sake, calm down, Blue—it's only a bloody croc. What the hell does it matter if he's a bit bigger than usual? You've seen it, anyway; it's so caught up in the bloody net that it can't hurt you.'

'That's what you think. Didn't you see those jaws open?'

'Come on, Blue, calm down. Think of the service you're going to be doing for Darwin. Christ, they'll probably give you a medal!'

'Sure, and just what the hell am I supposed to tell them I was doing with a net in Buckleys Creek?'

'Just get in the boat and shut up, Blue. You're making me madder by the minute.'

With Besser seated in the front, torch in hand, Bluey pulled the boat along the float line. It had been at least three minutes since Numunwari had last struggled, in a further attempt to free itself, and it lay beneath the surface, gathering energy for yet another attempt. When the bow reached where the floats disappeared beneath the surface, Bluey stopped pulling.

'You'd better get ready, the bastard's just down there.'

Besser picked up the axe and placed it on his knees. When he shone the light into the brown water, he saw only the reflections from the many, small suspended particles, with not a sign of the crocodile, whose head lay two metres below.

'Okay, Blue, I'm ready. Pull him up.'

The boat leaned over as Bluey pulled firmly on the float line, which started to come up. He could feel no movement on the line, only a large dead weight—he hoped the crocodile had already drowned, though doubted it.

Suddenly the line went slack in his hands.

'He's coming up!' he yelled as Besser stood, staring into the water, the torch in his left hand, the axe in his right.

Through the murkiness, they saw a black shape rising a fraction of a second before the grotesquely sculptured head, tightly bound in net, broke the surface a metre in front. The crocodile lay there, motionless on the surface as though resigned to its fate, its left eye glowing in the torch beam.

Besser and Bluey did not speak or make any sudden movement. Keeping the beam on Numunwari's eye, Besser carefully passed the torch to Bluey, whose hand was already extended and waiting for it. With the torch gone, both hands grasped the smooth wooden handle, and slowly raised the axe well above Besser's head; Numunwari exhaled, unaware of what threatened.

The contracted pupil registered the flash of light some two-hundredths of a second before the steel began to penetrate its skull. The bone where the axe hit was three centimetres thick and formed a square plate, protecting the tubular and delicate brain, and the blade penetrated two centimetres before jamming in its crevice.

Two responses to the urgent signal to dive occurred simultaneously with the blow. The huge tail drove through the water, pulling the animal backward, and the expanded webbed feet rose in the water, pulling Numunwari down, the axe still wedged in its prehistoric skull. Besser had no time to contemplate a reaction; with both hands tightly wrapped around the axe when Numunwari dived, he kept moving forward, and, less than half a second after he had started to swing the axe, he felt the rush of water in the creek over his body.

Numunwari's movements were instinctive and automatic. Once below the surface the tail ploughed through the water, driving him forward against the net, which still held firmly. He was no longer just restrained; he had been injured, he was being hunted, and every muscle responded to the frantic need to free itself.

The axe came out and sank.

Besser felt the solid head smash into his thigh while he floundered in the water; he also felt his right arm seized in a crushing grip, and he was being dragged beneath the surface.

Numunwari was aware of contact with a solid object in the water. The lower jaw instinctively slammed shut against the meshed upper jaw, and as the powerful jaw muscles contracted, the teeth tore through the skin of Besser's arm, breaking and crushing the bones. The fish net careered through the water as Numunwari swam, and Bluey felt the boat moving as he watched Besser disappear.

As the ropes held the moving net, the cords pulled against the entangled head, but with a final burst of energy the mighty animal fought for freedom. The meshes surrounding its head began to break; more broke as the same strength was pitted against fewer of them, and within a quarter of a second Numunwari was moving through a hole, dragging Besser against the net, where the strong cords held. Numunwari felt one further restraint as it moved through the net, but one jerk of its head and the crocodile was free and swimming against the tide towards the mouth of Buckleys Creek.

Besser also felt freedom, and kicked to the surface, clear of the net and gasping for air. His head broke the surface in front of the boat, where the beam of the torch was frantically moving back and forth.

Bluey stumbled forward to help his friend and grabbed the left arm which reached up to him. It was only then that Besser realised what had happened; his right hand and lower arm were gone, and all that remained was a shredded mass of bleeding tissue from just above the elbow.

'Your arm!' shouted Bluey.

'Get me in the fucking boat,' Besser yelled, trying to use the stub to hold the edge of the bobbing dinghy. Bluey hauled on his shirt to pull him from the water, but as Besser came he fell, banging his head on the seat as he tried to use his missing arm for support.

'It's got your arm. Your arm's gone!'

'Fuck the arm!' shouted Besser, trying to hold the stub with his powerful left hand, and amazed by his own calmness. 'Get me to the bank.'

Bluey frantically pulled the boat to shore, but when he helped Besser out, they both slipped in the mud. Instinctively Besser threw his right arm forward to break the fall, only to see the tattered, bleeding stub bury itself into the soft mud.

Dragging him free, Bluey hauled him up through the mud to the fire.

'Give me your belt, Blue, I'll have to stop the bleeding.' Tearing the leather belt from around his waist, Bluey wrapped it around the remains of Besser's arm. Blood squirted from the stub in distinct pulses, but as Bluey pulled on the belt, the bleeding slowed. Besser screamed and pulled away when Bluey gave it a final pull, but the bleeding stopped.

'That's got it. Now let's get out of here.'

Besser was in shock. His exhausted brain searched for something other than the water, the crocodile, or his arm.

'What about the net?'

'Fuck the net! Let's get you to a hospital, quickly.'

'The net's worth a fortune. You can't just leave it.'

'What's the matter with you?' shouted Bluey. 'If you don't get to hospital, you'll bleed to fucking death.'

'It's stopped bleeding,' said Besser, looking at the bloody mess that had been an intact arm.

'John, you need help, mate. Now let's get going.'

'You're not going to leave the fish too?'

Bluey realised what had happened. He ran to the Land Rover and opened the door, then grabbing Besser around the back and by the left arm, he walked him to the front seat. Besser was a man to whom tears were seldom known, yet he was crying. He climbed into the cabin and Bluey slammed the door before running to the right-hand side and climbing in behind the wheel. Within seconds the vehicle was moving, the accelerator flat to the floor.

No one was there to listen to the splashing as fish rammed into the remains of the net, still strung out across the creek. The flickering light of the fire illuminated the pile of carcasses and the tarpaulin stacked with over two hundred kilos of fillets. The blood-spattered aluminium boat drifted slowly upstream with the incoming tide.

Steve, Mac and Oondabund were a kilometre past the mouth of Buckleys Creek, when without warning, Oondabund stood up, startling Steve, who was almost asleep.

'What that noise?' he said softly. 'Him sound like white man he yell out loud, that one.'

The three of them listened, but there were no further sounds. Steve switched on the torch and scanned the deserted waters before switching it off and listening in the darkness. They all heard the sound of the Land Rover's four cylinders racing for Darwin.

'There that truck!' said Oondabund.

'Wonder who the hell that was?' asked Steve, turning to Mac, who shrugged his shoulders.

'Him been cry out loud, that white man,' said Oondabund seriously. 'Him proper hurt himself.'

'Well, whoever it was, he's on his way now,' said Steve.

Oondabund picked up the torch, and holding it level with his eyes and pointed back behind them, he switched it on. He moved it in a single slow scan, but, seeing nothing, switched it off again.

'Steve,' said Mac after they had drifted in silence for a few minutes, 'It's four o'clock, mate. Do you reckon we'd better give it away? I'm buggered; can hardly keep my eyes open.'

'I feel the same, but we'd better keep going a while longer. Splash some water on your face, that'll refresh you.'

Following Steve's advice, Mac leaned over the stern and with his hands cupped, threw water up on to his face, letting it run freely over his hair and down his neck. 'That feels better,' he said, running his fingers through his wet hair, not seeing a disapproving stare from Oondabund.

The crocodile swam underwater against the current until it reached the mouth of Buckleys Creek, where it surfaced and breathed deeply in the darkness. As air rushed into the tired body, Numunwari let himself be carried by the current, drifting upstream on the surface, with senses alert for any unnatural sounds, sounds that could be threatening.

A kilometre away, Mac harmlessly splashed water onto himself, but Numunwari's keen hearing perceived the distant disturbance, and the slit-like ear flaps vibrated in response. Instantly the mighty tail, which had been moving just enough to keep the crocodile on the surface, began to sweep faster through the water, Numunwari moving upstream faster than the current, upstream to where the injured fish flapped on the surface.

Doubting they would see their prey again, Steve nevertheless systematically searched with the torch every few minutes. As the beam approached the crocodile, he dived, now wary of the night light, and swam beneath the surface to reappear in the darkness. Here it lay motionless on the surface, watching, listening.

Again Mac dipped his hands into the water, and wiped the refreshing fluid over his forehead. It held back the sleep which otherwise would close his tired eyes.

Immediately Numunwari headed upstream again, cruising on the surface. The second splash was a good sign, a sign that whatever he had heard before was still there, and as the crocodile swam, the expanded pupils, specially developed for seeing in low light levels, searched the starlit river.

There! In midstream, a shadow. A night light flashed on, and the crocodile dived.

'Are we wasting our time, Oondabund?' asked Steve, moving the light around, but convinced they had seen the last of Numunwari.

'Him here somewhere, that crocodile. Maybe we find him.'

The torch switched off; again they waited in the silent darkness. Steve thought about what they would do in the morning, when the sun came up. It had been made very clear that the harbour could not be kept closed indefinitely, and the crocodile had to be caught or killed. Every hour that went by without success was an hour closer to a decision to kill rather than catch Numunwari, regardless of the arrangement with Oondabund. Earlier in the night they could have killed him easily, and Steve could guess what Barrett's response would be when they told him that they had had the crocodile so close, but had lost him. Numunwari's well-being depended on their catching him, but to the crocodile itself, it was a danger he used all his primitive instincts to resist.

For the third time, Mac dipped his hands into the water, letting them trail momentarily before cupping them together and dousing his face. It felt good. He lowered them again, and this time leaned down to get more water to his face before it trickled between his fingers. It was refreshing.

As his eyes blinked open, they saw it—a great rounded snout right beside the boat.

Hurtling sideways, Mac screamed as the jaws opened and slammed shut just behind him, the head crashing against the stern as the light flicked on. Oondabund was standing in the wildly rocking boat, the harpoon in his hands, and swinging backwards as the confusion of signals jumbled through Numunwari's senses—prey, night light, attack, dive. He was submerging as Mac clambered forward, and underwater the skilled spring exploded, driving the harpoon pole into the water where there was no longer a crocodile.

The dull thud and single line running over the side of the boat meant that a metre below the surface, the sharpened barbs had hit their mark.

'You're okay, you're okay, Mac!' shouted Steve, as he struggled to pin Mac down, but Mac fought to release himself from whatever held him. 'You're all right, Mac! Calm down,' Steve repeated.

Slowly the words took meaning, and the struggling stopped. Mac lay there, breathing deeply as his heart pounded inside, and his mind struggled for control. When his hand touched the cold, wet spotlight lying on the deck, he jerked forward again in momentary terror, but Steve held him firmly.

'Get 'im engine going,' ordered Oondabund, the line running through his capable fingers.

Leaving Mac, Steve stumbled to the stern and had the engine going in seconds. As the boat moved forward and Oondabund started pulling in the slack, Mac sat up, his body shaking uncontrollably.

'You're going to have to take the engine, Mac,' called Steve.

Mac looked blankly around. He saw Steve and then noticed Oondabund taking in the line. Only then did he realise what had happened; Numunwari was on the line again. He made his way to the stern, where Steve held his shoulder.

'You okay now?'

'Yeah. Christ, I thought it had me. I thought I must have been dead.'

'It was bloody close, Mac, but we've got the harpoon in. Quick, take the engine so I can help up front.'

'Grabbem harpoon!' yelled Oondabund, pointing to the floating pole that had drifted past them. Steve leaned over the side in time to retrieve it.

In the bow, Steve took the line from Oondabund, and shone the torch out in front to where it was slicing through the water, as Numunwari swam unseen. Oondabund jammed the second harpoon in the end of the pole, and coiled the first few metres of line before standing up on the seat.

'Hold it, Mac! He's on the bottom!' yelled Steve, as the boat began to overtake the line, causing it to go loose. Steve gathered in the slack, and with the boat stopped the line ran vertically downward. He gave it a gentle pull.

'No pull him!' yelled Oondabund. 'Him maybe in little one—we wait.'

The line went slack. 'He's coming up!' yelled Steve, pulling in the excess rapidly, but when he had pulled in three metres without feeling a weight he began to have doubts. After a further two metres, the horrible truth sank in.

'It's out! The bloody thing's out!'

Oondabund had not flinched. Poised with his back arched and the pole extended to its maximum length, his forefinger pressed on the end, he watched the water.

'Bugger the bastard!' yelled Steve angrily, as the harpoon head clattered over the side of the boat. He picked it up and threw it on to the deck. A mixture of disappointment and rage surged within; he flashed the torch on Mac, and opened his mouth to continue his tirade of despair.

A white man would not have seen Numunwari surface some six metres out from the boat, but as the head first broke the water Oondabund was launching the harpoon. Steve saw the movement and flashed the light back out in front, just in time to see the harpoon slam into Numunwari's neck, and hear the distinctive thud.

'Engine!' yelled Oondabund, and, as the boat sprang forward, he passed the line to Steve. Leaning over the side, he retrieved the floating pole, then picked up the second harpoon from the deck. Inspecting it, he saw that one point was bent, and gave Steve a reproachful glance before severing the line with a knife from the fish crate. After attaching a fresh harpoon head from his pocket, he forced it into the end of the pole, and once again stood up on the seat.

'Him in good one now, that harpoon,' he said quietly to Steve.

'Sorry about buggering the other one,' Steve answered, equally softly, but Oondabund merely put his hand on Steve's shoulder and gave it a gentle squeeze.

Numunwari swam for what seemed a long time, but which was only five minutes, before coming to rest on the bottom.

'Pull 'im up slow one,' said Oondabund, when the boat stopped.

Steve felt the line tighten, go slack and tighten, and let the line run from his fingers. 'He's rolling,' he told Oondabund.

'Poor feller, him proper buggered now. Him biggest fright.'

When the rolling stopped, Steve pulled firmly on the line and felt the massive body lift from the mud.

'Back off a bit, Mac,' he called. 'He's coming up.'

Oondabund waited, tensed, poised, and watched the white belly slowly appear in the moving waters. 'Hold him,' he ordered before the crocodile actually reached the surface.

Numunwari, wrapped in the line, was no longer resisting while being manoeuvred underwater, but was likely to thrash wildly once his head broke the surface. By holding the crocodile where he was, with the white belly exposed, they could wait until he rolled a little, just enough for the neck or tail to expose itself. Steve gently jerked the line, and, passively, the animal started to turn. No sooner had the neck appeared than the harpoon crashed through the water, quivering as the crocodile dived before the harpoon pole was separated from the head.

'It's in!' yelled Steve excitedly as both lines ran from the bow, and Oondabund threw the pole back into the boat.

As the boat moved forward, Oondabund took both lines, leaving Steve free with the torch. The crocodile swam strongly forward beneath the surface, each movement tugging at the taut lines.

Numunwari swam for ten minutes before finally coming to rest. By that time, Steve had taken two of the lengths of cord from the side of the basket, had slipped them in his pocket for easy access, had unravelled one of the catching ropes, and had opened the steel cable noose. As Mac joined them in the bow, he loosely tied the noose to the end of the harpoon pole with cord.

'Okay, we're ready; let's haul him up.'

No sooner had Mac and Oondabund begun pulling on the lines than the great crocodile began to roll, but this time there was no waiting. 'Pull him up, anyway,' said Steve. 'There's two harpoons in, and we can't give him time to recover.'

As they pulled, the rolling stopped. Steve extended the pole and noose out over the bow.

When barely two metres from the surface, Numunwari gave two powerful strokes of his tail. Oondabund and Mac had no option but to let the lines run. It was when Oondabund noticed that the lines were almost horizontal that he saw the crocodile, almost fifteen metres from the boat, lying motionless on the surface. Without talking, he pointed, and together with Mac slowly pulling on the lines, he made as little visible movement with his arms as possible.

Facing upstream, Numunwari was first pulled backwards towards the boat, the tail gently sweeping from side to side, keeping the lines taut. The whole of his back, from the tip of his snout to the tip of his tail was above the water level, as the crocodile slowly swam on the surface, being pulled closer and closer to the boat. When five metres away, Steve fully extended the harpoon pole, and allowed the noose to lower until it was dangling just above the water. The crocodile stopped swimming, and with his neck held to the boat he swung in the current to face his hunters.

There was absolute silence. Steve and Mac subconsciously held their breath for fear that the normal noise of breathing would be enough to frighten their quarry. Gradually the lines continued coming, the eyes watching the approaching boat from which the night light shone.

When three metres away, Oondabund and Mac stopped pulling and held the lines firm. The bottom of the noose gently swung in the stillness, two centimetres above the nostrils, which opened and closed obliviously. For thirty seconds the vigilance was maintained, neither man or animal breaking the tension; Steve's muscles began to flinch with the weight of the extended pole, and the noose began firstly to swing more, then to quiver above the snout.

Attracted by the light, two small garfish appeared between the bow and Numunwari's snout, darting back and forth in search of floating food small enough to be taken by their comical mouths. Barely ten centimetres long, they suddenly darted to one side, one passing the rounded snout, the other glancing off it and skipping across the water surface in fright, to dive in the darkness. Numunwari's head jerked sideways, and the whole of the body, except for the head, lowered in the water in preparation for a dive, but the jaws opened enough to slip the noose in.

Steve slowly lowered the moving noose towards the opening between the rows of teeth, and gently edged it forward until the cable touched the front teeth. Without warning, and leaving barely a ripple, Numunwari sank below the surface.

'Bastard!' said Steve lowering the pole and flexing his arms. 'That was bloody close. Christ, if he'd only opened his mouth a little sooner! I was going to tap him on the snout, but he's so big I wasn't game.'

'Them little fish bugger 'im,' added Oondabund, smiling as he held the moving line. 'Him got biggest sorry cut on him head that crocodile. You see that one?'

'Yeah, Steve,' said Mac. 'I saw that, too; a bloody big gash across the top of the platform.'

'Him stop swimming now,' said Oondabund, shining the torch

out in front, to where Numunwari again lay on the surface some twenty metres away.

Mac and Oondabund again eased in the lines, but this time the crocodile came in faster. Steve extended the noose out over the water as before, but waited until the crocodile was very close before supporting the full weight of the pole on his arms. The vigilance reestablished, Steve decided to wait no longer. He lowered the noose until it touched the nostrils, and when the crocodile did not move, he raised and lowered the pole just enough to make the cable tap the soft pad of tissue which held the nostrils on the rounded snout. Still Numunwari did not respond. He raised the pole further, and let the noose hit harder, and suddenly the head jerked up in the water, the jaws fifteen centimetres apart. The trunk and tail sank below the surface, leaving only the head to be seen.

'Look out, him come now,' hissed Oondabund, without moving the light from the crocodile's eyes.

Steve lowered the noose, tension mounting to a peak as he felt the conflict between catching Numunwari and avoiding being attacked by him. The now-quivering cable levelled with the gap between the teeth, and Steve extended the pole further, his muscles strained to their limit. The cable bounced across the teeth as the upper jaw slid within the bounds of the noose, but Numunwari was moving, moving forward.

Calmness shattered, Steve reefed the pole upwards, while jumping from the bow as the crocodile came forward. The noose closed, locking around the moving jaw, and simultaneously Numunwari threw his head sideways, slamming the mighty jaws closed, only to open them and bite into the air once more, before diving amidst a spray of water. Steve gave the rope a heavy jerk, to lock the noose even tighter around the top jaw, before letting the rope run.

'It's on!' he yelled excitedly. 'We've got him.'

Wrapping the rope around his hands, Steve lowered himself so that his knees locked in under the bow as the full weight of Numunwari reached him. He needed all his strength, and as his arms strained against his shoulders and the rope dug into his hands, he was thankful for the able black hands that joined his in grasping the rope. The boat began to move, relieving the weight, and as Steve's fingers pulsated with the blood flowing back through his hands, they watched grim-faced as Numunwari crashed out of the depths, rolling and thrashing violently on the surface in a desperate bid for freedom. The cable held, and he dived.

'Get another cable,' Steve called behind him.

When they pulled Numunwari up the second time, he rose vertically through the water, and when his snout was just below the surface, they stopped pulling. The mouth hung limply open, and Steve lowered the cable noose into the water so that it sank over the top jaw, with Oondabund pulling the head to one side to facilitate its slipping in over the teeth. Very gently, Steve leaned forward and tightened the noose, giving one final jerk to lock it in position as the crocodile erupted, thrashing, rolling and biting into the cables in an attempt to sever the thin steel bands.

'That's on,' said Steve, as both ropes ran. 'Pull him up again.'

While Mac and Oondabund hauled on the ropes, Steve removed one of the pieces of cord from his pocket, the thin braided cord that would lock both jaws together. Because the ropes were only on the head, Numunwari again came vertically through the water, and once more they stopped pulling when the tip of the snout was just below the surface.

With the cord, Steve made a large loose circle around both catching ropes, using a simple knot that could be tightened by pulling both ends. 'Now, for Christ's sake, take it easy,' he whispered as he leaned over the bow and lowered the circle to the water's surface above the snout.

Without needing further instruction, Oondabund and Mac slowly pulled on the ropes, and the bulbous snout eased to the surface within the circle, the jaws just slightly agape, with perhaps two centimetres separating the upper and lower rows of teeth. Still they pulled, until the first and then the second cable noose, both locked on the upper jaw, slid above the surface, then they stopped. With his hands just above the water, Steve drew the two ends of the cord, and the circle closed around both jaws, gently forcing them together.

When the cord could go no further, he knotted it, and reached for the second piece. Carefully, so as not to bump or knock the snout, he wrapped the second cord next to the first, tying it on both the upper and lower sides of the jaw. When he straightened up, both cords tied in position, Oondabund and Mac released the tension on the rope, and the snout slid beneath the surface, jaws immobilised.

'We've got the bastard!' said Steve in excitement, breathing deeply. 'Christ, I can't believe it.'

'An hour ago,' added Mac, 'I wouldn't have given two cents for our chances.'

As the three men sat in the drifting boat, the sky lightened as a prelude to morning. A light mist rose from the water's edge near the shore, where the current was less strong, and the tide, though still coming in, was almost high and covered the mudbanks below the mangroves.

'Him real buggered, that crocodile,' said Oondabund, smiling. 'Proper tired one after biggest try him run away.'

'Unless I'd seen it myself,' said Steve, 'I just wouldn't have believed a croc could fight for so long. It's no wonder he's "proper tired".'

As they spoke, Numunwari surfaced, the jaws bound together and the two cables locked in position; both harpoons still stuck unnaturally in the scaled skin of the enormous neck. The crocodile was beaten and confused. The relentless struggle had taken its toll, and he lay there breathing deeply and watching his captors. They in turn stared at Numunwari in silence, each deep in his thoughts.

Oondabund lashed the ropes and lines around the front seat, then jerked on the ropes; Numunwari dived, but only swam a short distance before coming to rest on the bottom.

After about fifteen minutes, they pulled Numunwari to the surface again, and brought him in next to the boat. As he lay next to them, Steve worked two ropes around the middle of the body, and a third around the butt of the tail, before letting the crocodile sink once more.

'Let's get the engine going while he's down, Mac,' said Steve, 'and then we'll pull him up slowly and lash the ropes short, to the front seat. We'll all come down the back to balance the boat and try reversing into shore.'

With the engine idling, the crocodile was raised and the ropes tied so that the front of the head was about half a metre from the bow. Then, with the three of them in the stern, they slowly reversed towards the eastern bank, the crocodile trailing in the water behind. Once he struggled, shortly after starting, but his rolling merely wrapped the ropes around each other and jerked the boat back and forth: Numunwari could not escape. Progress was hampered by the current, and by the time they reached the shore, they were a good three hundred and sixty metres upstream of where they had started, adjacent to a small clearing where the mangroves were sturdy but sparse.

One by one, the existing ropes were untied from the boat and retied around the gnarled trunks, with Steve tying on six additional ropes before being satisfied that the crocodile could not escape. The head was held in one position in the water by ropes going alternately in opposite directions, and from the body, ropes radiated out everywhere. Numunwari struggled only once during the tying, but for barely five seconds before sinking in the shallow water, so that all but his head was submerged.

The tying finished, Oondabund broke a thin green branch from one of the mangroves, and waded in until he was next to the near-black head. With considerable force he struck at the snout, just in front of the nostrils, causing the crocodile to throw its head from side to side, and violently roll the body in a bid to release the restrained head; but the ropes held, and the crocodile rolled back to his former position.

'Him not get away, that Numunwari,' Oondabund said confidently as he walked back to where Mac and Steve stood watching on the bank.

Hesitant to leave their captive, the three men sat on the bank watching it, quietly discussing the night's events. After a time Oondabund walked back down to Numunwari and stood by the head for almost a minute before beckoning to Steve and Mac, who then joined him. When he spoke, his expression showed considerable concern.

'That biggest cut him head,' he said, pointing to the conspicuous gash on the otherwise unmarked head. 'Him from axe. Someone been hunt this Numunwari with axe; try finish him.'

Steve looked from Oondabund to Mac, then back at the deep wound. It did look like an axe cut, and although he tried to think of realistic alternatives, none were forthcoming.

'This fresh one from tonight, maybe,' continued Oondabund. 'Someone him try finish him.'

'Well,' replied Steve, 'they didn't get him, and I'd say that's going to heal up without any problems. We'd better start heading back to the launch. They'll be wondering what the hell's happened to us.'

'Do you think it's okay to leave the croc, Steve?'

'Me stay with Numunwari,' replied Oondabund immediately. 'Someone round this place try kill 'im, that crocodile.'

'Well, I was going to suggest that, anyway,' said Steve. 'I'm not keen on leaving any big croc on its own. You'd better take some extra ropes just in case he manages to break out of some of the ones we've got on.'

'Him no get away,' said Oondabund, knowledgeably. 'Him happy now Oondabund here for him friend; him quiet one and have biggest sleep.'

Mac and Steve untied the dinghy and pushed it out into the stream. Oondabund waved as the engine burst into life and they moved off, sending back a series of small waves which splashed over the primitive head. Although tired, Mac and Steve were elated; catching Numunwari was an achievement of which they could feel proud, and they knew it, although they knew equally that they had attempted it only because of Oondabund's insistence that it could be done.

When Steve took one final look back, he knew that Oondabund had also received his rewards—he was sitting cross-legged on the bank in front of the crocodile's head, his mouth moving in song, the song Steve had last heard on the beach at Maningrida.

7

It was 8.30 am when the small boat rounded the last bend of the river from the police launch, still anchored in midstream. During the trip downstream, Mac and Steve had both been overcome by intense weariness, but their spirits rose when they sighted the launch, and they both began to anticipate the climbing aboard, the reporting of their success the changing of expressions from fear to relief. Bearing good news was pleasurable, doubly so when the bearers were responsible for it.

As they came alongside, Steve threw the bowline to the waiting hands of the skipper, whose eyes were fixed on the section of gunwale that Numunwari had ripped out. Each muscle in Steve's body ached as he pulled himself up onto the deck.

'What happened?' asked the skipper. 'Where's the Abo?'

Steve and Mac exchanged glances, both grinning cheekily as Barrett appeared at the doorway.

'We got him,' said Steve, loud enough so that both could hear; but there was no answer, nor the expected change in expression.

'We got him!' Steve repeated, a little louder. 'We had a battle, but we got him.'

Still there was no reply, and Steve looked questioningly from Barrett to the skipper. The smile on Mac's face had vanished.

'Have you killed it?' asked Barrett, eventually.

'Killed it?' repeated Steve, in complete confusion. 'What the hell's going on here?'

'It's a simple question, Harris. Did you or did you not kill the bloody crocodile?' His eyes wide open with anger, Barrett glared at Steve.

'Of course we didn't kill it. The deal was to catch it alive—we've spent the whole bloody night doing it.'

Barrett's gaze shifted from Steve to Mac, the small eyes probing deeply.

'Where is the bloody thing, Wilson?' he snarled. 'And where's that bloody Abo?'

'It's . . . ah, up the . . .'

'It's tied up in the mangroves and Oondabund is with it,' snapped Steve, his body quivering with anger. 'Now what's this all about? Cut the crap, what's going on?'

'It's tied up, is it?' said Barrett, ignoring Steve. 'Alive and being well cared for, I suppose. Well, it's not going to be for much longer. I'm sick to death of the fucking thing and we're going to kill it once and for all. You bastards have gone soft in the bloody head! People are what count—not bloody crocodiles!'

Steve stared at Barrett, but there was no explanation to be had, and he was beyond further questioning. He grasped Mac's arm. 'Come on, mate, let's get some coffee.'

Barrett stood his ground in the doorway as Steve approached. He was also angry, furious, and as they exchanged glances, Steve saw a trickle of saliva on the corner of the thin, cutting mouth.

'Get out of my way!' Steve almost snarled, his control rapidly disappearing.

Barrett moved half a pace to the side, but as Steve passed, as if as an afterthought, he grabbed at Steve's shoulder. Instantly Steve spun, his fist clenched and level with his right shoulder as Barrett dropped, releasing his grip. The skipper pushed between them.

'Calm down,' he said quietly, nervously. 'Come on, calm down.'

'Calm down, be buggered!' repeated Steve loudly and quickly. 'You guys sort out what the hell's going on and tell us. If anyone touches that bloody croc they'll be sorry—it's alive all right, and it's going to stay that way. That's the deal we made.' Without awaiting an answer, he turned and stormed down the steps to the galley. Barrett started to follow, but the skipper stopped him.

'People like Harris don't speak to me like that!' Furious, Barrett turned and walked to the side of the launch. When the skipper joined him, they both stood staring at the catching boat anchored beside. 'They've had a pretty rough time, Mr Barrett,' said the skipper quietly. 'I'll go down and have a talk with them.'

In the galley, Steve and Mac drank their coffee in silence. Within a matter of minutes, they had progressed from intense weariness and tiredness, to the high spirits of elation, only to be thrown into frustration and anger. Ten minutes later, they were joined by the skipper, who, after pouring himself a cup of strong black coffee, slid in on the bench beside Mac.

'Last night there was another attack. The croc ripped a bloke's arm off near the shoulder, and he was lucky not to be killed.'

'Yeah? Well, it wasn't this bloody croc for once. We were with it all night,' said Steve confidently.

'It was in Buckleys Creek around midnight, and they reckoned the croc was enormous—at least twenty-five feet.'

Steve and Mac stared in silence as they both remembered the scream Oondabund had heard, and the sounds of the vehicle. The skipper continued, 'These two blokes were up there line fishing for catfish, and they reckoned it just appeared in front of them and grabbed Besser before they could do a thing.'

'Besser!' repeated Steve. 'John Besser?'

'That's him. John Besser and . . .'

'Bluey Noakes,' continued Steve. 'Two of the biggest bloody fish and croc poachers in the Territory. It's a shame the bloody croc didn't take him altogether.'

'Poachers or not, the croc attacked them.'

'Attacked them? What, Besser and Noakes? You don't believe that story about line fishing for catfish, for Christ's sake?'

'All I know is what came over the radio.'

'You can take it from me, there's no way Besser and Noakes would go all the way out to Buckleys Creek to catch catfish with handlines. That's just got to be Bluey Noakes's story—Besser's too smart to come up with something like that. They were out there poaching! I'll bet they had a bloody net stretched from one side of the creek to the other. That's how they caught the croc.'

'What about that axe-mark, Steve?' asked Mac.

'Right. They caught the croc in a net and tried to kill it.'

'Even so, poachers are entitled to protection. They're still people,' the skipper pointed out.

'Well, they might be to you, but you don't have to spend half your life trying to catch them. Serves bloody Besser right; it's just what he deserves.'

'Anyway,' continued the skipper, 'Mr Barrett seemed to take that news all right. It was the telegram from the Minister that really upset him. It came over about half an hour ago; sent late yesterday afternoon. The Minister wanted Mr Barrett to ring him last night. He'd booked a seat on today's flight to Darwin, but wanted confirmation that the crocodile was still a problem before leaving. Mr

Barrett was almost frantic. He wanted me to take the boat back to Darwin, but I talked him into getting a telegram sent over the radio. But it wouldn't have arrived before the plane was due to leave.'

'Well, why didn't one of you tell us this when we got back?' asked Steve.

'I'm just the bloke who drives the boat, Mr Harris. But mind you, I was getting pretty worried myself. We hadn't heard from you since you left, and at four o'clock we get a report that someone's been attacked in Buckleys Creek, but it's not until five that we get the names. Up until then we thought it must have been you! We've been trying to contact you on the radio since four, and not an answer; nothing to let us know you were all right. It's not too pleasant just sitting, unable to do anything, at the same time wondering whether you lot are alive or dead. Then comes the telegram.'

'We weren't exactly having it easy out there, you know. We'd have called in, only the radio got soaked, and we couldn't take the time to come back. But we sure weren't expecting to get screamed at as soon as we got back—especially after finally catching the bastard!'

'It looks like a big misunderstanding all the way along, Mr Harris. Maybe if you and Mr Barrett have a talk you can sort it out. What are your plans, now that we've got the thing?'

'The original plan,' Steve replied firmly. 'The deal with Oondabund sticks, whether Besser's been attacked or not.'

Barrett was visibly more relaxed when he joined Mac and Steve in the galley. 'I believe you know about the attack in Buckleys Creek. This seems to throw a new light on the whole question of what we're going to do with the croc. If that thing goes back to Darwin alive, people won't only kill it, they'll probably kill us, too. As far as I'm concerned, there's only one way out of this. The croc's got to go back dead.'

'We discussed all this before,' replied Steve wearily. 'We've made a deal with Oondabund, and now we've got the croc it's no longer ours to do anything with. We wouldn't have got the thing except for him, and there's no way I'm going back on the arrangement; the crocodile stays alive, and we don't take it back to Darwin and make a great fuss. We stick to the original plan.'

'Do you seriously think you're going to be able to hide something like that in Darwin?' asked Barrett. 'You've got to be joking.'

'Look, we haven't time to argue. Oondabund's up the river waiting for us, and we can't just leave him there. If you want to kill it, get his permission, and I'll do it, but till you do we're sticking to the original plan.'

'Well, where the hell are you going to keep it?' demanded Barrett. 'What if it gets out?'

'It won't get out. We'll take it to the breeding pen like we planned before. The pen's two hundred yards from the others and was built especially so that there could be no public disturbance. It's surrounded by bushes, with a fence six feet high and four feet in the ground; there's no way it could get out, and no one ever goes near the place.'

'Well, what are you going to tell the public, Harris? We've got to tell them something, you know.'

'We'll tell them that it's dead!'

'The body?' questioned Barrett.

'Searched everywhere for it. Shot and harpooned it, but when we were towing the carcass back the rope broke and it sank.'

There was silence. Barrett thought only of the consequences if the deception were exposed, but Steve was trying to picture Numunwari in the breeding pen. The pool was large and deep, covered in emerald-green water-lilies around the edges, with floating weed in the middle. Once in there, it would be unlikely that anyone would see him for months, even if they were watching purposely. In a few months, they would announce that they had caught another big crocodile, and released it in the pen. From then on, it would not matter who saw it, as no one would be able to pick one big crocodile from another.

'Like I said before,' said Barrett, 'I'm not going to take any responsibility. As far as I'm concerned, I believed every word you told me, and that's exactly what I'm telling everyone, the Minister included.'

Mac thought about Barrett's dilemma. Either way, he was in a precarious position. If the deception were ever exposed, his name would be closely linked with it, whether he was prepared to take responsibility or not. On the other hand, if he did somehow manage to have the crocodile killed, there would be no telling what Steve and Oondabund would do; plenty of people were eager to back a full-blood Aboriginal with a legitimate claim. Either way, he was caught, and no doubt regretted having ever given in to the whole issue of catching it alive.

'What about the radio, Steve?' asked Mac. 'When do we tell Darwin?'

'Not yet; let's wait until we've got the croc away. We don't want to chance any other boats poking around.'

Steve turned to the skipper. 'Okay, then, let's get going.'

While the launch moved upstream, Steve and Mac had something to eat, and discussed the way in which they would move Numunwari from the river to the breeding pen. The nearest landing to where the crocodile was tied was the one in Buckleys Creek, and once they got him there they would be able to get the low loader in, and take it back by road. As the launch approached the site, they both walked out on deck and stood in silence, looking out over the river on which they had spent the night.

Steve's thoughts drifted back to the first large crocodile he had ever caught, and the lessons he had learned from that experience. The croc, about four metres long, had taken him three hours to catch and tie up at the bank, but when he had returned to it an hour later, there was nothing; it had struggled free. Since that time he had never left a large restrained croc, and if Oondabund had not agreed to stay with Numunwari, he would have done so himself.

As they came round the last bend, his eyes picked up the clearing and he pointed it out to Mac. Oondabund, standing knee-deep in water, was waving frantically. Steve's heart began to pound as he looked for Numunwari.

'What is it, Steve? What's the matter?' asked Mac anxiously.

Barely forty-five metres away, the launch slowed down. Steve could see the ropes still tied to the trees and leading to the water, but to nothing else. There was no crocodile.

'He's gone! He's got away!' he shouted to Mac.

'He can't have,' replied Mac, searching, tears in his eyes.

Steve could see Oondabund clearly. He had stopped waving, but there was a broad smile on his face. The ropes were all leading to one position. With a surge of relief, Steve realised what had happened.

'He's underwater! He's just under. Christ. Scared the hell out of me.'

The skipper nosed the launch into the bank before throwing mooring lines ashore. Steve and Mac went quickly over the bow and waded towards Oondabund, having secured the heavy lines to mangroves.

'Him been proper quiet for Oondabund. Not one time him fight.'

Barrett plodded slowly through the mud, giving the ropes to Numunwari a wide berth. On the bank he stood behind the others, but could see nothing in the murky water; he was anxious to see the crocodile, but equally hesitant to ask that he be pulled in for that purpose. Steve produced three of the tranquilliser darts, and indicated to Oondabund that they would anaesthetise the crocodile before towing it to Buckleys Creek; with the launch there to tow him, there was no chance he could be lost, once anaesthetised. Oondabund walked along the bank behind the mangroves, returning in a few minutes with a sturdy pole nearly three metres long, to which Steve bound the dart with cord, then he straightened up.

'Okay. We'll all pull him in a bit and Oondabund can spear this into the tail.'

In response to the pulling, Numunwari immediately rose to the surface, looking even larger than before.

'Hell!' exclaimed Barrett, after his first close look, but then he went silent, and just watched. It was not the beast's size that moved him, it was the huge, knobbled, black head, the head that had held Constable John Wiley and torn him apart, crushing bones and ripping flesh. He wanted to vomit. He looked up at Steve, who was smiling, then again focused on Numunwari's head. How could anyone want to keep the creature alive? He could kill him now, without a moment's hesitation; fire bullet after bullet into the repulsive object until all life in it ceased.

Improvised spear in hand, Oondabund waded into the water until level with where the tail lay, but three metres from it. Carefully he extended the pole and lowered it until the end of the dart lay on the tail butt; Numunwari did not move. Slowly and carefully, he eased it back towards him, until the tip of the dart was on the edge of the tail. He then looked momentarily at Steve and smiled cheekily, before plunging the pole against the side of the tail with one rapid movement, driving in the dart as he leaped backwards through the water and the animal exploded in a frenzy. Barrett jumped away, and was backing higher up the bank, as Oondabund, laughing heartily, reached the edge.

'Proper funny one, that Numunwari. Him fright like hospital needle.'

After ten minutes, Steve jerked on the rope again to determine

181

whether or not the drug was working. Numunwari tried to back off into deeper water, so, after hitching the rope to make sure the nostrils were above water, Steve left him for a further ten minutes. This time, there was no response to the pull, the head merely emerging further as they dragged him forward. Steve waded in to the head, and touched the naked eyeball with a piece of grass; like a camera blind shutter, the membranous eyelid flicked across.

'Just about out to it,' he mumbled. 'Another few minutes will do it.'

When Steve next touched the eye, there was no response; the drug had worked. Numunwari was unconscious and could be expected to remain so for at least the next two hours.

It took the four men half an hour to prepare Numunwari for the trip up Buckleys Creek. When the launch was ready to leave, two heavy ropes ran from its stern to the bow of the fibreglass dinghy, and Numunwari's head lay over the back of the dinghy, where the outboard engine had been, with ropes securing it to the seats; the body itself trailed in the water behind. Because of the crocodile's weight, the dinghy was out of the water at the front end and under at the back; only flotation prevented it from sinking. The snout rope and two additional ropes around the body ran directly from the crocodile to the launch in case the dinghy did sink, and its front and back legs were tied over the animal's back, to stop any struggling if the anaesthetic wore off. Oondabund laughed at all these precautions as the launch moved out into midstream, towing its cargo.

The tide was running out as they left, and in Buckleys Creek mud banks were already exposed. As they moved upstream to the landing, Steve watched the small bright red fiddler crabs on the mud banks, advertising their presence by waving their single freakish, enlarged claw. A single great-billed heron was the only other animal he saw, and it flew ahead of the procession, only to land and fly again as the launch drew nearer. Steve saw the net when they approached the landing, still stretched from one side of the creek to the other, and with at least two fish near the surface, both dead and bloated. He pointed it out to the skipper.

When the launch pushed into the bank, Steve, Mac and Oondabund set about manoeuvring the dinghy and crocodile into shore, and, having checked that the eye reflex was still negative, they untied the ropes that held it to the launch. With the three of them ashore, they pulled the dinghy free of the crocodile, then dragged the head as far out of the water as they could before resecuring the ropes to surrounding mangroves.

Up on the landing they saw the filleted carcasses that Besser and Noakes had left, and the neatly stacked piles of barramundi fillets, now swarming with ants and flies. Oondabund examined the tracks leading to the water, and having noticed the blood, he pointed it out to Steve. There had been two men, and he could clearly discern where the uninjured one had helped the other into the truck.

Using the dinghy, they rowed to the other side of the creek, where Mac had to follow the net's float line beneath the surface to find where it was tied to the tree before the tide came up. After trying in vain to untie the much-tightened knot, he cut the rope, letting the net drift downstream until held by the rope on the other side where Numunwari lay.

They then rowed to the drifting free end and began to bundle the net into the dinghy. It was an unpleasant task, as the net contained fifty-four dead barramundi, all bloated and already putrid. Of the three live barramundi in the net, Oondabund kept the biggest for himself, releasing the two others.

Steve felt no sympathy for Besser, and contemplated using the net and dead fish for evidence in a poaching charge; however, it was hopeless, and he knew it. He could imagine Besser's answer in court. 'Net? There was no net when we were there. Must have been some poachers who arrived after we'd left.' He had heard the same answer so many times before.

Oondabund chose to stay with Numunwari again, freeing Steve and Mac to return to Darwin in the launch and organise the truck. Steve left two extra darts with him, just in case the eye reflex returned, and bade him farewell. As the launch pulled away, there was a small fire on the bank, a prelude to the bed of coals in which Oondabund would cook his barramundi.

On the way back, the skipper radioed the message that the crocodile had been killed, and that they were returning.

Radio and television programmes were immediately interrupted with the news; its effect was electrifying. Everyone in the city seemed to be talking about it. The telephone lines to the south were jammed as reporters and agents competed to get the news to their southern contacts. On the jetty, where hundreds of people had congregated, the news was received with a loud cheer.

In hospital, John Besser stared blankly at the nurse who hoped the news would cheer him.

Anne Wilson cried, alone in the kitchen. It was over, and Mac was safe. Her son instantly became the hero of the kindergarten class.

At the police station most men babbled to one another with relief that the crocodile had been finally killed, but only a few showed real happiness or elation; the memory of how John Wiley had disappeared was still very fresh.

By the time the launch berthed, the crowd had swollen to some six hundred cheering spectators, including at least fifty reporters. Four television cameras were in the forefront again, anxious to record every movement and word that those on the launch could be goaded into offering.

On the launch itself, it had been agreed that Barrett would handle the newsmen and publicity, while Steve and Mac made their way as soon as possible to where the low loader was parked. Delays would increase the possibility of someone arriving at the Buckleys Creek landing, and the consequences of that would be disastrous. At Mac's suggestion, he, Barrett and the skipper agreed not to tell their wives the truth about Numunwari. Barrett again mumbled his displeasure at the deception, but fully realised the consequences of exposure. His wife was known as a gossip, and the magnitude of this deception would just be too much of a temptation. Mac knew he would tell Anne the complete story as soon as they were alone. She did not gossip and would agree that he had made the right decisions—she usually did.

As soon as they climbed the steps, the reporters flocked towards Barrett who moved to the right, leaving Steve and Mac to jostle through the crowd, where they received an occasional pat on the back, and a 'Good job, mate' from well-wishers. When nearly through the crowd, Mac saw Anne standing by the Toyota almost fifty metres back. He hurriedly pushed through the remaining people, and when he reached her, they fell into each other's arms. Tears trickled down their cheeks as they hugged tightly in silence. Suddenly realising Mac was not alone, Anne broke the embrace and looked up.

'I thought you'd never stop,' said Steve, from behind. 'Oondabund's okay, too; he's still upriver.'

As they drove to the Wildlife Section office, Mac told Anne what had happened during the night. She diplomatically refrained from comment when she learned, to her horror, that the crocodile was still alive, and was clearly upset when told that they had to pick up the truck immediately and drive back out of town. Mac did not tell her about being thrown out of the boat, nor about the crocodile's appearance behind him; he doubted that he ever would.

The Forestry low loader was parked outside the office as Mac had arranged, and while Steve briefly checked it over, making sure that the winch was functional, Mac rummaged through their store and came back with a large blue tarpaulin and some additional ropes. Within fifteen minutes of arrival, they were ready to leave once more.

Anne was not happy to see the truck move off, but knew that there was no use saying anything. She arranged for the three men to come back to the house when they had finished, knowing they would all be overtired and in need of food. She even offered to drive home and get food for them to take out now, but Mac and Steve refused, being eager to leave.

8

Mac was relieved when the truck pulled up at Buckleys Creek to see that no other vehicles were present, and that the area looked exactly as they had left it a few hours before. Steve was asleep in the cabin and he did not even wake when the truck stopped, so Mac had to shake him until his tired eyes opened. Oondabund, sitting in the shade of a mangrove, stood up and waved. High and dry on the top of the mud bank left by the falling tide, was Numunwari, half covered with the tarpaulin that had been under the fillets.

Oondabund gave the darts back to Steve. 'Him little bit wake up me give him one needle. Him sleep now.'

'Has anyone been out here?' asked Steve, pocketing the darts.

Oondabund shook his head. 'No one been come.'

Moving Numunwari to the back of the truck proved awkward. When they tried reversing the vehicle down the bank, the back wheels sank in the mud, and when they ran a cable from the snout ropes to the tow hitch and tried towing the crocodile up the bank, the only way they could get a steady pull was to ride the clutch and roar the engine. When they tried to winch the crocodile, the truck slid backwards, and it was only after they tied additional cables from the front of the vehicle to surrounding trees that Numunwari began to slide up the bank.

After the initial pull, the crocodile moved easily, sliding up the ramps and onto the loader without further trouble. Steve had worried that the force on the neck would cause damage if the body was caught and the winch kept pulling, but his worries were groundless. Once the crocodile was on the loader, they retied the ropes, and placed additional ones across the body, before covering the whole animal with bushes and branches and pulling the tarpaulin over the lot.

Before finally covering the head, Steve checked the eye but found no reflex. He stood back and examined the load with satisfaction; it did not in any way resemble a crocodile.

'You know, Mac, I'd really like to weigh that croc,' he said thoughtfully.

Mac stared at him, not sure at first whether he was being serious.

'Seriously, Mac. The dimensions of this one are as important as if it were a dinosaur.'

'Yeah, but where are we going to get scales and how the hell are we going to lift it? Remember we can't get any help.'

'What about the weighing station?'

'You've got to be joking! Those blokes check the truck over. It'd be too risky.'

Steve continued as though he had not heard Mac's reply. 'If we drove the truck in and got a total weight, we could unload the croc, then come back and get another weight. The difference would be the weight of the croc.'

'What about the inspectors?'

'They wouldn't see anything. They'd just think it was a load of brush. If anything happened to that croc and I hadn't weighed it, I'd kick myself for ever more; I'm going to take all the other measurements before we let it go in the pond.'

'Christ, Steve, I'm sure you'll be the death of me one day,' said Mac, only half joking.

The drive to Darwin took forty minutes and, before they turned onto the Stuart Highway, Mac stopped so that Steve could check Numunwari. There was no response the first time Steve touched the eyeball, but the second time there was a definite twitch, so he injected half the remaining dart full of anaesthetic before retying the tarpaulin ropes. Passing the turn-off to the research station, they drove five kilometres further, to the highway weighing station where a road train consisting of a bright red prime mover and three separate four-wheel trailers was pulling out as they came in.

An elderly man in khaki came over to Mac. 'You can go straight through, mate, you're not overloaded,' he said.

'We want a weight, mate,' replied Mac. 'Want to know how much we've got on.'

'Okay,' agreed the man, staring at Mac and noticing Steve and Oondabund for the first time. 'Move her up.'

Mac drove the truck up on to the weighbridge and after the weight was recorded, drove a little further to get the back wheels on. After a short delay the man came up to the cabin with a pink slip of paper.

'Here it is, mate. As I said, you've got no problems. What's your load, anyway?'

'Special trees, mate, for Forestry. They want to know the exact weight.' Mac hoped he sounded convincing.

'Well, it's down there to a kilogram,' he replied, a questioning look on his face. 'Where'd you pick 'em up?'

Perspiration formed in droplets on Mac's forehead. 'Out near Humpty Doo, mate. We'd better get going; thanks.'

Mac drove from beneath the covered weighbridge and back onto the highway while the man stood staring at them.

'I didn't like that,' said Mac as they straightened up on the road.

'He's okay,' said Steve, smiling, 'just a bit inquisitive. I'll bet he's like that with everyone. You'd better not take to robbing banks, Mac; you couldn't tell a good lie if your life depended on it.'

Mac smiled, knowing that what Steve had said was true. He was always self-conscious when he had to say anything but the truth, and it had been the reason he had failed so miserably in office politics. Still, he hoped the man at the weighing station hadn't noticed anything unusual.

When they arrived at the research station, Mac stopped the truck by the small office next to the house, while Steve ran inside to get the key to the breeding pen and the small kit containing the measuring tape, calipers and record book. When he came out, he walked past a row of pens and opened a wire mesh gate which allowed access to a forty-hectare field, in the centre of which was a prominent group of trees and a single fenced enclosure—the breeding pen.

Mac drove through the gate and along the red dirt track, crossing a treeless grassy area and climbing the gentle slope to the pen.

The pen itself was almost a quarter hectare in area, enclosed by a two-metre heavy mesh fence with four strands of barbed wire to deter inquisitive children from climbing in. Although basically square, the corners of the fence were rounded so that if crocodiles followed it around, they would not find themselves face to face with a wire mesh corner; if this happened, they would try and push their way through, damaging their snouts and teeth. The pond accounted for almost half the area enclosed, and was about five metres deep in the middle.

A variety of shrubs had been planted on the inside of the fence so that the pen could be approached without disturbing the crocodiles, but there were only two tall trees, both gums, within this perimeter. On the outside, a ladder against the fence led to a two-metre square wooden observation hut, from which in turn an elevated walkway extended out over the pond. Steve realised that the set-up was even more suited to their requirements than he had anticipated.

While Mac turned the truck around, Steve unlocked the steel gate which formed the only direct access, other than jumping from the walkway, and after three attempts, the truck was reversed in, bringing Numunwari to his new home. The ramps down, Steve tied the ropes from the crocodile's snout to the two gums, and as Mac slowly drove forward, Numunwari twisted, then slid to the ground. After retesting the eye reflex, they removed the many ropes, cords and cables before Steve opened the measuring kit.

Oondabund and Mac pulled the tail out straight and Steve made a mark on the ground level with its tip. They then straightened the head and Steve made a second mark level with the tip of the snout, and, using the tape measure, he measured the distance between the two marks.

'Seven hundred and seventy-one centimetres, Mac,' he called out before turning the tape over. 'That's twenty-five foot three and a half inches.'

Mac wrote the measurement down in the book. 'What's the biggest you've had before, Steve?'

'Fifteen feet, the one from the Daly. But the one those poachers killed a few years back was twenty-one feet.'

'What's the biggest known?'

'This one's the biggest that's well documented. There's talk of a big one shot in the Gulf in the fifties. Supposed to have been twenty-eight feet. I believe it, but there are no photographs or accurate measurements.'

Steve continued with the measurements of Numunwari, and the immensity of the animal took written form: The head was one hundred and six centimetres long, fifty centimetres high and sixty-six centimetres wide at the back of the jaws. The girth was over three metres and they had trouble measuring it until Oondabund suggested pulling a piece of cord under the animal and after tying a knot where the two ends met, pulling it out and laying it against the tape. It worked well.

Steve counted the number of rows of scales along its back, and examined the whole of the body for injuries and scars. Apart from the deep axe wound on the head, and a graze mark between the eyes, there was a cut on the side of the tail, which Steve guessed was where Barrett had shot it; some broken teeth, probably from the trawler fence; and only one old scar, which showed up as an irregularity in the scales on the side of the body. Where the harpoons had buried in, there were small puncture marks; Steve couldn't remember having removed them.

'Did you take the harpoons out?'

'Me take him out,' replied Oondabund smiling.

'What with?' asked Steve, knowing that it was almost always necessary to slit the skin to free the barbs.

'Me find him knife,' said Oondabund, pulling a long-bladed filleting knife from beneath his shirt. 'Him belong men with net. Proper good one.'

The measuring completed, Steve took a few photographs with a miniature camera from the kit, knowing full well he would have to develop the negative and print the photographs himself, but that didn't matter; there had to be a record.

Fifteen minutes after they had finished, the eye reflex returned, but although they waited a further twenty minutes, the crocodile made no obvious movement. Oondabund walked to the end of the tail and pushed down on the tip with his foot, eliciting a wave of quivering throughout the body; a sure sign it was coming out of the anaesthetic. It was almost an hour later that the great head rose, and with two powerful kicks, the crocodile slid down the bank and disappeared with a swirl beneath the floating vegetation.

'It's going to be some time before we see him like that again,' said Steve. 'He'll stay under now and just slip his snout up for a quick breath every now and again. Poor bastard, he'll be spooky for months.'

'Poor bastard be buggered,' replied Mac. 'It strikes me he's bloody lucky to be alive.'

'Guess you're right,' mused Steve. 'Let's get going anyway, it's almost five o'clock.'

At the weighing station, the man was surprised to see the low loader pull in again, and further surprised to see Steve driving. Steve explained briefly that they had a second load, and needed another weight, the pile of wilted leaves and branches looking insignificant on the long tray. Still, the man weighed it, filled in the pink form and stood scratching his head as the truck moved off, with Mac subtracting the second weight from the first. 'Your croc weighs two point eight tonnes, Steve; minus a bit for the branches drying.'

After parking the truck outside the Wildlife Section office, the three of them drove to Mac's house, where Anne had prepared a hearty evening meal. Throughout the day reporters had been either phoning or coming to the door trying to find Steve, Mac or Oondabund, and she had told them the same story, 'They're asleep and won't be answering questions until morning.' When three of the reporters refused to leave, she had phoned the police who moved them along. Barrett had telephoned twice to find out whether or not Mac and Steve had returned, but had not given her any information; just asked that Mac contact him as soon as possible.

When Mac phoned, Barrett told him that he had spent the afternoon in interviews with the media, and that he felt confident that no one suspected anything was other than what was being told to them. It seemed that the reporters were primarily interested in interviewing Steve. Their two most common questions were: Could it happen again? How big was the crocodile? Mac told Barrett what their movements had been, confirming that their charge was safely in its new home. After arranging a meeting for ten o'clock in the morning, they terminated the conversation, but only after Barrett relayed personal congratulations from the Minister, who unfortunately would not be able to get to Darwin.

After finishing what turned out to be an enormous meal, Mac and Steve each went to bed and were asleep within seconds of lying down. Oondabund, seemingly untroubled by lack of sleep, perched himself in front of the television, content to watch whatever was on. Anne spent a good portion of the evening answering the telephone, before in desperation leaving it off the hook, something she had never done in the past.

The seven o'clock television news was almost solely concerned with Numunwari. Barrett was interviewed at the jetty and later at his office, and was extremely convincing when he spoke of the way in which the crocodile had been killed, although he did point out that he had not actually been there himself. Again Anne found herself wondering just how many times he had lied so plausibly in public. She was pleased and proud to hear him single out Mac, Steve and

Oondabund as the people directly responsible for getting the crocodile, and those deserving of congratulations.

The film clip of Constable Wiley's funeral was depressing, and brought home to her the real danger associated with the crocodile, feelings that were amplified by the short interview with Bluey Noakes, who gave an imaginary but horrific version of how John Besser had lost his arm. The particular segment of the news was terminated with an interview with two local crocodile shooters, both of whom emphasised the menace crocodiles posed to the people of the Northern Territory, and both of whom seemed to be smugly saying, 'Well you were told—it had to happen sometime.'

The current affairs programme following the news started with an apology that Steve, Mac and Oondabund could not be present, but they were completely exhausted after the hunt and were recuperating, but it was hoped that they would be available the following day. The interviews with Barrett, Noakes and the crocodile shooters were repeated, and there were a number of additional interviews with various officials, dignitaries and local residents. The concensus of opinion was that *something* had to be done about crocodiles, though nothing specific was mentioned.

That the crocodile attacks were a major Australian and world news item was amply demonstrated from a variety of newspaper headline stories pictured. There seemed little doubt that next to Cyclone Tracy, which had nearly wiped Darwin out on Christmas Eve, 1974, and the uranium mining controversy, which had raged for years, the crocodile that had terrorised the city was one of the biggest stories to come out of the north for years. The crocodile attacks seemed to have appealed to the newsmen, who played on people's basic fear of crocodiles to the limit.

The next two days proved to be two of the most trying that either Steve or Mac could remember. After the meeting with Barrett, they went from interview to interview. Steve gave a factual account of the capture, except that he said they had shot the crocodile. He tried to answer all the interviewers' questions honestly and cordially, even though they were often framed to make crocodile protection seem the desire of madmen.

'You mean after four people have been killed, there's still reason to keep crocodiles protected? How much does a long-term commercial gain have to be worth to balance the lives of four people?

But, Mr Harris, most of the older generation Territorians say there's more crocodiles around now than there have ever been. Wouldn't it be a sensible thing to clear out the crocodiles within an eight-kilometre radius of Darwin? Who *is* responsible when a protected animal attacks an innocent citizen? Do you think the public should have some say in what happens to the crocodiles?' Throughout the interviews, Mac was reluctant to talk about just how they had killed the crocodile, though he did become involved when the issues of policy were discussed. Like Steve, however, he was relieved when each interview drew to a close.

Oondabund went to the interviews on the first day, when the cameramen photographed his face from every conceivable angle, but after realising his broken English was not what their viewers and readers were used to, they let it be known that he was not required further. This pleased him, because he preferred watching television to appearing on it, and it was a relief to Steve and Mac, who were never quite sure if Oondabund fully appreciated the consequences if anyone found out that Numunwari was still alive. Certainly he gave Steve a look of scorn when he began relating the details of how they had shot and killed his beloved crocodile, even though they had discussed the deception in detail beforehand.

Steve managed to get to the breeding pen once each day, but he did not see Numunwari, nor was there any indication that the serene pond, picturesque in its stillness, could mean instant death to anyone who approached the water's edge. Large numbers of cars began arriving to see the captive crocodiles in the pens near the house, so Mac stationed an Inspector there to redirect them to the local zoo.

On the night of the third day after the capture, Oondabund looked miserable, and after dining, Steve walked out into the back garden with him.

'Me time go home now,' he replied to Steve's question, while staring blankly at the ground.

'Well, that's nothing to worry about, there's a plane twice a week.'

'Me know that,' he replied indignantly, looking up. Steve waited to see whether he was going to continue, but he didn't.

'Is it money? I haven't organised any pay for you yet.'

'Me no worry for money, for Numunwari.' He looked into Steve's eyes. 'Who been going look after him that crocodile?'

'Well, I guess I am,' replied Steve hesitantly.

'No good that white man look after him. Aborigine man him need. Him special business one, that Numunwari.' Again Steve waited, hoping Oondabund would continue, but when he spoke, his voice was quiet, and his words slow. 'What about me come live Darwin look after him? Please?'

This possibility had not occurred to Steve, but he was not going to answer in haste. Having Oondabund in Darwin where he could see him often would be truly enjoyable, because they were close friends, but there was his family. If Oondabund came to Darwin he would have to live in the reserve, and what would that hold for his wife and children, and even himself? The answer was simple—they would lose all the dignity they had. As the children grew they would learn to drown their frustrations in alcohol, like most others who had done what Oondabund was suggesting. Even the proud man himself would not be able to resist the call of temporary oblivion.

'What about your family, Oondabund? What would happen to them when they were living in the reserve?'

'Them not stay reserve, them camp your place.'

This possibility certainly had not been considered before. Steve tried to imagine the family all living together in the house at the research station. It was probably big enough, a standard Government dwelling of three bedrooms, a kitchen, lounge room and laundry, but could it work? They led basically different lives, with different priorities based on vastly different cultures; relatives, either distant or close, would be coming around continually, with their cultural right to food and shelter, whether drunk or sober. Oondabund sensed Steve's doubts.

'Me maybe build little house next your one?' he asked hopefully.

'What about grog, Oondabund? It's a real problem and you know it better than I do. How the hell are you going to cope with that?'

'Me buy little bit grog, but me always bring 'im your camp. We drink together like long time you in Maningrida. You look after him for me your camp.'

Almost a minute elapsed before Steve spoke again. 'All right. We can all stay at my house first and see how it works out, but if it doesn't, then that's it. There's three conditions: you're not to go bringing drunks home; you've got to keep visitors to really close relatives; and your wife's got to keep the bloody place clean. How's that?'

Oondabund's face, alight in a broad smile, conveyed his answer as he gently held Steve's arm: 'Me go Maningrida next plane.'

Over the next two weeks, interest in Numunwari waned rapidly, and, surprisingly, saltwater crocodiles remained protected, though procedures for dealing with 'rogue' animals were formalised and given a high emergency priority. Oondabund went back to Maningrida, and returned with his family a week later. Steve was in the office when an airport official rang.

'There's a team of them here, and they asked me to ring you. Do you know 'em?'

'I've been expecting them, have they got much gear?'

'Not much, few cases and looks like a bundle of spears.'

'Well, if you tell them to hang on, I'll get down there in a few minutes. Thanks for ringing, mate.'

Steve felt excited as he drove through the outskirts to the airport. Since making the decision that Oondabund and his family could share the house with him, he had longed for their arrival, and had decided that he would make sure the arrangement proved satisfactory to them all. When he reached the airport and parked, he saw one of the children run inside the terminal with the news of his arrival. They were all standing by the time he reached them, each with a variety of cases, bags and blankets, the tightly wrapped bundle of spears at their feet.

'How are you?' Steve asked, shaking the dark hand.

'How that Numunwari?' Oondabund whispered, smiling. 'Him been good feller?'

Steve raised a finger to his lips. 'Shh . . . he's okay. Now, let's get your gear out to the Toyota.'

'Hello, Steve,' came a voice from behind.

Steve turned to see a smiling Nancy looking at him, carrying her wide-eyed baby daughter.

'What are you doing in here?'

'I come with Oondabund to our new house.'

'What about your husband?'

She smiled broadly. 'I'll tell you that story later.' Steve looked from her to Oondabund, who was laughing quietly to himself. He squeezed Steve's arm firmly before looking down at the ground; Steve's face flushed.

When they arrived at the house and began unloading the cases, Steve had a good look at the spears. There were two fish spears, which each had four thin iron prongs on the end, and five shovel-nosed spears, each about four metres long. On the end of each, bound with native string and the wax from wild bees' nests, was a thin blade of steel, some thirty centimetres long and five centimetres wide.

'What'd you bring all them for?'

'Hunting.'

'There's not much left to hunt round here, old man.'

'We go bush maybe some day. Get buffalo, wallaby.'

As Oondabund picked up the bundle, Steve thought about the shovel-nosed spears. In the past, they had been the single weapon with which the Arnhem Land Aboriginals protected themselves against the whites, and even as late as the 1940s some areas had remained basically unexplored because of the fear of these spears. Today most Aboriginals in Arnhem Land kept them, but they were only ever seen when words ceased to solve an argument. They were a frightening weapon in the hands of an Aboriginal, and had been responsible for terrible injuries to both man and beast. At one time there had been talk of banning them, which would only have resulted in them being kept hidden; and after all, they had been developed from the scrap iron and rubbish left by the early settlers and Macassan fishermen.

The luggage carried in, Steve heated some water for tea and prepared to discuss the living arrangements. The extra people meant that accommodation in the house was going to be cramped, though the thought of Nancy living under the same roof excited him more than he would ever have expected.

'What's been happening out at Maningrida?' asked Steve, hopeful of hearing the story about Nancy's husband.

'My husband's finished,' replied Nancy, smiling.

'How?'

'Something went wrong in his head. He got dizzy and kept falling over, then he went to sleep. Him never wake up.'

'This Nancy,' added Oondabund, 'she no promised anyone now; she free girl.'

Steve felt his embarrassment showing as his desire began to burn. 'Well, we'd better work out where everyone's going to sleep.'

Although trying to change the subject, Steve realised he had just brought it to a head. He continued quickly, 'For now, I'd say you and your wife take the first bedroom, Nancy the second, and the kids can go wherever they want. I'll go and get some more beds from town.' Everyone seemed to be smiling when Steve finished talking; even the children were looking up at him.

'Good one,' said Oondabund, standing.

'You fix your gear and I'll show you around the place.'

Most of the afternoon was spent showing Nancy and her mother how everything worked and the way in which Steve, as a bachelor, had kept his house organised. Nancy had participated in a home management course at school, and though she had been in the bush for a number of years since, she quickly remembered how to operate a white man's kitchen.

Steve and Oondabund walked up to the breeding pen and climbed into the observation hut; they waited an hour, but Numunwari failed to surface. When Steve decided to go back to the house, Oondabund remained, and as Steve walked down the hill, Oondabund started singing.

Steve drove into town and bought two extra beds, and when he returned, just after dusk, Oondabund ran in excitedly.

'Him come up.'

'What did?'

'That Numunwari, him come up, him look Oondabund and say "Hello"; then him go under again. Proper good one, that Numunwari.'

'That's terrific. I haven't seen him since we put him in there.'

'Me take him tucker in morning time.'

'He won't eat yet, will he?'

'Him eat. You see.'

Steve stared at Oondabund. 'It's bloody good to have you in here. Seeing it's your first night I'm going to get a few cans of beer; we'll celebrate.'

Oondabund dug into his pocket and produced a roll of well-worn twenty-dollar notes, which at a rough guess, Steve estimated must total six hundred dollars.

'Where the hell did you get all that?'

'That Nancy, she play card. Proper lucky one. I buy beer.'

'You hang on to your money,' said Steve. 'I'll get the grog.'

At the hotel Steve bought a carton of beer, and on the way home pulled into a take-away food bar and got a large carton of chicken. When he arrived home, everyone was watching television except Nancy, who was by the kitchen door.

'What you want for dinner?'

Steve smiled as he passed the carton to her. 'I've brought some home.'

Since his departure she had showered and her wet black hair clung tightly to her brown face. Her skin shone—she was truly beautiful.

Oondabund with his wife and children ate by the television set, while Steve and Nancy stayed at the kitchen table. Everyone apart from the children drank three or four cans of beer each; enough to take the edge off Steve's inhibitions.

'What did Oondabund mean when he said you were a free woman?'

'You know what he mean,' she replied shyly. 'He's not worried for me, that Oondabund. Before he was, because I was promised, but not now.'

Steve reached for a fresh can of beer, but her slender fingers were on it before him. 'You don't want more beer. Take me for walk.'

Steve wanted to say something, anything, but his mouth didn't respond. His eyes flashed towards the lounge room and back to Nancy.

'Him not worry now. He wants you and me to be together. I'm a free girl.'

Oondabund was suddenly beside Steve.

'She free girl, that Nancy, and she worry for you all long time. When you gone I move her suitcase your room.' He picked up a can of beer and walked back to the television. Steve stood, her slender hand in his.

Life for Steve changed rather dramatically from that night on. His new-found love rekindled old fires that had burnt strongly when he was married; before he came to the Territory. Although he wondered whether Susan would have understood his desire for Nancy, an Aboriginal woman, he knew she would have wanted him to be happy. Her last words before they took her away for the emergency operation to stem internal bleeding had been, 'If anything happens, Steve, find someone else. Don't become one of those sour old bachelors trying to bring up a child on your own.' She never knew that their only son was already dead, and she failed to recover consciousness after the operation.

Steve had lived on his own for over five years, having found no one with whom he wanted to be all the time, until Nancy. Overnight his dwelling had become a home, there were children present, and she was there.

Most nights they spent talking. One evening, Oondabund told Steve about the burial rites, Nancy translating as he talked in his own language. Halfway through, Oondabund got up, walked into the bedroom, and came back with a suitcase, which contained human bones; the polished bones of his father. Beside the sightless white skull was a woven grass bag painted with ochres and blotched with the down feathers of what Steve thought must have been wild geese.

Nancy explained that this was her father's dillybag, which contained a variety of items, all considered sacred; protruding from the end were brightly-coloured parrot feathers, woven into some type of belt or band. When they were alone, Oondabund told Steve that the piece of skin cut from his penis, when he was circumcised at the age of twelve, was inside, too.

The dillybag was Oondabund's most important link with his people, and it was only worn on truly sacred occasions, hanging across his chest from bush string cords around his neck. Nancy spoke of how unscrupulous whites had somehow managed to separate dillybags from their rightful owners and when the dillybags ended up in museums, their original owners remained ostracised and in continual disgrace. Steve was not surprised that Oondabund's suitcase remained locked and beneath his bed, but felt privileged to have been shown its contents.

Mac managed to organise a tracker's salary for Oondabund, which paid $130 per week, and was a welcome addition to Steve's pay packet as far as household expenses were concerned. Oondabund was paid to look after the few crocodiles in the pens, and, of course, Numunwari.

Each morning he would walk up the slope to the breeding pen, climb the ladder and walk through the observation hut to the walkway, where he sat cross-legged on the end and sang to the water below. Occasionally the huge head would surface for a moment, but usually the only sign of Numunwari was the movement of floating surface vegetation as the huge tail moved beneath the surface.

Oondabund always took food with him, usually a fish or small shark, and after slapping the water with a fish spear, he lowered the morsel on a piece of cord so that it hung just above the surface of the water; but Numunwari refused to go near it.

An unexpected development was the steady flow of very old Aboriginals from Maningrida and other Arnhem Land settlements who came into Darwin to see Numunwari.

When the first group arrived, Steve was horrified. Oondabund had promised not to tell anyone that Numunwari was alive, yet it seemed that everyone in Arnhem Land knew. It soon became apparent, however, that the existence of Numunwari was still a very well-kept secret, and only the very old men who had strong religious and cultural ties with the animal knew about it. For most of them, who were no longer able to walk up into the stone country, it was their last chance to see the great animal before they died. Exactly why they should want to see Numunwari before dying remained a mystery to Steve, and although he asked both Oondabund and Nancy about it, the only answer he could get was that they 'love him that crocodile'. Steve did not pursue the matter, though he did find himself wondering what the reaction of white Christians would be if they heard that Jesus Christ was in an enclosure at Maningrida, but that He would be killed if the authorities found out.

The old men usually only stayed a day, arriving and returning by charter flight. At night, they sat around the fire, talking and singing; the same song over and over, the word 'Numunwari' being called out into the night.

In the morning they all went up the hill with Oondabund and sat patiently waiting for the head to break through the weeds, and once this happened, Nancy organised a taxi to take them back to the airport.

By the end of the fourth week, virtually nobody was interested in crocodiles except for people in Wildlife Section and the old Aboriginals. Oondabund achieved remarkable success with Numunwari, who would come up beneath the overhead walkway whenever he splashed, rising out of the water and taking food now lowered on the fish spear. Steve was surprised he had quietened so quickly, having predicted that it would be at least three months before the crocodile fed.

It was during the fifth week that Numunwari first ventured out of the water and lay on the red earthen bank in the sun, appearing to take no notice of Oondabund, who could walk up and down on the walkway while Numunwari lay beneath. However, a splash in the water, with either fish spear or stick, and the crocodile would slide back in and come up beneath the walkway for its food.

Mac was delighted when Steve told him of the progress; having Oondabund on site relieved many of their worries. He either heard or saw anyone who came near the house, and there was no way people could get to the breeding pen without his knowing. In addition, with the crocodile so quiet, even Mac and Steve could occasionally sit and observe him, something they would not have thought possible. To watch Numunwari, lying unafraid in the sun, was an awe-inspiring experience. It was easy to understand how Numunwari had achieved such reverence in Aboriginal culture.

The sixth week saw a change in weather. The nights became relatively cold and the days windy. Numunwari stopped feeding and spent most of the daylight hours on the bank, trying to absorb what heat he could from the little sun that penetrated the high cloud.

9

No one in Darwin was awaiting the arrival of the thin, sallow-faced individual who walked among a group of others from a recently-landed jet. His acquaintances down south knew him to be a professional opportunist in the guise of a journalist, prepared to do anything if the money was right. His arrival in Darwin was partly the result of negotiations with two leading national magazines. One wanted an article on the anti-uranium movement in Darwin itself; the city was the closest centre to the controversial and fabulously extensive Alligator Rivers uranium deposits—surveyed and confirmed, but as yet unmined. The other magazine wanted a series of articles on crocodiles. These were intended to set forth the arguments for and against crocodile protection, and were a direct result of the interest created by the attacks. At this time, neither magazine realised that two contracts had been let; this was the way that the journalist, David Ryan, usually tried to plan his jobs, as he was able to claim double expenses for travel and accommodation, and get two straight fees.

Ryan was no stranger to Darwin, having been one of the first outside reporters to get into the city after Cyclone Tracy struck. He had been in Brisbane when the first indications of devastation came through, and immediately chartered a light aircraft and headed north. He had landed without a permit to enter the city, but talked his way around the Civil Defence officials within minutes. Once in the streets his camera and notebook recorded the disaster quickly, and he had taken off for Sydney within hours—the expedition had returned a handsome profit.

On his present trip, the two contracts were what Ryan considered his bread and butter, the basic salary. There were second strings to his bow with both assignments. He had privately negotiated with a multi-national uranium mining consortium to supply details of the individuals involved with the recent upsurge in the anti-uranium movement in Darwin; the money for that was worth more to him than both the legitimate contracts. Similarly, his enquiries in Sydney about the crocodile articles had placed him in touch with the tannery that had been the major exporter of Australian crocodile hides before protection. There were very strong indications that the Singapore-based principals of the tannery would be prepared to reward him handsomely if his articles concluded with the recommendation that the crocodile hide industry should once again be started—that protection was no longer required.

In addition, Ryan was always on the lookout for additional sources of finance. He anticipated finding further stories in the northern Australian city, which he could either follow up himself or, for a price, give to others. At this stage he didn't know what they would be, but he would find something—he always did.

'I'd like to hire a car,' he said at the hire car counter within the terminal. 'What do you have available?'

'There's a Ford Cortina outside, sir, it's fuelled and ready to go,' the uniformed girl replied.

'I'll take it.' Ryan placed his briefcase at his feet, in preparation for filling out the multitude of forms safeguarding the company against any conceivable responsibility. 'And could you tell me the best motel in Darwin?'

It took Ryan ten minutes to drive to the new multi-storeyed motel erected on the edge of Darwin Harbour. After a short exchange at the reception, he took the lift to the sixth floor, and in his room, unpacked a portable electric typewriter and a small tape recorder. Pushing the button on the recorder's side, he counted, 'One, two, three . . . ten', before rewinding and playing it back. Satisfied, he placed it on the imitation antique table next to the typewriter and searched in vain for a telephone directory. Apart from Gideon's Bible, and a neat sachet of writing paper and tourist information, the room was devoid of the written word; he picked up the phone.

'Reception,' came the answer.

'I don't seem to have a telephone directory in my room.'

'There are none in any rooms, sir, who are you trying to call? I'll look it up.'

'I need to make a lot of calls. Could I have a book?'

'Well, it's against regulations, but if you return it to me personally, I'll lend you one.'

'Thank you. Could you send someone up with it?'

'There's no room service, sir.'

'I'll be down for it,' he replied, banging down the phone. At this time, Ryan was not sure just whom he really wanted to phone, but when he returned with the directory, he sat on the bed and began flicking through it. Within fifteen minutes, he had underlined four numbers.

The first two calls were to the Darwin newspaper offices, where Ryan arranged to talk with the reporters who covered both the uranium issue and the crocodile attacks. He also enquired about access to the files of clippings, which formed a good starting point for any story, and arranged to visit both offices during the afternoon.

When he called Wildlife Division, the telephonist connected the call through to Mac.

'My name's Ryan, David Ryan. I've just arrived from Sydney to do a series of articles on crocodiles and was wondering if you people could help me.'

After telling Ryan to hold the line, Mac contacted Steve at the research station. 'Got a reporter for you, Steve. He wants information on crocs for a series of articles down south.'

'Okay,' agreed Steve resignedly, feeling he had spoken to enough reporters over the past few weeks to last him a lifetime. 'What's his name?'

'David Ryan. He's from Sydney, but that's all I really know.'

'Never heard of him,' said Steve. 'Can you get him to come out here in the morning, say 8.30?'

Mac confirmed the time with Ryan, who thanked him and hung up.

The next phone call was to police headquarters. Here he contacted the public relations officer, and after a short delay was able to explain his interest in both the uranium issue and the crocodile attacks. An interview was organised for the next afternoon.

Ryan spent the afternoon discussing both issues with local Darwin reporters, and made a start on the extensive clipping files in both offices. By late afternoon, he was very satisfied with his progress, and returned to the motel. Here he put his notes in order, showered, and was the first person to be seated when the doors of the motel's restaurant were opened. After a modest meal, he walked out of the air-conditioning into Darwin's warm night air, and started towards the centre of the city, looking for suitable hotels.

Ryan had learnt many times in the past that hotels were often valuable sources of information, because people were usually far more relaxed and unguarded after drinking for an hour or two. There was always a problem separating truth from fantasy, but with the type of stories he wrote, the distinction was not critical. He disliked drinking in crowded public bars, preferring quiet secluded clubs where the noise level was low, and the lights were tastefully dimmed. Unfortunately, such places were not conducive to meeting strangers, the people who often had the information he wanted.

The first hotel he approached was by the waterfront, and the centre of activity was a large bar in which a three-man band was blaring out music, to the apparent delight of some two hundred people, mostly seated in fours and fives around individual tables. Ryan moved over to the bar, and within minutes was talking with three men from a prawn trawler. All were well-dressed in anticipation of a last night out before heading back to the prawn fishing grounds off the north coast of Melville Island. As they talked, one of the men anxiously kept scrutinising his watch, though none mentioned why, or what he was awaiting.

The trawler men knew Collins well, and were able to tell Ryan quite a bit about the man whose leg Numunwari had almost torn off. One of the men also told him about how the crocodiles had appeared in Darwin Harbour after the cyclone, and how they were supposed to have taken a number of the seamen who had been washed overboard or cast into the water when their boats sank. Ryan noted the information, deciding to clarify its validity with Steve Harris during the interview next morning.

Around 8.30 pm, when Ryan was preparing to move on to another hotel, the trawler men were joined by a group of nurses, equally intent on a good night out. They were supposed to have arrived an hour earlier, and excused their delay by blaming the driver of a bus —a bus which had returned from the Ranger uranium site, where they had all been involved with the first anti-uranium protest for nearly five months. Much to the consternation of the trawler men, who were no longer interested in discussing anything with Ryan, the girls were eager to tell him all about the protest, and how they had almost taken over the administrative office. Ryan made a note of their names, and procured a phone number where they could be contacted, before finally making moves to leave, much to the pleasure of the trawler men. The girls had had a lot to tell him, and he felt sure that they would accept an invitation to dine with him at the motel's restaurant, after the trawler had sailed.

The centre of town was almost deserted when Ryan walked through it, the only people in sight being four girls outside the battery of public telephones at the post office. The quietness was a welcome relief after the almost painfully loud music at the hotel he had just left.

When Ryan saw the Newcomer Inn, he guessed its character immediately—there was at least one hotel like it in every town. The clientele were almost exclusively local residents, and when a stranger walked in, all conversation would stop and the intruder would receive blank stares from everyone. Places like the Newcomer Inn were hotels that thrived on a small number of regulars, who could be expected to arrive every night, and Ryan often called them 'Christian' pubs, because Christian names, never surnames, were used at the bar.

When he walked in and approached the bar, Ryan felt the eyes following his every step. Unperturbed, he ordered a pint of beer, a drink he detested, pulled up a bar stool, and fixed his eyes on the painted photographs of local trotting horses which covered the yellow-tiled wall behind the bar.

'Where you from, mate?' asked the short rotund barman as he filled the glass.

'Sydney,' replied Ryan, without smiling or even hinting at his true desire to talk.

'What you doing up these parts?' The barman was clearly the spokesman for all in the room.

'Writing a few articles for the newspapers down south. They want to know about the anti-uranium movement—you'd reckon they'd be sick of it by now.'

'What do they want to know about it?' enquired the barman, as the people on both sides of Ryan listened.

'You know, the sorts of people involved, who's putting up the money, how effective they are, what the average person thinks about them.'

'I can tell you what sort of people they are,' said the man standing beside Ryan. 'They're bloody shits. Most of 'em are on the dole and they're stirred up by blokes like you, from down south.'

Within twenty minutes, five of the sixteen men in the room were on either side of Ryan, giving him their opinions. To a man they supported uranium mining, and violently opposed the anti-uranium demonstrators. Ryan acted as though intensely interested in their points of view, and as they talked, he began jotting down the occasional note and asking a speaker his name. Within half an hour he had the attention of all in the bar—all except two men who sat alone in one corner, drinking quietly on their own.

Four pints of beer later and about as much of the uranium issue as Ryan thought he could stand, he brought up the second topic. He did so simply, in a manner he thought suited to his audience. 'What about the crocodile that grabbed a few people a couple of weeks ago? You guys know anything about that?'

The smiles disappeared from their faces, and Ryan knew he was mining near gold. After a good half minute, during which time four of the men walked away, one of them answered him quietly, almost whispering: 'We don't talk about that much in here, mate. You see, one of our mates got grabbed by that thing. Lost his arm. That big bloke over there in the corner.'

Ryan looked across and his eyes met Besser's. The two men stared at each other for perhaps two seconds before Ryan called to the barman, 'Shout a beer for everyone,' and after placing a note on the bar crossed the room to the corner, with Besser stolidly watching each step he made.

'Sorry to hear about your arm, mate.'

'Not as fucking sorry as I was,' came the gruff reply. 'Anyway, what's it to you?'

'I'm writing a story on the crocodile attacks for a Sydney newspaper.'

'So what?' asked Besser dryly. 'How much are you prepared to pay for first-hand information? And what's your name?'

'Ryan, David Ryan. It depends on the information. Say twenty bucks?'

Besser's expression moulded into a wry smile as he caught Bluey's attention, before looking back at Ryan. 'You'd better piss off, Mr Ryan, you're wasting our time.'

'Well what do you think it's worth, then?' he replied, undaunted.

'At least a hundred, wouldn't you say, Blue?'

Ryan stared at the man before him: the face was hard and the mole made it repulsive. There was little doubt the man himself could be both cruel and vicious, his single powerful arm being sufficient to beat respect from everyone in the room.

'Okay, then, one hundred bucks.'

'In advance,' Besser snarled unrelentingly.

Ryan took fifty dollars from his pocket and laid it on the table, half covered with his hand. 'Half now, and half when we finish talking, otherwise no deal.'

'Get your beer and join us,' said Besser, picking up the money and draining the last of his glass. 'Better get one for me and Blue while you're there.'

Their discussion lasted until the bar closed at ten o'clock. Besser told him everything that had happened at Maningrida and on the fateful night he and Bluey poached fish at Buckleys Creek. Bluey was quick to add details Besser overlooked, and seemed excited by the interest Ryan devoted to him. It was exactly the type of information Ryan needed, and while they talked, he jotted down notes continually. It was easy to imagine Besser standing over the trapped crocodile with an axe, and Ryan was convinced Besser could still do it, given the opportunity, with his single arm and thick chubby hand.

'I'd have liked to kill that bloody crocodile,' he mused quietly when the discussion neared its end. 'I'd give me other bloody arm to get that head.'

'What happened to the head?'

'No one knows. The Wildlife bastards killed the croc that same night, but they lost the bloody body when they were towing it back —broke the ropes and sank. Lots of people searched for it and there must have been twenty boats cruising around waiting for it to float up, but it never did. The bloke from the Tourist Office said he'd pay five thousand bucks for the head, but no one came in with it. Anyway, I'd have paid that much for it, just to have it.'

'Did you both go out looking for it?' asked Ryan, without raising his eyes from his notebook.

'Bluey here did, but I was in hospital.' He tapped his powerful hand against his shoulder, 'getting this sewn up.'

'Well, what do you think about crocs now?'

Besser shrugged his shoulders. 'If you're a fisherman, they're just a bloody menace and you kill every one you can. But they're nothing like that big bastard; he was something different. That bastard was mean and enjoyed killing people whenever he could; a real man-eater, that one.' When he had finished, his face was twisted in a sneer, and he stared blankly at the glass in his hand. 'You know, I think of that fucking croc every day, every time I see me arm. I'd have liked to do to him what he did to me.'

Ryan waited for perhaps thirty seconds before continuing. 'I'd like to get a photograph of the pair of you together.'

'It'll cost,' replied Besser instantly, snapped from his thoughts. 'Another fifty.'

'I'll think about it, then,' Ryan replied, standing. From his wallet he took fifty dollars. 'Here's the money I owe you for now. They're closing the bar; we'd better be going.'

Besser grabbed at the money and, after counting it, pushed it into his shirt pocket; Ryan was already at the door.

Besser laughed. 'You see, Blue, mate? Never let a good opportunity pass by without making the most of it.'

Steve was surprised when the thin, well-dressed man introduced himself as David Ryan; for some reason he had imagined him to be a short, stocky man. They sat in the office talking for nearly two hours, and Steve told him everything he could about crocodiles and Numunwari, and also gave him copies of all the official reports he had written. Ryan took some notes, but had the tape recorder going throughout the interview so that details and statistics could be checked if necessary. When they finished, he had a comprehensive summary of the biology of saltwater crocodiles, and a detailed account of just how unusual the 'rogue' crocodile had been.

When they walked around the pens, Steve showed him different-sized crocodiles and an old nest with eggs. Oondabund joined them, and Ryan took photographs of him and Steve together, with the largest crocodile at the station, a three-metre male from the Daly River.

'What's that up there?' Ryan asked when the isolated pen on the hill caught his attention.

'It's a breeding pen. We've got a small female up there nesting, and don't let anyone near it to disturb her. We want to know whether or not an undisturbed female nests more successfully.'

Satisfied, Ryan asked about how Cyclone Tracy had affected the crocodiles around Darwin, and Steve told him that the reported abundance was largely a myth. Ryan made relevant notes, but had already decided that he would use the information given to him by the seamen; it was what the public would want to read. After thanking Steve profusely and agreeing to send copies of the published articles, he drove back into Darwin, leaving Steve confident that their secret was in no way threatened.

On the drive back, Ryan detoured to the Newcomer Inn and, after paying Besser another fifty dollars, he took a series of photographs of him and Bluey. It was midday when he finally sat down with the typewriter and began to draft the article on the crocodile attacks. After talking with Steve, he had decided that in addition to the 'loathsome cunning killer' which would feature in one of the series, he would prepare another complete article featuring 'a confused and ancient visitor from the past'—that slant would be perfect for the format of another southern weekly.

At 2 pm, he drove to police headquarters and sought out their public relations officer as planned. He spent until 5 pm discussing the crocodile attacks, and arranged to return the following afternoon to discuss the anti-uranium protests. Following a quick meal, he was back at the typewriter. The first two articles in the crocodile series flowed smoothly, and he knew he only needed one more interview to complete them; he wanted to contact Wiley's wife and find out how she had managed since the death of her husband. This interview alone would be a welcome article for a women's magazine, and Ryan began to feel that his speculative trip was going to be financially rewarding.

By 2 am, the first draft was complete, except for the other interview and a summary of the life cycle of crocodiles, which were on the tapes from the interview with Steve.

Next morning, Ryan phoned the nurses' quarters and arranged to take two of the three girls to dinner, he was relieved that the most vocal of the group could come, as she was also the most attractive. He then phoned a charter company and arranged a flight for the following morning. He wanted to fly over the Alligator Rivers area and photograph the controversial sites in which the proposed mining was to take place.

It was when Ryan was back at the typewriter writing about the life cycle of crocodiles that he first realised something was wrong, though he was not at all suspicious, and merely made a note to contact Steve. On the tapes, Steve had said saltwater crocodiles built a nest of grass and mud and laid about fifty eggs at the start of the wet season, and it was because of this that most nests were lost to flooding each year. The pen on the hill, the breeding pen, was supposed to have a small crocodile in it with a nest, yet the wet season was not due for another four months. The apparent contradiction did not worry Ryan, who assumed he had misinterpreted something Steve had said. Maybe the crocodile in the pen was a freshwater crocodile, because Steve had said they nested in the dry season, pointing it out when talking about the way in which one species had overcome the problem of nest flooding whereas the other had not.

Ryan spent the afternoon at police headquarters, where he discussed the recent upsurge in anti-uranium protests, and got the address of Wiley's wife and phoned her about an interview. She was hesitant, but agreed to see him during the afternoon of the next day.

Back in the motel room, Ryan began outlining the uranium article and pinpointing a number of specific questions to which he wanted answers. Around 7 pm, he showered, dressed, and went down to the restaurant in time to see both girls arrive.

His evening was as successful as the previous night with Besser and Noakes, in that he obtained masses of information on the people involved with the anti-uranium movement, their backgrounds, motivation and future plans. For his part, he feigned complete and dedicated objection to the mining of uranium in Australia and elsewhere, and made it obvious that his articles were intended to publicise this point of view. This, combined with three bottles of a good wine, spurred the girls on further, and he eventually got around to where the financial backing was coming from. As far as they knew, however, the anti-uranium movement in which they were involved depended on the participants in a demonstration funding it themselves. Around midnight, when Ryan realised the girls were simply repeating themselves, he decided to call it a night. A half-hearted attempt to further the discussion in his motel room was smilingly refused, though there was sufficient encouragement to indicate that a similar proposal would not always be treated so. He rang them a taxi, went back to his room, and for half an hour summarised what he had learned.

By seven the next morning, Ryan was in the air heading out towards the Alligator Rivers. The plane he had chartered had removable ports in the perspex window through which a camera lens could be inserted. When they reached the area, the pilot flew back and forth over the proposed mining sites, and in barely thirty minutes, Ryan was sure he had the pictures needed to accompany the article.

Ryan found the flight back into Darwin excruciatingly boring, as he neither cared for nor recognised the country below. It was only when the pilot began to follow the Stuart Highway that Ryan realised where he was, as he had driven out along it for the interview with Steve at the research station. Being the opportunist that he was, an idea flashed into Ryan's mind—an aerial photo of the research station would clearly show the layout of the pens and would look good in the article.

'Take her over that way,' he said, pointing towards the research station. 'I want to get a few photos of the crocodile pens.'

As he did every morning, Oondabund climbed the ladder and stood on the walkway above Numunwari, who lay motionless, basking on the bank in the morning sun, outstretched and relaxed; there was no food for the crocodile, because it had been windy and Numunwari refused to eat when cold. Squatting on the wooden planks, Oondabund talked loudly in his native language, for his companion, Numunwari, did not understand the white man's language, yet this was the time of day when much had to be discussed between them, as it was each morning.

Oondabund ignored the sound of the plane when he heard it, because planes flew back and forth throughout the day, but never passed over the research station. When the original site had been chosen, considerable effort had been directed into avoiding known flight paths because low-flying aircraft frightened the crocodiles, and were a threat to successful captive breeding.

When the sound of the plane increased, Oondabund ceased talking and looked up. Eight hundred metres away, and barely a hundred and sixty metres from the ground, a light aircraft was heading straight towards him, descending as it came.

'Turn her over on my side when you're above the station,' yelled Ryan, with his camera ready.

The realisation that the plane was definitely coming over the station on a path leading to the breeding pen, caused a surge of panic in Oondabund—Numunwari was exposed on the bank for all to see.

He grabbed the fish spear and drove it at the enormous restive animal below, and as the four prongs struck, the mighty crocodile exploded in confusion. The hind feet clawed into the ground as the head and tail swung and thrashed wildly, and the great mass moved towards the water. The spear shaft shattered, and amidst a spray of floating vegetation and water, the pond was reached as the plane flew overhead.

Ryan took one photo as they approached the station, and a second when they were above the pens, but was still looking through the viewfinder when they passed over the breeding pen. He saw the splash, and the wave of water spreading across the pond, and he thought he saw a tail, a huge tail with rows of jagged scales forming a crest.

'Bring her round, *quick* !' he yelled to the pilot.

Steve was in the office writing when he heard the plane come overhead, but was outside in time to see it bank and turn, and start in on its second run; he recognised the aircraft as one belonging to a charter company.

On the second run, Ryan paid particular attention to the apparent size of the three-metre crocodile near the station, and compared it with the width of the pathway through the floating vegetation in the breeding pen. There was no way they could match, and the tail he had seen was almost the size of the three-metre specimen. And there was the Aboriginal, standing on the walkway, yet no one was to go near that particular pen. There was no need for a third run, and Ryan felt the familiar tingle of excitement. He knew why people were kept away from the breeding pen, and he knew why there had been an irregularity in his information from Steve about crocodile breeding; more importantly, he knew why no one had ever found the carcass of the dead crocodile. As the plane straightened on a path to the Darwin airstrip, he was smiling broadly, having found a source of funds much greater than those to be had from his other interests.

'Mr Ryan, initial D, from Sydney,' was the reply to Steve's immediate phone call to the charter company. As he hung up, Oondabund came crashing through the door, crying loudly and talking in an unintelligible mixture of his native language and broken English. Nancy was behind him, and Steve looked to her for interpretation.

'He's sure the plane saw Numunwari. It was on the bank and he

213

threw a spear at it to chase him back into the water, but he was too late.'

'Take him into the house and look after him. I'm going down to the airport, but while I'm gone don't let anyone near the place. Ring Mac if you have to and tell him someone's seen the crocodile; he'll understand.'

Steve drove the ten kilometres in six minutes, and went straight to the charter company office. From where he parked he could see the single-engined plane, and he watched as Ryan and the pilot climbed out and walked towards the office. Not sure of exactly what to say when he confronted him, Steve knew only that the crocodile's existence had to remain secret.

While the account was being prepared, Ryan walked to the window of the office and slid the curtain apart just enough to see Steve waiting by the parked Toyota; smiling, he walked back and paid the secretary. His smile had gone when he walked from the office door.

'I'd like to talk to you,' said Steve, as he intercepted Ryan on his way to the parked Ford Cortina.

'And, Mr Harris,' Ryan replied confidently, 'I most certainly want to talk with *you*. What about coming to my motel room where we can talk undisturbed?' He stared into Steve's eyes as he spoke, leaving no question as to who held the trump cards.

'I'll follow you,' was Steve's quiet reply.

The drive from the airport into town gave Steve time to think, and he was thankful for it. Ryan had seemed reasonable when they were talking two days ago; in fact it was because he appeared so genuinely interested in crocodiles that Steve had given him all the information he could. Even now, at the airport, he had been reasonable in view of what he had seen. Steve decided to explain the whole thing to him, and just hoped Ryan would appreciate why they had done what they did. When he pulled in behind Ryan at the motel he felt confident of winning the day.

However, there was one question to which he needed an intimate answer. 'Did the pilot see anything?' he asked as they walked through the doorway.

'No,' replied Ryan, leading the way to the lift.

In his room Ryan offered Steve a chair, then poured two glasses of whisky. When he sat on the edge of the bed, he seemed calm and relaxed.

'It was purely accidental, Mr Harris. I was trying to get photographs for the uranium story I'm working on, and when we passed near your place, I thought I'd get a few photos for the croc story. It just stood out. I'm amazed no one else has seen it.'

'What are you going to do?'

'Depends,' replied Ryan quietly. 'You'd better tell me all about it; the truth this time.'

Impressed by Ryan's directness, Steve slowly unravelled the story of Numunwari, emphasising the uniqueness of the crocodile and the bond between it and Oondabund. When he neared the end, he misinterpreted Ryan's blank stare for one of sympathy. 'Well, that's it,' he concluded. 'The croc you saw was Numunwari.'

There was a momentary silence and Steve finished the whisky he was drinking and placed the glass on the table; Ryan stood.

'I don't know how you bastards can live with yourselves. You might as well be harbouring a murderer. What about Constable Wiley's wife? What about John Besser? Don't you think they've got some rights? You blokes have just taken the law into your own hands. That animal's a killer, a murderer. It should be shot.'

Steve sensed danger. He had told Ryan the whole story, complete with names and details.

'I know it seems wrong; in some ways it's wrong to me too, but we did the only thing we could—get the croc away from the water and give it to Oondabund alive as promised. What else could we do?'

'What bullshit! All you blokes did was deceive the public and lie, and that includes Rex Barrett and the Inspector; you should all be kicked out of the place. Give me one good reason why I shouldn't spread the story over every newspaper and television station in the country.'

'I can't,' said Steve after a pause, knowing there was little to be gained from arguing.

Ryan poured two more glasses of whisky, gave one to Steve, then sat on the bed again. He was deep in thought, though he never took his eyes from Steve's.

When he spoke, his voice had lost all emotional overtones; he talked casually, as though with an old friend. 'You know, Mr Harris,' he said, 'the life of a reporter isn't an easy one. The average guy'd be lucky if he got five really big stories in his lifetime. I mean big stories, like this one; the sort that makes headlines all over Australia, and in most overseas papers as well; the sort that sells millions of papers—yet the story's exclusive to one writer. It's a pretty big thing.

'I've only ever had one of those stories. It was a freak find; happened a couple of years back. I met a girl who swore she'd had affairs with two of our biggest politicians, and had been blackmailing both of them since. Not for money—she was a smart bitch; she had building projects passed, all over the city, and the developers paid her each time her two ex-lovers passed the projects. There were major disasters as a result of two of those buildings, and she only came to me because she was sure they'd try and get rid of her. She told me the story and left the country, but before she went she signed statements about the whole business.' He paused and looked at Steve before continuing.

'That story would've blown the political and building scenes right open.'

'Would have?' questioned Steve.

'It was never printed, Mr Harris. Never even offered for sale.'

Steve could see the path Ryan was following, and his muscles tensed. Now he knew what he was up against.

'How much did they pay you, Ryan?' he managed to get out between clenched teeth.

'Pay, Mr Harris? How much are they *paying*, I think you mean.'

'Yeah, all right, how much?' Steve was talking loudly and Ryan seemed to be enjoying his game.

'That's not really relevant, is it? What I want to know is, what's it worth to keep quiet about the crocodile? There's you, Barrett, the Inspector and Wilson. I'd say about ten thousand flat.'

'What if we can't pay?'

'I'm a ruthless man, Mr Harris. If you can't pay, I sell the story. I've got photographs of the crocodile and they're right beside that old blackfeller for scale.'

'What do you think it'll do to that old man? You know what the crocodile means to him.'

'I couldn't give a damn about the old bastard. As far as I'm concerned, he and his mates are like crocodiles—the country'd be better without them. Let's not play games, Harris. I'm interested in one person, me. I've made you an offer and you've got till ten o'clock tonight to come up with an answer. Ten thousand dollars or the story's all over the country. Think yourself lucky I'm even talking to you about it.'

There was no change in the expression on Steve's face as he stood. Ryan assumed he was seeing himself to the door, and turned to look out of the window. The view was superb; the only asset he considered the motel had. Once Steve left, he would ring Sydney and prepare them for the story of the year. Ten thousand dollars or not, it was going to cover the front page.

Instinct made him turn. Steve was before him, wild, animal wild. Ryan tried to shout but the first punch crashed into his chest driving out his breath, and as he lay on the floor, gasping, unable to move, Steve waited above.

'Suppose you think you're a pretty good photographer, do you?' said Steve after a minute, and as he picked up the the $2,000 German single-lens reflex camera.

Ryan didn't answer.

Unlatching the back of the camera, Steve exposed the roll of film, then walked to the large glass doorway connecting the room to its private balcony and slid it open. The deserted car park was below, six storeys below. Steve looked at Ryan, held the camera over the edge, and dropped it, before re-entering the room.

'Get up!' he ordered.

Ryan did not move. He lay there, frightened and wary, cursing himself for having misjudged Steve.

'I said, get up!' Steve grabbed him by the shirt and hauled him to his feet.

'What are you going to do?' stammered Ryan.

'It's not what I'm going to do, Ryan, it's what you're going to do. You dropped your camera—go and get it.'

'You're mad,' stammered Ryan. 'You're insane.'

Steve pushed him backwards out on to the balcony, and walked slowly towards him as Ryan backed off until he was against the iron railing.

'I'll pay you. Anything.' Ryan's throat was dry and he spoke with difficulty.

Steve grabbed him by the arms and with a seemingly effortless movement lifted him from the ground. Ryan screamed as he hurtled back through the doorway into the room, and when he landed, his arms clutched the leg of the bed. Steve sat down, his own heart pounding, his eyes fixed on the blubbering, frightened man clinging to the leg of the bed.

'Shut up, Ryan!' he ordered after a minute.

Ryan looked up, wanting to call for help, but afraid to open his mouth.

'Get up!' Steve snapped.

Slowly Ryan rose from beneath the bed, his hands reluctantly leaving the safety of the bed end. Steve did not shift his gaze, and watched each movement. Ryan was quivering, and having difficulty in mouthing words as he spoke. 'I didn't mean it; I just . . .'

The words rolled around in Steve's mind; he had heard them before. I didn't mean it . . . I didn't mean it . . . It was dark; there was a woman screaming, another was being dragged from the twisted wreck which had been a car; a small body lay on the road, covered with a blanket; there was a siren blaring; two men in blue uniforms struggled to hold a man too drunk to stand, who leaned on a vehicle, saying 'I didn't mean it.'

'. . . an accident, I didn't have the slightest idea the crocodile was there.'

Steve stared at Ryan without speaking. 'You were going to blackmail me, Ryan, remember?'

'You've got to understand my position. Reporters don't make much.'

'Neither do Wildlife Officers.'

'I'm sorry. I don't know what else to say.'

'You ever seen a big croc feeding?'

'No . . . why? What are you talking about?' Ryan's body began to tingle all over again.

'You'd like it. They tear their food apart before they swallow it—in big chunks.'

'What are you talking about?' stammered Ryan.

'Nothing that goes in ever comes out. Even rocks just roll around in the stomach, till they wear away.'

'You're crazy.'

'It's twenty minutes to eleven. You gave me till ten o'clock tonight to get ten thousand dollars. I'm not going to be so generous. You've got till three o'clock this afternoon to be out of Darwin. There are two planes for Sydney after lunch—be on one of them.'

'What if . . . what if I can't get a booking?'

'That's your problem. But I'll tell you one thing for sure. I'm going to come looking for you at three o'clock. If you're still here, you're going to find out just how big crocs like live food. And I'll tell you something else you'd better not forget. If there's one word about the crocodile in the papers, I'll hunt you down like a dog, Ryan. Believe me, I mean what I say.'

'Don't worry, I'll be gone.'

Steve walked to the door, half opened it and turned to face Ryan. 'Think yourself bloody lucky you didn't go over the balcony.'

Thoughts of falling through the air rushed through Ryan's mind as Steve walked out. Within seconds the door was locked and Ryan was leaning against it, his eyes closed, his chest heaving, his head aching. The phone rang.

Steve walked briskly from the lift across the foyer to the main door, noticing that the girl behind the reception desk had the phone held to her ear, and the shattered remains of Ryan's camera before her.

On the drive back to the research station, Steve tried to think rationally about what had happened. Numunwari was threatened, yet Ryan surely would not have the guts to pursue it any further. Mac had to be told, but should he tell Barrett? He would panic. Would the wisest thing be to move Numunwari? What if Ryan stayed? A shiver ran down Steve's spine when he thought of the balcony. It had been close. He had wanted to throw Ryan over, and was now so thankful he had not.

When he reached the station and walked towards the house, Nancy, tears in her eyes, ran to meet him. 'Oondabund's been crying. Him worry for Numunwari, for throwing spear at that crocodile. You come and talk with him, Steve. He's proper sad one.' She grabbed Steve's hand tightly, and walked with him to the house.

Ryan had two large whiskies before phoning the airline company. He waited nervously while the bookings were checked, and was relieved when told there was a seat available; departure time was 2 pm, and he would need to be at the airport half an hour early.

As he calmed, he seethed with bitterness towards Steve. Leaving Darwin now meant no story; a wasted trip. He had lost a camera and a considerable financial investment in the charter flight; the air ticket to Sydney and back was worth $500 itself, and there was the accommodation cost, too. Not to gain from a trip was one thing—losing your own money was another. Ryan wanted revenge, but without the risk of incurring the wrath he had been threatened with. He was not a fool—he had seen men placed in situations where they became desperate before, and Steve Harris was in such a position.

He thought about it for a few minutes more before reaching for the telephone. As he dialled, a slight smile came over his face. 'Put me through to the Public Bar, please,' he said.

At the research station, Steve also had the phone in hand. He was waiting for someone to find Mac.

'Hello, Wilson here,' came the reply.

'Steve here, Mac. You got a few minutes?'

'Sure. You coming to the office this afternoon?'

'Don't know yet. There've been a few problems out here.'

'What?'

'You remember that reporter, Ryan? The one you sent out yesterday? He thought he'd take some photos of the station for his story—some aerial photos.'

'So what?' replied Mac, wondering what Steve was leading to.

'Guess what he saw when he flew over?'

'I wouldn't have . . .' Mac stopped in mid-sentence. 'He didn't.'

'He sure bloody well did. Sitting up on the bank as large as life when he went over. Oondabund threw a spear to try and chase it into the water, but he was too late.'

'Shit!' Mac closed his eyes and pictured Numunwari lying in the sun, as it would be seen from a plane. He posed his next question quietly. 'What's he going to do about it?'

'I've had a talk with him, and I don't think he'll do anything, but I don't trust the bastard.'

'What about Barrett? He know yet?'

'Christ, no! I haven't told anyone—only you.'

'What the hell are we going to do? What's he like, this bloke Ryan? Do you think he'll keep his mouth shut?'

'He's a first-class bastard, Mac. That's what I'm worried about. I've got a nagging feeling inside that says "don't panic", but on the other hand, it says "don't be a bloody fool—move the croc". I think we'd better get together and work things out. If we're going to move it, we'll need to be quick.'

Mac looked at his watch. 'I'll be over by half-past twelve,' he said, and put the phone down thoughtfully.

In the Newcomer Inn, the one-armed man picked up the phone which lay on the bar. 'Besser here. Who is it?'

'David Ryan, the reporter.'

'What do you want?' Besser snapped.

'The other night I paid you for information, remember?'

'Course I do.'

'Well, now I've got something to sell you—but, by Christ, it's going to cost.'

'You bloody mad or something?' sneered Besser. 'Why would I want anything from you. Piss off, I'm busy.'

'Shut up, Besser!' said Ryan. 'The croc that took your arm isn't dead. It's alive and hidden and I know where it is—I saw it today.'

There was silence on the line, and Ryan waited patiently.

'I might have only one arm, mate, but if you're lying I'll break your fucking neck.'

'It's alive. They didn't kill it,' repeated Ryan. 'They caught it. That's why no one found the body.'

'Where is it?' shouted Besser. In the bar everyone stopped talking and looked at the one-armed man; there was deathly quiet.

'When you have the money.'

'How much?'

'Two thousand.'

'Where the fuck am I going to get that sort of cash?'

'Your problem, Besser. I'll ring you at 12.30, and if you want the information, have the money.'

Ryan was smiling to himself as he hung up and poured another whisky. In an hour's time he would ring Besser. Meanwhile, the hire car and motel account had to be paid, and the post office checked for mail. Apart from that, he was ready to go.

Besser was furious when he replaced the phone. He ordered a double rum and was sipping it when Bluey walked up. 'Who was that?'

Besser didn't answer, but his face betrayed his anger.

'What's up? What's the matter?'

'How much do you reckon your truck's worth, Blue?'

'I don't know. Couple of thousand, I suppose. Why?'

'Couple of grand,' repeated Besser, ignoring Bluey's question.

'Yeah, but it's not bloody well for sale.'

'Remember that Ryan? The bloke in here the other night? That was him on the phone.' Besser's hand tightened on the glass. 'He reckons the croc's still alive. Says he saw it.'

'What a lot of bullshit.'

'He wasn't bullshitting. He saw it all right.'

'You don't believe him, do you?' asked Bluey.

'He wouldn't have the guts to pull one like that. No, he's on to something. Those Wildlife bastards caught and hid it. Doesn't surprise me one bit; Harris thinks more of bloody crocs than he does of people. He'd do something like that.'

'Caught it!' repeated Bluey. 'How the fuck could anyone catch it? He's lying. Forget him.'

'He wants two thousand bucks before he'll tell me where it is.'

'He must be fucking mad. Does he think we're stupid or something?'

'I've got an hour to get the cash, Blue. We'll have to sell your truck.'

Bluey stared at him. 'You're joking.'

'Finish your beer and let's get going.'

'I'm not going to sell me bloody truck to give that bastard two grand. No way.'

Besser was shaking with fury when he turned on Bluey. 'I've got one stinking hour to get two grand. One hour. If I don't have it, that's it. No second chance. I'm not asking you, Blue, I'm telling you; we're going to sell your truck. It's the only way.'

'All right,' said Bluey eventually. 'If you reckon he's on the level, we'll sell it.'

The dealer of the first car yard they came to was eager to purchase the vehicle; four-wheel drives were good property in Darwin. He offered $1,500, but Besser demanded $3,000; within minutes they settled on $2,500, with Besser stipulating the cheque be made out to cash. They returned to the bar after stopping at the bank and converting the single note to a roll of fifty-dollar bills; it was 12.45 pm, and they ordered two beers while waiting by the telephone. Since agreeing to sell the truck, Bluey had said little, and when he did speak his voice lacked humour. 'What if he doesn't ring?'

'He'll ring,' snarled Besser, with confidence.

Mac arrived at Steve's house at 12.20 pm. They sat in the kitchen, and while Nancy got them coffee, Steve told him what had happened.

'I'm glad you didn't throw him over,' said Mac. 'Christ, imagine trying to explain *that*; the whole thing's hard to believe. Who is the bastard anyway?'

Steve shrugged his shoulders. 'He said he'd been up north a couple of times and reckons he's well-known, but I've never come across him before.'

'Doesn't really matter, I suppose; the big question is, what now?'

'We're going to have to move it, Mac. I've been thinking about the whole thing since I rang you and you just couldn't trust a bastard like Ryan; he'll end up telling someone.'

'But where the hell can we take it?'

'Yarbalonga Reserve—no one goes out there any more and with a bit of work the old pen near the homestead would hold him. I've already had a talk with Oondabund, and he's prepared to go out there once we set it up.' Mac didn't answer, and was clearly trying to envisage the great crocodile in the small deep pool that lay next to the deserted homestead.

Steve continued: 'Anyway, as soon as this is over, we could stage the recatch of a big croc, and bring Numunwari back as the new croc caught in one of the Mary River billabongs. The scar on his head is almost completely healed, and there's nothing really to tie him in with the one that was "killed".'

'The sooner we get that over and done with, the better,' replied Mac. 'For the time being, Yarbalonga sounds a sensible alternative; if Ryan's like you say, we'd be taking a hell of a risk just leaving it in the breeding pen.'

'That's the way I see it too, Mac; in fact, I think it's bloody urgent we move it out. What about getting everything ready this afternoon and going out first thing in the morning? It won't be hard to catch, now that Oondabund's got it quiet.'

'Okay then, Steve,' replied Mac, looking at his watch. 'I've got to get back to the office but I'll organise a truck there. I'll bring it over later this afternoon.'

'That you, Besser?' the voice said, when the one-armed man grabbed at the ringing phone.

'Yeah.'

'You got the money?'

'How about a thousand? I can't get two.'

'Well, that's bloody bad luck, isn't it? Sorry I bothered you—be seeing you some time.'

'Hold it!' shouted Besser. 'I've got it, you bloodsucking bastard.'

'Flattery'll get you nowhere, Besser. Is the money in cash?'

'Fifties.'

'You got a car?'

'Just sold the fucking thing.'

'Well, use a taxi,' said Ryan without sympathy. 'Have one waiting in exactly one hour, and I'll phone and tell you where to come to. If you're late you miss out, and there'll be no second chance.' The line went dead.

Besser turned to Bluey as he slammed the telephone down. 'I'd like to break his fucking neck.'

'What'd he say?'

'He's going to ring back in an hour. We've got to have a taxi waiting. I'll get that bastard.'

'He's playing games,' said Bluey, hoping there might be a chance of buying his vehicle back.

'Shut up, Blue. I'm sick and tired of your whingeing. It's my fucking arm, and if that bastard croc's still alive I'm going to make sure I get it.'

Ryan ordered a taxi and paid his account at the motel, having left the hire car in the parking lot as arranged with the company.

Fifteen minutes later, he arrived at the airport, checked in his bags and received a seat allocation; the plane, he was told, could be expected to leave on schedule at 1400 hours. After thanking the attendant, he climbed the stairs to the waiting lounge and looked around until his eyes centred on the counter near the departure doorway, where passengers were subjected to a routine weapons check before boarding. The two inspectors, members of a private security company, were armed, and they were talking with a policeman. It was an ideal place to meet Besser.

At exactly 1.30 pm, he rang the Newcomer Inn from a public phone booth. Besser was waiting.

'I'm at the airport, Besser. Come out alone in the taxi and when you get there, walk straight through the main doors and up the stairway to the lounge—I'll be waiting there for you, near the departure exit. My plane leaves at exactly two o'clock, and I'll be boarding five minutes before, which means you've got exactly twenty minutes to get here.' He hung up.

Besser's huge frame burst through the door seven minutes before the plane was due to leave, and as instructed, he ran up the stairs and entered the waiting lounge; it was crowded, and on his first scan of the room, he did not see the man he sought. However, Ryan sighted him.

Seated next to the weapons check counter, Ryan had removed a cigarette from its packet three minutes before Besser arrived, and with it unlit in his hand, had sat patiently watching the doorway. The moment Besser appeared, he was on his feet with the cigarette conspicuously displayed, seeking a light from the armed policeman behind the counter; the end glowing, he thanked him courteously, rechecked the departure time, and turned to meet Besser's stare from across the room.

The sight of the policeman shattered any illusions Besser had had of retrieving the money at the last minute. He was dealing with a professional, and such people planned carefully, leaving nothing to chance.

'You bring the money?' asked Ryan.

'Yeah,' replied Besser, holding a well-used brown paper bag where it could be seen, but not taken. 'Where's the croc?'

'Let's have the money first, thank you.'

Besser looked from Ryan to the policeman, who was talking with the two armed inspectors. There was nothing he could do. The single powerful hand held out its contents, which Ryan casually removed, folded tightly and slipped into his inside coat pocket; there was no need to count it.

Unafraid, he stared into Besser's anxious face for nearly ten seconds before speaking. 'It's out at the crocodile research station, in a pen they call the breeding pen, about two hundred yards from the house. You can't miss it, it's the only pen away from the house and it's surrounded by a wire fence with shrubs and a few trees.'

'How do you know it's the same croc?' growled Besser.

'How do you think I got this?' said Ryan, gently touching a large bruise on his left cheek. 'Harris threatened to kill me if I told anyone.'

'Well, if it's not there, Ryan, I'll kill you. I've got a lot of old friends in Sydney, mate, and they're the type of people who specialise in collecting bad debts. If the crocodile's not there, they'll not only track you down, they'll break every bone in your body. Now, I'm gonna ask you once more—is it the same crocodile?'

'I saw the thing myself this morning, and when Steve Harris found out that I had, he told me the whole story. He was trying to get me to shut up about it. They're all in it; Barrett, Harris, Wilson. When Harris realised he hadn't convinced me, he went berserk, bloody nearly killed me. It's the same croc all right.'

The conversation was terminated by an announcement over the loudspeaker requesting passengers to Mt Isa, Sydney and Melbourne via Brisbane to board through gateway two. Ryan picked up his brief-case and placed it on the counter, then took the three steps necessary to bring him to the archway where electromagnetic waves would check whether or not there was metal in his pockets. As he began to walk through, he signalled to the one-armed man that he had something else to say.

'There's one more thing,' he said quietly when Besser was beside him: 'It's a damn shame the crocodile only got *one* arm.' He was through the arch before Besser could respond.

IO

At the Newcomer Inn, Besser ordered a double rum as he reached the bar.

'How'd you go?' asked Bluey, still hoping that somehow he would get his truck back.

'Harris's got it. He's got the fucking thing out at that research place,' Besser snarled.

'I don't trust that Ryan bastard. You're sure, are you?'

'I'm sure. Ryan's got more guts than I'd have thought, but he's not stupid. It's there all right.'

'What are we going to do?' asked Bluey.

'We're going to kill it, Blue. I'm not sure how yet, but I'm going to kill that croc.' Besser finished his rum and ordered another.

'Well, these blokes in here'll help you if you need 'em. Why not tell them all about it?'

'Yeah,' said Besser slowly, staring blankly at the ceramic tiles on the wall. 'Get 'em over, Blue; we might need some help with this little job.'

The men in the bar, all regulars, were drinking in three groups, and Bluey went to each with the news that Besser wanted to see them. Each man had his glass refilled, and they congregated in silence around the back of the man who seemed to ignore them; but when he did turn, he held their undivided attention.

'You all know how I lost this,' he said, using a near-empty glass to tap the skin of the rounded shoulder which just protruded from a sleeveless shirt, 'and you all know what it meant to me—you can't catch fish and work nets with one arm. Well, the fucking croc who did it was supposed to have been killed—at least, that's what everyone was told.'

No one liked being close to Besser when he talked about the crocodile, because his hatred for it made his behaviour unpredictable, he was just as likely to fly into a rage and take it out on the closest person. The regulars in the Newcomer Inn had accordingly learned to back quietly away whenever the subject was raised, because without an audience, Besser would usually calm down and forget about it. But with the suggestion that the crocodile hadn't been killed, no one moved—everybody listened intently as he continued.

'Everyone went looking for the croc's body after it was shot, but no one found it. Why? Crocs always float up after a few days. Why didn't this bastard?'

His question met with silence, no one being prepared to speak, though all anxiously awaited details. 'I'll tell you why,' Besser continued loudly, with his face showing anger. 'Because it wasn't fucking well shot! It was caught alive! Those Wildlife bastards caught it and hid the fucking thing until everyone forgot about it.' Besser was shouting, and some of the men took a step backwards. 'All that crap about how they shot it was bullshit. The fucking croc's still alive, and it's out at that bloody research station!'

There was a quiet murmur. 'How do you know?' asked one of the men.

'That bloody reporter, the one in here the other night—that Ryan bastard. He saw the fucking thing and thought he'd cash in on it. But he went to Harris to get cash for keeping his mouth shut, and Harris beat the shit out of him, said he'd kill him if Ryan told anyone what he'd seen. Harris's got the bastard out there, all right.'

'What you gonna do?' asked another of the men.

'I'm going to kill the fucking thing, that's what I'm gonna do; but I might need help. That's why Bluey asked you lot over.'

'Well, I'll bloody well help,' answered one man, immediately. 'I've got a score to fix with Harris.'

'Me, too,' replied another. 'I've lost two boats and all me nets because of that bastard.'

'What about the cops?' asked a third man. 'What'll they do if we kill it?'

'The fucking croc *ate* one of the bastards!' shouted Besser. 'They'd help us if we asked 'em.'

'Don't forget the bloke from the Tourist Bureau said he'd pay five thousand dollars for the head,' said the barman, who had been leaning on the bar listening.

'It cost us two grand to get the fucking information from that bastard Ryan. Had to sell Bluey's truck to get it.'

'Two grand!' repeated the barman. 'Shit, he's a bit of an asker.'

'Yeah, but it's cheap at the price. Anyway, we'll get that back for the head.'

'Right,' said Bluey. 'Who's going to be in it?'

After a short discussion everyone agreed to help, and Besser ordered a round of drinks, which were eagerly accepted.

'You worked out how you're going to get it?' asked one of the men.

'Got a rough idea,' replied Besser. 'Still haven't worked it all out, though. There're not many blokes out at that research place now, only Harris and maybe one other bastard. Gotta work out how to get him away, then just go and shoot the croc in its cage; Ryan reckoned it was up on a bit of a hill away from the house.'

'Worth trying to get a look at it before we go out?' asked Bluey. 'Just to make sure it's there.'

'No,' scowled Besser. 'If Harris gets wind of what's going on, he'll have a fucking army out there. Let's just keep it quiet and stay away from the place.'

'You sure he hasn't moved it?' asked one man.

'You don't just move a croc like that, even if it's dead. Ryan only saw it this morning and Harris thinks he's shut Ryan's mouth. It'll be there tomorrow—we can go out early in the morning to be sure.'

'Getting Harris away's going to be a bit of a problem, isn't it?' asked Bluey.

'Haven't worked out how to do it yet,' said Besser, slowly and obviously deep in thought.

'I'll tell you a way.' All eyes turned to the barman. He quickly whispered in Besser's ear. Besser beamed as the plan unravelled.

'Brilliant! That'll work for sure.' He turned to the others. 'We'll get Harris away. Tomorrow morning we'll do it—that bastard croc's going to get it this time.'

The small group gathered around Besser at the bar, while the barman refilled each glass. 'Drink 'em up, fellers,' said Besser cheerfully. 'The grog's on me—I've got something to celebrate for a change.'

Bluey Noakes was the only person who failed to give a cheer of delight. Although he was as excited as the others, the 'free' drinks were coming from the $500 left over from the sale of his truck.

At the research station, Oondabund walked back up to the breeding pen and sat cross-legged on the walkway, singing to the water below, waiting for Numunwari to appear. Steve, alone in the office, stood when he heard the truck coming through the driveway.

The new brightly-painted blue semi-trailer crawled through the narrow entrance, and with a hiss from the air-brakes pulled up outside the office.

'How d'you like this one?' asked Mac, as he climbed from the cabin. Steve walked around it, admiring the new vehicle. 'What happened to the low loader?'

'They're using it out at the Alligator Rivers. This was the only one left in the vehicle pool that'd have any chance of carrying the crocodile. They weren't real keen on giving it to me, because it's brand new—only done a thousand kilometres, but to drive it's like a car.'

'It'll do the job,' said Steve. 'We'll need to pick up a set of big ramps from somewhere, and get a few hand winches, then all we need are ropes, a tarpaulin and a stack of branches and leaves to cover the croc with—why don't we get on to that now?'

By sunset, everything needed to move Numunwari had been assembled and checked, and both Steve and Mac felt confident that the operation would go without a hitch. It was as Mac drove home that Steve heard Oondabund walk up behind him.

'He come up, that Numunwari," he said excitedly. 'Me sing him long time and me say sorry for hit 'im spear. That crocodile him climb up on bank and him say, "Me know why you throw spear Oondabund, thank you very much for help me". Him proper friendly one.'

Steve placed his arm on Oondabund's shoulder. 'We might have to hurt him a little bit when we try and move him tomorrow.'

'Him not worry. I tell him that story and him very happy to go new camp. No trouble for him that crocodile.'

'First thing in the morning we'll start. Let's go and have a beer.'

At the Newcomer Inn the atmosphere was electric. Besser had been buying drinks for everyone, and for the first time in months was laughing and joking. He was even telling stories about when he had been a doorman at one of Melbourne's less reputable nightclubs, something he had never even mentioned to Bluey in the years they had worked together.

'What about tomorrow?' shouted one of the men, and the noise level dropped. 'What time do we leave?'

'I guess we'd better sort that out,' said Besser, smiling. 'What say we leave early, round seven in the morning?'

'Meet here?' questioned Bluey.

'Can't see why not. It's sort of fitting, anyway. Meet outside at seven and bring every gun you've got—we don't want the bastard getting away this time.'

There was a cheer from the men before the noise level rose and everyone settled back to his drinking, with Besser the toast for the beer they consumed. People milled around him, patting him on the back and urging him on with his stories.

The men drank until the bar closed at ten, and, after reaffirming their decision to meet at seven the next morning, all staggered off in different directions. In the bar, Besser and Bluey finished a last rum with the barman.

'You pair take it easy tomorrow, don't do anything stupid. Remember it's the croc you're after, not Harris.'

Besser stared at the barman with glazed eyes. He felt hatred at the mention of Steve's name, because, although the crocodile had done the damage, Harris was really reponsible for the loss of his hand.

Steve, Nancy and Oondabund sat up talking until late at night, while Oondabund's wife and children watched television until the last programme ceased. Steve talked about the plans for the following day and told Oondabund about Yarbalonga Reserve and the pool in which Numunwari would be kept. They also discussed the way in which the 'recatch' of a big crocodile would be staged, and how, once this was done, Numunwari would no longer need to be hidden. He could be shown to the world, though his true origins would always have to remain a closely guarded secret.

When they did all go to bed, Nancy was unable to sleep, and after an hour, she shook Steve's shoulder gently until he woke. 'I can't sleep, Steve. I'm worried for that crocodile,' she said.

'What's the time?' he said, rubbing his eyes and trying to focus on the luminous dial of his watch. 'Christ, it's two o'clock.'

'I can't sleep,' she repeated.

Steve sat up and cuddled her against his chest. 'Everything will be okay. We've got all the gear ready, and as soon as it's light we'll get cracking. There's nothing to worry about.'

'I keep dreaming a bad dream.' A tear trickled down her cheek, and Steve saw the reflection of it in the moonlight and held her tightly. 'I'm frightened for Oondabund and Numunwari,' she whispered.

'There's nothing to worry about, loved one. Mac'll be here and we'll have it on the truck in a few hours. Calm down, come on, just relax.' Steve lay back down and was asleep within minutes, but Nancy's wide brown eyes watched the moon through the window until the sky lightened and the stars disappeared. If anything happened to Oondabund, Nancy was responsible for Numunwari. It was her birthright, and something she considered of the utmost importance.

When Nancy got up, Oondabund was already at the table, and as they prepared some tea, she told him about her dreams. He neither answered her, nor tried to console her, but the expression on his face showed that he, too, took the dreams as a bad sign.

At 6.15 am, Nancy woke Steve, and they were all just finishing breakfast when Mac arrived.

'Feel like a cup of tea before we start, Mac?' asked Steve the moment he was in the door.

'Just had one, but could do with another. Has all been quiet out here?'

'Yeah, not a sign of anyone. I checked the motel and Ryan's gone, so I guess he mustn't have told anyone here, at least.'

'Thank Christ for that,' replied Mac as he sat at the table. 'How are we going to catch the croc, Steve?'

'Well, I thought we'd have to harpoon it again, but Oondabund reckons it will eat this morning, so that changes things. Last night we mixed up a small dose of anaesthetic and slipped it inside a piece of mackerel, and as soon as we finish here Oondabund's going to go and feed it. It'll come straight out on the bank and bask, and hopefully the drug'll put it to sleep for fifteen or twenty minutes. When it starts to come out, we can give it a proper dose in the tail. That'll keep it out for hours.'

'How long does the first dose take to work?'

'Not long,' replied Steve. 'I'd say about fifteen minutes to half an hour. The croc's so bloody quiet that it's just going to sit there trying to digest the fish, and as long as the stomach's being used the drug should go straight into the blood system.'

Besser and Bluey were on the steps outside the Newcomer Inn at 6.45 am, waiting for the others to arrive. Bluey doubted that they would be late; Besser was the sort of person few people kept waiting if they could help it.

The first vehicle, with two men in it, arrived at five minutes to seven, and the second, a Toyota with three men in it, two minutes later.

'Where the fuck're Fred and Dan?' said Besser impatiently.

'They were pretty pissed when they went home last night. If no one's got 'em up, I'd say they'd still be asleep. I didn't think they were real keen on coming anyway.'

'Bugger 'em; we'll go without them.' Besser climbed into the front of the car, while Bluey got in the back of the Toyota, and within seconds they were driving through the slowly-awakening streets of Darwin.

When Oondabund climbed the steps and walked out across the walkway, Numunwari was just crawling out of the water. As he watched, the huge crocodile swayed his way up the earthen bank and lay with his side facing east to catch the morning sun. Oondabund tied the mackerel he was carrying to a piece of thin cord, then squatted on the planks singing quietly to his companion, and waiting for Steve and Mac to arrive. While he waited, he let the fish drop in the water and sink, so that it would be wet and slippery enough for the great crocodile to swallow.

'When we get up there,' whispered Steve as they neared the fence, 'just take it real easy. He doesn't seem to worry about Oondabund, but if we make any sudden moves he might dive in.'

Mac failed to see the crocodile when he first peered through the fence and shrubs, but Steve pointed him out, then signalled to Oondabund to feed him. As if in anticipation, the great crocodile was lying with his mouth open, the first rays of sunlight striking the back of the head. The crocodile didn't move when the fish was manoeuvred across, but when Oondabund swung it out so that it almost touched the lower teeth, he suddenly exploded into activity, lunging forward and slamming his jaws shut around it. One sideways jerk of the head and the cord broke, and, throwing its head in the air twice, the crocodile first manoeuvred, then swallowed the fish head first, before all activity stopped. Steve tapped Mac's shoulder and indicated they should move back away from the fence, and signalled to Oondabund to remain where he was. It was important to keep a constant watch on the crocodile, because, if he did go back into the water, they would need to probe for him immediately, harpoon him, and get his head back to the surface before the drug worked and he drowned. Oondabund was confident that Numunwari would stay on the bank, but they could take no chances.

'That bloody croc's huge,' said Mac when they were well back from the fence. 'He's bloody bigger than when we caught him—he's still growing!'

'Yeah, I've thought that too. Ever since he started feeding, he seems to have packed on weight. We've got a list of everything he's eaten, so that really you could work out how much of that has been converted to body mass—if you had his body weight.'

'Steve,' said Mac, 'you're not figuring on that bloody weighing station again?'

Steve smiled. 'Well, look, Mac, we know exactly what he's eaten and how long we've had him, so we could get the conversion factor. If he is still growing, it'd be a bloody valuable bit of data.'

'It's going to be a bit of buggering around—is it really worth it?'

As Mac expected, Steve nodded his head in reply.

'Okay then,' said Mac resignedly, 'but I'm taking the *empty* truck this time, and you can take it down when the croc's on. I couldn't look that guy in the face if he asks any more questions.'

'It shouldn't take us much time, Mac. If you take the truck down now, Numunwari will be only just out to it by the time you get back, and once we've got him on, it'll only take an extra ten minutes to get the second weight. All the branches and the tarp are already on the back.'

The engine burst into life at the turn of the key, and with a, 'See you in a few minutes', Mac headed back out of the research station and along the track to the highway. Steve was watching it go when he heard Nancy call from the front door of the house.

'Telephone, Steve; they want you urgently.'

'Steve Harris?' the voice on the telephone questioned. 'It's George

Watson here. I'm the attendant down at the main Darwin wharf. There's a bloody huge crocodile in under the end bearers, and no one's game to go near their boats. The police said to contact you.'

'Don't let anyone near it!' shouted Steve. 'I'll be down in about fifteen minutes, but for Christ's sake keep everyone away from it.'

Five kilometres away, a man walked from a roadside telephone booth and held his hand out towards a parked truck and car on the side of the road. He gave the thumbs-up signal.

'He's on his way. Be there in fifteen minutes, he said.'

'We'll sit and wait till he goes past,' said Besser, stretching back in the front seat of the car.

Oondabund was already halfway down the hill when he saw Steve run from the house, yell and wave to him. He quickened his pace, but without waiting for him, Steve ran to the storage shed and threw open the doors. By the time Oondabund got there, the red plastic fish crate was in the back of the Toyota and the harpoon poles tied to its side.

'Another croc, Oondabund. There's a big one in under the wharf again. Give us a hand with the boat.'

As they lifted the aluminum dinghy, Oondabund relayed his message. 'That Numunwari sleep now. Him proper tired one. Me touch him eye and that eye not move no more.'

'Well, we might have to start all over again. I'll get the tranquilliser gun, you check the harpoons; they're in the crate.'

As Steve ran towards the office, Nancy came down the stairs, a frightened look on her face. 'What the matter, Steve?' she asked frantically.

'There's a big croc in under the wharf and we've got to get down there right away. When Mac comes back, tell him what's happened, but tell him not to come down; we'll ring here if we need any help.' Steve turned to run to the Toyota, then hesitated. Turning back, he looked into her eyes. 'Don't worry, we'll be back in a little while,' he said, giving her a squeeze and a gentle kiss on the forehead.

Besser watched the Toyota swerve around the corner on to the highway, and accelerate in the direction of Darwin Harbour.

'They don't muck around, do they?' he said quietly before turning in the seat and catching the attention of the driver in the truck parked behind. The man waved and Besser heard its engine start.

'Right,' he said as he straightened. 'Let's go get the bastard.'

Nancy was surprised to hear the Toyota pull into the yard, and ran to the door and down the steps, thinking Steve and Oondabund were returning. As she watched the men getting out, her small heart began to beat faster and fear spread throughout her body. Besser's single arm ran to a wide-bladed axe, which was new and shone in the sun. Bluey carried a rusted double-barrelled shotgun into which he was inserting two solid slugs, and the other five men were all carrying arms. She knew why they were there, and only she stood between them and their prey. Slowly, bravely, she walked towards them.

'What you mob want?' she asked angrily, when she was about six metres away.

Bluey looked up when she spoke, then turned to Besser. 'Who's the black bitch?'

'I don't know. There was an Abo in the truck with Harris.'

'What do you want?' Nancy repeated. 'Steve Harris isn't home.'

'The crocodile, love,' said Besser. 'That's all we want. Now you'd better get inside before you get hurt.' Axe in hand, he started along the path between the pens, but Nancy walked quickly and stood her ground in front of him.

'You leave now!' she demanded. 'You come back when Steve Harris here.' Besser stopped momentarily. 'You go!' Nancy frantically yelled again.

Bluey, who had walked up next to Besser, back-handed her across the face, knocking her to the ground. He then leaned over her, his ugly unshaven face close to hers as the frightened brown eyes stared up. 'Didn't you hear him?' he said, laughing as he reached out and grabbed her left breast, squeezing it hard. 'Not a bad tit you got there.'

Nancy kicked up at him, hoping to hit the one region she knew would double him up in pain, but her bare foot missed and buried into the inside of his thigh. Furious, he dropped the gun, and taking hold of her with both hands, he hauled her to her feet. She fought wildly, but in vain.

'You fucking black bitch,' he shouted, tearing her dress open and exposing her two well-formed breasts. He sunk his fingers into one and began slapping her face with his other hand.

'Leave her,' yelled Besser angrily, as Bluey threw her to the ground. 'Piss off, gin.'

Nancy stood quickly and glared defiantly at him, as he breathed deeply and stared back, his forced smile hiding the painful throb from the inside of his leg.

'For fuck's sake leave her !' Besser shouted, furious at the diversion.

The two brown hands flew for Bluey's face, the fingernails gouging deeply into the skin below each of his eyes. He screamed in pain as he tried to push her off him, but she clung tightly, digging in her fingers, biting at his thrashing arms, and trying to kick wherever her foot could land.

In an instant, Besser was there. He was wild, and his eyes flashed from Bluey to Nancy, both of whom were rolling in the dirt, entangled in a moving mass of arms and legs. Dropping the axe, Besser grabbed a handful of Nancy's long black hair and hauled her off Bluey. Momentarily she stopped struggling, but had barely looked up at Besser when she saw the single powerful arm moving. With all his weight behind it, Besser drove his fist towards her face, and as she instinctively tried to move, it connected with her slender brown neck. The crack as it connected resounded above the curses coming up from Bluey, causing a look of horror on the faces of the two men. Nancy instantly collapsed and lay motionless on the ground; her head lay to one side at such an angle that there was little doubt its supporting vertebrae had been shattered.

'The fucking bitch, just about tore me bloody eyes out,' said Bluey, rubbing his bleeding face as he stood.

'Well, she's not going to give you any more trouble. Now, let's go,' snapped Blesser angrily. He pointed up the hill to the group of trees. 'That's the pen up there.'

As the seven men walked through the gate into the open field, an older Aboriginal woman ran across to the motionless body lying on the gravel. She rolled it over, but there was no movement. Beneath Nancy's exposed breasts were three scars running across her chest, scars from cuts she had received from a tribal elder when she was fifteen, sixteen and nineteen years of age. Between her breasts was a large knot of scar tissue; another tribal mark. Her mother lifted the frail shoulders and began to cry; Nancy's head hung loosely downwards.

Some of the men turned when they heard the mournful wailing. 'What the fuck's that?' said one of them.

'Just another Abo,' said Besser. 'Now for Christ's sake let's worry about the croc.'

As they continued up the hill, Nancy's mother cradled the head and shoulders in her arms, and rocked back and forth. The high-pitched cry radiated throughout the small research station, but no one who heard it cared.

Steve and Oondabund screeched to a halt beside the attendant's hut at the entrance to the wharf. It had been a hectic drive, Steve having had to swerve twice to avoid colliding with cars trying to force their way into the stream of morning traffic. A grey-haired old man walked from the small office and stood beside Steve's window.

'What boat you after?'

'We're down for the croc,' said Steve, frantically. 'Where is it?'

'Ain't no boat by that name here, mate.'

'Crocodile!' yelled Steve. 'Not a boat.'

'What? Down here? I've been here since six, mate, and I've seen nothing.'

The truth sank into Steve immediately, and he felt his heart pound. 'Is there a George Watson down here?'

'Yeah, that's my name. What's going on?'

Steve did not answer. He spun the vehicle into a tight turn and, with the engine roaring, he took off with his foot flat to the floor. Beside him, Oondabund knew something was wrong, terribly wrong, but he did not know what, and there was no way Steve could tell him.

Besser signalled to the others to stop when they were fifty metres from the pen, and beckoned them to come over to him. He whispered instructions. 'I'm going to sneak up and have a look, but you lot wait here until I come back. Get your guns ready to go now, so we don't make any noise once we get there.'

Leaving the group, he slowly crept up to the fence, crawling the last six metres, still with the axe in his hand.

At the fence, he carefully raised his head and peered through the layer of shrubs and bushes, but on his first scan saw nothing, not even an indication that the pen contained any living creature.

Suddenly he became aware of the huge object on the bank, barely five metres away, and instinctively he lowered his head and remained still, hesitant to even look at the prey he had surprised within reach, for fear it would see its hunter and take flight.

The membranes slid across Numunwari's eyes. For over fifteen minutes the drug had held the great crocodile motionless, but now, as its kidneys worked to filter the anaesthetic from its bloodstream, the crocodile was once again becoming aware of its surroundings. It had seen Besser's head raised and lowered, and had heard the shuffling of grass as Besser retreated back down the hill. Very slowly, the huge legs began to respond to the surges of signals racing back from the brain, but the transmission was impaired, the movements uncoordinated.

'It's there!' Besser whispered excitedly when he joined the others. 'Sitting out on the bloody bank just through the fence. Now for Christ's sake, sneak up real quiet and get yourselves a position on this side. Me and Bluey'll go first and get the gun on him while you blokes get ready, just in case he moves before you all get there. If he doesn't move, when I reckon you've had time I'll tell Blue here to fire, and when you hear the first shot open up. Now we don't want the bastard to get back into the fucking water, so once you start shooting keep it up until I tell you to stop—you all clear on that?'

Besser and the men approached the fence cautiously with Besser and Bluey ten metres ahead of the others. Positioning himself near where Besser had lain, Bluey extended the barrel very carefully through the wire mesh, being careful not to scrape it as it went. Again Numunwari's eyelids flicked across the naked eyeball. Air rushed slowly in and out of the huge lungs as the crocodile registered the moving gun barrel and shuffling sounds. Bluey looked along the barrel and moved the weapon just enough to bring the front sight level with an imaginary target on the head, eight centimetres below the square bony platform that protected the brain. Bluey did not lift his eyes, nor did he move his fingers from the two triggers, while the others slowly crawled up to the fence.

Within Numunwari's body, the last of the small dose of anaesthetic was filtered through the primitive kidneys.

The Toyota slid across the gravel road as Steve turned from the highway on to the lane leading to the station. Oondabund's eyes searched the road in front, waiting for the station to come into view.

As their vehicle swung through the station gateway, they sighted the Toyota and car in front of the office, and Oondabund's wife leaning over Nancy's body. Oondabund began to whimper, and jumped from the Toyota before it skidded to a halt. On the hill, he saw the men around the fence.

The threshold of disturbance that eventually caused Numunwari to move could not be attributed to any single event. All around the pen were the sounds of movement, and the aged sensory system perceived them all. As the second rifle protruded through the fence, Numunwari responded. From its position flat on the ground, the great head rose half a metre, while the hind limbs moved forward and positioned the claws in the ground to give them enough grip to move the body. The instant the head moved, Bluey fired one barrel, but although the solid lead slug tore through the lower jaw, splintering and smashing bone as it went, the brain was untouched and the signals to escape rushed freely to the limbs. As the great beast swung, two of the other men fired. One bullet missed completely, but the second penetrated the left eye and buried into the solid bone of the right upper jaw.

The sound of the first shot instantly brought each man to his feet, and before the crocodile reached the water, blood pouring from its head, each man frantically tried to line up the stricken animal and fire. Bullets tore into the body, where they had little immediate effect, apart from spurring Numunwari on in his frantic effort to reach the water.

Only Bluey kept calm. His eyes not lifting from the barrel, he watched as the animal turned, waiting for a second view of the prehistoric head. It came quickly, and as the square platform moved into the sight, he squeezed the trigger. The solid lead slug tore through the bone next to the slit-like ear, and within a fraction of a second it obliterated the delicate brain which lay within. Numunwari was aware only of an explosion of flashes as each nerve responded to the physical impact of lead and bone cutting and smashing. The body slumped, and although the tail still swung, and the limbs moved, the huge animal was oblivious to the impact of the bullets which now rained down upon him. Blood welled in the gaping wounds in the head before spilling over and running down the side to the moist red earth of the water's edge.

Besser yelled for them to stop shooting, and three of the men cheered loudly. Bluey stood up proudly, prepared to contest any claim that it was not his bullet that had finally stopped the crocodile.

Oondabund stopped crying when he heard the explosions. He stood from where he knelt by Nancy, and looked up the hill. Steve, too, his eyes fixed on the pen, heard the cheers and watched the men slowly standing. All at once his legs began moving, and he was running; he leaped the fence at the end of the pens. Oondabund walked back past his wife to the house.

'Well, well, well,' said Besser, turning to face the man rapidly approaching up the hill. 'Will you just look who's coming.' But the smiles rapidly vanished from the faces of the others.

Steve ignored the group of men and ran straight to the fence, but as soon as he saw Numunwari, he knew he was too late. Blood was pouring from the wounds onto the ground, from where it ran to the water, clouding it in red; there was no movement in the pen. When he turned, his fists were clenched tightly and his chest heaved in and out with each breath. He looked from man to man through the tears which welled in his eyes. Only one man was smiling, the one-armed man with the axe. 'Thought you were pretty fucking smart, didn't you, Harris? But you just weren't smart enough.'

Without warning, Steve leaped at him, driving his fists into the sneering face. Besser went over backwards with Steve still on top, raining punch after punch into any part of his body that he could reach. His hands found Besser's throat and began to tighten, as his knees continued crashing into the writhing, struggling body.

When Steve leaped at Besser, the others jumped back, reluctant to be involved. Within seconds, however, Bluey rushed to the assistance of the one-armed man, driving his boot into Steve's ribs as Besser's hand fought for a grip on Steve's face. In desperation, Bluey grabbed his shotgun by the barrel and slammed the wooden stock over Steve's back, smashing the woodwork from the rusted barrels. As if by a prearranged signal, the others rushed forward and dragged Steve off, and although he fought wildly, he was no match for them. They forced him up against the heavy wire mesh fence as Besser slowly rose to his feet, his face cut and bruised.

The single arm reached down for the axe.

'I'm going to kill you, Harris,' Besser snarled, as a trickle of blood ran from his mouth.

'Put the bloody axe down, for Christ's sake,' said Bluey, sensing Besser's rage.

'I'm going to kill you,' repeated Besser, slowly approaching Steve, axe in hand.

The other men sensed danger. Killing the croc was one thing; killing Harris was murder. Bluey grabbed a bolt action rifle from the man beside him and worked the action quickly.

'Put the axe down, Besser!' he yelled, realising that for the first time he was standing up to the man who usually ordered him around. Besser stopped and stared blankly at Bluey, and the rifle which pointed at his stomach—slowly the axe came down and dropped to the ground. Turning his attention once more to Steve, Besser glared into his face. The single arm crashed forward into the lower part of Steve's chest, and when the two men holding him released their grip, Steve slumped to the ground, gasping for breath. As he fell, Besser kicked out, connecting with the side of his head.

'That'll do!' yelled Bluey. 'For Christ's sake, leave him.'

Besser didn't answer. He stood above Steve, unconcerned by his agony, and delivered another kick into his back, before spinning to face Bluey.

'Let's get the fucking croc head and piss off,' he said.

The lock on the gate was shattered by a single blow with the axe. Inside, Numunwari lay where it had fallen, a pool of blood surrounding the great head. Besser walked up to it slowly and drove his foot into the animal's side, but there was not even a flinch. Satisfied, he passed the axe to Bluey. 'Cut the head off here,' he demanded, pointing to where his foot lay on the neck, and reasserting his control of the group.

Unable to stand, Steve crawled to the fence. Through swollen cheeks and puffed eyes he watched as the axe rose and fell, and though his ears were ringing with pain, he heard the thuds as it buried into muscle and bone. Each blow sprayed blood and small slivers of tissue around the pen, and the axe man was soaked by the time the final cut separated the last piece of skin from the body.

Besser leaned down and felt the weight of the head before straightening and looking around the pen. 'Get that bit of rope,' he ordered, pointing to a piece hanging near the walkway.

Following Besser's instructions, Bluey made a loop around the upper jaw, then with the two ends, tied the mouth closed. Both he and Besser grasped the loop, and after an initial pull to ensure it was tight, dragged the head between them to the gateway. As the group started down the hill, Besser stopped and turned to Steve, who still leaned on the fence, unable to stand. 'Think yourself lucky it wasn't you, Harris,' he said.

Again Steve tried to stand, but his legs failed to respond.

'The feet!' said Besser suddenly. 'We didn't get the feet.'

'Leave 'em,' said Bluey, his enthusiasm for the venture gone.

'Leave 'em be buggered!' growled Besser. 'They're worth money. Run back and hack 'em off, Blue.'

Besser's axe in hand, Bluey ran back into the pen and chopped off both hind feet, and the two hands. When he returned with them, everyone in the small group was looking down the hill.

Steve was mumbling something, and trying to stand, but no one heard or saw him. 'No, no . . .' he repeated over and over.

'Who the fuck's that?' asked Bluey, following their gaze and passing the blood-covered limbs to one of the men.

'Another Abo,' said Besser. 'It's that bastard from Maningrida. The one who pissed off on me. Don't fucking worry about him. He won't come near me.'

Led by Besser and Bluey dragging the severed head, the strange procession moved slowly down the hill in silence, gradually approaching the solitary figure who stood motionless one hundred metres away.

Oondabund watched them, but there were no longer tears in his bloodshot eyes, and nor was he dressed in the shorts and shirt of a white man. Around his head was a white band made from wallaby skin, which was streaked in red and brown, with clay and blood. Through his nose was a short bone, the only item which had been taken from the tightly-woven dillybag that now hung around his neck. His chest was bare, and the sun reflected from and highlighted the six wide bands of scar tissue that circled his chest, and the thin line of small scars that ran from his left shoulder to his left nipple. His only clothing was a square of red cloth, tied tightly in a knot on each hip. In his right hand, he held five spears, each with a broad blade of steel on the end; in his left hand was a short piece of wood with a recurved hook on the end—his woomera. Behind him, a woman's voice wailed, but he did not turn: he watched each movement of the men on the hill with only a low guttural sound hissing from between clenched teeth.

'The bastard's got spears!' said Bluey when they where within twenty metres of the Aboriginal, who stood with his weight on one leg and his other foot resting on the side of his ankle. The group stopped walking.

'Fuck off!' yelled Besser. 'Or you'll get it, too.'

'Go on black feller,' joined in Bluey, 'Piss off!'

Still Oondabund did not move, and Besser turned to those beside him. 'He won't do anything,' he said confidently. 'He's shit scared; they all are when you really come to it. Come on, let's just get out of here.'

They continued their trek down the hill, dragging Numunwari's head between them, the sacred head, dragging in the dirt, disfigured with gaping wounds and covered in blood to which grass was now clinging.

When ten metres from the solitary figure, he moved. Without needing to look, Oondabund slid the recurved point of the woomera into the notch at the end of the first spear.

'Look out!' yelled Bluey, dropping the rope and leaping to one side as the Aboriginal ran towards them.

Oondabund swerved sideways when barely five metres away from the scattering group. The first spear had already left his hands and before he straightened, the second was fitted to the woomera.

Besser's eyes had been fixed on the black figure who had suddenly sprung to life, and he barely saw the first spear move. The blade cut through his chest, slicing the side of his heart and opening one lung before forcing an exit through his back. As he fell, the damaged organ pumped frantically, pouring blood into the inside of his body, and out along the wooden shaft which protruded from it.

Confronted by Oondabund within a second of the first spear being launched, Bluey raised the broken shotgun in defiance, but it was not even loaded, and the Aboriginal knew no fear. The blade cut through the side of Bluey's neck, opening up his pulsating throat as blood spurted out. Bluey tried to run, and the shaft buried in the ground before his feet. When he fell, it broke, but Bluey did not get up again.

Oondabund's eyes fixed on the back of a third man, running to the vehicles. The third spear was launched as he ran, but buried into the ground just behind the moving heels. One of the men turned and fired his rifle, but the shot went wild. Oondabund was rapidly approaching.

The blue semi-trailer pulled into the yard as the fourth spear found the woomera's pointed end. Two of the men had reached the car and were frantically trying to start the engine, but a third, fighting with the door, screamed as the spear cut through his back and opened the metal of the door. Another man jumped to the open door of the moving vehicle, kicking the spear which protruded from the back of the man who lay dying face down on the gravel.

Mac jumped from the truck as the car swerved around him and amidst a cloud of dust, sped from the gate. 'Oh God, no!' he cried.

The last man fought to open the door of the Toyota, with Oondabund barely ten metres away, his last spear held ready, quivering high above his head. The man pulled frantically at the handle, but the simple lock prevented his entry as Oondabund walked slowly forward, watching his every movement.

The man turned—he was carrying a rifle. There was a loud groan from the dying man on the ground as he tried to crawl but failed.

'Don't, Oondabund!' yelled Mac, starting to move forward.

'Stay back or I'll shoot!' shouted the man, working the action of his rifle.

Step by step Oondabund approached, stalking the cornered prey, methodically raising each foot and sliding it forward, alert for any sudden attempt to escape.

'I'll shoot you!' yelled the man again, levelling the rifle.

'Oondabund!' shouted Mac.

'Get him back or I'll shoot!' The man was backing away from the Toyota, not taking his eyes from Oondabund, whose quivering speartip was only five metres away.

'Stop him, Mac, stop him . . .' came Steve's groaning voice from behind. He was at the end pen, trying to run forward, but he collapsed. 'Stop him!' he groaned from the ground.

Oondabund recognised the voice of the friend he thought dead, and turned his head suddenly. He was pushed backwards by the impact of a bullet, which broke the bone in his nose and punched a hole through his cheek, shattering the skull within. He stood momentarily, his balance regained, but the poised spear fell and clattered on the gravel an instant before the proud body collapsed.

No sooner had he fired than the man with the rifle was running past the semi-trailer on to the road. Crawling on all fours, Steve reached the dead Aboriginal and cradled the limp head. His tears mixed with the blood now flowing from the opened cheek. Speechless, Mac stood staring at the carnage both in front of him and on the gentle slope to the breeding pen. Steve was trying to wipe the blood from the dark skin, crying and sobbing, repeating the same word over and over: 'No, no . . .'

EPILOGUE

Four months after the incident in Darwin, the Aboriginals in Maningrida congregated for a ceremony that would ensure the peaceful rest of Oondabund's spirit. It had been done for his father and his grandfather before that, and Aboriginal law insisted that it be done for Oondabund. The men, both old and young, danced and sang on the beach, watched by the women and children who wailed and cried throughout the day and into the night. Oondabund's grief-stricken wife called out to her husband regularly, telling him in his language that she worried much and would one day join him. Beside her, a young Aboriginal woman sat proudly watching, and quietly crying.

The ceremony had waited until Nancy returned from Darwin Hospital. Besser's blow had fractured the vertebrae in her neck, and the doctors felt she was extremely lucky to have been knocked unconscious. Had she been able to move, the injury could have been substantially compounded and even paralysis could have resulted; as it was, however, she had healed well. With Oondabund dead, she had obligations in Maningrida, and although she wished to stay with Steve, she was unable to do so. Reluctant to see their relationship end, Steve wanted to plead with her to stay, but he could not. Oondabund would have expected her to accept the responsibilities of their people, and this much at least was owed to him.

The morning after the ceremony, Nancy and one of the old men slipped out of the settlement as the sun appeared on the horizon. They followed the path on which Oondabund had brought Besser back, and passed within thirty metres of where Numunwari had tipped Besser from the boat. The two of them travelled in silence; he carried only a spear and she held a single bag made from loosely-woven bush twine.

By sunset, they reached the edge of the Arnhem Land plateau and slept in the open around a small fire. Here the water was fresh, and the mud and mangroves of the tidal part of the river were replaced by pandanus palms and the dry scrub of the upper reaches of the river. The rich soil of the flood plains was gone, and they now walked on sand, and could see the rocky country in front. They were on the edge of the stone country.

For the next two days walking was more difficult. The country was dry and the rock and sand were hot on their bare feet, heated by the sun which beat down mercilessly, the trees shielding the wind which in other areas brought relief. But still they walked.

On the fourth day, the sky was clouded; not the normal cloud that appeared during the dry season, but rain cloud. What little wind there was changed direction and now came from the north. Although the old man noted it, he said little and continued walking. He walked until he had reached an area where the grass was long and green, and the trees tall and strong, and here he stopped and pointed it out to Nancy. They had reached their destination, a region in the heart of the stone country where there was deep and permanent water.

They walked down through the trees until they came to the edge of a large billabong, with fresh clear water. After drinking, they retired back to the shade of a low bush where they sat and waited, talking quietly. The old man frequently looked up at the sky, where the clouds built even more, then back at Nancy, shaking his head. It was too early for the rains; it was not good.

Two hours before sunset, the old man wandered off with his spear to one of the trails made by wallabies coming down to drink. Hidden in the bushes beside it, he waited patiently until he heard their distinctive pad on the rocks above. The spear flashed, a wallaby stumbled and staggered as two others scattered, but the spear had found its mark well, and pinned both legs; a single blow with a dead branch and the animal stretched and straightened in its last movement of life.

Removing the spear, the old man slung the dead animal over his shoulder and walked back to where Nancy waited. She then removed a small knife from the woven bag, and, opening the animal's belly, carefully cut out the warm liver, which she placed on the sand. Again reaching into the bag, she removed a small parcel wrapped in paperbark and tied with bush twine. A simple cut, and the bark unwrapped to reveal two bones, Oondabund's bones. Making a slit in each lobe of the liver, she inserted one bone in each, and with the twine, bound the two lobes together in a single bundle. As she did so, the first drops of rain began falling, and again the old man looked up and shook his head in disbelief.

As the sun neared the horizon behind cloud, the old man, who had moved to the edge of the billabong, began to sing. It was an old custom song, but one which had been heard at Maningrida when the Aboriginal child was taken, and one which had been heard from around the fires whenever the old men had come into Darwin to see Numunwari. When Nancy joined him, the old man continued singing and, in time with certain notes, he beat the water with the end of his spear. Nancy sat motionless and silent, watching the still clear water being disturbed only by the slap of the spear, and the light sprinkling of rain.

Suddenly there was something, a swirl, in fact made by a fish frightened into activity by a predator below. The surface of the water parted and a great head rose through the water to rest on the surface. The singing stopped as the membranes flicked across the eyeball and air rushed from the nostrils.

The old man pushed the point of the spear into the tightly-wrapped liver, and extended it until it lay on the sand a few centimetres from the tip of the great snout. Within seconds the jaws opened as the head moved sideways forward and slammed shut on the liver. Before them, the enormous crocodile raised its head in the air and in a single movement the meat disappeared between the rows of teeth—then, without warning, it sank below the surface. The rain intensified, and the old man looked up and spoke to Nancy. Early rain was a bad sign. It had come last year and meant that there would be a heavy wet season.

Nancy stood and walked back up the slope to the bush under which she had waited during the day. To the old people the answer to Numunwari was simple—he could not be killed by white men and had returned to his home. But to her, who knew the ways of the white man, there were many questions to which she had no answers.

As she sat, the old man, who squatted unafraid by the water's edge, oblivious to the warm rain, once again began singing. A word echoed across the billabong, as it had done for generations past, and as it would do in the future for as long as Aboriginal culture could withstand the onslaught of modern civilisation ... 'Numunwari, Numunwari'.